THE CLOUD PAVILION

Laura Joh Rowland

A Novel

MINOTAUR BOOKS

NEW YORK

This is a work of fiction. All of the characters, organizations, and events portrayed in this novel are either products of the author's imagination or are used fictitiously.

www.minotaurbooks.com

The Library of Congress has cataloged the hardcover edition as follows:

Rowland, Laura Joh.
    The cloud pavilion / Laura Joh Rowland.—1st ed.
      p. cm.
   ISBN 978-0-312-37949-0
    1. Sano, Ichirō (Fictitious character)—Fiction. 2. Samurai—Fiction.
3. Japan—History—Genroku period, 1688–1704—Fiction. I. Title.
   PS3568.O934 C58 2009
   813'.54—dc22

                      2009028468

ISBN 978-0-312-65255-5 (trade paperback)

First Minotaur Books Paperback Edition: December 2010

10 9 8 7 6 5 4 3 2 1

To my fellow longtime members of the George Alec Effinger writers' workshop: Andy Fox, Mark McCandless, Marian Moore, and Fritz Ziegler. My deepest thanks for your advice, support, and friendship through these many years.

And in memory of our mentor, George Alec Effinger (1947–2002). I owe you more than you ever knew, and I never thanked you enough. May we meet again someday.

THE CLOUD PAVILION

Edo
Genroku Year 14, Month 5
(Tokyo, June 1701)

Prologue

The pain pierced like knives into her breast and jarred her out of black unconsciousness. A gray blur swirled across her vision, as if she were looking up at a sky filled with windblown mist and clouds. Through dizzying nausea flashed pure, visceral terror.

Where was she? How had she come to be here?

A touch grazed her thigh. She gasped as fingers caressed her. The clouds had hands! Hands that were warm, and damp with the mist. As they stroked her hips and groin, she became aware of movement around her, of human flesh pressing on hers. The clouds inhaled and exhaled quick, hoarse gasps. There was a man with her. He and she floated together, suspended in the clouds, somewhere far above the earth. Her terror worsened.

Who was he?

She couldn't see him through the clouds, but she smelled the foul stench of his sweat; she sensed his lust. She knew what his caresses on the most intimate parts of her body portended.

She called for help, but the clouds absorbed and dissipated the sound. She tried to push the man away, but her arms, her legs, her muscles and bones, seemed disconnected from her will. She couldn't feel them, or any part of herself, except where the man's hands touched. Her heart was a disembodied pulse that thudded with panic.

Black waves of sleep welled up around her. Although she craved merciful oblivion, instinct compelled her to fight for her life. The blackness permeated the clouds, drawing her into its depths. She struggled to retain consciousness.

A new stab of pain, in her other breast, revived her again. The shape of the man, clothed in mist, spread above her eyes. He lowered his weight upon her. The clouds swayed under them, buoyed them while he gasped louder and faster. She felt an awful, tearing thrust between her legs. Thunder reverberated.

His face suddenly protruded through the swirling clouds. They stretched like a tight, opaque skin across his features. Two holes that appeared cut in the mist revealed his eyes, which glittered with desire and cruelty. Beneath them opened another hole, his mouth. The lips were red and swollen and moist; sharp teeth glistened with saliva. She smelled the hot, noxious rush of his breath.

She screamed.

For only an instant did she glimpse him. The clouds veiled her eyes as he took her. His every move within her was agony, flesh sawing flesh. The waves of sleep rose up and drenched her in a black fountain, obliterating his shape from view, the sensations from her awareness. The thunder crashed, distant and faint now. She heard the clatter of rain falling.

Then she plunged into a dark, silent void.

1

Conch trumpets blared a battle cry. War drums boomed. On the opposite banks of a small lake stood two generals clad in leather armor and metal helmets. They waved their war fans and shouted the command.

"Attack!"

Two armies of mounted troops plunged into the lake and charged. Chamberlain Sano Ichirō rode at the forefront of his yelling, whooping comrades. Water splashed his armor as his horse galloped toward the onrushing enemy legion. He and his army drew their swords while their mounts swam into the deep middle of the lake. The opposition met them, swords waving, lances aimed. On shore the generals barked orders to stay in ranks, but in the lake it was utter chaos.

Soldiers hacked wildly at one another with their swords and lances. The noise of wooden weapons battering armor and metal deafened Sano. As he fought, he sat in his saddle waist-deep in water that was filthy with mud and manure. His army's mounts buffeted his horse, rammed his legs. Sano thanked the gods for iron shin guards. He swatted his opponent, knocking the man off his mount. A rider armed with a lance charged at Sano. Sano whacked the lance with his sword. Unbalanced, the rider toppled into the lake. Cheers and applause resounded.

The audience was crowded in stands alongside the artificial lake and leaning out of windows in the covered corridors that topped the walls which enclosed the Edo Castle martial arts practice grounds. Spectators laughed as they egged on the armies, enjoying the tournament.

But Sano and everyone else who competed in them knew that these tournaments were almost as dangerous as real battles. Somebody always got hurt. Sometimes players were killed. Audiences enjoyed that the best. It was the most exciting part of the game.

The lake grew crowded with men who'd fallen in. They frantically swam, trying to avoid being kicked or crushed by the horses. Fighters howled in genuine pain from the blows dealt by the blunt yet heavy wooden weapons. Sano took a whack on his shoulder and knew he'd have a big bruise tomorrow. As he parried his opponent's strikes, he thought that perhaps, at his age of forty-three years, he was too old for tournaments. But it was his duty to participate for as long as he could.

"Stop!" cried a shrill, reedy voice.

The battle suddenly halted. Men reined in their horses and froze as if turned to stone. Sano sat with his sword crossed against his opponent's. In the lake, men treaded water. Blades hovered, suspended in the act of striking.

"Hold that pose!" the shogun called from inside a pavilion that stood on a rise near one end of the lake.

Thunder grumbled, and a drizzly rain began to fall from the misty gray summer sky, but nobody dared move.

Tokugawa Tsunayoshi, the supreme dictator of Japan, knelt at a table spread with paper, ink-stones, and jars that held brushes and water. He wore a smock over his silk robes, and the cylindrical black cap of his rank. He squinted at the battle scene, then sketched rapidly with his brush. An admirer of all forms of art, he dabbled in painting, and equestrian scenes were among his favorite subjects. Sano had seen his work and thought it not bad, certainly better than his leadership over Japan.

"That's enough," the shogun called. "Continue!"

The battle resumed with increased gusto. Soldiers swung, blades whacked, more riders fell. Sano fought with less care for martial arts technique than determination to avoid a ludicrous accidental death. He had to admit that tournaments were rather fun, in addition to serving purposes even more important than entertaining his lord.

Edo, the capital of the Tokugawa regime, was a city populated by more than a million people, some hundred thousand of them samurai. That equaled too many armed men with not enough to do during a peacetime that had lasted almost a century with only minor interruptions. There hadn't been a battle since Lord Matsudaira had defeated his rival, Yanagisawa Yoshiyasu, seven years ago. A conflict had then flared up between Lord Matsudaira and Sano, but had ended with Lord Matsudaira's ritual suicide last spring. Now the troops were restless.

Tournaments not only occupied the samurai class and offered it a chance to improve martial arts skills that had declined. They burned off energy that would otherwise be applied to brawling, starting insurrections, and generally causing trouble.

A bell clanged, signaling the battle's end, not a moment too soon for Sano. He and his army rode, swam, and trudged to one side of the lake while the enemy forces retreated to the other. The judge counted the men who hadn't fallen in the water, then announced, "Team Number One is the winner."

The men on Sano's side cheered, as did the audience. The opposition looked disgruntled. Sano urged his horse up the bank, then jumped out of the saddle. He slipped on the mud and would have fallen, but a strong hand gripped his arm. He turned to see who'd caught him. It was a tall samurai in a black armor tunic with red lacings. The samurai took off his helmet. Sano beheld the handsome face of Yanagisawa, his onetime foe.

"Many thanks," Sano said.

"It was my pleasure," Yanagisawa said.

He and Sano had a long, bitter history. Yanagisawa had been chamberlain when Sano had entered the shogun's service twelve years ago. Yanagisawa had once viewed Sano as a rival, had schemed to destroy him. A murder investigation on which they'd been forced to collaborate had resulted in a truce, and later his conflict with Lord Matsudaira had taken Yanagisawa's attention off Sano. Lord Matsudaira had capped his victory by exiling Yanagisawa to Hachijo Island. But Yanagisawa had escaped and sneaked back to Edo, where he'd operated behind the scenes, stealing allies from Sano and Lord Matsudaira, pitting them against each other, and engineering Lord Matsudaira's downfall. Last spring Sano had forced Yanagisawa out of hiding. Yanagisawa had made a triumphant comeback that coincided with Lord Matsudaira's suicide.

With Lord Matsudaira dead, the game was once again between Sano and Yanagisawa. They'd done unforgivable things to each other, and Sano had expected Yanagisawa to renew his attacks with a vengeance. Sano had braced himself for the fight of his life.

It hadn't come.

Now Yanagisawa smiled in the same friendly fashion with which he'd treated Sano since a few days after he'd made his reappearance on the political scene. He smoothed his hair, which had grown back since he'd shaved his head to disguise himself as a priest while in hiding. It was too short to tie in the customary samurai topknot, but thick and glossy and black even though he and Sano were the same age and Sano's hair had begun turning gray.

"You fought a good battle," Yanagisawa said.

Sano listened for nuances of hostility in Yanagisawa's tone but heard none. "So did you."

Yanagisawa laughed. "We slaughtered those poor bastards."

Not once had he lifted a hand to harm Sano. For over a year he and Sano had coexisted in a peace that Sano hadn't thought possible. Not that Sano minded a reprieve from feuding and assassination attempts, but their pleasant camaraderie felt all wrong, like the sun shining at midnight.

He and Yanagisawa took their places at the head of their rowdy, cheering army. The judge said to them, "Your team wins the top prize for equestrian combat in water—a barrel of the best sake for each man. I commend your excellent coaching."

"Isn't it a good thing we're on the same side now?" Yanagisawa said to Sano.

"Indeed," Sano said with feigned enthusiasm.

Yanagisawa was up to something. Sano knew.

So did everybody else. Sano had overheard their colleagues in the government speculating about what Yanagisawa had in store for him and taking bets as to when Yanagisawa would make his first move.

The shogun came hurrying up to them. He was thin, frail, and looked a decade older than his fifty-five years. A servant held an umbrella over his head, protecting him from the drizzle. "Ahh, Sano-*san*, Yanagisawa-*san*!" he exclaimed. Delight animated his weak, aristocratic features. "Congratulations on your, ahh, victory!"

Sano and Yanagisawa bowed and made modest disclaimers. Yanagisawa didn't try to hog the credit or make Sano look bad, as he would have in the past. Sano didn't trust this radical change in behavior.

"You make such a good team," the shogun said. "I think I, ahh, made the right decision when I appointed both of you as my chamberlains."

They shared the post of chamberlain and second-in-command to the shogun. That honor, which had first belonged solely to Yanagisawa, had passed to Sano when Yanagisawa had been exiled. When Yanagisawa returned, he'd expected to regain the post, and Sano had been ready to fight to keep it. But the shogun, always loath to exercise his judgment, had been unable to choose which one of them he preferred and made the unprecedented move of splitting the job between two men.

Two men whose antagonism could wreak havoc in the government and tear Japan apart.

Some said it was the most foolish decision ever made by this dictator not known for wisdom. Nobody thought the partnership between Sano and Yanagisawa would last a day without a blowup. But it had defied the odds.

Sano had expected Yanagisawa to oppose everything he did, to undermine his standing with the shogun, to try to turn every powerful man inside and outside the regime against him and run him out of office. But Yanagisawa had cooperated fully and, to all appearances, gladly with Sano. Together they'd overseen the huge, complicated machine of the *bakufu*—Japan's military government—with smooth, startling efficiency.

Yanagisawa lifted his eyebrow at Sano. "Imagine all the good we could have accomplished years ago if we'd been working together."

Instead of you trying to kill me and me trying to fend you off, Sano thought. "Two heads are better than one," he said out loud.

"Yes, yes," the shogun agreed happily.

Because he hated and feared conflict, he was glad to see his two dearest friends getting along so well. He didn't know they'd ever been enemies or had once vied for control of his regime, which was tantamount to treason. He was astoundingly oblivious to what went on around him, and Sano and Yanagisawa enforced a conspiracy of silence to keep the shogun ignorant.

Often Sano suspected the shogun knew the truth perfectly well, but acknowledging it would require him to take action for which he hadn't the stomach.

"Well, the fun's over," Yanagisawa said. "It's back to business for us, Honorable Chamberlain Sano."

"Yes, Honorable Chamberlain Yanagisawa," Sano said.

Although his former enemy's words were spoken with no trace of a threat, Sano searched them for hidden meanings. He knew the game between him and Yanagisawa was still on, and he was at a serious disadvantage.

Sano's spies hadn't managed to dig up a single clue as to what Yanagisawa was plotting. To all appearances, Yanagisawa had decided that it was better to join forces with Sano instead of risking his neck again. Yanagisawa had reportedly told his allies among the top officials and the *daimyo*—feudal lords who governed Japan's provinces—that he wasn't interested in fighting Sano anymore. And he'd not tried to recruit Sano's allies to his side.

Yanagisawa had changed the rules of the game, but Sano didn't know what they were. He felt like a blind samurai heading into battle. He could only wait, a sitting target.

The audience departed; the armies dispersed. Waterlogged troops trudged off to drink, celebrate, commiserate, or bathe. Grooms took charge of the horses. The shogun climbed into his palanquin, and his bearers carried him toward the palace. Yanagisawa looked past Sano and said, "I believe there's someone who would like your attention."

Sano turned. He saw, some thirty paces away, an elderly samurai waiting alone beside the stands, watching him. Recognition jolted Sano. Into his heart crept a cold sensation of dread.

2

Sano stood perfectly still as the samurai walked across the martial arts ground toward him. Everyone else receded to the edges of his awareness. Sano felt as if he and the samurai were alone on the muddy, trampled field. He suppressed an irrational urge to draw his sword. Its blade was wooden, and this encounter wasn't a duel.

Then again, perhaps it was.

The samurai stopped a few paces from Sano. He was in his sixties, his physique lean but strong, his shoulders held squarely rigid. He wore a metal helmet, and a leather armor tunic with the Tokugawa triple-hollyhock-leaf crest embossed on its breastplate over a silk robe and trousers striped in dark gray and black. An insignia on his helmet showed that he held the rank of major in the army. His forehead was severely creased, as if from too much frowning. Harsh lines bracketed his tight mouth.

"Good day," he said, bowing. "Please permit me to introduce myself." His deep voice had a faint quaver of old age and an oddly familiar ring. "I am Kumazawa Hiroyuki."

"I know," Sano said.

He'd never met Major Kumazawa face-to-face; they'd never spoken. But he'd observed the man from a distance and knew everything about him that the official government records, and Sano's own spies, could tell. In Sano's desk was a dossier on the entire Kumazawa clan. Sano had compiled it after a murder investigation that had revealed secret facts about his own background.

His parents had led him to believe that his mother came from humble peasant stock. Not until last spring, when she'd been accused of a crime hidden in her past, had Sano learned the truth: Her kin were high-ranking Tokugawa vassals. They'd disowned her because of a mistake she'd made when she was a girl, and she'd never seen them again.

Now Sano felt a flame of anger heat his blood. Major Kumazawa was the head of the clan that had treated Sano's mother so cruelly. Sano said, "Do you know who I am?"

Major Kumazawa didn't pretend to misunderstand, didn't give the obvious answer that everybody knew the famous Chamberlain Sano. "Yes. You are the son of my younger sister Etsuko." He spoke as if the words tasted bad. "That makes you my nephew."

It was just as Sano had suspected: Although he had long been ignorant of his connection with the Kumazawa, they had been aware that their blood ran in his veins. They must have kept track of his mother and her son through the years; they must have followed his career.

The flame of Sano's anger grew. The Kumazawa had spied on him and never deigned to seek his acquaintance. That casting off his mother and refusing to recognize her offspring was what any high-society family would have done under the circumstances did not appease Sano. He was insulted that his uncle should treat him with such disdain. He also experienced other emotions he hadn't expected.

Since learning about his new relatives, he had intended to get in touch with them, but kept putting it off. He was busy running the government and advising the shogun; he didn't have time. Or so he'd told himself. But he'd entertained secret fantasies about summoning his uncle to his mansion and impressing him with how well he had done without any help from their clan. The fantasies shamed Sano; he knew they were childish. Now, here he was, face-to-face with his uncle, soaked with water polluted by horse dung. He felt less like the shogun's second-in-command than an outcast.

"I don't suppose you approached me in order to inquire about my mother," he said in his coldest, most formal tone.

"No," Major Kumazawa said, equally cold. "But I will ask. How is she?"

"Quite well." *No thanks to you*, Sano thought. "She was widowed eleven years ago, when my father died." *My father was the rōnin—the lowly masterless samurai—that your family forced her to marry, to get her off your hands.* "But she remarried last fall." *To the man with whom she had an illicit affair, the results of which caused your clan to disown her.* "She and her new husband are living in Yamato."

The murder investigation had reunited Sano's mother with the one-time monk she'd fallen in love with as a girl. Loving him still, she'd happily given up her home and her old life in Edo to join him in the village where he'd settled.

"So I've heard," said Major Kumazawa. "Of course, I'm not responsible for what became of your mother."

Sano was glad she'd found happiness after years of disgrace and misery inflicted by her relatives, but she'd left him with unfinished business. "Not directly responsible, perhaps."

Major Kumazawa frowned, deepening the wrinkles in his forehead, at Sano's bitter tone. "My father disowned Etsuko. When he died and I became head of the clan, I merely honored his wishes. Were you in my position, you'd have no choice but to do the same."

Sano didn't think he'd have been so unyielding for the sake of mere convention. He knew it was unreasonable for him to be disturbed about something that had happened so long ago, which his mother had forgiven. Yet he felt that a personal injury had been done to him by Major Kumazawa. He had the strange sensation that they'd met before, although he knew they had not.

"So you upheld your family's ban on contact with my mother, which extended to me," Sano said. "Why break it now?"

Major Kumazawa spoke reluctantly, as if fighting an internal struggle against tradition and duty. "Because I need a favor."

"Ah," Sano said. "I should have guessed." Since he'd become chamberlain, thousands of people had lined up outside his door to ask for favors. Sano regarded his uncle with disgust.

"Do you think I like crawling to you, the son of my disgraced sister?" Major Kumazawa said, angry himself now. "Do you think I want to ask you for anything?"

"Obviously not," Sano retorted, "so I'll spare you the grief."

He turned and started to walk away toward the gate in the stone wall that enclosed the martial arts ground. Beyond the gate lay the shogun's palace, the official quarter, and Sano's own spacious compound—the rarefied world in which he'd earned a place. He wasn't even curious about what his uncle wanted. It had to be money, a promotion, or a job for a friend or relative. It always was.

"Wait. Don't go," Major Kumazawa called.

The anger had disappeared from his voice, which now resonated with such pleading that Sano halted. "I can understand why you don't like me or want to help me," Major Kumazawa said. "But the favor I need isn't for my benefit. It's for someone who had nothing to do with what happened to your mother, who's never done wrong to you or anybody else. Someone who is in serious danger."

That got Sano's attention. His conscience and his honor wouldn't let him walk away from an innocent person in danger. Facing his uncle, he said, "Who is it?"

The sternness of Major Kumazawa's expression had hardened, as though he were trying to keep his emotions at bay. "It's my daughter."

Sano knew that Major Kumazawa had three daughters and two sons—Sano's cousins. All of whom Sano had never seen.

"Her name is Chiyo," Major Kumazawa said. "She's my youngest child."

"What about her?" Sano recalled her name from the dossier. She was thirty-three years old, the wife of a captain in the army of a rich, powerful *daimyo*. She'd married very late, at age twenty-seven. Informants had told Sano that she was her father's favorite and Major Kumazawa had delayed her marriage to keep her at home while he found her the best possible husband.

"She's missing," Major Kumazawa said.

Sano remembered that terrible winter when his own son had been kidnapped, and he and his wife, Reiko, had suffered the pain of not knowing what had happened to their beloved child while fearing the worst. His resistance toward his uncle began to crumble.

"I know Chiyo is none of your concern, but please hear me out," Major Kumazawa said with the gruffness of a man unaccustomed to begging.

"All right." Sano had to listen; he owed his uncle that, if nothing else.

"Chiyo disappeared the day before yesterday. She had gone to the Awashima Shrine." Obviously relieved that Sano had given him another chance, yet hating his role as a supplicant, Major Kumazawa explained, "She gave birth to a child last month. A boy." It was the custom for mothers to take their new babies to shrines to be blessed. "She went with her attendants. There was a big crowd at the shrine. One moment Chiyo was there, and the next . . ."

Major Kumazawa held up his palms. "Gone." Anguish showed through his rigid expression.

Whenever Sano thought of the night his son, Masahiro, had disappeared—during a party at a temple—he shivered. "What happened to the baby?"

"He was found lying outside the shrine. Thank the gods he's safe," said Major Kumazawa. "Chiyo's guards couldn't find her. They went home and told her husband what had happened. He told me. We both gathered all the troops we could and sent them out to search for Chiyo. They're still out looking, but there's been not a sign of her. It's as if she just vanished into the air."

Sano knew that his uncle commanded a Tokugawa garrison outside Edo, and Chiyo's husband must have many men serving under him, but the city was too big for them to cover thoroughly. "Did you report Chiyo's disappearance to the police?"

"Of course. I went to their headquarters. They took my report and said they would keep an eye out for her." Major Kumazawa expelled his breath in a disdainful huff. "They said that was all they could do."

The police had their hands full keeping order in the city, Sano knew. They couldn't drop everything to search for one woman, even if her father was a Tokugawa army officer. A major didn't rate high enough.

"Could Chiyo have run away on her own?" Sano asked.

"That's impossible. She wouldn't have left her children and husband without so much as an explanation."

"I suppose you've considered the possibility that Chiyo was kidnapped," Sano said.

"What else could I think?" Worry about his daughter showed through Major Kumazawa's sarcasm. "People don't just drop off the face of the earth."

"Can you think of anyone who would want to hurt Chiyo?"

"Nobody. She's a good, decent, harmless girl."

"Do you have any enemies?" Sano asked.

"Every man with some standing in the world has enemies," Major Kumazawa said. "You of all people should know that. I talked to a few men who have grudges against me, but they insisted that they had nothing to do with Chiyo's disappearance. I think they're telling the truth. They treated me as if I'd gone insane," he added morosely.

"There's been no ransom letter?"

"No letter," Major Kumazawa said. "I'm at my wits' end. You have a reputation as a great detective. That's why I've come to you—to ask you to find my daughter."

Sano could not refuse, for reasons almost as important as saving a woman in peril. His son, Masahiro, wasn't the only member of his family who'd been kidnapped. So had his wife, Reiko, seven years ago. Had Sano not managed to rescue her, he would have lost his wife and Masahiro his mother. Sano couldn't withhold his help from another family facing a similar disastrous situation.

"You don't owe me anything," Major Kumazawa said. "You're bitter about the past. But don't hold it against Chiyo. She wasn't even born when my parents disowned your mother. She had no say in the matter of our clan keeping ourselves apart from you. For her sake, not mine, please help me. Do you want me to beg? I will. I'll do anything to save my daughter!"

Major Kumazawa dropped heavily to his knees, as if the tendons behind them had been slashed. Alone on the muddy field, he looked like a general who'd lost a battle and must commit suicide rather than live with the disgrace. He took off his helmet. The damp wind ruffled gray hair that had escaped from his topknot. For once he seemed human, vulnerable. He gazed up at Sano, his eyes fierce with entreaty and humiliation.

Sano had once imagined forcing his uncle to kneel to him, subjugating the man who'd maintained his mother's banishment from her family. But now he felt no satisfaction. He had too much sympathy for Major Kumazawa's plight.

"Very well," Sano said. "I'm at your service."

He had wanted a chance to know his new clan, and here it was. Perhaps he could even reunite his mother with her family, which he knew she'd always longed for.

Major Kumazawa bowed his head. "A thousand thanks." His tone held less relief than resentment, as if he'd done Sano a favor. Although Sano understood that his uncle had lost face, a painful blow to a proud samurai, he was offended at being treated with such a lack of respect or appreciation. Then again, what else could he have expected?

"Don't thank me yet," Sano said. There was no guarantee that he would find Chiyo alive. She'd been gone two days, long enough for the worst to happen. "I'm not making any promises."

3

The corpse of a young samurai lay amid the irises and reeds beside a pond coated with green algae. Blood covered the front of his kimono. A mosquito alighted between his closed eyes.

His hand flew up and swatted the mosquito.

"Don't move!" cried Chamberlain Sano's son, Masahiro, from behind a nearby tree. Almost ten years old, dressed in kimono, surcoat, and trousers, with two swords at his waist, he bore a strong resemblance to his father. He wore his hair in a forelock tied above his brow, the custom for young samurai who hadn't reached manhood. "You're supposed to be dead!"

"I'm sorry, young master, but these bugs are eating me up," the samurai said contritely. "How much longer do I have to lie here like this?"

The boy tiptoed slowly across the grass toward the samurai. "Until after I discover your body."

From inside the mansion whose wings enclosed the garden, Lady Reiko stepped out onto the veranda. She was beautiful in a green silk summer kimono patterned with dragonflies and water lilies. Lacquer combs anchored her upswept hairdo. "What's going on?" she called.

"I'm playing detective," Masahiro answered. "Lieutenant Tanuma is the murder victim."

"Not again!" Reiko sighed.

She wasn't sure what to make of her son's game. On the one hand, she was proud of his cleverness, his imagination. Most boys his age only played ball or fought mock battles. On the other hand, Reiko was concerned about his preoccupation with violent death. He had seen too much of it in his short life, and had even killed, in self-defense. Reiko and Sano blamed their life at the center of political turmoil, and their habit of talking too freely about the murder cases they'd investigated together. They'd thought Masahiro was too young to understand what they were saying, but they'd been wrong.

Masahiro pretended to stumble upon Lieutenant Tanuma. "What's this?" he exclaimed, and laughed. "Oh, a corpse!"

Reiko didn't know whether to be glad he had a sense of humor after everything that had happened to him, or worried that his experiences had made him callous, or simply horrified that he'd invented such a ghoulish pastime.

"What is that red substance on Lieutenant Tanuma's clothes?" she asked, hoping it wasn't actually blood.

"It's ink," Masahiro said.

"You shouldn't make Lieutenant Tanuma play with you," Reiko said. "It's not his job."

Tanuma was her chief bodyguard when she went outside the estate. "I don't mind," he said. A homely, serious young man, he'd replaced Reiko's favorite, Lieutenant Asukai, who'd died last year in the line of duty. Reiko still missed the handsome, gallant, and adventurous Asukai, who had saved her life more than once. But Tanuma did his own, solemn best. "Anything to entertain the young master."

"Don't spoil him," Reiko protested.

Masahiro was rummaging through the reeds. "Where's the murder weapon? I put it right down here."

Giggles issued from behind a flower bed. Out peeked Masahiro's two-year-old sister, Akiko. She held up a dagger whose blade was stained red.

"Hey! You stole it!" Masahiro said. "Give it to me!"

As he stalked toward Akiko, she ran. "Come here, you little thief!" He chased her while she waved the dagger and laughed, her pigtails and the skirt of her pink kimono flying. She was happy to have the attention of the big brother she adored, who was always too busy to play with her. Reiko gasped in alarm.

"That's a real dagger! Masahiro, you know you shouldn't leave weapons lying around where your sister can get at them. She could hurt herself!"

Reiko joined the chase. When she finally caught Akiko, she was breathless and perspiring, her hair windblown. She took away the dagger and said, "The game is over."

Lieutenant Tanuma got to his feet, bowed, and made a quick exit. Masahiro said, "But Mother——"

"Don't you have lessons to study?" Reiko said.

"I'm finished."

"Then practice martial arts."

"I already did."

"Can't you play other games that don't involve weapons or murder?"

"Yes, but this is the most exciting." As he traipsed off toward the house with Akiko tagging after him, Masahiro added wistfully, "It's been a long time since anything exciting has happened around here."

It had been more than a year, Reiko thought, since Lord Matsudaira's death had put an end to the political strife that had threatened their family. Reiko shuddered to think of that dreadful time, when she and her children had lived in a state of siege, prisoners in their own home, under constant guard. Lord Matsudaira's final attack had come from assassins he'd planted in the household. Reiko and the children had barely escaped death. She still had nightmares. She didn't miss those days, and she was disconcerted to see that Masahiro did.

She had to remind herself that Masahiro was too young to realize how serious their situation had been. Children, especially strong, brave boys like her son, believed they were invincible. And Masahiro thrived under conditions that most people found traumatic. No wonder he thought the current state of peace was boring.

Today Reiko realized that she agreed.

At first she'd been thankful for the peace and quiet. She'd been glad that Yanagisawa apparently didn't intend to continue his hostilities against Sano. She'd wanted only to raise her family without fear; she was glad not to worry every day about whether Sano would come home alive. For the past year she'd devoted herself to being a good mother and wife. She'd become very domestic, taking up feminine activities such as flower-arranging. Since the political situation had stabilized and Sano seemed likely to hold his position for a while, people had flocked to curry favor with him. Prominent men had sent their wives to cultivate Reiko because she had strong influence with the chamberlain. The wives brought their children to play with hers. Reiko found some of the wives dull and catty, but others intelligent and stimulating. She'd made new friends and enjoyed the social whirl.

But enough was enough.

As Reiko stood alone in the garden, her old, adventurous spirit revived. She looked up at the gray clouds, ever-present during this extremely wet rainy season. The leaves of the trees, the shrubs, and the grasses were lush and green. She felt the mist in the air, heard birdsong. She appreciated the natural beauty around her, but where was the challenge?

She wasn't meant for the circumscribed existence that was normal for women of her class. She missed the days when she'd run a service that helped women in trouble, when she'd helped Sano solve crimes. Reiko inhaled deeply, as if trying to breathe her native air of excitement and danger.

She was eager to take on a new investigation. But how? And when?

4

Sano rode his horse out the northern portal of Edo Castle toward the temple where his cousin Chiyo had last been seen. Although peace had blessed the capital for more than a year, troops still stood sentry outside the massive iron-banded gate and occupied the guardhouse above. More troops manned the watchtowers. Political or civil unrest could start up again any day. A squadron from his personal army accompanied Sano. He wouldn't put it past Yanagisawa to attack him after lulling him into complacence.

His chief bodyguards, Detectives Marume and Fukida, trotted their mounts beside him along the road that sloped down from the castle. Below them spread the gray tile rooftops of the vast city, whose far reaches disappeared into the mist and rain that cloaked the hills. The brawny, cheerful Marume drew a deep breath of the humid air and said, "It feels good to be out and about again. We've been cooped up inside the castle forever."

"I'm sorry your cousin is missing, Sano-*san*, but I'm glad to have a new investigation," said Fukida, the serious half of the pair.

Sano shared his men's renewed sense of energy and excitement. The thrill of the chase was a relief after sitting at a desk, shuffling papers, conducting meetings, and defusing crises in the government. That was one reason he'd decided to lead the search himself, even though he'd had to put off other important business.

"And guess what," Marume said. "This is the first time we're not working for the shogun."

"For once he won't be holding the threat of death over our heads," Fukida said.

"Thank the gods for small favors," Sano said.

He and his men laughed, enjoying their unusual freedom. But darker currents of emotion ran beneath Sano's high spirits.

He had a blood connection to the missing woman even though he'd never met Chiyo. He couldn't leave her fate to someone else, not even his most trusted subordinates. And what if he didn't find her? What if she was dead when he did? Not only would a father lose his favorite daughter, a husband his wife, and two children their mother, but Sano would lose an opportunity to know this member of his new family.

"My gut tells me that we'll find your cousin," Marume said.

"Your gut has gotten fat from sitting around and eating too much," Fukida teased with a straight face.

Marume reached behind Sano, swatted at Fukida, and said, "No, I'm telling you, this is our lucky day. But even if we don't find her, at least Major Kumazawa can't kill us."

Nevertheless, Sano feared disappointing Major Kumazawa. He shouldn't care what this relative who'd ostracized him from their clan thought of him, but he did. Meeting his uncle had reawakened feelings of inferiority that he'd believed he'd shed years ago. That short time with Major Kumazawa had reverted him to the mere son of a *rōnin* he'd once been. If he didn't find Chiyo, his uncle's low opinion of him would be justified. And even though the strong, independent part of Sano said, *to hell with Major Kumazawa*, that would hurt.

"It must be strange to meet relatives that you spent most of your life never knowing you had," Fukida said.

"You can't imagine," Sano said.

Asakusa Kannon Temple, dedicated to Kannon, the Buddhist deity of mercy and salvation, was Edo's most popular temple. The route to Asakusa district lay along the Ōshū Kaidō, the northern highway. Beyond the edge of town, the highway was built up on a wide earthen embankment above rice paddies. A few peasants, water buffaloes, and tiny huts dotted the lush, green paddies. The air stank of the nightsoil used for fertilizer. Even on this wet afternoon in the rainy season, Sano and his entourage found the highway crowded with traffic.

Bands of religious pilgrims, carrying staffs and chanting prayers, marched in step. Itinerant priests trudged, laden with heavy packs.

Families traveled to Asakusa for blessings. Samurai rode, the privilege of their class; commoners walked. But not all the traffic was connected with religion.

Once Sano and his party had to steer their horses to the edge of the highway to make way for a cart drawn by oxen and heaped with roof tiles. Carts like this, owned by the government, were the only wheeled vehicles permitted by Tokugawa law. This restricted the movement of war supplies and prevented insurrections, at least in theory.

Many of the other travelers weren't going to Asakusa at all. Beyond the temple lay the Yoshiwara licensed pleasure quarter, the only place in Edo where prostitution was legal. Merchants riding in palanquins, gangs of townsmen on foot, and samurai on horseback streamed toward Yoshiwara's brothels. The law banned samurai from the pleasure quarter, but they went in droves anyway. Yoshiwara was good for business in the temple district. Men traveling to Yoshiwara often stopped at the temple for rest, refreshments, and prayers, combining the profane with the sacred.

"What was your cousin doing in Asakusa? If she wanted to go to a shrine, why not one in town?" Marume asked.

"The Kumazawa family estate is out there," Sano said.

His uncle was in charge of guarding the shogun's rice depots, located on the river east of Asakusa. He also commanded the troops that patrolled the district. The Kumazawa house was the one in which Sano's mother had grown up, but Sano had yet to lay eyes on it.

Perhaps he soon would.

Within an hour, Asakusa appeared on the misty horizon. Originally a small outpost of the city, the site of a temple since ancient times, it had grown into a large, flourishing suburb. Other temples clustered around Asakusa Kannon like chicks around a hen. Above the rooftops rose the graceful silhouettes of pagodas. The rice fields gave way to houses on streets that branched off the highway. The neighborhood soon grew as dense as any in town. Hawkers wooed customers into shops that sold Buddhist rosaries, incense, shoes, fans, umbrellas, and other merchandise— a bargain-priced sampling of the goods sold at the big market inside the temple precinct. Balconies adorned with potted plants sheltered the crowds from the drizzle that began to fall. The streets narrowed; Sano and his men rode in single file. Marume led, scouting a safe passage.

"Have you any ideas about what happened to your cousin?" Fukida said, trailing behind Sano with the other guards.

"The only thing I know for sure is that Chiyo is either gone from this district or still inside it," Sano said. "We'll try to determine which is the case."

He dismounted at a gate that divided one block from the next. These gates were features common to all cities. At night they were closed to keep residents confined and prevent trouble; by day, they served as security checkpoints. "This is as good a place to start as any."

Marume backtracked to join Sano and the other men. "Isn't this territory that your uncle has already covered?"

"He might have overlooked something," Sano said, then addressed the watchman at the gate. "I'm looking for a missing woman," he began.

The watchman was a young peasant; he'd been chatting with a tea-seller who'd put down his bucket and cups and stopped to rest. His round face blanched with fright. "I haven't seen her, I swear!" He fell to his knees, bowed, and cringed, almost in tears. "I haven't done anything wrong!"

"If you haven't done anything wrong, then why are you so afraid?" Sano asked.

The tea-seller, an older man with the bluff, confident air of a street merchant, said, "Because of that other samurai who came by yesterday, asking about a missing woman. He and his soldiers roughed up anyone they thought was hiding something or who didn't answer fast enough."

Dismay spread through Sano. "Who was he?"

"I don't know. He didn't bother to introduce himself. He had deep wrinkles here, and here." The tea-seller drew his finger across his forehead and down his cheeks.

"Major Kumazawa," Sano said grimly.

The tea-seller gestured at the watchman. "He gave my poor friend here quite a beating."

"It sounds like your uncle hasn't exactly smoothed the way for us," Marume said.

"I understand how desperate he must be to find his daughter," Fukida said, "but beating up witnesses won't help."

Sano had thought this would be one investigation he could conduct without interference. "My apologies for what happened to you," he said to the watchman. "Now tell me if you've seen a strange woman wandering by herself, or being forced to go with someone, or looking as if she were in trouble."

The watchman swore that he hadn't. So did the tea-seller.

"She's thirty-three years old, and she was wearing a lavender kimono with small white flowers on it," Sano said. He'd asked his uncle what clothes Chiyo had been wearing. "Think hard. Are you sure you haven't seen a woman who matched that description?"

Both men said they were. Sano believed them. He and his comrades moved on, along a street of food-stalls. Vendors grilled eels, prawns, and squid on skewers over open hearths, boiled pots of rice, noodles, and soup. Fragrant steam and smoke billowed into the drizzle.

"I'm hungry," Marume said.

"You always are," Fukida said.

Sano hadn't eaten since morning, before the tournament. He and his men bought food. After they ate, they questioned more people. They soon learned that Major Kumazawa and his troops had already passed through the whole area that surrounded the temple, intimidating, torturing, and offending everywhere. And Sano's attempts to trace Chiyo proved as futile as his uncle's.

"No, I haven't seen her," said one vendor, shopkeeper, and peddler after another.

"Nobody's hiding a woman on my block," said the headmen of every street.

"Major Kumazawa threatened to have my head cut off if I didn't help him find his daughter, so I've been looking for her on my rounds," said a *doshin*—police patrol officer. "I've questioned everyone I've met, but no luck."

"It's looking as if she left the district," Sano said as he and his men led their horses through an alley, "whether on her own or against her will."

They turned down a road that bordered a canal under construction. Laborers armed with shovels and picks were digging a wide, deep trench. Peasants hauled up dirt and loaded it onto oxcarts. Sano, Marume, and Fukida gazed into the trench, at the lumpy, freshly exposed earth on the bottom.

"Are you thinking what I'm thinking?" Marume asked.

Sano refused to consider the possibility that his cousin had been killed and buried here or someplace else. "We'll keep looking. Let's go to the shrine."

As they headed farther into Asakusa district, the drizzle turned into sprinkles, then a fierce downpour. Rain boiled up from tile roofs, cascaded off eaves, and puddled the streets. The air dissolved in mist. Sano, the detectives, and his other men took cover under a balcony while their horses stoically endured the deluge and people ran for shelter.

"There go our witnesses," Fukida said glumly.

Lightning flashed. The dark sky blazed bright white for an instant. Thunder cracked. The world outside the small dry space where Sano and his men stood was a streaming gray blur. Down the vacant street, a lone human figure emerged from the storm and stumbled in their direction.

"Somebody doesn't know enough to get out of the rain," Marume said.

The figure drew nearer, limping and crouching. Sano saw that it was a woman. Her black hair hung in long, dripping tangles. Torn and drenched, her dark red and pale lavender kimono was plastered against her slim body. With one hand she held the garment closed over her bosom; with the other she groped as if she were blind.

"What on earth—," Fukida began.

Now Sano saw that the red streaks on her kimono weren't dyed into the fabric. The rain washed them down her skirts, into the puddles through which she limped barefoot.

She was bleeding.

Sano ran toward the woman. The storm battered him; he was instantly soaked to the skin. She faltered, her eyes wide and blank with terror. Rain trickled into her open, gasping mouth. She wasn't young or old; she could be in her thirties. Her features were startlingly familiar to Sano. She recoiled from him, lost her balance. He caught her, and she screamed and flailed.

"Don't be afraid," Sano shouted over a crash of thunder. "I won't hurt you."

As she fought him, the detectives hurried to Sano's aid. The woman began to weep, crying, "No! Leave me alone. Please!"

"Stand back," Sano ordered his men. They obeyed. "Who are you?" he urgently asked the woman.

Her gaze met his. The blankness in her eyes cleared. She stopped fighting Sano. Her expression showed puzzlement, wonder, and hope. Sano was astounded by recognition. As the rain swept them, he flashed back to a memory from his early childhood.

In those days his mother had often taken him to the public bathhouse because they didn't have room for a tub in their small, humble home. He remembered how she'd dunked under the hot water and come up with her hair and face streaming wet. His mind superimposed this picture of his mother upon the woman in his arms. The woman was his mother's younger image.

"Is your name Chiyo?" Sano shouted.

"Yes," his cousin whispered, her voice drowned by the storm. Her eyes closed, and she went limp in Sano's grasp as she fainted.

5

Light from a round white lantern cast a lunar glow in the room where Yanagisawa and his son Yoritomo lay side by side, facedown, on low wooden tables. Their long, naked bodies were identically proportioned, Yanagisawa's almost as slender, strong, and perfect as twenty-three-year-old Yoritomo's. Their faces, turned toward each other, had the same dark beauty. Their skin glistened with oil as two masseurs kneaded their backs, working out the aches from the morning's tournament. Incense smoke rose from a brass burner, sweet and pungent, masking the odors of dampness and decay. Outside, rain poured down; thunder rumbled.

"Father, may I ask you a question?" Yoritomo said, respectful and deferential as always.

"Of course," Yanagisawa said.

He didn't hesitate to talk in front of the masseurs. Other people had blind masseurs, an ancient tradition. Yanagisawa's were deaf and dumb. They wouldn't hear or spread tales. And although he usually hated being interrogated, he made an exception for Yoritomo. He distrusted and disliked most people, with good reason; he'd been stabbed in the back so many times that it was a wonder he hadn't bled to death. But his son was his love, the only person to whom he felt a connection, his blood. He had four other children, but Yoritomo was the only one that mattered. He would gladly tell Yoritomo all his secrets. Or almost all.

"Are things really settled between you and Sano?" Yoritomo asked.

"For the moment," Yanagisawa said.

But some scores could never be settled.

"I don't understand how you can be friends with him," Yoritomo said. He and Sano had once been close friends, Yanagisawa knew. During the three years that Yanagisawa had been in exile, Sano had taken the opportunity to cultivate Yoritomo, who was the shogun's favorite lover and companion. Yoritomo had grown attached to Sano and bravely defended him against his enemies. But no more. "Not after what he did to us!"

Yoritomo spoke with the indignation of trust and affection betrayed. Last year Sano had accused Yoritomo of treason, and had staged a trial and fake execution, in order to force Yanagisawa into the open. "I've never been so terrified in my life!"

Neither had Yanagisawa, when he'd heard that his son was to be put to death.

"Even though Sano apologized, I'll never forgive him," Yoritomo said, his voice hard, his sweet, gentle nature turned hateful by Sano's trick. "How can you?"

Yanagisawa couldn't. Whenever he thought of that day, he shook with fury. But he controlled his emotions, lest they goad him into rash action. And he had to convince Yoritomo to follow his example. "One can do whatever one must. Don't dwell on what Sano did to you. It'll only make you feel worse."

Yoritomo stared in amazement. "Can you honestly say that you don't hate Sano as much as I do? After all, it's not just me that Sano has humiliated." Yoritomo was so upset that he forgot his polite manners. "Look at yourself, Father! Once you were the only chamberlain, the shogun's only second-in-command. Now you have to share the honors with Sano. And he's not only stolen half your position—he has your house!"

The shogun had given the chamberlain's compound to Sano when Yanagisawa had been exiled. The very idea of Sano in his home rankled terribly with Yanagisawa, who now lived here, in a smaller estate in the castle's official quarter, among his subordinates. His new mansion was too close to the street; he could hear voices and hoofbeats outside. He felt crowded by his servants and troops. How he missed the space and privacy he'd once enjoyed! It was too bad that the traps he'd installed in his old home hadn't killed Sano.

"Why don't you punish him?" Yoritomo said, hungry for revenge. "Why do we have to act as if everything is all right? Why can't we fight back?"

"Because we would lose," Yanagisawa said bluntly.

"No, we wouldn't," Yoritomo protested. "You have lots of allies, lots of troops."

"So does Sano."

"Your position is stronger than his."

"That's what I thought when I went up against Lord Matsudaira. I was wrong. His troops slaughtered mine on the battlefield." Yanagisawa's thoughts darkened with the memory. "My allies defected to him like rats fleeing a sinking ship. No," he declared. "I won't risk another war."

"But—"

"But nothing," Yanagisawa said, harsh in his determination to convince his son. "We were let off easy last time. You were allowed to stay in Edo." The shogun had insisted on keeping Yoritomo with him, even though Lord Matsudaira had wanted to exile Yanagisawa's whole family. "I was banished instead of killed. Next time we won't be so fortunate."

Yoritomo beheld Yanagisawa with a mixture of resignation and disappointment. "You're saying you've given up. Because you're afraid of losing, afraid of dying."

The masseur pressed his fingers deep into Yanagisawa's shoulder joints, touching tender spots. Yanagisawa winced. His son had always idolized him, but now Yoritomo had accused him of being a coward. The accusation was unjust.

"Sometimes fear is a better guide than courage is," he said. "Courage has led many a man to do the wrong things, with disastrous results. I learned that lesson when I took on Lord Matsudaira: We can't seize power by force. You should have learned it, too. But you're young." He watched Yoritomo blush, shamed by the implied accusation of stupidity. "You don't understand that when a strategy fails, you shouldn't rush out and do the same thing again. If you want different results, you have to try a new strategy."

Hope brightened Yoritomo's gaze. "Do you mean you have a new plan for defeating Sano and putting us on top of the regime?"

"Oh, yes." Yanagisawa smiled with pleasure as his masseur worked the stiffness out of his back muscles. "Never let it be said that I don't have a plan."

"But how can you win without going to war?"

"The time for war was over more than a century ago, when the Tokugawa clan and its allies conquered their rivals and unified Japan,"

Yanagisawa said, wise in hindsight. "This dictatorship won't be won by military maneuvers, I see now. Today's political climate calls for more subtle tactics."

"What are they? What are you going to do?" Apprehension shadowed Yoritomo's beautiful face. "Is there a part in your plan for me?"

Yanagisawa was touched by his son's wish to be included in whatever he did, no matter the dangers. Yoritomo was so good, so loyal. "Never fear," Yanagisawa said. "You're key to my whole scheme." Yoritomo was Yanagisawa's best hope of one day ruling Japan. Yanagisawa had big plans for him. "Now listen."

6

Sano and his retinue escorted his cousin Chiyo home.

She rode, semiconscious, in a palanquin carried by bearers that Sano had hired. The storm decreased to a light rain and the afternoon faded into dusk as he and his men accompanied the palanquin through the samurai enclave near the shogun's rice warehouses along the river. The rice was used to pay the Tokugawa retainers their stipends. Heavily guarded by Major Kumazawa's troops, it was sold to rice brokers, and converted to cash, by a bevy of officials.

Lanterns flickered outside the walled estates where Major Kumazawa and the officials lived. Sentries in guardhouses looked up to watch Sano's procession pass. This part of town was older than the rest of Edo; the white plaster on the walls was patched, the roof tiles weathered, the roads narrow and serpentine. Sano didn't think he'd been here before, but the double-roofed gate that displayed a banner emblazoned with the Kumazawa family crest—a stylized bear head in a circle—struck in him an eerie chord of recognition.

He and his men dismounted, and Sano ordered the sentries, "Tell Major Kumazawa I've brought his daughter home."

The sentries rushed to open the gate. Sano found himself in a court-yard lit by fires in stone lanterns outside the mansion, a low, half-timbered building raised on a stone foundation. Rain trickled off the overhanging eaves. Major Kumazawa rushed out the door, trailed by a gray-haired woman. They halted on the veranda. Déjà vu assailed Sano. Images surfaced from the depths of his mind.

He had a vision of this same courtyard, of Major Kumazawa and this woman who must be his wife. But they were younger, their hair black, their faces unlined. Sano heard a woman pleading and weeping, somewhere out of sight. Dizziness and chills washed through him. For a moment he couldn't breathe.

His vision was a memory. He had come here before. But when? And why?

The images, sounds, and sensations vanished as Major Kumazawa and his wife hurried to the palanquin. Major Kumazawa opened the door. Inside, Chiyo lay motionless, covered by a quilt that Sano had bought in a shop. Her eyes were closed, her head wrapped in a white cotton cloth stained with blood.

Major Kumazawa's wife cried out in dismay. The major demanded, "What happened to her?"

He didn't thank Sano for bringing Chiyo home. Detectives Marume and Fukida frowned at this affront to their master, but Sano recalled how he'd felt when reunited with his own kidnapped child. Courtesy had been the last thing on his mind.

"There's a cut on her head," Sano said. That, as he'd discovered, was the source of the blood on her clothes. "She hasn't any other injuries, as far as I could see. But you should send for a doctor."

Major Kumazawa barked orders to the servants who appeared on the veranda, then asked Sano, "Where did you find her?"

"On a street in Asakusa district," Sano said.

"I'll bring her in the house." As Major Kumazawa lifted his daughter, she awakened. She began to struggle.

"No!" she cried. "Don't touch me! Go away!"

"It's all right, little one," Major Kumazawa said, his voice as gentle as if he were talking to a child. "It's Papa. You're home safe now."

Her struggles ceased; she quieted. "Papa," she whispered.

As he carried her toward the house, his wife bustled along with them, stroking Chiyo's pale, muddy cheek, murmuring endearments. Major Kumazawa looked over his shoulder at Sano.

"I'm indebted to you," he said gruffly. "If you and your men would like to come in, please do."

"Right this way, Honorable Chamberlain," said a servant.

Sano could tell that his uncle didn't want him here, but he was curious to see the house. Perhaps it would trigger more memories. Furthermore, Sano had a stubborn streak.

"Come on," he told his detectives, and followed the servant inside the mansion.

They left their shoes and swords in the entryway. They were led down a corridor with polished cedar floors, past rooms concealed behind lattice and paper partitions. They arrived in a reception room with a dais backed by a landscape mural and an alcove that held a vase of chrysanthemums. The house seemed familiar to Sano, but only because it had the same architecture and décor as other samurai homes including his own. His own was much bigger than this, but he looked at his uncle's home through the eyes of the child he'd once been.

His family had lived in a tiny house behind the martial arts school that his father had operated. Compared to that, Major Kumazawa's estate was a palace. Sano thought of how his mother must have felt, banished to what had surely seemed like squalor to her. He recalled days when food had been scarce, winters when their house had been freezing because they couldn't afford enough coal. He knew his mother had suffered more than he had.

Major Kumazawa must have known about her poverty. He could have helped but hadn't.

Sano thought of the memory he'd experienced outside. He tried to dredge it up into the light where he could examine it, but it slipped away, elusive as a ghost.

After a long interval, Major Kumazawa entered the room. "Chiyo is being cared for by her mother and her maids." He gestured to Sano and the detectives and said, "Please sit."

Sano knelt in the position of honor by the alcove, the detectives near him. Major Kumazawa seated himself on the dais. He didn't offer refreshments, not that Sano would have accepted. Major Kumazawa was clearly ill at ease: He didn't like entertaining a stranger who was his blood kin and an outcast. Sano himself didn't exactly feel at home.

"I looked all over Asakusa district and didn't find Chiyo," Major Kumazawa said. "How did you find her?"

"I spotted her wandering in the rainstorm," Sano said.

"What a stroke of good luck." Then Major Kumazawa seemed to realize how ungracious he sounded. "But you brought my daughter back to me. I apologize for my bad manners." For once he seemed honestly contrite about how he'd behaved toward Sano. "A thousand thanks."

Sano bowed, accepting the thanks and the apology. He began to realize that Major Kumazawa's treatment of him wasn't entirely personal. Old samurai often became curmudgeons. If that was true of his uncle, Sano could live with it.

"How did Chiyo get there?" Major Kumazawa asked.

"It would seem that someone kidnapped her, then dumped her in the street," Sano said.

"Who?" Major Kumazawa clenched his fists; his expression tightened with anger.

"Your guess is as good as mine," Sano said. "While I was tending to your daughter, I sent my men to look around the area. It was deserted because of the rain. They didn't see anyone."

Major Kumazawa brooded darkly. "Two days Chiyo was gone. Where was she? And what happened to her during all that time?"

The sound of a sob interrupted the conversation. Sano, the detectives, and Major Kumazawa looked up and saw Chiyo's mother standing in the doorway. Tears streaked her contorted face. Major Kumazawa rose and went to her. She whispered in his ear, then fled. He returned to his guests, clearly shaken.

"My daughter," he began, then swallowed and drew a deep breath. "When my wife undressed and bathed Chiyo, she saw . . . injuries. And blood." He finished in a low, broken voice, "My daughter has been violated."

Her torn clothes had suggested the possibility of rape to Sano, but he was dismayed to have his suspicions confirmed. Major Kumazawa sank to his knees, stricken with horror and anguish. Rape was a terrible thing to happen to a woman, perhaps worse than death. Rape contaminated her body and spirit, destroyed her chastity and her honor. Sano and the detectives bowed their heads in sympathy.

Indignation transformed Major Kumazawa's face into a hideous mask so flushed with red that Sano thought the man would burst a vein. "This thing that has been done to my daughter is a disgrace! But it's not against the law!"

Tokugawa law didn't recognize rape as a crime. Men could take their sexual satisfaction where they chose, against a woman's will, and not be punished. But Chiyo's case was different.

"Your daughter was the victim of a kidnapping," Sano said, "and she was injured. The violation constitutes an assault. Kidnapping and assault are both illegal. The law won't let whoever hurt Chiyo get away with it."

This rapist had earned a stay in prison and torture by the jailers. He could also be sentenced to live as an outcast for a term set by the magistrate. And since he'd chosen a victim with political connections, he might even get the death penalty.

Major Kumazawa grimaced. "Tell that to the police. They wouldn't do anything to find Chiyo. They won't catch her attacker. No," he said, pounding his fists on the floor. "If I want him punished, I'll have to do it myself. But first I'll have to find him." He fixed his bitter gaze on Sano. "I must trouble you for another favor. Will you help me catch the bastard?"

Sano realized that he and his uncle had found common ground: They both wanted justice for Chiyo. Sano saw the attack on Chiyo as a personal offense to himself as well as her immediate family. He felt a new, unexpected kinship with his estranged relatives.

"Of course," he said. "I'll start at once. The first thing I need to do is speak with Chiyo."

"Why?"

"To ask her what happened."

Resistance flared in Major Kumazawa's eyes. "She was kidnapped and violated. What more do we need to know? I don't want her forced to relive it. She's been through enough."

Sano saw that working with his uncle would be no easy partnership. "Chiyo will relive what happened to her whether she talks about it or not." Sano knew that although Reiko seldom spoke of the episodes of violence in her life, she still had nightmares about them. "And right now Chiyo is our only source of information about her attacker."

"I don't want you to upset her," Major Kumazawa said, obstinate. "We should go out and shake up everyone in the district until somebody talks."

They might have to resort to that eventually, but Sano couldn't ignore their best lead, the victim who'd witnessed the crime. And he was getting fed up with his uncle's interference. "Understand that I don't need your permission to question Chiyo." Sano rose; so did his detectives. "You can be present while I do it, but I will question her, make no mistake."

Detectives Marume and Fukida looked gratified because Sano had put his foot down. Major Kumazawa stared in offense because Sano had pulled rank on him. How he must resent that Sano the outcast had risen so high in society!

He obviously realized that he'd been given an order he must obey, but he said, "Can't you at least wait until tomorrow?"

"No." Sano was loath to cause further pain to Chiyo, but the passage of time could erase important clues from her mind. He added, "I'll be careful with her. I give you my word."

Major Kumazawa rose reluctantly. "Very well."

In the women's quarters, Sano and Major Kumazawa entered a room where Chiyo lay in bed, her mother and the physician kneeling on either side. She looked small and delicate under a thick quilt. Her eyes were closed. The right side of her head had been shaved around an ugly red cut, crossed by stitches. Major Kumazawa stared at it, appalled.

The physician was a middle-aged man who wore the dark blue coat of his profession. "The cut wasn't deep." He covered it with salve and a cotton pad, then wound a bandage around Chiyo's head. "It should heal perfectly."

"What about the inside of her head?" Major Kumazawa said.

"It's too soon to tell."

"Is she unconscious?"

"No, just drowsy. I've given her a potion to ease the pain and let her sleep." The physician picked up a tray that held his instruments, jars of medicine, Chiyo's hair clippings, and a bloodstained cloth. "I'll come back to check on her in the morning." He bowed and departed.

Major Kumazawa knelt at the foot of the bed, obviously disturbed by his daughter's condition. His wife glanced up at Sano. She seemed too shy as well as too upset to speak. Chiyo's eyes fluttered open. She looked around, her pupils dilated wide and black by the drug. Her gaze fixed on Sano. Her lips formed broken, halting speech: ". . . thanks . . . rescuing me . . . grateful . . ."

Sano was moved by her effort. Even in her condition she had better manners than her father did. Sano knelt near her and noticed again her resemblance to his mother. She had the same sweet, pretty features set in a rectangular face. He thought of a time when he'd interrogated his mother about a crime, when she'd lain drugged and sleepy just like this. But Chiyo was the victim, not the accused.

"Chamberlain Sano is going to catch the person who did this to you," Major Kumazawa told her. "But first he needs to ask you a few questions." *Only a few*, his gaze warned Sano.

Chiyo nodded weakly. Sano began in a quiet voice, "Do you remember wandering in the Asakusa district before I found you? Can you tell me how you got there?"

Vagueness clouded her eyes. "I woke up lying in an alley. My head hurt. It was raining. When I stood up, I was so dizzy I could hardly walk. I didn't know where I was. But I kept going. When I was a child, Papa told me that if I were ever lost, I should walk until I saw something I recognized, I shouldn't just cry and wait for help."

Sano admired her bravery. He also approved of how Major Kumazawa had taught his daughter to be self-reliant. "Did you see anyone around when you woke up?"

Her forehead wrinkled. "No. I don't think there was anyone."

For now Sano avoided the subject of what the kidnapper had done to Chiyo. Maybe he could get enough information about the man without discussing the rape itself. He said, "Do you remember going to the Awashima Shrine with your baby?"

"My baby . . ." Alarm agitated Chiyo. "Where is my baby?" She tried to sit up, gasping and frantic.

Her mother gently restrained her, whispering, "It's all right, dearest. He's safe at home."

"I want to go home," Chiyo cried. "I want to see my children. They need me. I want my husband."

"I've sent for him," Major Kumazawa said. "He'll take you home as soon as you're well enough to go." He asked Sano, "Are you almost finished?"

"Almost." Sano asked Chiyo, "What happened at the shrine?"

She made an obvious, labored effort to calm herself. Her gaze wandered, as if into the past. "My baby started crying. He wasn't used to so many people, so much noise. I thought that if I took him someplace quiet, he would settle. So I left my attendants and carried him into a garden. That's the last thing I remember until . . . until . . ."

Chiyo's eyes and mouth opened wide in horror, at something that only she could see. She screamed, "No! Stop! Please!" and thrashed under the quilt. "Help! Help!"

She was remembering the rape, Sano realized. Her mother tried to soothe her, but she burst into a torrent of weeping. Major Kumazawa said to Sano, "That's enough." His paternal protectiveness outweighed his duty to obey Sano and their mutual wish to catch Chiyo's rapist. "Please go."

7

High on a hill above the city, Edo Castle's massive conglomeration of stone walls, gabled roofs, and watchtowers shimmered, hazy and insubstantial, in the rain and fog. As dusk deepened into evening, lights from its many lanterns wavered as if submerged in the sea.

Inside the castle, Sano's estate occupied an enclosed compound. The mansion's many wings angled around courtyards and gardens. Within the private chambers at the center of the estate, Reiko began the nightly ordeal of putting her daughter to bed.

"Time to go to sleep," Reiko said, patting the futon laid out on the floor.

"No!" Akiko said.

Reiko sighed. Akiko was a moody child, all sweetness one moment and all temper the next. Reiko wondered whether bad experiences she'd had while pregnant had affected her daughter's personality. Or maybe Akiko had never forgiven Reiko for leaving her behind when she and Sano had gone to rescue Masahiro after he'd been kidnapped. Sometimes they got along fine, but often they clashed wills like enemy warlords.

"Come on, Akiko, it's late, and you're tired," Reiko said.

"No tired," Akiko protested.

Her face bunched into a frown that portended one of her horrific tantrums. She didn't have them for anybody except Reiko, who, determined to learn to handle her child, resisted the temptation to call the nurse to deal with Akiko.

"No more arguments," she said gently but firmly. "You're going to bed now."

Akiko sobbed, screamed, and beat her head and heels on the floor as if possessed by a demon. Reiko soothed, scolded, and pleaded. By the time Akiko had worn herself out and fallen asleep, Reiko felt as beaten up as if she'd lost a battle.

She stepped out the door and saw Sano coming. He smiled, but an air of tension around him caused her heart to race. "What's happened?"

"No new political upheavals," Sano reassured her. "I met my uncle, Major Kumazawa, today."

"Ah," Reiko said, thinking that it was about time.

She accompanied Sano into their chamber, where he removed his rain-damp clothes. Reiko opened the cabinet, took out a robe, and helped him into it. "Why did you finally decide to make contact with your uncle?"

"I didn't. He came to me, to request my help." Sano explained that the man's daughter had gone missing and he'd spent the day searching for her in Asakusa.

Reiko felt a stir of excitement. Here, perhaps, was a new investigation for her to join. "Did you find any clues?" she said as she heated sake on a charcoal brazier.

"Better than that," Sano said, kneeling opposite Reiko. "I found Chiyo herself. She's alive."

Reiko was amazed at his quick results. "That's wonderful!" But even though she was glad for Chiyo's sake, she couldn't help feeling disappointed. The investigation was over already.

"I took her to my uncle's house," Sano said.

"The place where your mother grew up? What was it like?"

"About what you would expect. Typical for his rank."

Men weren't good at describing places in the detail that women wanted, Reiko thought. She sensed that the visit to his ancestral estate had caused Sano feelings he would rather not discuss. "Your uncle must have been very pleased and grateful."

"Pleased, I would have liked. Grateful, not exactly." Sano sounded nettled beneath his humor. "He's a stern, hard man—a real old-style samurai."

"Well, a plague on him," Reiko said, offended on Sano's behalf. "You brought his daughter home safe and sound."

"Not exactly sound." Sano described Chiyo's dazed, weak condition and the injury on her head. "And it appears that she was violated."

"How awful," Reiko murmured, recalling the time she'd been kidnapped by a madman who'd nearly ravished her. And she knew that the consequences of a rape could be even worse than the pain and terror.

Masahiro padded barefoot into the room and asked, "What does that mean, 'violated'?"

Reiko and Sano exchanged perturbed glances. They tried not to talk about adult matters when their son could hear, but Masahiro had sharp ears. He could sense when something had happened, and often showed up at the scene before his parents knew he was there. Reiko gestured at Sano. *You're his father; you explain.*

Sano told Masahiro, "It means she was hurt."

"Hurt how?"

Sano looked as flustered as Reiko felt. Masahiro was familiar with the facts of life; he'd seen animals mating, their offspring born. But he was too young and innocent to know about rape.

"Never mind." Sano put on a stern expression that closed the subject.

"Who did this to Chiyo?" Reiko asked. "Has she said?"

"She doesn't remember much." Sano puffed out his breath with frustrated concern. "And she became so upset that Major Kumazawa put a halt to my questions."

"Is Major Kumazawa my uncle, too?" Masahiro asked.

"He's your great-uncle," Sano said.

"Can I meet him?"

Reiko herself was eager to meet Sano's family. She wanted to know what her husband came from, to see his traits reflected in the faces of strangers. But she said, "Someday." A family that had suffered such an ordeal would be in no shape to contend with new relations. She asked Sano, "What are you going to do about Chiyo?"

"Major Kumazawa has asked me to find and punish the kidnapper."

"And you agreed?"

"Of course," Sano said.

Reiko heard misgivings in his voice, but they didn't put off her desire to collaborate in the investigation. "Can I help?"

Sano smiled with appreciation. "As a matter of fact, you can. Major Kumazawa doesn't want me to talk to Chiyo again. I could force him to cooperate, but after what Chiyo has been through, she probably wouldn't want to discuss it with a man. She might be more comfortable with a woman. So I asked Major Kumazawa if he would permit her to be questioned by my wife. He agreed, although reluctantly. Will you do it?"

"I'd be glad to," Reiko said. Not only did she welcome a chance to help catch a criminal and obtain justice for Chiyo; perhaps she could smooth Sano's relations with his newfound family.

"Chiyo insisted on going home to her husband and children," Sano said. "Her husband is a Captain Okubo; he's a retainer to Lord Horio, *daimyo* of Idzuma Province. They live inside the *daimyo*'s estate. You can talk to her there."

"I'll go first thing tomorrow," Reiko said.

"I'll be needing more help," Sano said. "I've sent for Hirata." Footsteps approached down the corridor, their gait slightly heavier on one leg. "Here he is now."

Into the room strode Hirata, the shogun's *sōsakan-sama*—Most Honorable Investigator of Events, Situations, and People. He'd inherited the post from Sano seven years ago, when Sano became chamberlain. He was also Sano's chief retainer and close friend, although their respective duties kept them much apart.

"Greetings," Hirata said, bowing.

He wasn't tall, and he wore modest garb, a gray and black kimono, surcoat, and trousers. His face was broad and ordinary; he didn't stand out in a crowd. But appearances were deceiving, Reiko knew. Seven years ago, Hirata had been seriously injured in the line of duty. A lesser man would be dead or an invalid, but Hirata had apprenticed himself to a mystic martial arts master. Rigorous training had whittled every spare bit of fat from his body, which was now all muscle, sinew, and bone as strong as steel. Secret rituals had conditioned his mind, had replaced his youthful, naïve mien with an expression of preternaturally mature wisdom. And he'd gained a reputation as the best martial artist in Edo.

Masahiro yelled, "Hah, yah!" and launched a flying kick at Hirata. Hirata took the kick in his stomach, howled in comic pain, and fell backward with a floor-shaking thud. Masahiro threw himself on Hirata. As they wrestled and Masahiro laughed, Reiko protested, "Masahiro, that's no way to greet a guest!"

Hirata let Masahiro pin him facedown. Masahiro sat on Hirata's back, crowing, "I win!"

"I surrender," Hirata said. "Let me up." Masahiro climbed off Hirata, who asked Sano, "How can I be of service?"

Sano told him about the kidnapping and assault while Reiko poured cups of sake for the men. "Right now I've no idea who might be responsible. After I spoke with Chiyo, I questioned her attendants, but they didn't see anything. I need you to help me beat the bushes for leads."

"I'll do my best." Hirata didn't mention any other work he might have pending. He had a detective corps to cover for him, and his first duty was to Sano, his sworn master. "I have some contacts who might be useful."

Masahiro had been listening with a pensive frown on his face. He blurted, "I want to help, too."

The adults regarded him with surprise. Sano said, "What? How?"

"I can look for clues," Masahiro said eagerly. "I can interrogate witnesses and suspects." He stammered the difficult words. "I'll catch the bad man."

Hirata chuckled. "Here's a pinecone that didn't fall far from the tree."

"Our son spends too much time playing detective," Reiko said with a laugh.

Masahiro bristled. "I'm not playing! I'm practicing!"

"Yes, and that's good," Sano said, "but this is a real investigation, not a game. We can't have you chasing a bad man who won't want to be caught. It could be dangerous."

"If anybody attacks me, I can defend myself," Masahiro insisted.

He'd proved he could, Reiko knew, but she said, "A real investigation is too complicated. It's for grown-ups, not children."

"You're too young," Sano said.

"I'm not. I'm almost ten!" Masahiro said.

"Your manners are worse than if you were half that age," Reiko rebuked him, but gently because she understood what it was like to want to be a detective and not be permitted. Once Sano had refused to let her participate in his investigations on the grounds that women weren't capable or allowed by tradition. Only by taking matters into her own hands, and proving her worth, had she prevailed. "Don't contradict your parents."

Masahiro bowed his head. "I'm sorry. Please forgive me." He was a good, considerate boy who only forgot courtesy when carried away by youthful impetuousness. "How long do I have to wait before I can be a detective?"

Reiko could feel Sano thinking that he didn't want their son following in his footsteps, investigating murders for the shogun, facing the constant threat of death. Neither did she. Sano said, "Until you're fifteen."

That was the official age of manhood for samurai, when they could marry, earn their keep, fight in wars, and take on other adult responsibilities. Time went so fast, Reiko thought with a pang of sadness; before they knew it, Masahiro would be a man.

"That's forever!" Masahiro protested. Although strong, mature, and self-controlled for his age, he looked on the verge of tears. "Isn't there something I can do?"

"No," Sano and Reiko said together. They both wished to protect Masahiro from the world. He'd already seen too much. Even though this case was within the family, without the danger of working for the shogun, it had its own particular horrors to which a child shouldn't be exposed.

"But—"

"Don't argue," Sano said sternly, although Reiko knew he hated to disappoint their son. "Our decision is final."

The rising sun shone pale and diluted through storm clouds as Sano left his compound with Detectives Marume and Fukida and his entourage. As they rode along the passage, water dripped from the eaves of the covered corridors atop the stone walls, onto their wicker hats and straw rain capes. Their horses' hooves splashed in puddles on the paving stones. High above them, far beyond Edo Castle, rain obliterated the green eastern hills outside the city. The pealing of temple bells echoed, then quickly faded, as if drowned by the humid summer air.

Sano and his men came upon another procession of mounted samurai, led by Yanagisawa. "Good day, Sano-*san*," Yanagisawa said. He and Sano exchanged polite bows. "I was sorry to hear about what happened to Major Kumazawa's daughter Chiyo."

He sounded genuinely concerned and sympathetic, but Sano's guard went up at once. "News travels fast," Sano said. He took for granted that Yanagisawa kept abreast of his business; he did the same for Yanagisawa. But Sano was alarmed by how efficient Yanagisawa's informants were.

"News travels especially fast when it concerns the uncle and cousin of a man as important as yourself," Yanagisawa said.

He was also aware of the relationship between Sano and the Kumazawa clan, Sano observed. "What other facts do you have stored up in case they should come in handy?" Sano said in a light, jocular tone.

Yanagisawa responded with a pleasant smile. "Not half as many as you do, I'm sure. I assume you're on your way to hunt down the person who perpetrated this crime against your clan?"

"You assume correctly." Sano wondered if Yanagisawa had planted a spy inside the Kumazawa estate because he'd figured Sano would eventually show up there.

"Well, I wish you the best of luck," Yanagisawa said. "And I'll be glad to help, if you like."

Memories flickered through Sano's mind. He saw himself and Yanagisawa rolling in the dirt together, locked in mortal, savage combat. He heard Yanagisawa howling for his blood. Yanagisawa's current behavior was truly perplexing.

"I'll keep your offer in mind," Sano said. "Many thanks."

They bowed, said their farewells, and rode in opposite directions. Fukida glanced over his shoulder and said, "*He* wants to help? How about that?"

"Maybe a rat can change its whiskers," Marume said, "but he's got a trick up his sleeve, mark my word."

"Obviously," Sano said.

"What are you going to do?" Fukida asked.

"I'm going to stop relying on spies who can tell me what Yanagisawa ate for breakfast but can't find out what's in his mind," Sano said. "It's time to bring in an expert."

Escorted by a squadron of guards, Reiko rode in her palanquin through the district south of Edo Castle, where the *daimyo* and their hordes of retainers lived. Her bearers carried her down wide boulevards thronged with mounted samurai, past the barracks that enclosed each huge, fortified estate. Rain began to patter on the roof of Reiko's palanquin as her procession stopped at the gatehouse of the estate that belonged to the lord of Idzuma Province. Lieutenant Tanuma said to the guards, "The wife of the honorable Chamberlain Sano is here to see the wife of Captain Okubo."

The guard opened the gate and called someone to announce Reiko's arrival. Reiko had read the Kumazawa clan dossier and knew that Chiyo was a lady-in-waiting to the *daimyo*'s womenfolk. She hoped Chiyo was receiving good care here.

After a brief interval, a manservant put his head out the gate, spoke with the guard, and shook his head. The guard told Lieutenant Tanuma, "Sorry, Captain Okubo's wife doesn't live here anymore. She's staying at her father's house in Asakusa."

Sano and his entourage rode across Nihonbashi, the bridge that had the same name as the river it spanned as well as Edo's merchant quarter. The bridge was jammed with traffic. Porters carried trunks for samurai traveling in palanquins; peasant women armed with market baskets jostled begging priests and children; foot soldiers patrolled. Below them, barges floated on the murky brown water. Wharves stacked with lumber, bamboo poles, vegetables, and coal occupied shores lined with warehouses. Drizzle hung so thickly in the air that it muted the sounds of seagulls shrieking, oars splashing, and voices raised in laughter and argument. The wet atmosphere intensified the stench from the fish market at the north end of the bridge. Sano scanned the crowds, looking for Toda Ikkyu, the master spy.

Earlier, he'd stopped in the chambers within Edo Castle that housed the *metsuke*, the Tokugawa intelligence service. A secretary had informed him that Toda was working at the bridge. He knew from experience that Toda was hard to pick out of a crowd. Toda was so ordinary in appearance, so utterly lacking in distinctive features, that Sano could never remember what he looked like even though they'd known each other for more than a decade. Neither could most other people. That was an advantage in Toda's line of work.

As Sano eyed the faces of samurai who passed him, he thought of what he'd learned from Toda's dossier some months ago. Toda had begun his life as a *sutego*—an abandoned child, one among legions that roamed the cities. No one knew who his parents were. Toda had fended for himself by stealing. One night, when he was twelve, he sneaked into the estate of a rich *daimyo*. There he lived for three months, filching food from the kitchen, sleeping under the raised buildings. The *daimyo*'s men noticed things missing and found traces of Toda, but they couldn't catch him until the dogs cornered him. They brought him before the *daimyo*.

"I can use a boy with your talents," the *daimyo* had reportedly said. "From now on you're in my service."

He put Toda to work spying on his retainers, reporting any hint or act of disloyalty. This went on for ten years, during which Toda was granted the rank of samurai. Then the *daimyo* ran into financial trouble; he couldn't pay the cash tribute required by the shogun, Tokugawa Ietsuna. He presented Toda to the shogun and said, "A good spy is worth more than any amount of money, and this young fellow is the best."

So the legend went. Toda had risen within the ranks of the *metsuke* until he became the chief spy. To him and his subordinates belonged much of the credit for keeping the Tokugawa regime in power.

Now Sano heard a voice call, "Greetings, Honorable Chamberlain Sano. Are you looking for me, by any chance?" He saw a samurai who appeared to be Toda, leaning against the bridge's railing. Toda was ageless, his body neither tall nor short, fat nor thin, his face composed of features seen on a million others. He wore the ubiquitous wicker hat and straw rain cape, and an expression of world-weary amusement that was vaguely familiar.

"Yes, as a matter of fact." Sano jumped off his horse and joined Toda; his men halted; traffic streamed around them. "I'm not interrupting any secret operation, am I?"

"Not at all," Toda said. "I haven't done much of that since Lord Matsudaira's death. Things have been quiet lately. I'm just conducting school."

"What kind of school?" Sano asked.

"For the next generation of *metsuke* agents. Political strife will flare up again eventually, and we'll need new spies who know the craft."

Sano looked around. "So where are your students?"

"They'll show up soon. What can I do for you?"

"I want you to put Chamberlain Yanagisawa under surveillance," Sano said.

Interest enlivened Toda's expression. "Why? Have you reason to believe he's plotting against you?"

"Only that he's been too nice for too long."

"Indeed he has. As I said, things are quiet." Toda added, "I must tell you that Yanagisawa already has us spying on you."

"That doesn't surprise me," Sano said. Yanagisawa was far more careful of potential rivals than Sano had ever been.

"And since I've told you about his spying, I also have to tell him about yours, just to be fair."

"That doesn't surprise me, either." Sano knew that the *metsuke* had to serve all the top officials in the regime, keep them happy, and offend none. That was how Toda and his kind rode the shifting tides of political power. "Do what you must."

"Wouldn't you rather use your own men?" Toda said, hinting that they were more trustworthy than himself.

"They're on the job, too."

"But they've come up empty, and that's why you're calling on us," Toda said, wisely superior.

"I might as well deploy all the ammunition at hand." Although Sano couldn't entirely trust Toda, he'd run out of other options. "Begin your surveillance today. Handle it personally."

"I assure you that my agents are trained and competent."

"But you're the best."

Humor crinkled Toda's eyes. "Flattery is nice, but what I would really like—"

His gaze suddenly moved past Sano and sharpened. He called, "Kimura-*san*! Ono-*san*! Hitomi-*san*!"

Three people walking across the bridge stopped abruptly. One was a stout woman with a shawl that covered her hair and a basket over her arm. One was a water-seller carrying wooden buckets that hung from a pole across his shoulders. The other was a filthy beggar dressed in rags.

Toda beckoned, and the three lined up before him. "How did you know it was us?" said the woman. She pulled down her shawl, revealing a shaved crown and hair tied in a samurai topknot.

"That's not a bad costume, Kimura-*san*, but you walk like a sumo wrestler," Toda said. "Nobody on the lookout for a spy would mistake you for a woman." He turned to his other students. "Hitomi-*san*, your buckets are too light; I could tell they're empty. Don't be so lazy when you're on a real job. It'll get you killed. And you, Ono-*san*," he said to the beggar. "I saw a merchant throw a coin on the ground, and you didn't pick it up. A samurai like you wouldn't because it's beneath you, but a real beggar would have."

The students hung their heads. Toda said, "You all fail this lesson. Go back to the castle."

They slunk off. Sano said, "Ah, a class on secret surveillance."

"Weren't you a little harsh on your boys?" Marume called from astride his horse. "I didn't see through their disguises."

"You weren't paying attention," Toda said. "But you should be. You might miss someone who's stalking your master."

Marume looked chastened. A chill passed through Sano. Did Yanagi-sawa plan to assassinate him? Was he acting friendly because he knew Sano wouldn't be around much longer?

"What I would really like," Toda said, resuming their conversation, "is for you to ensure that if there's a political upheaval and you come out on top, I'll survive and prosper."

That was a fair deal as far as Sano was concerned. "Find out what Yanagisawa is up to, and I will."

9

The rain turned into a downpour while Reiko and her escorts traveled to Asakusa. By the time they reached Major Kumazawa's estate, the roof of her palanquin was leaking and her cloak was damp. She alighted in the courtyard, under a roof that was supported on pillars and covered a path leading up the steps of the mansion. She'd been curious to see Sano's clan's ancestral home, but the streaming rain obscured the buildings.

An old woman met her on the veranda, bowed, and said, "Welcome, Honorable Lady Reiko. We've been expecting you." She was in her sixties, gray-haired, modestly dressed. Her plain, somber face was shadowed under the eyes, as if from a sleepless night. "My name is Yasuko. I am Chiyo's mother." She ushered Reiko into the mansion's entryway, where Reiko removed her shoes and cloak. "I'm sorry you had to make such a long journey in this weather." She seemed genuinely regretful. "It would have been easier for you to see Chiyo at her home in town, but she is unable to return there. Her husband has cast her off."

Reiko was shocked, although she realized she shouldn't be. Society viewed a woman who'd been violated as disgraced and contaminated. Rape was considered akin to adultery, even though the victim wasn't to blame.

"When he came last night to fetch Chiyo, he found out what had happened to her," Yasuko explained. "He no longer wants her as his wife. He means to get a divorce."

"How terrible," Reiko said as the woman escorted her through the mansion's dim, dank corridors.

52

Her husband could divorce Chiyo by simply picking up a brush and inking three and a half straight lines on a piece of paper. And that was a mild punishment. He could have sent her to work in a brothel if he so chose.

"What is worse, her husband has kept their children, and he won't even let her see them," Yasuko said. "She is very upset."

She slid open a door, called inside, "Lady Reiko is here," and stood aside for Reiko to enter.

Chiyo was sitting up in bed, propped by pillows. A quilt covered her from bosom to toes, even though the room was warm and stuffy. Her lank hair spilled from the bandage that swathed her head. Her features were so swollen from crying that Reiko couldn't tell what she looked like under normal circumstances. Chiyo's mouth quivered and her chest heaved with sobs.

Reiko knew that state of profound grief that possesses mind and body like an uncontrollable force. She'd experienced it once in Miyako, when she'd thought Sano had been killed, and again when she'd gone north to rescue Masahiro and found evidence that he was dead. Now Reiko faced a woman who'd lost her husband and children even though they were still alive. She forgot that she'd once been ready to dislike Sano's relatives because they cared more for social customs than for their blood kin. Her heart went out to Chiyo.

She knelt beside Chiyo, bowed, and said, "I am so sorry about what happened." She felt inadequate, unable to think of anything else to say but, "Please accept my sympathy."

"Many thanks." Chiyo's voice broke on a sob. "You're very kind."

Her mother offered Reiko refreshments. Reiko politely refused, was pressed, then accepted. The social routine gave Chiyo time to compose herself. Yasuko went off to see about the food. Reiko sensed that she didn't want to listen while Reiko questioned Chiyo and hear disturbing answers.

"Honorable Lady Reiko, I appreciate your coming to talk to me," Chiyo said humbly.

"There's no need to call me by my title," Reiko said. "My name will do."

"Very well, Reiko-san. A thousand apologies for causing you so much trouble."

Reiko liked Chiyo for caring about other people's feelings even after her terrible ordeal. "I'm sorry we had to meet under such circumstances."

Chiyo's face crumpled.

Reiko had to force herself to say, "My husband wants me to ask you about what happened. Can you bear it?"

Chiyo nodded meekly. A tremulous sigh issued from her. "But what good will it do?"

"It will help my husband catch the man who hurt you."

Tears trickled down Chiyo's drenched face. Her eyes were so red that she looked as if she were weeping blood. "Suppose he does. Nothing will change. My husband won't take me back. Last night he told me I was dead to him, dead to our children. Once he loved me, but he doesn't anymore. He looked so stern, so hateful." She wailed, "I'll never see my babies again!"

Reiko could hardly bear to imagine her own children ripped away from her. Alarmed at Chiyo's suffering, she urged, "Wait a while. Your husband may feel differently."

"No, he won't," Chiyo insisted. Reiko's sympathy and family connection made Chiyo speak more frankly than she might have with another stranger. "He's a good man, but once he makes up his mind, he never changes it."

How Reiko deplored male obstinacy and pride!

"He thinks I've dishonored our family." Chiyo sobbed. "I think maybe he's right."

"Why?"

"Because I brought it on myself."

"No, you didn't," Reiko said firmly. "My husband told me what you said happened at the shrine. You left your group because your baby was upset. You got kidnapped. That wasn't your fault."

"That isn't all that happened. I remember more than I told your husband. It's coming back to me in bits and pieces."

Controlling her eagerness for information, Reiko spoke gently: "What else do you remember?"

"I took my baby into the garden, and I nursed him." Chiyo's arms crept out from under the quilt and cradled around the infant who should have been there but wasn't. "I heard someone moaning behind a grove of bamboo. He called for help. I went to see what was wrong."

Women were taught from an early age to put themselves at the service of others, and Chiyo had an obliging nature. Reiko understood what must have happened, and she burned with anger at the rapist. "He lured you to him by playing on your kindness."

"But I was stupid!" Chiyo cried. "I fell for the trick. I deserve for my husband to divorce me and take our children."

Women were also taught to be humble and accept responsibility for whatever ills came their way. "No!" Reiko said. "You couldn't have known it was a trick. Neither could anybody else. Don't blame yourself."

Weeping contorted Chiyo's face. "My husband does."

So would most other people, Reiko thought sadly. "Your husband is wrong."

"I'm fortunate that my father hasn't cast me off, too."

Most fathers probably would shun a daughter who'd been violated. The fact that Major Kumazawa hadn't bespoke his love for Chiyo. Perhaps Sano's picture of him as a rigid, tradition-bound samurai wasn't completely accurate.

"Your father has put the blame exactly where it belongs—on the man who hurt you," Reiko said. "He wants to catch him and punish him. So do I." She felt her own taste for vengeance. "Don't you?"

"Oh, I don't know." Chiyo looked worried at the thought of taking direct action against anyone. She probably didn't have a vengeful bone in her body, Reiko thought. "But if that's what everyone else wants . . ."

"We want justice for you. But we need your help."

"All right." Chiyo was clearly used to obeying authority. "What do you want me to do?"

"Tell me everything you can remember about the kidnapping and the attack. Let's begin with the man who tricked you. What did he look like?"

Chiyo pondered, frowned, then shook her head. "I don't know. I recall walking up to the bamboo grove. After that, everything is a blank until . . ." A shudder wracked her body. "Until I woke up." Chiyo turned her face into the pillow, as if hiding from the recollection.

Reiko speculated that Chiyo had been grabbed, then forced to drink a potion that rendered her unconscious and erased memories. She leaned forward, bracing herself to hear the awful details of the rape. She spoke quietly, trying not to pressure Chiyo. "Then what happened?"

"He . . . he touched me where no one but my husband has ever touched." Chiyo drew deep breaths and swallowed hard. "He suckled milk from me. And . . . he bit me."

She opened her robe. On her breasts, around the nipples, were curved rows of tooth marks, red and bloody. Reiko winced. "Did you see his face?"

"Only for a moment. Everything was misty and blurry. It was like . . ." Chiyo fumbled for words. "I once read a poem about a pavilion of clouds. It reminded me of that."

Reiko wondered if the clouds had been a hallucination caused by a drug.

"The clouds covered his face, except for his eyes and mouth," Chiyo said.

He'd worn a mask, Reiko deduced.

Chiyo shrank against the cushions, reliving her fear. She whispered, "He was so ugly and cruel. Like a demon."

"Was he someone you recognized? Did he seem familiar?"

"No. At least I don't think so."

"Would you recognize him if you saw him again?"

"Perhaps," Chiyo said uncertainly.

Reiko hid her dismay at the idea that the rapist might get away with his crime because Chiyo had so little memory of it. "Can you remember anything that might help us identify him?"

More shudders convulsed Chiyo. "His voice. While he did it, he muttered, 'Dearest mother. My beloved mother.'"

Reiko felt her own body shiver with disgust at the rapist's perversion. "Did you hear anything besides his voice?"

"The rain and thunder outside."

That didn't help narrow down the location; it had been raining all over Edo for days. And maybe Chiyo had imagined the clouds she'd seen. "Clouds and rain," was the poetic term for sexual release. Maybe the drug had conjured up the clouds and linked them with the rain, and her violation, in her dazed mind.

"Think again. Can you remember anything else at all?" Reiko said hopefully.

"I'm sorry, I cannot." Chiyo sighed, exhausted and weakened from reliving her ordeal. "I went back to sleep."

Then she froze rigid, her muscles locked in a sudden, brief spasm. Her expression alternated among shock, fright, and horror. "No! Oh, no!"

"What's wrong?" Urgency seized Reiko. "What do you remember?"

"Something new. I woke up again. Just for an instant. Because he slapped my face." Chiyo touched her cheek. "And I heard him say that if I told anybody what he'd done to me, he would kill me, and kill my baby, too."

Her voice rose in hysteria. "I told! And I shouldn't have! Now I'll be punished. Now my baby is going to die!"

"That's not going to happen," Reiko assured Chiyo. "You're safe here. Your father will protect you. My husband and I will catch the man before he can make good on his threat." Reiko would do everything in her power to deliver the monster to justice. Even though she knew there was no guarantee that she would succeed, she said, "I promise."

10

Sano and his entourage arrived in the street where he'd found Chiyo. The rain had stopped for the moment. The balcony that had sheltered him and his men belonged to one of several shops in a row that sold confectionaries. Lines of customers extended outside the doors. Sano worked his way down the row, asking shopkeepers if they'd seen Chiyo stumbling through the rain yesterday.

"I saw her," said one man as he wrapped cakes. "I thought she was just a drunken whore."

Sano retraced Chiyo's footsteps around a corner and down another block, whose shops sold religious supplies. Two dealers had seen Chiyo; the rest hadn't. Dividing the shops was an alley, wider than the usual narrow space that ran between buildings. It was a firebreak, designed to reduce crowding and prevent the spread of fires, and apparently used as a side street. Sano and Detectives Marume and Fukida walked down the alley, skirting puddles. Balconies overhung recessed doorways and malodorous nightsoil bins. As he examined the paving stones, Sano spotted blood that had collected in the cracks. He pictured Chiyo falling, hitting her head.

"This is where Chiyo was dumped," Sano said.

An old woman with a tobacco pipe clamped between her teeth hobbled out on a balcony, picked up a quilt that had been left out in the rain, wrung out the soaked fabric, and cursed. Sano called up to her, "Did you see anyone come through here yesterday, during the storm?"

"An oxcart. They take a shortcut instead of going around the block."

The woman puffed on her pipe, which gave off foul smoke. "There's just enough room for them to squeeze through, but they scrape the walls. And the oxen leave dung. Filthy beasts! I pick up the dung, save it in this bucket, and throw it at the drivers." She cackled.

"Chiyo must have been dumped from that oxcart," Sano said to his detectives, then asked the woman, "Did you get a look at the driver? What was the cart carrying?"

"No. I didn't see. It was covered by a piece of cloth."

"He hid her under the cloth so no one would see her," Fukida said.

"But who is 'he'?" Marume asked.

"That's the question," Sano said. "Let's go find that oxcart." He recalled the construction site they'd passed yesterday. "I know where to start."

The Hibiya administrative district near Edo Castle was thick with samurai. They filled the streets where government officials lived and worked in mansions protected by high stone walls. Some of them wore the silk robes of high rank, some the armor tunics of soldiers; all were equipped with the customary two swords of their class. Some rode in palanquins or on horseback followed by attendants; the lowlier trudged on foot. They all moved aside to make way for Hirata.

As he rode down his cleared path through the crowd, his reputation as the top martial artist in Edo cloaked him like a golden suit of armor. Rumor said he could read minds, see behind him, anticipate an opponent's every move, and communicate with the spirit world.

There was truth to the rumor. His training had developed mental powers that everyone had to some degree but few ever learned to exercise.

Part of his perception focused on his surroundings. It noted the faces he passed, the plod of hooves and sandals on wet streets, the rustle of straw rain capes, the bright umbrellas. The other part, honed by arcane training rituals, sensed the energy auras around each human being. In each pattern of heat and light and vibration he could read personality and emotion. Some pulsed faintly, the auras of weak wills; others flared with confidence. In battle, the aura functioned as a warrior's first line of defense, a shield. A strong aura could deflect blows as effectively as a sword could and defeat an enemy without a single strike.

In present company, no aura was as powerful as Hirata's.

Now Hirata perceived a configuration of arrogance and recklessness in three auras among the crowd. They belonged to three young soldiers who came riding toward him. The men jumped from their saddles and blocked his path. The tallest one had eyebrows like black slashes, an out-thrust square jaw, and the lean, muscular physique of a man who spent much time at martial arts practice, unlike many samurai. His armor tunic sported the Tokugawa crest. He swaggered up to Hirata and said, "I challenge you to a duel."

Hirata experienced a sinking sensation. "You don't want to do this," he said.

"What's the matter? Are you scared I'll beat you?" the soldier taunted. "Come down and fight!"

This wasn't the first time Hirata had been challenged. A reputation like his had certain disadvantages. He'd lost count of how many samurai had accosted him, eager to prove their fighting skills superior to his. So far none had succeeded. But they'd caused Hirata serious problems nonetheless.

The soldier's companions yelled, "Coward! Loser!"

A crowd gathered around Hirata and the samurai, avid for a fight. "Well?" the soldier shouted. "Aren't you going to defend your honor?"

"I'm going to give you a chance to save your life," Hirata said. "Go, and we'll pretend this never happened."

The soldier went red with anger. "Are you saying I'm not good enough to fight you? In front of all these people?"

"I'm saying don't be foolish."

"I'll make you fight me," the soldier huffed. He looked around the audience and spied a teenaged peasant boy, a servant. "Hey, you! Come here."

The boy looked dismayed to be drawn into the argument. The soldier's friends grabbed him. They shoved him at the soldier, who drew his sword and said to Hirata, "If you won't, I'll fight this boy instead."

Hirata was appalled at the lengths to which men would go in order to provoke him. "Wait," he said, and jumped off his horse. He couldn't let an innocent bystander suffer.

The spectators cheered as he strode forward. He seized the friends, twisted their arms, and flung them to the ground. They shrieked. The boy scampered off unharmed. The soldier yelled and charged at Hirata, waving his sword.

Hirata's mind and body instinctively united in action. He drew a deep breath that aerated his entire body. His heart pumped blood and energy through his veins as a mystic trance came upon him. His perception expanded. He projected his vision into the future. It showed him ghostly images where the people would move in the next few moments. He saw the soldier coming as if in slowed motion, his ghost one step ahead of him. The ghost's sword traced curving, shimmering lines that the real blade would soon follow. Hirata glided between the lines. The soldier's sword whistled harmlessly around him. Hirata launched a kick at the ghost.

A split instant later, his foot struck the soldier's stomach. The soldier howled, flying backward into the crowd, which scattered to get out of his way. He hit the side of a building. His head banged against the wall. His face went blank. He slid down the wall, leaving a red smear where his head had hit. He sagged onto the ground, his scalp bleeding profusely.

Hirata's awareness reverted to normal. The ghostly images and energy auras faded; his breathing and pulse slowed. He found himself in the center of a silent, awestruck audience. The soldier lay crumpled, motionless. His friends rushed to him, crying, "Ibe *san*! Are you all right?"

"He'll wake up soon," Hirata said with more confidence than he felt. He was good at gauging the force necessary to subdue attackers without killing them, but he hadn't anticipated the wall meeting Ibe's head.

"Let this be a lesson to anyone who wants to challenge me," Hirata announced.

The crowd dispersed. As the friends of the soldier hoisted him onto his horse and led it off, along came a *doshin* Hirata knew from his police days. The *doshin*, named Kurita, was an older man with a rough, cheerful face, dressed in a short kimono and cotton leggings. In addition to his swords he wore a *jitte*—a metal wand with a hook above the hilt for catching an attacker's blade—standard police equipment. His three assistants followed him, armed with rope for restraining criminals.

"Well, if it isn't Hirata-*san*," he said. "Not another duel! Haven't you been warned about that?"

"Yes, by the shogun himself, no less."

The shogun had heard reports of the duels and not been pleased. He abhorred violence, and he'd ordered Hirata to cease dueling and threatened him with banishment if he didn't stop.

"We can't have you killing and maiming Edo's best young men, especially those from the Tokugawa army," Kurita said.

"If Edo's best young men would leave me alone, there'd be no problem," Hirata said.

He rode to police headquarters, a walled compound in the southern corner of the Hibiya district. Guards let him through the ironclad gate, into a courtyard surrounded by barracks and stables. A few criminals, recently arrested, their hands bound with rope, huddled miserably under the dripping eaves, awaiting an escort to jail.

Hirata strode into the main building. The reception room was a cavernous space divided by square pillars that supported a low ceiling. Messengers crouched on the floor and smoked pipes that fouled the air. Closed skylights leaked water into buckets set on the platform where three clerks knelt at desks. The chief clerk greeted Hirata and said, "It's been a long time."

"Greetings, Uchida-*san*," Hirata said.

Uchida was a middle-aged samurai with flexible, comic features. He'd held his job since Hirata had been a child, and was a trove of information about crime, criminals, and all police business in Edo.

"What can I do for you today?" Uchida asked.

"I need your help with a case I'm investigating." Hirata explained, "Chamberlain Sano's cousin Chiyo was kidnapped."

"So I've heard." Uchida's mobile features drooped with concern. He lowered his voice. "Raped, wasn't she? Poor girl. Well, I'm glad she's home safe. I hope you catch the bastard. How can I help?"

"Her father told Chamberlain Sano that when she went missing, he reported it to the police," Hirata began. "Have you heard about that, too?"

Uchida pulled a grimace. "Major Kumazawa stalked in here like a conquering general. He demanded that we drop everything and look for his daughter. But we couldn't, could we? Put every man on the search and let the criminals run wild in the meantime?"

"Of course not," Hirata agreed. "But I hope someone made an effort to find Chiyo."

"Sure we did," Uchida said. "A missing person is a missing person. We were duty-bound to investigate even if Major Kumazawa didn't exactly make us eager to do it."

If Major Kumazawa hadn't been so high-handed, the police might have worked harder and rescued Chiyo sooner, Hirata thought. "What did the investigation turn up?"

"Nothing," Uchida said. "Our officers in Asakusa had a look around the shrine where she disappeared, but nobody there saw anything. But I've got a bit of news that might be related to the crime."

"What?" Hirata said, surprised. "Did you tell Major Kumazawa?" The man hadn't given Sano any information from the police, as far as Hirata knew.

"I didn't get a chance," Uchida defended himself. "He threw a fit because we didn't all jump at once, then he stormed out of here before I could speak."

"Well, cough it up," Hirata said.

Uchida paused, letting the suspense build, until prodded by a frown from Hirata. "Chamberlain Sano's cousin isn't the only woman to be kidnapped lately. There have been two others."

11

"Is anyone following us?" Yanagisawa said.

"No, master," said one of his two bodyguards.

They were riding along a rain-swept quay in the Hatchobori district. Their wicker hats concealed their faces; their straw capes covered the identifying crests on their garments. Yanagisawa glanced furtively over his shoulder at the watercraft moored at the quay. He didn't see anyone except laborers hurrying goods from barges to warehouses. But this was a time for extra caution.

The other guard said, "Your precautions seem to have worked."

After leaving Edo Castle, Yanagisawa and his guards had traveled by palanquin to the estate of a *daimyo* who was an ally. They'd borrowed horses, donned rain gear, and ridden out the back gate. They'd surely lost anyone who'd followed them from the castle. Now they turned down a street where shops, restaurants, and teahouses occupied narrow storefronts. The street was deserted except for a samurai—one of Yanagisawa's own troops—who stood outside a teahouse distinguished by a giant conch shell hung above its entrance.

Yanagisawa's party dismounted. The samurai opened the door. Yanagisawa and his bodyguards stepped inside, where two more of his soldiers waited in a room with a *tatami* floor and a low table for drinks, otherwise empty. They'd cleared out the proprietor and customers in advance of Yanagisawa's arrival.

"Are they here yet?" Yanagisawa asked, shedding his wet hat and cape.

The soldiers pointed to a doorway covered with a blue curtain. As he moved toward it, Yanagisawa felt excitement speed his pulse. He was embarking upon the plan he'd outlined to his son last night. His success depended upon the people he was about to meet.

Pushing aside the curtain, he stepped into another room. On the *tatami* floor knelt two old women. Both in their sixties, they wore rich silk robes patterned in muted colors that gleamed in the gray light from the barred window. Their faces were made up with white rice powder and red rouge, their hair upswept and anchored with lacquer combs. They both looked out of place in these humble surroundings. Otherwise, they could not have been more different.

The younger woman boldly spoke first. "You have kept us waiting for more than an hour." Her speech was crisp, precise, high-class. She had an emaciated figure on which her rich garments hung like cloth on sticks. Her face was narrow, with elegant bone structure, but the right side was distorted, its muscles bunched together, the eye half closed, as if in pain.

"It was best that we not arrive at the same time and be seen together," Yanagisawa explained.

"Still, you took far too long getting here, Honorable—"

Yanagisawa raised his hand. "We'll not use our real titles or names," he said, kneeling opposite the women. "You can call me 'Ogata.' I'll call you 'Lady Setsu.' "

"Surely such theatrics are not necessary here." She swept a disdainful gaze around the shabby room, the window that gave a view of an empty alley in a neighborhood where no one they knew ever came.

"There are spies everywhere," Yanagisawa said, "as you well know."

"Lady Setsu" nodded, conceding his point. Her right eye leaked involuntary tears.

"Me, what about me?" the elder woman piped up. She had a babyish voice and a doughy face that reminded Yanagisawa of a rice cake dusted with powdered sugar. "What shall I be called?" She giggled. "I've always liked the name 'Chocho.' "

Butterfly, Yanagisawa thought. *How inappropriate for such an old, fat woman.* " 'Lady Chocho' you shall be," he said, putting on his most gallant, charming manner. "It's most suitable. You are as pretty and graceful as your namesake."

Lady Chocho preened, delighted by his flattery. Yanagisawa smiled. He'd already won an ally. But her companion frowned.

"It was quite inconvenient and uncomfortable to travel so far in such bad weather," Lady Setsu said, "particularly since my health is poor, as you well know."

Yanagisawa knew she suffered from terrible headaches that caused spasms in her face. "Yes, I do know, and I apologize for bringing you all the way out here," he said contritely.

Lady Chocho had borne the fruit that was key to his plan, whose acquisition was the object of this meeting. But Lady Setsu had a say in the matter, too.

"I didn't mind coming," Lady Chocho said, beholding Yanagisawa with the admiration that he often excited in both women and men.

Lady Setsu shot her a glance. Lady Chocho quailed and bowed her head. Lady Setsu had much influence over her friend, Yanagisawa knew from his informants.

"Why did you choose such a squalid dump?" Lady Setsu brushed at her sleeves as if afraid of fleas.

"Because it has no connection to us, and we'll never use it again," Yanagisawa said. "Those are my favorite criteria for places to hold secret meetings."

"Very well. I suppose you have a good reason for summoning us?" Lady Setsu's voice hinted that it had better be good. Even though he was the shogun's second-in-command, her age, her pedigree, and the irritability caused by her pain made her insolent.

"Yes," Yanagisawa said. "I've a proposal to make."

Suspicion narrowed her good eye. "What sort of proposal?"

"For a collaboration that would benefit us both."

Lady Setsu permitted herself a thin, bad-humored smile, which only appeared on the side of her face not distorted by the headache. "What can you offer that would induce us to collaborate with *you*?"

She pronounced the last word as if she thought him a demon incarnate, which she probably did. Yanagisawa didn't mind. He would rather be feared and reviled than discounted.

"I can offer you a chance at what you most want in the world," he said.

Lady Chocho tugged Lady Setsu's sleeve. "What's he talking about?"

"Quiet," Lady Setsu ordered. To Yanagisawa she said, "Why do you think that we want for anything? We're quite comfortably situated."

"That could change." Yanagisawa paused to let her absorb the ominous impact of his words. "The shogun's health is uncertain."

Lady Setsu regarded him suspiciously. "His Excellency was well enough to attend the martial arts tournament yesterday."

She was well informed, Yanagisawa observed. "Just last month he was wretchedly ill. You must be aware that he grows feebler with every passing year."

"Well, yes. But he often fancies himself ill when he isn't really."

"Still, he's an old man. He's expected to die sooner rather than later."

Lady Setsu hastened to say, "He's been threatening to die for ages." Just as Yanagisawa had hoped, the prospect of the shogun's passing deeply worried her. "He hasn't yet."

"Nobody lives forever," Yanagisawa pointed out. "And when he does die, the regime will change hands. The new dictator will have little use for people close to the past shogun." In case she missed his hint, he added, "People such as you."

Fear flashed across her expression. Yanagisawa knew he had her in his grasp now. "People such as yourself," she retorted.

"True," Yanagisawa said. "I'd like to know that when the dictatorship does change hands, I'll be safe. Wouldn't you?"

Lady Setsu said grudgingly, "I see your point."

"I don't," Lady Chocho said, pouting because they'd left her out of their discussion.

Yanagisawa turned to her with his most charming smile. "My point is that we have so much in common that we're destined to be great friends."

"Oh, I'd like that." Lady Chocho simpered.

Lady Setsu flicked a tolerant glance at her companion, then said to Yanagisawa, "What is your proposal?"

He hid his glee that he'd coaxed her this far. He must exercise caution. "The first step would involve a wedding."

"I love weddings!" Lady Chocho clapped her hands in delight. "Who's getting married?"

Comprehension dawned on Lady Setsu's face. "Your nerve is astounding. You take my breath away."

"He takes mine away, too," Lady Chocho said with a giggle.

"So you don't like my plan?" Yanagisawa prepared to argue, cajole, and eventually convince.

"I didn't say that." Lady Setsu's manner expressed reluctant admiration for his ingenuity. "But you realize there are serious obstacles."

"None that I can't get around."

Her painted eyebrows rose in surprise; she shook her head. "I always knew you were ruthless, but until this moment I didn't realize how much so."

"Well, what do you think?" Yanagisawa said. "Shall we be partners?"

"I say yes," Lady Chocho said, ready to join him in anything he proposed whether she understood it or not.

But Lady Setsu said, "I refuse to make a major decision in such a hurry. There are other people whose future is at stake."

"Of course," Yanagisawa said. "I didn't mean to imply that the interests of all parties wouldn't be taken into account. Forgive me if I gave you that impression. I was about to suggest that everyone involved should meet and have a chance to approve of the plan."

For a moment Lady Setsu beheld him with silent outrage that he would forsake all sense of propriety and ask her to be his accomplice. But they both knew how much she dreaded the future, the unknown. Better to ally herself with a demon who was familiar than to depend on the whim of strangers.

"I will take the next step, but that is all I will commit to now," she said.

"Good enough," Yanagisawa said. "Shall we have a drink?"

"Oh, yes," Lady Chocho said.

Yanagisawa poured cups of sake from a decanter on the table. Lady Setsu covertly removed a vial from her sleeve and dosed her sake with opium potion. Yanagisawa said, "Here's to our joining forces in the near future."

"I can't wait," Lady Chocho said, batting her eyes at Yanagisawa.

"We'll see about that," Lady Setsu said.

They drank and bowed. The women left the teahouse first. Then Yanagisawa and his men took their leave. As they rode home in the rain, he congratulated himself on a mission almost accomplished.

In the alley outside the teahouse, beneath the window of the room where Yanagisawa had met the two women, a pile of trash stirred. Broken planks shifted; an old bucket foul with rotten fish entrails rolled free as a man dressed in beggar's rags emerged. Toda Ikkyu stood and flexed his cramped muscles. He'd overheard everything Yanagisawa and the women had said. The paper panel that covered the window had blocked out sights but not sound. Now Toda had interesting news to report to Chamberlain Sano—or not.

12

Below the highway between Asakusa and Edo, raindrops pattered into the rice fields. Sano and his entourage rode past pedestrians who looked like moving haystacks in their straw capes. Ahead Sano saw Hirata galloping on horseback toward him from the city.

"Any luck?" Hirata said as he turned his mount and rode alongside Sano.

"Yes and no," Sano said. "We located the place where my cousin Chiyo was dumped by her kidnapper. An oxcart was seen there, but we couldn't find it."

"When you don't want oxcarts, they're all around, blocking the streets and stinking up the city," Marume said. "When you do, there's not a single blessed one in sight."

Sano had led his men back to the construction site where they'd seen oxcarts yesterday, only to find the site deserted due to the rain. Sano and his men had combed the Asakusa district, but all the oxcarts seemed to have vanished.

"We'll have to go to the stables and track down the drivers who were working in Asakusa yesterday and when Chiyo was kidnapped," Sano said.

"Maybe I can save you the trouble," Hirata said.

Sano had figured that Hirata must have good news or he wouldn't have come looking for him, but he was surprised nonetheless. "Don't tell me the police actually investigated Chiyo's kidnapping and turned up some suspects?"

"No," Hirata said, "but their chief clerk says that two other women were kidnapped before your cousin was. Both were missing for a couple of days. Both were found near the places where they were taken."

Sano felt a mixture of excitement and dismay. He hated the thought that two more women had suffered, but the other crimes might provide clues. "Who are these women?"

"One is an old nun named Tengu-in," Hirata said. "She lives in a convent in the Zōjō Temple district."

"Merciful gods," Fukida said. "Who would rape a nun?"

"She was taken on the first day of the third month and found two days later," Hirata said. "The other is a twelve-year-old girl."

That shocked the detectives speechless. Sano, thinking of his own young daughter, felt sick with horror.

"She was kidnapped on the third day of last month, found two days later. Her name is Fumiko," Hirata said. "I happen to know her father. His name is Jirocho."

"The big gangster?" Sano said.

"None other."

The gangster class had proliferated since the civil war era some hundred years ago, when samurai who'd lost their masters in battles had become *rōnin* and wandered Japan, raiding the villages. Brave peasants had banded together to protect themselves. Today's gangsters were descendants of these heroes. But times had changed. The Tokugawa government enforced law and order throughout Japan. No longer needed to protect the villages, the gangsters had turned to crime. Their ranks had swelled with thieves, con artists, and other dregs of society.

"When I was a police officer, I arrested Jirocho a few times," Hirata said, "for extorting money from market vendors." There were two distinct types of gangster—the *bakuto*, gamblers who ran illegal gambling dens, and the *tekiya*, who were associated with trade and sold illicit or stolen merchandise. Jirocho belonged to the latter type. "He made them pay him for not stealing their goods, driving their customers away, and beating them up."

"Why's he still on the loose?" Marume asked.

"Friends in high places," Fukida said.

Hirata nodded. Sano knew that Jirocho and other gang bosses bribed government officials to let them carry out their business. As chamberlain, Sano tried to discourage this corrupt practice, but it was hard to catch the officials colluding with the gangsters, and the gangsters actually benefited the government. They helped to keep the growing merchant class under control and provided public services such as money-lending and security. Still, Sano thought this cooperation between government and gangsters boded ill for the future.

"Well, now Jirocho is a possible witness in a crime rather than the perpetrator," Sano said. "Marume-*san*, you and Fukida-*san* will go to the stables and track down our oxcart driver. Hirata-*san*, you can question Jirocho and his daughter. I'll take the nun."

The Zōjō Temple district was a city within the city, home to forty-eight subsidiary temples, the Tokugawa mausoleum, and thousands of priests, nuns, monks, and novices. The high stone walls of Keiaiji Convent shut out the noises from the marketplace, the traffic of pilgrims and peddlers in the streets, and the chanting of prayers in nearby monasteries. Pine trees cleansed the air in spacious grounds landscaped with mossy boulders and raked white sand. The large building resembled a samurai mansion rather than the typical convent in which nuns lived in cramped, impoverished austerity. The abbess received Sano in a room furnished with a pristine *tatami* floor and a mural that showed Mount Fuji amid the clouds.

"I've come to inquire about Tengu-in, your nun who was kidnapped," Sano said.

The abbess wore a plain gray hemp robe, the uniform of Buddhist holy women. Her head was shaved; her scalp glistened with a thin fuzz of silver hair. She was as short and sturdy as a peasant, with broad features set in a square face and an air of authority.

"Ah, yes. It was a dreadful thing to happen," she said. "And to such a virtuous woman, yet."

Sano inferred from her hushed tone that the nun had been raped as well as kidnapped. "My condolences to her, and to you and her sisters," he said. "It must have been very upsetting for everyone here."

The abbess shook her head in regret. "Yes, indeed, especially since Tengu-in was such a favorite."

Her use of the past tense didn't escape Sano. Had her community ostracized Tengu-in because she'd been violated? "Is she still here?"

"Yes, of course," the abbess said. "She's a member of our order for life. What happened to her doesn't change that."

But the abbess's manner suggested that she'd become an unwanted burden, Sano thought.

"Tengu-in has been with us for eight years," the abbess said. "She joined our order after her husband died. They had been married for forty-five years."

Widows often did join convents, sometimes because they were devoutly religious, sometimes because their husbands' deaths left them impoverished and homeless. Tengu-in must be in her sixties, Sano deduced. That someone would kidnap and rape a woman who was not only a nun but so elderly!

"Her husband was a high-ranking official in Lord Kuroda's service," the abbess went on. "She came to us with a very generous dowry."

That explained how the order could afford such a nice home. When a rich woman entered a convent, she brought with her gold coins, silk robes, and expensive artifacts. This order had been lucky to get Tengu-in.

"But that isn't why we were so fond of her," the abbess hastened to say. "She is a good woman. She never expected special treatment because she was from high society. She always had a kind word for everyone."

Sano pitied Tengu-in, who hadn't deserved to suffer any more than Chiyo had. "Exactly where was she kidnapped?"

"Outside the main temple. Some of our nuns had gone there to worship. She got separated from the group. When it was time to go home, they couldn't find her. All of us looked and looked, and I reported her missing to the police."

Those circumstances sounded ominously familiar. "Where did she turn up?"

"Outside the temple's main gate, early in the morning," the abbess said. "Some monks found her. They brought her back to the convent."

Sano thought of the oxcart seen in the alley where his cousin had been dumped. "On the day the nuns went to Zōjō Temple, were there any oxcarts in the area?"

"They didn't mention it."

"What about near the gate on the day Tengu-in was found?"

"I don't know. But there has been work done on the temple buildings lately."

The government supported religion and had probably furnished ox-carts to bring supplies for repairs to the temple. "The reason I'm interested in Tengu-in is that the same thing recently happened to my cousin. I suspect that the same man is responsible for both crimes. I want to catch him, and I need Tengu-in's help. May I speak with her?"

"I'm afraid she won't tell you anything. She hasn't even told me. She's very upset."

"That's understandable," Sano said, "but I must insist. She may be my only chance of catching the criminal."

"Very well." The abbess rose and said, "I'll take you to her. But I beg you not to expect too much."

13

Jirocho the gangster boss lived in Ueno, one of Edo's three temple districts. Ueno was situated in the northeast corner of the capital, known as the unluckiest direction, the "devil's gate." Its temples were supposed to guard the city from bad influences, but evil existed there as well as every place else.

At first glance Jirocho's street was no different from any other in an affluent merchant quarter. Between the neighborhood gates at either end stood rows of large two-story houses with tile roofs, their entrances recessed beneath overhanging eaves. Four men loitered, smoking pipes. A casual observer would never suspect that one of Edo's notorious gang bosses lived here. But Hirata, riding up the street, spotted the signs.

The men were tattooed with blue and black designs that showed at the edges of their collars and sleeves. Once the tattoos had been used by the authorities to brand outlaws; now they were insignias that represented wealth, bravery, and other desirable traits. They declared which clan a gangster belonged to and were worn as proudly as samurai crests.

When Hirata dismounted outside the largest house, the gangsters converged on him. "Looking for something?" one gangster said. His manner was devoid of the respect usually shown by a commoner to a samurai. The tattoo on his chest depicted a dragon, symbol of Jirocho's clan. He was probably one of its low-level soldiers.

"I want to see Jirocho," Hirata said.

"What makes you think Jirocho would want to see you?"

"Tell him Hirata is here."

They froze at the sound of Hirata's name: His reputation had spread into the underworld. Gangsters hated to admit they were afraid of anybody; they would kill on the slightest provocation, and they fought savagely with rival gangs, but they were more inclined toward self-preservation than the samurai who constantly challenged Hirata. These four gangsters chuckled as if they'd been playing a joke on him. Three pretended an interest in reloading their pipes. The other ambled into the house. Soon he reemerged and beckoned Hirata inside.

Led down a corridor, Hirata saw rooms where gang members lounged, awaiting orders from their boss. They eyed him, silent and hostile. A group of them knelt in a circle, playing *hana-fuda*—the flower card game. They wore their kimonos down around their waists, displaying their tattoos. One man threw down his cards. The others laughed and exclaimed, "*Ya-ku-za!*"

Eight-nine-three. It was the worst hand possible, but the gangsters seemed to feel an affection for it. Maybe they thought it symbolized their no-good selves, Hirata speculated.

His escort left him in a reception room. The *tatami* floor mats were bound with embroidered ribbon and so thick that they felt like cushions under Hirata's feet. The mural on the wall depicted a garden of brilliantly colored flowers beside a blue river highlighted with ripples of silver and gold paint. Black lacquer screens sported gold-inlaid birds. Brass lanterns suspended from the ceilings dangled gold pendants. Shelves held a collection of gold figurines. Hirata got the message: Jirocho was filthy rich. But he hid his wealth behind closed doors. Not even a top gangster boss dared violate the sumptuary laws that prohibited commoners from flaunting their wealth.

Two women brought refreshments to Hirata. They were as beautiful and stylishly dressed as the most expensive courtesans in the Yoshiwara licensed pleasure quarter. They wordlessly served the tea and food and departed. Hirata listened to the gangsters talking and joking at their card game. His keen ears also picked up the sound of distant sobs.

He followed the sound down a passage to a door that was open just enough for him to peer inside. He saw a young man kneeling and weeping, arms extended on the floor. Two older gangsters stood over him. "I hear you've been keeping some of the money you collected from the vendors," said a deep, scratchy voice. Hirata couldn't see the man who

76

spoke, but he recognized the voice as Jirocho's. "Did you really think I wouldn't find out?"

"I'm sorry," the young man cried. "I shouldn't have done it!"

Hirata knew that gangsters had a code of honor consisting of three rules: Don't touch the wife of a fellow member; don't reveal gang secrets to outsiders; and, above all, be loyal to the boss. *If the boss says crows are white, you must agree*, the saying went.

One of the two gangsters standing grabbed the young man and yanked him upright. The other shoved a heavy wooden table in front of him and offered him a cleaver. Even as he sobbed in fright, the young man took the cleaver in his left hand. He positioned his right hand with its little finger laid against the table, its others curled into a fist. He raised the cleaver, screamed, and hacked off the tip of his finger.

Hirata blinked. He'd seen many acts of violence, but this one shocked him even though he knew it was common among gangsters. One who broke the rules would lose a finger joint for each offense. Samurai who violated Bushido were punished by compulsory suicide, but Hirata thought this forced self-mutilation was bizarre.

Pale as death, the trembling young man accepted a white silk cloth from one of the other gangsters. He wrapped his severed finger in the cloth and offered the package to Jirocho.

"You're forgiven this time," Jirocho said. "Don't let there be a next time."

Hirata silently slipped away and returned to the reception room. Soon Jirocho entered. "Well, well, Hirata-*san*. This is a surprise."

Now in his fifties, Jirocho had changed in the twelve or so years since he and Hirata had last met. Beneath the gaudy silk robes that he wore in private defiance of the sumptuary laws, his figure was pudgier because he sat around and gave orders instead of prowling the streets and fighting as he'd done in his youth. His hair had turned gray and he'd gone bald at the temples; his jowls sagged. But his sharp eyes gleamed with the familiar look of controlled aggression. His thick mouth wore the same predatory smile that Hirata remembered.

The biggest change had less to do with Jirocho than with Hirata's own expanded perception.

For the first time Hirata saw Jirocho's shield. It exuded a magnetic attraction as well as sheer ruthlessness. Once Hirata had wondered how

Jirocho had climbed the ranks from petty thief to boss of his own gang. Now he knew. Jirocho drew weaker men like a magnet draws iron specks.

"Have you come to arrest me again?" Jirocho's smile broadened: He knew he was safe, protected by the same government that Hirata served.

"Not today," Hirata said. "I'm here about a crime, but not one that you committed."

"What crime?"

"The kidnapping of your daughter."

Jirocho's smile vanished. He abruptly turned away. "I won't talk about that."

"I'm afraid you'll have to," Hirata said. "Chamberlain Sano and I are investigating another kidnapping that may be related to your daughter's. We need information."

"You'll have to get it somewhere else," Jirocho said, his back turned, his voice cold.

"How about if I talk to your daughter?"

"My daughter Fumiko is dead."

"What?" Hirata was surprised. "The police say she was found alive."

"She's dead to me." Jirocho turned to face Hirata, who saw that his eyes were wet and ablaze with angry tears. "Some filthy monster ruined my girl. She was disgraced."

Her kidnapping had one more thing in common with Sano's cousin's, Hirata realized. Fumiko, too, had been raped.

"I had to disown her, for the sake of my clan's honor," Jirocho said.

"Where is she?"

"I don't know. I threw her out of the house."

"You threw a twelve-year-old girl out to fend for herself?" Hirata was horrified by Jirocho's attitude.

Jirocho gave him a hostile stare. "I loved Fumiko with all my heart, but things have changed. Wait until it happens to your daughter, then let's see how you react."

Hirata thought of little Taeko, whom he would always love and protect no matter what. But he wasn't as bound by conventions as Jirocho was in spite of his outlaw background. And he shouldn't criticize Jirocho if he wanted his cooperation.

"All right," Hirata said, "I understand. But I still need your help. Perhaps you would let me talk to Fumiko's mother?"

"Her mother died when she was a baby," Jirocho said. "I raised her myself."

Hirata made one last try. "Chamberlain Sano's cousin was kidnapped and violated, perhaps by the same man as Fumiko. We're seeking justice for her. Don't you want to avenge your daughter?"

"Oh, indeed, I do. Make no mistake." Jirocho spoke with a savagery that darkened his face. This was the man who forced his henchmen to cut off their own fingers as punishment for crossing him. He would never let anyone get away with violating his daughter, even though he'd forsaken her. "But I'll do it myself, my way."

Things had been bad enough when Major Kumazawa had conducted a search for his daughter, offending and threatening people wherever he went. Now Hirata was appalled by the idea of the gangster boss out for blood.

"You stay out of this," he ordered Jirocho. "Let Chamberlain Sano and me handle it. Just tell me what you know about your daughter's kidnapping."

Jirocho's face was stony, closed. "With all due respect to you and Chamberlain Sano, this score is mine to settle personally. Now please leave."

The gangster who'd escorted Hirata into the house escorted him out. When they reached the street, Hirata asked, "Where can I find Jirocho's daughter?"

"If Jirocho won't tell you, neither will I," the gangster said. "I don't talk about his business."

Hirata observed that the gangster's energy shield was weak. This was the kind of man he could manipulate. "Where is she?" Hirata said, projecting the force of his will at the gangster.

"In the marketplace," the gangster said obediently.

"Where was she kidnapped and found?"

"By Shinobazu Pond." Now the gangster's eyes widened in fright because he realized he'd broken a gang rule.

"Thank you," Hirata said. "I won't tell your boss."

The abbess led Sano into the convent's chapel, which was shaded by pine trees and darkened by closed shutters. Inside, a low altar held a gold Buddha statue that sat amid gold lotus flowers, lit candles, and brass incense burners that emitted pungent, bittersweet smoke. Before the altar knelt a nun, shrouded in a gray hemp robe, her head covered with a white drape. She rocked slowly back and forth.

"Since she was kidnapped, all she does is pray," the abbess said in a quiet, sad voice. "She won't talk to anyone. It's as if she's living in a world of her own."

Now Sano understood why the other nuns considered her a problem. As he and the abbess moved toward her, he noticed someone else standing in an alcove, like a guardian deity. It was a girl in her teens, with an innocent, pretty face, her hair tied in a kerchief.

"That's Ume," the abbess said. "One of our novices. I've assigned her to watch over Tengu-in." She whispered, "When she first came home, she took a knife and cut her arm."

Had she been trying to punish herself for the rape, which many people would consider her fault? Sano felt a terrible pity for the old woman. He knelt at the altar, far enough away from her that she wouldn't feel threatened by his presence, but close enough to see her clearly. Now he observed that her body was emaciated; her robes hung on her skeleton.

"She won't eat," the abbess said, "or sleep, either."

Her profile was sharp with facial bones visible through taut, waxen skin. Her eyes were closed tight, their lids purplish. Her lips moved, but she made no sound.

"Tengu-in," Sano said quietly.

She seemed not to notice him. Her lips kept moving; she rocked to some inner, secret rhythm.

"Can you hear me?"

There was no response. The novice gave a faint, desolate sigh. The abbess said sadly, "I warned you."

But Sano couldn't give up. "Tengu-in, I'm Chamberlain Sano. Tell me what happened when you were kidnapped."

She continued her silent praying. Her face was expressionless, animated only by the flickering candlelight.

"Who took you?" Sano persisted. "Was it someone you recognized?"

No answer came.

Sano appealed to the kind nature that the abbess had said Tengu-in had once possessed. "I believe this man has kidnapped and attacked two other women besides you. One of them is my cousin. I must catch him before he hurts anyone else. And I need your help."

His words didn't penetrate the invisible shell into which she'd re-treated. In an attempt to reach her, he spoke louder, urgently: "What did he look like? Where did he take you?"

"It's no use," the abbess said as Tengu-in prayed, rocked, and ignored everyone. "Even if she's listening, she won't speak."

Sano rose, reluctantly. He didn't want to leave empty-handed. "I need to question everyone who was with Tengu-in on that trip to Zōjō Temple."

"Ume was." The abbess beckoned to the novice.

The girl crept over to Sano and bowed, her eyes open wide with anxiety.

"What happened?" Sano said. "How did Tengu-in just suddenly disap-pear?"

"I don't know," she said in a barely audible whisper. She clenched her hands under her sleeves and cast a nervous glance at the abbess.

Sano said to the abbess, "I'd like to speak with Ume privately."

Disapproval crossed the older woman's face, but she couldn't deny his request. She said, "I'll be right outside," and departed.

Sano said, "Whatever secret you don't want her to know, it's safe with me."

The girl's face crumpled. Tears shone in her eyes. "It's my fault Tengu-in was kidnapped."

Sano couldn't believe that this innocent-looking girl was in any way responsible for the crime. "How so?"

"We were supposed to stay with her. I should have watched out for her." Ume sobbed as she gazed down at Tengu-in, who seemed oblivious. "Instead, I ran ahead with the other novices. She was too slow. She couldn't keep up."

Sano envisioned the old woman hobbling through the temple grounds in the wake of the young, exuberant girls. Perhaps they had been negli-gent, but he said, "You're not to blame. You couldn't have known she was in danger."

"But I was doing something I shouldn't have been." Shamefaced yet eager to unburden herself, Ume said, "There was a group of novices from the monastery down the street. We—the other girls and I . . ."

The picture became clear to Sano. The girls had wanted to flirt with the young monks, so they'd run away from their chaperone. Joining a religious order didn't rid people of their natural human desires.

"I feel so guilty," Ume said as she wept. "I wish I could make up for what I did."

"Here's your chance," Sano said. "Help me catch the man who hurt her. When you were at the temple, did you see anyone or anything that looked suspicious?"

"No," Ume said, wiping her tears on her sleeve. "I've tried and tried to remember, but I don't."

Whoever had kidnapped Tengu-in couldn't have just suddenly appeared out of nowhere, swooped down on her like an eagle from the sky, and spirited her away, Sano thought. He would have had to single her out of the crowd, to await an opportunity to take her without anyone seeing.

He must have been watching her.

"Think back to the time before you and the other girls left Tengu-in," Sano said. "Did you notice anyone paying particular attention to your group?"

Ume pondered, then shook her head.

"Anyone following you?" Sano persisted.

"No. I'm sorry. I was busy looking at the monks." Then she frowned, as if startled by a memory forgotten until now.

"What is it?" Sano asked.

"I did see someone."

"At the temple?" Sano's pulse began to race in anticipation.

"No, not there. And not then. It was the day before. Outside the convent."

Maybe the kidnapper had had his eye on the nuns. Maybe he'd been spying on the convent, lying in wait for his chance to kidnap one. "Tell me what happened," Sano said urgently.

"It was after morning prayers. I sneaked outside." Ume's face flushed. "The monks walk past the convent on their way to the city. There's one that I—well, when he goes by, he smiles at me." Pleasure and guilt mingled in her voice. "That day, I missed him. But I saw a man standing in the street."

"Who was he?"

"I don't know. I'd never seen him before. Nor since."

"Can you describe him?"

"I didn't get a very good look. As soon as he saw me, he turned and walked away." Ume squinted, trying to bring the remembered glimpse of him into focus. "He was tall and strong. His hair was so short, the skin on his head showed through. He was old, about thirty."

Sano winced: He himself was forty-three, which she probably considered ancient. "What was he wearing?"

"A dark blue kimono."

Every commoner in Japan owned a cotton kimono dyed with indigo. And many of them cut their hair short to discourage fleas and lice. "Did his face have any distinctive features?"

"He looked like he hadn't shaved in a while." Ume brightened at a fresh recollection. "He had a big scab, here." She touched her right cheekbone. "I remember thinking he must have been in an accident or a fight."

That wasn't unusual, either. Sano pressed for more details, but Ume could provide none. "Did you see an oxcart?"

"No. I'm sorry," she said, gazing unhappily at Tengu-in, who prayed, rocked, and apparently had not heard any of the conversation.

But the oxcart could have been parked nearby, out of sight. The man she'd seen could have been the driver, who might have kidnapped Tengu-in, Chiyo, and Jirocho's daughter, too.

"You've been very helpful," Sano said.

"You'll catch him, won't you?" she said, with touching faith.

"I will," Sano vowed. He dared to think that he had a lead at last.

14

The marketplace in Ueno extended along the approach to the foot of the hill where Kannei Temple stood. Hirata rode past shops that sold boxwood combs and ear-cleaners and teahouses where customers ate rice steamed in lotus leaves, a local specialty. The street widened into the Broad Little Road, home to stalls and booths crammed with all sorts of goods. A few dancers, puppeteers, and acrobats entertained crowds diminished by the rain. Beneath the lively, colorful bustle of the market, Hirata saw its dark underpinnings.

Tattooed gangsters roamed, looking for any traders who didn't belong there, keeping an eye out for thieves. This was Jirocho's domain. He controlled the allocation of the stalls, shops, teahouses, and booths, collected rents from the vendors, paid tributes to the temple and taxes to the government, and kept a generous cut of the profits for himself. Here his daughter had sought refuge after he'd turned her loose.

Hirata rode down the aisles of stalls, looking for a twelve-year-old girl on her own. The market swarmed with children unaccompanied by parents. The orphans of Edo flocked to its temple markets in hope of food and alms. Children with dirty faces and dirtier bare feet, dressed in rags, grabbed scraps of food dropped outside the stalls and begged coins from the customers. They were such a usual part of the city scene that Hirata had never paid them much attention. Now he scrutinized the girls for some hours until he found one who looked to be the right age. She squatted on the ground, gnawing a rice ball. Long, matted hair hung over her face. She wore a white kimono printed with green leaves; it was torn and muddy.

"Fumiko-*san*?" Hirata called.

The girl looked up. She had elfin features marred by fading bruises around her eyes and scabs on her cheeks. Surprised to hear her name, frightened by the sight of Hirata, she crammed the food into her mouth and ran.

Hirata jumped off his horse and chased her. Fumiko was quick, darting through the crowds. But his longer stride gave Hirata an advantage, and he could follow the unique, starburst pattern of her energy. He tracked her to the narrow back streets where local brothels employed illegal prostitutes. Dressed in their trademark aprons, the women bargained with customers outside their rooms. Hirata cornered Fumiko in a doorway. She stood with her hands inside her sleeves, panting and trembling.

"Don't be afraid," Hirata said.

Her eyes gleamed with feral panic. After two months of living on the streets, she already looked more animal than human.

"I'm not going to hurt you." Hirata introduced himself, then said, "I want to help you."

Incredulity wrinkled her dirt-smeared brow. Hirata wasn't surprised that she didn't believe him. Why should she trust any man, after one had kidnapped, raped, and apparently beaten her, and her own father had cast her off?

His heart went out to the girl. Extending his hand, he said, "Come with me. I'll take you to a place where you'll be safe, and—"

Fumiko whipped her right hand out of her sleeve. She lashed at his face with a knife clutched in her fingers. Startled, he leaped backward just in time to avoid a nasty cut. Fumiko lunged around him and fled.

"Hey!" Hirata called. "Wait!"

But she was gone.

Sano arrived home in late afternoon. The sun was a pale, shimmering pearl behind gray clouds. In the courtyard, grooms took charge of his and his men's horses, which were spattered in mud from hooves to flanks. On the veranda of his mansion, servants rid Sano of his wet hat and cape. His secretary appeared and said, "Major Kumazawa is here to see you."

Sano was surprised that his uncle would come, without advance notice or invitation. They'd not parted on very good terms yesterday. "Show him into the reception room."

"I must inform you that the treasury minister and the judicial council are ahead of him in the queue."

"I'll see Major Kumazawa first."

Sano felt a strange attraction to his uncle, the pull of blood to blood, even though they didn't get along. He discovered in himself a yearning for the sense of family that had been diminished when he'd moved out of his parents' home, when his father had died, when his mother had remarried. The Kumazawa were his closest senior kin in town.

In the reception room, he found Major Kumazawa marching slowly back and forth like a soldier at a drill. His face was as stern and hard as ever, but his restlessness told Sano how distraught he still was about his daughter.

"I wanted to ask if your investigation has made any progress," Major Kumazawa said. "My apologies for showing up like this, but I thought I'd save you the trouble of another trip to Asakusa." He sounded much more polite than before, but of course this was Sano's territory.

"You knew where to find me," Sano said.

His tone hinted at the fact that his uncle had kept track of him since his birth. He saw a glint of antagonism in Major Kumazawa's eyes, but the man simply nodded and said, "I've been here before. When this place belonged to Yanagisawa."

That his uncle had been in his house, without his knowledge until this moment, gave Sano an eerie feeling, as if he'd just learned that his home was haunted by a ghost whose presence he'd never suspected. He recalled the vision he'd had at Major Kumazawa's house. He still didn't know what it meant.

"Please allow me to welcome you back," Sano said evenly.

They exchanged wary glances, both bracing for another clash. But Sano was determined to keep things civil. He didn't want a quarrel that would be overheard by his subordinates, or bad blood with his uncle to contaminate the peace of his home.

"How is Chiyo today?" he asked.

"I went home to check on her this afternoon. She was asleep. The doctor had given her a potion." Major Kumazawa's expression was grim. "My wife says that after your wife came to see Chiyo, she was very upset."

His gaze accused Reiko, and Sano, of upsetting Chiyo. Sano refused to seize on the pretext for another argument. "It stands to reason that she would be upset by talking about the crime. But if I'm to catch the man who kidnapped her, I must know as many details about it as possible. However, I may not need any more help from Chiyo. I discovered some clues today."

"Oh?" Major Kumazawa's eyebrows and tone lifted in surprise. "What sort?"

Sano couldn't help feeling pleased that he'd exceeded his uncle's expectations. He told Major Kumazawa about the oxcart spotted by the witness.

"An oxcart." Major Kumazawa looked disappointed, and skeptical. "If nobody saw Chiyo put into or thrown off it, how can you be sure it had anything to do with what happened to her? Even if it did, there are hundreds of oxcarts in Edo. They all look alike, and you said your witness didn't see the driver. How are you going to find the right one?"

"I'll find it." Sano had people out searching now. He'd expected Major Kumazawa to find fault with his results, but that didn't make the carping any less unpleasant. He would almost rather be working for the shogun, who always complained about his lack of progress and threatened him with death, but sometimes appreciated his efforts.

Sometimes.

At least Sano could tell himself that the shogun was a fool. Criticism from someone more intelligent was harder to stomach.

"I've also made another discovery: Two other women were kidnapped before Chiyo was." Sano told Major Kumazawa about the gangster boss's daughter and the nun. "The kidnappings may be related."

After he described what he'd learned at the convent, disapproval crossed his uncle's features. "You said you were going after the man who kidnapped my daughter, but you've been investigating this other woman?" Major Kumazawa said.

Nettled by the implication that he'd wasted time, Sano said, "The other crime is a new source of clues."

"I suppose so, but it doesn't sound as if you got anything out of the nun. With all due respect, you would do better to concentrate on Chiyo. Especially since you can't be sure that the crimes are related."

"I found other witnesses at the convent, and there are similarities between Chiyo's case and the nun's," Sano said, his patience slipping. "Both women are from samurai families. Both were kidnapped at places of worship, then found nearby."

"What about the gangster's daughter?"

Sano was at a disadvantage because he hadn't any information about that. "My chief retainer is investigating her case. I expect news from him soon."

"So maybe the cases are related," Major Kumazawa said. "Or maybe you're going down the wrong path."

Fed up now, Sano spoke more sharply than he'd intended: "Maybe you're not qualified to decide how this investigation should go."

They exchanged stares in hostile silence. Then Major Kumazawa said, "By the way, I met your father a few times."

Sano felt his muscles tense, but he said coolly, "I can guess when that was. When he asked your parents for my mother's hand in marriage. At the *miai* where he was formally introduced to her. Then, at their wedding."

Those were the instances when social custom had forced the Kumazawa clan to associate with the lowly *rōnin* who'd married Sano's mother.

Major Kumazawa nodded. His eyes narrowed, scrutinizing Sano. "You take after your father."

Sano knew that Major Kumazawa wasn't referring to the physical similarities. His uncle was implying that he'd inherited bad character traits, chiefly his determination to follow his own will. And Major Kumazawa was blaming heredity on his father's side for what Major Kumazawa perceived as Sano's mishandling of the investigation. Sano burned with rage, and not only because Major Kumazawa would disparage his bloodline.

"It's obvious you didn't get to know my father very well," Sano said coldly. His father had been an old-style samurai with conventional notions about duty and bowing to authority and a distaste for individual initiative—everything Sano was not. "Making snap judgments about people based on limited acquaintance isn't very smart. Perhaps *you* take after *your* father."

Now it was Major Kumazawa's turn to bristle. "Perhaps I was wrong about you, Honorable Chamberlain. Perhaps you're more like your mother."

He must think that was the ultimate blow, to be compared to a disgraced woman. But Sano had reason to be proud of his mother, of her blood that ran in his veins. "If you say so, then I must thank you for the compliment. My mother did a great service for Japan." She'd been accused of murder and, in a startling instance of irony, emerged a heroine. "The shogun holds her in the highest esteem. He's pronounced himself in her debt forever."

The shogun had not only attended her recent wedding; he'd insisted on providing her dowry. He'd given her and her second husband enough gold to support them for the rest of their lives.

"My mother has managed to distinguish herself," Sano said, "probably more than anyone else in her family has." The bitter antipathy in Major Kumazawa's eyes said he resented Sano for pointing out the truth that his mother had risen above her estranged clan. Before Major Kumazawa could retort, Sano thought of something he'd been wanting to know. "After my parents were married, did you ever see my mother again?"

Caught off guard, Major Kumazawa said, ". . . No."

Sano didn't miss the pause before his answer. "Did you ever see me when I was a child?"

"Of course not."

"Are you sure?"

"Are you calling me a liar?" Major Kumazawa demanded.

"Only if you deserve the name," Sano said evenly.

"I never saw her, or you," Major Kumazawa said. "That's the truth, whether you believe it or not."

But Sano knew his uncle was lying. He was sure now that he had been to the Kumazawa house, had seen his uncle and aunt, who had seen him, too. He didn't know when or why, but he intended to find out, later.

Major Kumazawa started to speak, but Sano raised a hand. "That's enough about the past. Our main priority is catching the kidnapper. We should put our differences aside and concentrate on the investigation."

"I couldn't agree more," Major Kumazawa said with controlled hostility. "And since you insist on pursuing the matter of those other women, I will lead my own troops in a hunt for the man who raped my daughter."

"I've been meaning to speak to you about that," Sano said. "When

I was looking for Chiyo, I came across many people that you and your men had bullied and threatened while you were looking for her."

"So we shook them up a little," Major Kumazawa said. "I did what I had to do."

"That's not the way to conduct an investigation," Sano said. "At best, it'll make people less willing to cooperate than if you treated them politely. At worst, you'll get false confessions, punish innocent folks, and waste your time. If you keep on, you'll only make my job harder. So don't interfere."

Major Kumazawa glared. "It's my daughter who was hurt. It's my right to avenge her."

"I certainly understand your position." If Akiko were hurt, Sano wouldn't let anyone stand between him and her attacker. "But I'm not going to change mine. Stay out of the investigation. That's an order."

Major Kumazawa flushed with humiliation because Sano had pulled rank on him yet again. "And if I don't obey?" he said, even though they both knew he must.

"You saw all the people in my anteroom. Hundreds of them come to see me every day. They all want me to do things for them. I don't need this investigation to keep me busy."

Now Major Kumazawa laughed, scorning Sano's hint that he would abandon the quest for justice for Chiyo unless Major Kumazawa cooperated. "No, but you won't walk away from Chiyo. Everybody knows your reputation. Once you've committed to doing something, you don't give up. You're an honorable man, I'll give you that. You would never break your word."

That had always been true in the past. Sano kept his promises and stayed the course even at the risk of his life. But things had begun to change when his mother had been accused of murder and Sano had learned that his background was different from what he'd always believed. During his investigation into the murder, he'd done things he'd never thought himself capable of; in particular, staging the trial and execution of Yoritomo, his onetime friend. Sano felt as if discovering the truth about his family had altered him in some fundamental way.

He no longer knew what he would or wouldn't do.

He wanted justice for Chiyo, but he was vexed by how his uncle treated him even while he was doing the Kumazawa clan a favor. Come to think of it, Sano was fed up after years of other people, the shogun among them, demanding service from him while throwing obstacles at him. Bushido dictated that he do his duty to his lord and his family without minding how they treated him or expecting rewards, but still . . .

Might he walk away from this investigation before it was done?

It wouldn't hurt to let his uncle think so.

"There's always a first time," Sano said.

15

Shinobazu Pond was a popular attraction in the Ueno temple district. Lotus plants bloomed on its wide expanse. A causeway led from the shore to an island in the middle, upon which stood a shrine dedicated to the goddess Benten. Along the embankments around the pond, teahouses offered splendid views and rooms for lovers to spend the night.

Today Hirata found the pond desolate in the rain that had started to fall again. Egrets stood like white specters among the lotus leaves in the mist. Lumber lay piled in the mud near the approach to the causeway. Teahouse proprietors stood on their verandas, gloomily surveying the scene. When they saw Hirata climb off his horse and walk toward them, they brightened and called, "Welcome, honorable master!"

One youthful, agile man with an ear-to-ear smile ran from his teahouse and intercepted Hirata. "Come in, come in. May I serve you a drink?"

"Yes, please," Hirata said, glad to get out of the rain.

Inside a room that smelled of mildewed *tatami*, the proprietor heated sake over a charcoal brazier. Two other men wandered in, perhaps hoping to woo Hirata to their establishments later. Hirata drank. The liquor was cheap and harsh, but it relieved the chill of the wet day. Introductions were exchanged; then Hirata said, "I'm investigating the kidnapping of Jirocho's daughter."

The three men nodded. The proprietor, whose name was Kanroku, said, "We heard about it. Such a terrible shame."

"I wouldn't wish that on anyone, not even Jirocho," said another man, called Geki. He was in his fifties, with a sardonically humorous face accented by bushy eyebrows.

"Did you see anything suspicious the day Fumiko was kidnapped?" Hirata said.

"Not a thing. We didn't even know she was gone until Jirocho sent his men looking for her," Geki answered.

The third man, named Hachibei, who was old, white-haired, and spry, said, "Neither did anyone else we know. Everybody said it was as if she'd vanished into thin air."

Just as Chiyo had, Hirata recalled. "What about when she turned up?" he asked.

"That I did see," Geki said, "being that I'm the one who found her."

"Tell me what happened," Hirata said.

"It was an hour or so before dawn. I woke up because I needed to make water. When I was finished, I heard whimpering out there." Geki pointed toward the embankment. "I went to have a look." His humorous face turned somber. "She was lying on the ground. Her clothes were torn and she was bleeding between her legs. I recognized her right away. She used to hang around here a lot."

"She was always either by herself or with some young toughs from her father's gang," Kanroku the proprietor said. "I thought it was wrong for Jirocho to let her run wild like that."

"Me, too," old Hachibei said, "but who are we to tell a gang boss what to do?"

"I always said Fumiko would get in trouble someday, and I was right," the proprietor said wisely.

"People are saying that she wasn't kidnapped, that she went with a man, and then he got tired of her and dumped her," Geki said. "If it's true, then Jirocho was right to throw her out. I'd have done the same."

People were eager to blame the victim for the crime, Hirata thought. He asked, "When you found her, did you see anyone else around?"

"Not until I called for help and people woke up and came outside. Then I sent a servant to tell Jirocho. He came and took her home."

And then, upon learning she was damaged goods, he'd punished her.

"Did you hear anything?" Hirata asked.

Geki shook his head, then stopped as a look of sudden, surprised recollection came over his face. "Wait. I did."

Hirata felt a stir of excitement. "What?"

"Wagon wheels clattering," Geki said. "An oxcart."

Maybe it was the same one that had been sighted in the alley where Sano's cousin had been dumped. "But you didn't see it or the driver?"

"Not then," Geki said, "but maybe the day before. It could have been the fellow who brought that lumber outside."

"Who was that?"

"I don't know his name."

"Can you describe him?" Hirata said hopefully.

"He was about twenty-five," Geki said. "He had two missing teeth." He pointed at the two teeth to the right of his own big, yellowish front ones.

"Yes, that's right," the proprietor said. "I saw him, too. If he's the man that hurt Fumiko, I hope you catch him, the bastard."

After Major Kumazawa left, Sano felt simultaneously fatigued and riled up, as if he'd been in a fight that had no winner. And so he had. He rolled his shoulders, easing tense muscles. He'd put off his usual business of governing Japan, and he still had a long day of work ahead of him. He received the rest of his callers. By the time everyone was gone, it was late in the evening. Seated at his desk, Sano reviewed the most urgent reports and correspondence until his secretary came to the door and said, "Toda Ikkyu is here."

"Bring him in."

Toda entered, knelt, and bowed. He resembled a shadow in his gray clothes, in the dim light, his nondescript face bland.

"What have you to report, Toda-*san*?" Sano asked.

"I spent the day following our friend Yanagisawa."

"How did you manage that?" Sano's own men had been unable to follow Yanagisawa very long before he shook them off his trail.

"It's easy when you know the art of stealth," Toda said. Most samurai looked upon stealth as a dark art, unworthy of the Way of the Warrior. But that never bothered Toda, or Yanagisawa. "If he goes inside a building, don't wait for him at the front door; he'll come out the back. Don't expect him to look the same as he did when he went in—he'll have put on a disguise. And you should change your own appearance occasionally, or he'll spot you. You don't need a fancy disguise; a different hat will do."

"Thank you for the tips," Sano said. "I'll pass them on to my men. Where did Yanagisawa go?"

"To a teahouse in Hatchobori district, for what appeared to be a secret meeting."

Intrigued, Sano said, "With whom?"

"Two old ladies."

Sano had expected to hear that Yanagisawa had met with some *daimyo*, presumably to enlist their support in another bid for power. "Who were they?"

"I don't know," Toda said. "They were already secluded inside the teahouse when Yanagisawa and I arrived. And I didn't get a good look at them when they left. He called them 'Lady Setsu' and 'Lady Chocho.' But those are false names. He said as much. I did overhear some of their conversation."

"And just how did you manage that?"

Amusement crinkled Toda's eyes. "You don't want to know."

"What did they talk about?"

"The possibility of a marriage between someone connected with the ladies and someone connected with Yanagisawa."

"That doesn't sound like anything out of the ordinary," Sano said, feeling let down. "Yanagisawa does have four sons, including Yoritomo, all single and all of marriageable age."

"And a daughter. Don't forget Kikuko."

Sano would never forget Yanagisawa's beautiful but feeble-minded daughter, Kikuko. She'd once almost drowned his son. And her mother—Yanagisawa's deranged wife—had once tried to kill Reiko. When Yanagisawa had been exiled to Hachijo Island, his wife and daughter had gone with him. When he'd escaped, they'd stayed behind, but they'd recently returned and he'd installed them in a mansion in Kamakura. Sano had spies watching them, in case they should come back to Edo and threaten his family again.

"It stands to reason that Yanagisawa would want to marry off his children," Sano said.

Toda nodded. "He needs to make politically advantageous matches for them."

"But why the secrecy?" Sano said.

"Your guess is as good as mine." Toda shrugged.

Sano thought about how oddly Yanagisawa had been acting. Maybe he had decided that if he couldn't seize power by military might, he would achieve it through marriage. But with what family? A quick mental review of prominent clans and their eligible sons and daughters didn't provide the answer. There were so many, and no apparent explanation for why marriage negotiations with them should need to be kept under wraps.

"Continue your surveillance on Yanagisawa," Sano said. "Find out who those women are and who's the prospective bride or groom."

"Will do." Toda bowed and rose.

As he left the room, Sano wondered if there was anything Toda had heard or seen but neglected to mention.

As he mounted his horse outside the teahouse at Shinobazu Pond, the witnesses waved to Hirata from the veranda. He waved back and had started to ride away in search of other witnesses who'd seen the oxcart, when a sudden strange sensation came over him. It was an energy aura so powerful that the damp, drizzly air throbbed and scintillated. Not he, not even his teacher or the other venerable mystic martial artists he knew, had an aura as strong. Filled with awe, he yanked on the reins, brought his horse to a stop. He looked around for the source of the energy.

The embankment was deserted and dark. The teahouse proprietors had gone inside their buildings, and there was no one in sight. Rain pelted the lotus leaves in the pond. All appeared as peaceful and desolate as before. But Hirata felt alarm raise every hair on his body. Someone he couldn't see was watching him. His hand instinctively flew to his sword. His heart began to race, his own energy gathering in preparation for combat. He'd seldom had cause for fear; there were few men in all of Japan that he couldn't beat. But then why did he feel so certain that he was in the presence of danger?

The impulse to flee vied with the impulse to hunt for the person whose aura threatened him. Before Hirata could succumb to either urge, the aura vanished as suddenly as if some great, cosmic machine had ceased to run. All Hirata heard or felt was the rain. He was alone.

Down the corridor from Sano's office, Masahiro crouched on the floor, lining up his toy soldiers. He watched the man dressed in gray come out of the office. As the man walked away from Masahiro, he looked over his shoulder and smiled faintly before he vanished around a corner.

Masahiro told himself that he hadn't meant to listen in on his father's business.

Well, maybe he had.

He was curious about what Father did. Someday he would inherit Father's position. Father had said so. He should try to learn as much as he could, shouldn't he? There was nothing dishonest, sneaky, or wrong with that. He wasn't hurting anyone.

He'd overheard Father's whole conversation with the man named Toda. Now Masahiro thought about what they'd said. Toda seemed to be a spy. Father had sent him to follow Yanagisawa, the evil enemy who had tried over and over to destroy Father. Masahiro had heard Father and Mother trying to figure out why Yanagisawa wasn't attacking them anymore. Masahiro was interested in the secret meeting with the two old ladies. Why was it important whom Yanagisawa's children married?

And what did "politically advantageous" mean?

Masahiro had heard the term spoken around the estate, but the adults never explained. But he understood that Yanagisawa was up to something, and Father thought it was bad. Masahiro wished he could help Father. While he played with his toys, he felt sorry for himself. If only he could grow up quicker!

A sudden idea lit up his mind like the fireworks that were shot into the sky over the river in the summertime. Masahiro smiled. He knew what he could do!

Father had said to stay out of the kidnapping investigation, but this should have nothing to do with it. And Masahiro didn't think it would be dangerous. Father and Mother shouldn't mind.

The door to the office slid open. Before his father stepped out, Masahiro snatched up his soldiers, darted around the corner, and hid. He felt guilty because he suspected that Father wouldn't like him eavesdropping.

He wouldn't tell Father or Mother what he was going to do. They might say no. It would be a surprise for them. Masahiro was sure they would be pleased.

16

The sound of children laughing enlivened the private chambers of Sano's estate. In the main room, Reiko chatted with her friend Midori, who was Hirata's wife, as Akiko played with Midori's little girl and boy. The children turned somersaults across the floor. Servants cleared away the remains of the evening meal.

"Take it easy," Midori cautioned the children good-naturedly. "You'll get dizzy and throw up."

Masahiro lay on his stomach beneath the lantern, writing a lesson assigned by his tutor. Reiko peeked over his shoulder. He didn't need her to supervise his homework, but she enjoyed seeing how good his calligraphy was, and how well he expressed his ideas, even at such a young age. She smiled proudly, enjoying the peaceful, cozy evening.

The rain had stopped, and the open windows let in the cool, damp breeze that blew in from the garden, where crickets chirped and cicadas hummed in rhythm to the drip of water from the trees. Frogs sang in the pond. The garden was radiantly silver with moonlight. Life was good tonight, Reiko thought.

Sano entered the room. "Papa!" cried Akiko.

She ran to him, and he lifted her onto his shoulders. Masahiro jumped up and said, "Look at what I just wrote."

As Sano read and admired Masahiro's composition, Reiko took pleasure in the company of her family. She was glad to see Sano, for she was bursting with questions about his investigation and eager to tell him what she'd learned.

She was also relieved that he'd come home safely. She still felt a lingering anxiety from the dangerous days when they'd been threatened by war at every turn.

In walked Hirata. His children clung to his legs, and he trudged under their weight while they rode and cheered. Midori greeted him, smiling and giggly. Reiko knew they'd had marital troubles in the recent past. Hirata had been gone for the better part of five years, pursuing his mystic martial arts studies, Midori had suffered from his absences, and they'd grown apart. They'd since reconciled, and Reiko was happy for them. She wanted to enjoy the peace, however long it lasted.

"Have you eaten yet?" she asked Sano and Hirata. "Are you hungry?"

"I forgot to eat, I was so busy," Sano confessed.

"Same here," Hirata said.

"Oh, you men," Midori chided. "If it weren't for us, you'd starve to death."

Reiko ordered the servants to bring food. She made hot tea on the charcoal brazier and served cups to Sano and Hirata.

"Any luck today?" Sano asked Hirata.

Midori glanced at Reiko. Both women knew that talk about serious subjects was coming, and they didn't want the children to hear. "It's time for us to go," Midori said.

Her children groaned and protested. Hirata said, "I'll be home soon and tuck you into bed."

"Come along," Midori said, and departed with her family.

The nurse led Akiko away. Masahiro picked up his things and followed without argument. Reiko was surprised. He'd been so interested in the investigation that she'd expected him to beg her and Sano to allow him to stay and hear about it. She hoped he was outgrowing his penchant for detective work.

"Don't keep me in suspense," she said to Sano and Hirata. "What happened?"

"I went to see Jirocho," said Hirata.

"The gangster?" Reiko had heard about him from her father, Magistrate Ueda, in whose court Jirocho had appeared more than once. "How is he involved in the kidnapping?"

"There were two other women kidnapped before Chiyo," Hirata explained. "One is Jirocho's daughter."

"Is her case related to Chiyo's?" Sano asked.

"I don't know. Jirocho wasn't very cooperative. He wouldn't tell me anything." Hirata described his conversation with the gangster boss. "He wants to handle the case himself."

Concern showed on Sano's face. "So does Major Kumazawa. I talked to him today. He's not happy with my investigating two other crimes that we don't know for sure are related."

Reiko was offended that Sano's uncle would criticize Sano's work. To ask a favor after all these years of family estrangement, then object to how it was carried out! But Reiko kept silent. She didn't want to fan the fire that was obviously heating up between Major Kumazawa and her husband.

"Did you have any better luck with Fumiko?" Sano asked.

"Even worse." Hirata reported that her father had thrown the girl out and she was living in the marketplace.

"That's awful!" Reiko exclaimed. All day she'd felt bad for Chiyo. Now she deplored that a young girl's life had been destroyed. Which was crueler, the rapist or society?

"When I tried to talk to her, she tried to stab me, and then ran away." Hirata sounded rueful. "But I did turn up a witness—the man who found her by Shinobazu Pond. He heard an oxcart."

Sano nodded, gratified. "Maybe it was the same one that transported Chiyo."

"Speaking of oxcarts," Detective Marume said as he strode into the room with Fukida, "we went to the stables. The man in charge says there weren't any oxcarts assigned to work in Asakusa on the day we found Chiyo there—or on the day she was kidnapped."

"Whoever drove that oxcart, he wasn't there on legitimate business," Fukida said.

"We spent the rest of the day trying to track down drivers who hadn't been where they were supposed to be," Marume said. "But—" He turned up his empty palms.

"Maybe we can narrow down the search," Sano said. "Hirata-*san*, did you get a description of the driver who was seen near Shinobazu Pond?"

"No. The witness didn't see him. But he said it could be someone who'd been working in the vicinity—a fellow about twenty-five years old, with two teeth missing."

Sano frowned as he drank tea and pondered.

"But that's good news, isn't it?" Reiko said. "Now you have an idea of whom to look for."

"The problem is, I got a description of a suspect, too," Sano said, "and mine doesn't match Hirata-*san*'s." He told of his trip to Zōjō Temple district. Reiko was aghast to learn that the third victim had been an elderly nun. "My suspect is a big, muscular man in his thirties, with a shaved head, an unshaven face, and a scab on his cheekbone. The novice who saw him outside the convent didn't mention any missing teeth."

"We could have two or three different criminals," Hirata agreed. "What did the nun say?"

"Nothing, unfortunately." Sano explained that she was apparently so distraught that all she did was pray.

At least Chiyo still had her wits, Reiko thought. But that was a mixed blessing. Chiyo couldn't escape her misery by withdrawing into religion.

Sano asked Reiko, "Did you learn anything from Chiyo?"

Reiko felt his hope. "I'm sorry I have so little to report." She told them about the man at the shrine who'd called to Chiyo for help. "But Chiyo doesn't remember actually seeing the man. She does remember what he did to her." Reiko described the bites on Chiyo's breasts, how the man had suckled on her and called her "dearest mother, beloved mother," and the threats he'd made against Chiyo and her baby.

Sano shook his head in horror and disbelief. "Chiyo didn't see him while all that was happening?"

"No. I think he wore a mask." Reiko explained about the demonic face and the clouds Chiyo had seen, or imagined.

"It sounds like she was drugged," Sano said.

"That's what I thought," Reiko said.

"When the mind is disturbed, it can play tricks on itself, with or without drugs," Hirata suggested.

"By the way, Chiyo is still at her father's house. Her husband has cast her off," Reiko explained.

Sano looked disturbed but not surprised. "As if she hasn't suffered enough already." Setting down his tea bowl, he added, "We've covered a lot of ground, but we only have an oxcart that might or might not be involved, and descriptions of two suspects who might or might not be the culprits in any of the kidnappings."

"I started a search for mine," Hirata said.

"So did I," Sano said, "I sent my whole army out on the street to post notices and circulate my suspect's description."

"I hope it works." But Reiko knew how many men among Edo's million people probably fit those descriptions. Personal regret weighed upon her. "I wish there were something more I could do."

"There is," Sano said. "Talk to Chiyo again. Maybe she'll remember something else. And I want you to interview Fumiko and the nun. Maybe you can get more information from them than Hirata and I did."

17

For a brief moment when the sun ascended over the hills outside Edo, the rooftops of the city gleamed bright as gold. Then clouds rolled down from the hills, chasing and overtaking the rays of the sun. Edo was cloaked in a silvery mist.

Inside Sano's estate, Sano and Masahiro knelt opposite one another, some ten paces apart, in a shadowed courtyard. Each wore white martial arts practice clothes, his hand on the long sword at his waist. They sat perfectly still, their expressions serene yet alert.

Sano drew his sword. In one fluid motion, he whipped his blade out of its scabbard, leaped to his feet, and lunged. Masahiro followed suit. They slashed at each other; they parried and whirled, attacked, and counterattacked. Their wooden blades never touched, never made contact with their bodies. At last they retreated, sheathed their swords, and bowed.

"Your form is improving," Sano said, "but you were slower than usual."

Masahiro hung his head. "I'm sorry, Father."

Sano disliked criticizing his son. That was why he'd hired a tutor to teach Masahiro. He remembered his own childhood, when his father had taught him swordsmanship, and how much his father's constant, merciless tongue-lashings had hurt. He and Masahiro enjoyed practicing together; it was their special time to share during his busy day. But Sano couldn't ignore his son's faults.

Uncorrected, they might be the death of Masahiro someday. His own father's stern discipline was the reason Sano had fought and lived to fight again.

"You weren't paying attention," Sano said. "If this had been real combat, you'd be dead."

"Yes, Father, I know," Masahiro said, chastened.

Sano was concerned because Masahiro usually took martial arts practice very seriously. He knew better than other children how crucial good fighting skills were.

"What's the matter?" Sano said.

"Nothing," Masahiro said, with a haste that aroused Sano's suspicions.

"Is something on your mind?"

Masahiro fidgeted with the hilt of his sword. "No."

The gate opened, and Detectives Fukida and Marume appeared. "Please excuse the interruption, but there's good news," Fukida said.

"Can I go now, Father?" Masahiro said.

Sano studied his son's eager, nervous face. Masahiro was normally enthusiastic about their sessions and reluctant for them to end. His behavior today puzzled Sano.

But Sano said, "All right," and didn't press for an explanation. His own father had made him practice for long hours every single day. He'd often wished for time off to play with other children, wander the city and see the sights, or simply do nothing.

Masahiro hurried off. Sano said to the detectives, "What is it?"

"We just went back to the oxcart stables," Fukida said. "We asked the boss if any drivers fit your description of the man from the convent. He knew of one."

Hopeful excitement rose in Sano. "Good work. Where is he? Have you arrested him?"

"Not yet," Fukida said.

"He's working right near our doorstep," Marume said. "We thought you'd like to be in on the action."

Before Reiko left home, she stopped at the kitchen, where an army of cooks prepared food for the hundreds of people who lived in Sano's estate. Cooks slung vegetables and fish, grilled, stewed, and fried amid a din of cleavers chopping, pans rattling, and hearths roaring. Powerful aromas of garlic and hot oil permeated the steam from boiling pots.

Reiko packed fried dumplings stuffed with shrimp, grilled eel, raw tuna strips fastened to rice balls with seaweed, noodles with vegetables, and cakes filled with sweet chestnut paste into a lacquered wooden, compartmented lunchbox. She filled a jar with water, then carried the feast to her palanquin. She climbed inside and said to the bearers, "Take me to Zōjō Temple district."

After hastily changing his martial arts clothes for his regular garments, Sano donned his swords, mounted his horse, and left his estate with his detectives. They stopped to fetch Hirata on their way out of the castle. Marume and Fukida led the way through the northwestern gate. They brought their horses to a stop on the avenue that circled the castle. The avenue separated Edo Castle from the *daimyo* district, where the feudal lords and their thousands of retainers lived in vast compounds. Traffic that consisted mainly of samurai on horseback avoided the roadside by the castle, where piles of rocks, scrap lumber, and dirt overflowed into the street. Sano looked up at the construction site.

It was a dilapidated guard turret atop the wall, partially demolished, its upper story gone. Laborers hacked at the remains with pickaxes. They dropped the debris onto the pile on the roadside below, where two pairs of oxen, each yoked to a cart, stood patiently, tails swishing off flies. The two drivers—men dressed in short indigo kimonos and frayed sandals—loaded the debris on their carts.

One man was big, muscular, in his thirties. He wore his hair shorn down to a black fuzz on his scalp. His face sported several days' growth of whiskers. As Sano rode closer, he saw the large, pale scar on the man's right cheekbone.

"It looks like the man that the novice at the convent saw," Sano said.

The man spoke to his fellow driver, who grinned.

Hirata, riding beside Sano, said, "Look at the other fellow. He's younger and has two teeth missing from the right side of his mouth. That's my suspect."

"That's why a different man was at the scenes of two different kidnappings," Sano said. "We haven't got two separate criminals. They're a team."

"What a piece of good luck, finding them together," Marume said as he followed with Fukida.

When Sano and his men approached the oxcarts, the drivers spied them. The humor on their faces turned to caution, then the fear of guilty men cornered by the law. They dropped the timbers they'd lifted. They both jumped in one oxcart, and the big man snatched up a whip.

"Go!" he shouted, flailing the oxen.

The oxen clopped down the avenue, dragging the cart filled with debris. Workers on the turret yelled, "Hey! We're not done. Wait!" Sano and his men surged forward in pursuit. The driver with the missing teeth shouted, "Faster! Faster!"

But the heavy cart was no match for horsemen. Sano's party quickly caught up with it. The drivers jumped off the cart and ran.

"Don't let them get away!" Sano shouted as the drivers fled through the crowd and people swerved to avoid them.

Hirata leaped from his horse, flew through the air, landed on the younger man's back, and quickly subdued him. Marume and Fukida rode down the other man. When they caught him, he punched, kicked, and thrashed. By the time they'd wrestled him to the ground, they were panting and sweating.

From astride his horse, Sano surveyed his captives. "You're under arrest," he said.

"Didn't do anything wrong," the big man protested, his scarred cheek pressed into the mud.

"Neither did I," said his friend, pinned under Hirata.

"Then why did you run?" Sano asked.

That question stumped them into silence.

"Well, well," Marume said, "our new friends don't seem to have a good excuse."

Reiko rode in her palanquin, accompanied by Lieutenant Tanuma and her other guards, along the misty streets of the city. Peasants on their way to work avoided soldiers on patrol. Peddlers selling water, tea, baskets, and other merchandise hawked their wares. Neighborhood gates slowed the crush of traffic. Shopkeepers arranged their goods on the roadside to catch customers' eyes. At the approach to Zōjō district, pilgrims streamed toward the temple, while priests, monks, and nuns headed out to the city to beg. Reiko found the marketplace already crowded, with the children out in full force.

They'd emerged from the alleys where they slept at night. Ravenous, they begged at the food-stalls. Reiko was sad for the ragged, dirty boys and girls. She wished she could adopt them all. In fact, she had once adopted an orphan, the son of a woman who'd been murdered, but it hadn't been entirely successful. The boy's nature had been so affected by painful experiences that he'd not warmed to Reiko, despite her attempts to give him a good home. He shunned people, preferring to work in the stables with the horses. He would be an excellent groom someday, able to earn his living, if not overcome his past. Now Reiko watched for a twelve-year-old girl in a green and white kimono. Maybe today she could help another child in trouble.

Dogs barked. Reiko put her head out the window and saw, up the road, a pack of big, mangy black and brown hounds. They growled and lunged at something in their midst.

Feral dogs were plentiful in Edo. They came from the *daimyo* estates, where in the past they'd been bred for hunting. But the shogun, a devout Buddhist, had enacted laws that protected animals, forbade hunting, and prohibited killing or hurting dogs. He'd been born in the Year of the Dog, and he believed that if he protected dogs, the gods would grant him an heir. The result was that dogs proliferated unchecked. The *daimyo* still kept them as watchdogs, and when too many litters were born, they couldn't drown the puppies because the penalty for killing a dog was death. Samurai could no longer use dogs to test a sword. Unwanted dogs were simply turned out to fend for themselves. They roved in packs, foraging and competing for food. They befouled the city and posed a danger to all, and too often their victims were the helpless children.

Among the dogs now gathered in the marketplace, Reiko spied a flash of green, from a kimono worn by a girl who'd fallen on the ground. She cringed as the dogs snapped at her.

"Stop!" Reiko cried to her bearers. The moment they set down her palanquin, she was out the door. She called, "Lieutenant Tanuma! Save that girl!"

He and two other guards jumped off their horses. Shouting and waving their swords, they chased the dogs away. People nearby paid scant notice; the public had learned not to get involved in dog attacks. Nobody wanted to hurt a dog and be arrested and executed. Reiko hurried over to the girl, who scrambled to her feet. Near her lay a half-eaten fish that she and the dogs had been fighting over.

"Fumiko-*san*, are you all right?" Reiko said.

The girl started at the sound of her name. The fright on her dirty face turned to scowling distrust. "Who are you?"

"My name is Reiko. I'm the wife of Chamberlain Sano." Reiko extended her hand. "I want to help you."

Fumiko recoiled. "Don't touch me!" Her voice was gruff, boyish. "Leave me alone!" She turned to run.

"Don't let her get away," Reiko ordered her guards.

Lieutenant Tanuma put out his hand to grab the girl; the other men surrounded her. Reiko warned, "Look out—she's got a knife!" just as Fumiko slashed it at Tanuma. He jerked his hand back. Fumiko cowered within the circle formed by the guards and Reiko, as terrified of them as she'd been of the dogs.

"Shall I take the knife away from her?" Tanuma asked.

"No. Wait." Reiko ran to the palanquin and fetched the lunchbox. She opened the lid and showed the contents to Fumiko. "I brought this for you," she said. "Do you want it?"

Her eyes glazed with hunger, Fumiko breathed through her open mouth as she stared at the food.

"Put your knife away and come sit with me inside my palanquin," Reiko said, "and I'll give it all to you."

Fumiko hesitated. Reiko read in her gaze the fear of what might happen if she put herself in the hands of a stranger. "What do you want?" she asked.

"Just to talk," Reiko said.

18

Fumiko tucked her knife under her sash, climbed into the palanquin with Reiko, and fell upon the food. She crammed fish, rice, dumplings, noodles, and cakes into her mouth. She gulped and slurped, hardly bothering to chew. It was like watching a wild animal feed.

In the close confines of the palanquin, Reiko could smell Fumiko's stench of urine and unwashed hair and body. Fumiko ate and ate until the lunchbox was empty. She washed the food down with water from the jar Reiko had brought. Then she lunged for the door.

Reiko held it closed. "We'll talk first."

"Let me out, or I'll kill you." Fumiko reached for the knife.

Reiko grabbed Fumiko's wrist. It was skin and bone, thin and fragile.

"Let me go!" Fumiko cried.

As she struggled to pull free, their gazes met, and something unspoken passed between them. Maybe it was a sudden realization that they were both women in unusual circumstances—Fumiko the gangster's daughter who'd become a wild, starving street child; Reiko the samurai lady who'd ventured outside her own society to befriend an outcast. Maybe they had more in common than both of them recognized. Fumiko stopped fighting. When Reiko let go of her wrist, she scowled, but she stayed.

"Talk about what?" Fumiko said.

"Your kidnapping," Reiko said.

Now Fumiko looked surprised. "How do you know about that?"

"A friend of mine heard it from the police."

"The police?" Fumiko glanced out the window in sudden fright, as if she suspected a trap. "We don't want them in our business."

"We" meant her father's gangster clan, Reiko supposed. Not all the police were in cahoots with Jirocho, and he undoubtedly steered clear of those who tried to enforce the law.

"Don't worry, I didn't bring the police," Reiko said. "They only knew about the kidnapping because your father reported it to them."

"My father?" Hope appeared on Fumiko's face, breaking through her distrust like the sun through clouds. "Did he send you?" She sounded puzzled but eager.

Reiko realized that Fumiko thought Jirocho had sent the chamberlain's wife to rescue her, as improbable as that would be. Hating to disappoint the girl, she said, "No, I'm sorry," and watched Fumiko's expression turn woeful. "My husband sent me. He and I want to catch the person who kidnapped you."

Fumiko frowned, her suspicion renewed. "Why?"

"Because he hurt you," Reiko said. She didn't mention Sano's cousin and the nun who'd also been kidnapped; she didn't want Fumiko to think she cared only about them. She felt an affection for this savage little girl. "He should be punished."

"If I ever see him again, I'll kill him myself," Fumiko said. "That's the way we do things. We don't wait for other people to get revenge for us."

Reiko began to wonder what kind of life Fumiko had led within the gangster clan. Maybe she'd been wild and violent even before she'd been disowned. "Still, I want to help you," Reiko said. "Tell me about the man who kidnapped you. What did he look like?"

Confusion shadowed Fumiko's face. She pressed her lips together.

"You don't remember, do you?" Reiko said gently. When Fumiko remained silent, Reiko said, "Tell me what happened."

Fumiko bowed her head and mumbled through the tangled hair that fell over her face: "I was at Shinobazu Pond, feeding the fish. After that, it's all mixed up in my head. There was a little monkey . . ."

Confused, Reiko said, "A monkey? Where?"

"A man had it on a leash. He said that if I came with him, he would let me play with it."

"Who was he?"

"I don't remember." Fumiko sighed.

The kidnapper had used the monkey as bait for the girl, Reiko deduced. Fumiko must have gone with him, perhaps to an oxcart in which he'd carried her away. This was a different ploy than Chiyo's kidnapper had used. Reiko considered the disturbing idea that there were two rapists, possibly three.

"I was playing ball with the monkey," Fumiko said. "Then I woke up and it was gone. Everything was gone." The puzzlement she must have felt sounded in her voice. "I was someplace that was filled with clouds."

That did match Chiyo's story. "Was the man there?" Reiko asked.

Fumiko nodded.

"But you didn't see him?"

"No. Because of the clouds."

"What did he do?" Reiko asked.

She expected Fumiko to be so overcome with shame that she couldn't bear to tell the tale. But Fumiko spoke with startling matter-of-factness. "He pawed me all over. He put his thing in my mouth for me to suck."

Reiko remembered that Jirocho ran illegal brothels. Perhaps Fumiko had seen sex there, between the male customers and girls as young as herself.

"I tried to fight him off, but I couldn't move," Fumiko said. "I screamed and cursed at him. He called me a naughty girl. He spanked my behind until I cried. Then he shoved himself into me and did it."

Reiko was disturbed, and not only by what Fumiko had suffered. The man in Fumiko's case seemed to have different tastes in women and sexual practices than the one in Chiyo's. Still, Reiko believed that Chiyo and Fumiko had both been drugged; maybe their minds had been affected, and that explained the discrepancies. But despite the similarities in the stories, Reiko couldn't dismiss the possibility that there was more than one rapist.

"That's all I remember," Fumiko said. "The next thing I knew, I was lying on the ground beside Shinobazu Pond."

"The man hit your face, didn't he?" Reiko said. Although loath to make Fumiko dwell on bad experiences, she must probe the girl's memory for information about the criminal.

Fumiko touched her bruised eye. "No. My father did. He said I led the man on. He said I disgraced myself and our clan."

Here was the most tragic similarity between her story and Chiyo's. Both women had suffered insult heaped upon injury.

"I begged him to forgive me," Fumiko said. Tears trembled beneath her gruff, sullen manner. "I offered to cut off my finger." She added, "That's how we make it up to my father when we've done something wrong."

Reiko had known about the gangsters' rule, but the idea that a little girl should take it for granted was shocking.

"But my father wouldn't listen," Fumiko said. "He threw me out."

At that moment Reiko hated Fumiko's father, and Chiyo's husband, as much as she hated the man—or men—who'd assaulted the women. "I'm sorry about what happened to you. It wasn't your fault, no matter what anybody says. You're a brave, good girl. And I want you to know that my husband will catch the man who hurt you."

But even as she spoke, Reiko remembered that Sano's objective was to punish the man who'd kidnapped and raped his cousin. If a different man had kidnapped Fumiko, would Sano avenge her? He had enough else to do. Reiko made a private vow that if Sano didn't deliver Fumiko's rapist to justice, then she herself would. In the meantime, she could offer Fumiko other assistance.

"For now, you're coming with me," she said, then called to her bearers, "Let's go."

They hoisted the beams of the palanquin to their shoulders. As the vehicle began moving, Fumiko looked aghast. "Go where?"

"To my house," Reiko said, "inside Edo Castle."

"I can't!" Fumiko protested.

Reiko thought the girl must be afraid of a strange place. "Yes, you can," she said soothingly. "I'll give you as much food as you want, clean clothes, and a nice place to sleep. You'll be quite comfortable."

"Please stop," Fumiko said as the bearers carried her and Reiko past the market stalls. "I can't leave!"

Bewildered, Reiko said, "Here you have to sleep outdoors; you have to eat garbage. Why do you want to stay?"

"My father knows I'm here." Fumiko was frantic. "His gangsters have seen me. If I go someplace else, he won't be able to find me."

"Why would he want to?" Reiko asked. "He threw you out."

"After he thinks I've been punished enough, he'll take me back." Fumiko sounded desperate to believe it.

"I'll send word to your father that you're at my house, so he'll know to look for you there."

"He might not like that. He might get even angrier."

"You were just attacked by dogs," Reiko reminded Fumiko. "You might not be saved next time. You might not survive until your father decides to bring you home."

Fumiko flapped her hands, as if to ward off Reiko's logic. "I'm not going with you! Here is where I belong!"

She picked up the empty lunchbox and hurled it at Reiko. Reiko flung up her arms. Fumiko bounded out the door.

"Wait!" Reiko cried. "Fumiko, stop!"

The girl ran away into the marketplace, where the throngs absorbed her. Lieutenant Tanuma called, "Should I go after her, Lady Reiko?"

"No, don't."

Sighing, Reiko closed the door of the palanquin. She wouldn't force Fumiko to accept shelter against her will. Perhaps Fumiko was right in her belief that Jirocho would relent, and when he came to fetch her, she had better be here, or he would change his mind. Reiko didn't understand gangsters well enough to know otherwise. And she had another task to perform for Sano.

"Take me to the Keiaiji Convent," she called to her escorts. "Maybe I'll have better luck with the nun."

Chamberlain Yanagisawa's estate was one of many inside the quarter within Edo Castle where the shogun's top officials lived. Guards opened its gate, and out came Yanagisawa, his son Yoritomo, and their guards, all on horseback. Clad in rain hats and capes, they rode down the street amid mounted soldiers going in the same direction.

One soldier wasn't really a soldier. The face under his helmet belonged to Toda Ikkyu. As he followed Yanagisawa and Yoritomo, they didn't notice him. Neither they nor Toda noticed the boy riding a pony, trailing in their wake.

Masahiro wore, in addition to the rain cape and hat that hid his face and clothes, a flag bearing the Tokugawa crest on a pole attached to his back. He carried a leather sack of bamboo scroll containers. The flag, sack, and scrolls were the standard equipment of messenger boys. He'd borrowed them from Father's office. He hoped Father wouldn't mind. The scroll containers were empty; they were part of his disguise.

He'd gotten the idea for the disguise from Mother. She sometimes dressed as a servant, the better to avoid attention when she went out investigating. Masahiro had also taken a hint from the spy who'd come to visit Father last night. Under the scrolls in his sack were a spare hat and jacket.

As he trailed Yanagisawa, Yoritomo, and their procession along the stone-walled passages that wound downhill through the castle, his heart beat fast with excitement. This was his first day as a real detective. He meant to find out what Yanagisawa was up to.

The procession stopped at a checkpoint, two gates that led in and out of a square enclosure designed to trap invading enemies during war. In peacetime, the guards merely eyed the folks who came by and let them pass. Yanagisawa rode through with his party. Masahiro waited impatiently, stuck behind the people who blocked his view. He mustn't lose track of Yanagisawa. He worried about whether his disguise would pass inspection. Would the guards notice that he was too young to be a messenger? He drew himself up to his full height, held his breath, and silently prayed.

The guards let him through without a second glance. Relieved, Masahiro hurriedly rode after Yanagisawa. But as they approached the castle's main gate, he felt serious qualms.

He'd never gone outside the castle by himself. Father and Mother said it was too dangerous. He didn't want to admit that he was afraid to go out, but he was. The city was a big place filled with scary people. Masahiro carried a dagger hidden beneath his cape, but what if he got attacked by someone too big and strong for him to fight? He also worried about what would happen when Father and Mother found out he'd broken their rule.

Ahead loomed the gate. Masahiro saw Yanagisawa's procession riding through the portals. What should he do?

He drew a deep breath for courage and followed Yanagisawa.

Tonight, when he told Father and Mother what he'd learned about Yanagisawa, they would be so proud of him that they wouldn't be angry.

Inside the bedchamber at the convent, two novices held the nun Tengu-in, who sat on a futon atop a wooden pallet. Another novice spooned miso soup into her mouth. The old woman struggled weakly, spat, and whispered prayers.

"It won't do you any good to talk to her," the abbess said, standing in the doorway with Reiko. "See for yourself."

Reiko watched with dismay as Tengu-in coughed and retched, while the novices poured water into her. The force-feeding seemed like torture, but it had probably kept the old nun alive. "I must try," Reiko said.

She walked toward Tengu-in across the big room where the other nuns slept at night on the pallets laid out in a row. The abbess and the novices bowed and left. Tengu-in lay on her bed, eyes closed, exhausted. In the misty daylight that shone through the paper windowpanes she looked like a corpse. Her face was sunken, her skin so thin that the spidery blue veins pulsed through it on her bare scalp. Her skeletal hands clutched a rosary of round, brown jade beads strung on a thick leather cord.

"Tengu-in?" Reiko said, kneeling beside her. "Can you hear me?"

The nun's lips formed silent prayers. Her fingers counted beads. Chiyo and Fumiko seemed well off compared to her. At least they were more physically and mentally sound, no matter how they'd been treated.

"I'm sorry to bother you," Reiko said, "but my husband sent me to talk to you. He's Chamberlain Sano. He came here yesterday. Do you remember?"

Tengu-in didn't answer. She continued her wordless praying as her fingers slid beads along the cord.

"I need to know what happened to you when you were kidnapped," Reiko persisted. "Maybe if you tell me, you'll feel better."

No response came. Reiko tried a different tack. "Two other women besides you have been kidnapped and attacked. My husband and I think it was the same man." Although Reiko wasn't so sure, after hearing Fumiko's story and comparing it to Chiyo's. "We want to catch him. You may be the only person who can help us. Can you try, for their sake as well as your own?"

As moments passed and the nun seemed unaware of Reiko's presence, Reiko had the eerie feeling that she was alone. Tengu-in's spirit had retreated into another, faraway realm. How could Reiko bridge the distance?

"I'll tell you what I think happened," Reiko said. "Can you give some sign whether I'm right?" It was like talking to herself, but she began to recite the story she'd learned from Sano. "You went to the main temple that day. With the novices. You couldn't keep up with them. They left you behind. That's when he came and took you."

Did Tengu-in stiffen with anxiety? Reiko wondered if it was only her imagination.

"He pretended he was hurt and he asked for your help," Reiko suggested, recalling the ploy that had lured Chiyo.

Tengu-in's expression of stoic suffering didn't alter.

"He had a pet monkey. He said he would let you play with it if you went with him." Even as she spoke, Reiko knew that although the monkey trick had worked for Fumiko, it probably wouldn't have for an old woman, and the kidnapper was smart.

A hoarse whisper came from the nun. Her eyes opened. Filmy and blank, their lids crusted, they gazed at nothing.

"What did you say?" Reiko kept her voice gentle; she hid her excitement.

"Place of Relief," whispered Tengu-in.

That was the polite term for the privy. "Do you need to go?" Reiko asked.

Tengu-in's lips moved, and for a moment Reiko thought she'd resumed praying. But her words were audible now, although barely. Reiko leaned closer to hear.

"I went to the Place of Relief," she said. "I was inside. He opened the door."

Reiko realized that she was talking about that day she'd been kidnapped. Finally her silence had broken. Reiko didn't know why. Perhaps the time had simply come. Reiko pictured Tengu-in crouched over the hole inside a public privy in the temple grounds, and the door opening. The kidnapper had cornered the helpless old woman there.

"Who was he?" Reiko asked urgently.

Tengu-in's head rolled from side to side on the pillow.

Reiko said, "Was he a big man with a shaved head and a scab on his cheek?"

". . . I don't know."

If he wasn't the suspect sighted outside the convent, maybe he was the one Hirata's witness had seen by Shinobazu Pond. "Did he have teeth missing?"

"Couldn't see," whispered Tengu-in. "The light . . ."

The daylight behind the man must have left his features in shadow. "What happened next?" Reiko asked.

The nun's gaze shifted rapidly; her eyelids lowered.

"Then you woke up," Reiko prompted, anxious to prevent Tengu-in from withdrawing beyond her reach. "You were in a place filled with clouds."

"Clouds," Tengu-in echoed in a voice like the wind sighing.

"You couldn't move. The man was there."

A low, fearful whimper resonated through Tengu-in. Her body quaked.

"He nursed at your breasts," Reiko suggested. "He called you 'dearest mother,' and 'beloved mother.'"

Again Tengu-in's head tossed.

Reiko ventured, "He forced you to suck on him. He said you were naughty and beat you?" Tengu-in mumbled something Reiko couldn't hear. "What was that?"

"Pray," whispered Tengu-in. "He made me pray while he had me." Her voice rose to a loud, shrill pitch: "*Namo Amida Butsu! Namo Amida Butsu!*" *I trust in the Buddha of Immeasurable Light.* She was praying to be delivered from this life of suffering and reborn into the Pure Land, a heaven of beauty and enlightenment. Her voice trailed off while her lips kept moving. Her eyes closed as she withdrew behind the barrier of her private hell.

19

"I'm bringing these prisoners in for interrogation," Sano told the sentries outside Edo Jail. Behind him, the two suspects knelt in their oxcart, their wrists and ankles bound with rope, guarded by Detectives Marume and Fukida and Sano's other troops. Above him loomed the jail's high, mossy stone walls and guard turrets. "Let us in."

The guards obeyed. Sano and his entourage crowded into a courtyard surrounded by barracks. His soldiers brought in the oxcart and unloaded the two prisoners. His party marched into the dungeon, a building whose dirty, scabrous plaster walls rose from a high stone base. It was a reflection of Edo Castle in a dark mirror—one edifice designed to safe-guard the regime's highest society, the other to cage its lowest.

The interrogation rooms, situated along a dank passage that smelled of sewers, had ironclad doors with small windows set at eye level. Hirata marched the young suspect with the missing teeth into one room. Sano, Marume, and Fukida took the other suspect into a room at the passage's opposite end. Shouts, moans, and weeping emanated from the rooms in between. Sano's room was just large enough to hold four people and swing a sword. Dim light seeped from a barred window near the ceiling. The walls were marred with cracks and gouges, discolored by old blood-stains. Marume and Fukida shoved the suspect down on the straw that covered the floor. Sano smelled urine on the straw, which was trampled and grimy; it hadn't been changed since the last interrogation. He stood over the suspect.

The big man stared at the wall behind Sano, his gaze sullen beneath his heavy brow. His unshaven face was mud-streaked from his tussle with the detectives. Sweat plastered his blue kimono against his muscles. He hadn't uttered a word since he'd been captured.

"What's your name?" Sano asked.

The suspect tightened his jaw. Marume kicked his thigh and ordered, "Speak up."

"Jinshichi," the suspect said. His deep voice was thick and raspy, as if he'd swallowed sand mixed with pitch.

"Well, Jinshichi," Sano said, "you're under arrest for kidnapping my cousin."

"Didn't kidnap anybody."

He spoke with conviction, but Sano didn't believe him. Something about the man didn't smell right.

"Let me refresh your memory," Sano said. "My cousin is the woman you met at Awashima Shrine. She'd gone there with her new baby. You hid in the bushes and called to her that you were hurt. She came to help you. You took her and left the baby."

"I never," Jinshichi said, adamant.

"You gave her a drug that put her to sleep." Sano kept his voice calm, but anger mounted inside him. "You locked her up."

"Never."

"Then you raped her," Sano said, controlling an urge to lash out at Jinshichi for hurting Chiyo, to wipe that hard, defiant look off his face.

"You're wrong." If Jinshichi was afraid, it didn't show.

Standing on either side of him, Marume and Fukida exchanged glances. They looked at Sano, who saw that they had doubts about the man's guilt.

"You kept her for two days," Sano said. "When you were finished with her, you dumped her in an alley, as if she were a sack of garbage."

Jinshichi muttered. Fukida smacked his head, and he said, "Wasn't me. I'm innocent."

"I suppose you didn't kidnap Tengu-in, either," Sano said.

"Who?"

"The nun. She was taken from the Zōjō Temple precinct on the first day of the third month. You were seen outside her convent the day before."

"Couldn't have been," Jinshichi said. "Wasn't there."

"Then where were you?" Sano demanded.

Jinshichi eyed Sano with incredulity. "That was a long time ago. Damned if I can remember. Working, probably."

"Working where?"

"Around town. Hell if I know!" Jinshichi grew loud, impatient. "I didn't do anything wrong. Can I go now?"

"If you really want to," Sano said. "You can go straight to the court of justice and be tried for two kidnappings and two assaults."

For the first time, Jinshichi's face showed fear. It was common knowledge that almost every trial ended with a guilty verdict.

"Better yet," Sano said, "we'll just skip the trial and take you straight to the execution ground."

"But I didn't kidnap those women." Jinshichi strained against the ropes that bound him. "I swear!"

Sano burned with rage at the man's denials. But even though Sano was sure Jinshichi was lying, he couldn't ignore the obvious reason that the man might not be.

There was a second suspect right down the hall.

In the other interrogation room, Hirata studied the prisoner who knelt on the straw at his feet. "Tell me your name," he ordered.

"Gombei, Honorable master." The man bowed and grinned.

He was slender and wiry, the type that was far stronger than he looked. He could probably lift loads as heavy as himself. Even with his wrists and ankles tied up, he exuded a bounding energy. Hirata could hear his rapid heartbeat, his blood swift beneath his skin. Despite his missing teeth, his face wasn't unhandsome. Long, wavy hair, fallen from his topknot, grazed his shoulders and framed roguish features. His eyes sparkled with vitality and cunning.

Trained perception and samurai instinct told Hirata that Gombei had plenty to hide.

But even as Hirata prepared to extract Gombei's guilty secrets, only half of his attention was focused on the job at hand. He couldn't stop thinking about the presence he'd sensed at Shinobazu Pond yesterday. Who was it? What were the man's intentions?

Now, half of Hirata's mind was attuned to the world beyond his sight, waiting for the mysterious presence to return. He believed that even though he didn't know who it was, it knew who he was. He found himself constantly glancing over his shoulder, sensing that he was being watched. He felt like a coward rather than the best fighter in Edo. The presence had planted a seed of fear in him. Hirata felt the seed growing, feeding on his confusion, against his will.

What would happen the next time he encountered the presence?

There would be a next time, but when?

Gombei's voice brought Hirata back to Edo Jail and the investigation. "Honorable master, please believe me when I say that I am a decent, honest citizen who's never broken the law." He had the kind of earnest, charming manner that Hirata automatically distrusted. "Ask anyone who knows me. My family, my friends, my neighbors, my boss, they'll tell you that I'm—"

"Quite the talker," Hirata interrupted. "Well, let's talk about the little girl you kidnapped."

Amazement snapped Gombei's eyes wide. His full lips silently repeated the word *kidnapped*. "What little girl?"

"The one at Shinobazu Pond."

"With all due respect, I didn't do it." Gombei oozed earnestness. "I would never hurt a child. In fact, I would never even hurt a fly. Except if it's the biting kind."

"You were in the area," Hirata said. "A witness saw you."

"I've done work over there. A lot of people must have seen me. If I may say so, that doesn't mean I kidnapped somebody."

"I say you did. You kidnapped that girl, put her in a cage, and raped her."

"I didn't!" Gombei bristled with indignation.

He had a combative streak beneath his charm, Hirata observed. He wasn't as harmless as he took pains to appear. But Hirata couldn't discern more about the man. Preoccupation had weakened his mental energy.

"If I want a good time, I don't need to kidnap and force anybody, and besides, I don't go for children. I like women." Gombei's grin turned lecherous. "And they like me. I've got a wife, a mistress, and ladies all over town."

"Not even a big ladies' man like you can have whoever he wants," Hirata said. He couldn't summon the power to see through lies or manipulate Gombei into confessing. He must rely on verbal tactics. "What if you want somebody you can't get?"

"Pardon me, but I can't imagine who that might be."

"How about the chamberlain's cousin? She's a high-ranking samurai woman with a new baby. She was kidnapped, too." Hirata asked, "Do you like to drink mother's milk straight from the breast while you have sex?"

"What?" Disbelief and outrage lifted the pitch of Gombei's voice. "No, indeed."

"How about a sixty-year-old nun? Do you get a thrill out of raping holy women?"

Gombei sputtered. "With all due respect, only a man who's sick in the head would do such things."

"Like your friend?"

"You could save yourself a lot of trouble if you would just confess," Fukida told Jinshichi.

"And save us the trouble of torturing you," Marume said.

They both knew that Sano didn't approve of torture because it often produced false confessions.

"Go ahead," Jinshichi said, his eyes glittering with bravado. "Tell you right now, I say what you want, it's not true."

Today Sano would have been glad to make an exception for Jinshichi, but he had at least one other ploy to try. "Maybe you're right," he said, in such a quick about-face that Marume and Fukida looked at him in surprise. "Maybe you're not the culprit."

"Been telling you all along," Jinshichi said, half relieved, half wary of a trick.

"Maybe it's your friend," Sano said. "What's his name?"

"Gombei." The man sneered. "He didn't do it, either."

"Somebody did," Sano said. "Somebody's going to be punished. Right now my choice is him or you. Which is it going to be?"

"Not him. Not me," Jinshichi insisted. "Like I said, you got the wrong folks."

"Your friend is under interrogation as we speak," Sano said. "My chief retainer is asking him the same kind of questions that I've been asking you. What do you think he's saying?"

Jinshichi shrugged. "That we're both innocent."

"Don't be too sure about that," Sano said. "He puts the blame on you, he goes free."

"He wouldn't," Jinshichi said staunchly.

"Of course he would, if it means he lives and you die."

"You're trying to pit us against each other," Jinshichi said. "Won't work."

"I'm trying to help you see reason," Sano said. "Any moment, my chief retainer is going to walk in here and say that your friend turned on you. Then it will be too late for you to take advantage of the deal I'm offering."

Suspicion lowered Jinshichi's heavy brow. "What deal?"

"Be the first to turn. If your friend kidnapped and raped those women, you tell me everything you know about it, and I'll let you go."

Sano hoped this deal would induce Jinshichi to provide details about the crimes that would help him figure out which, if either, man had committed them. But Jinshichi squared his muscular shoulders and set his jaw.

"Forget it," he said. "Gombei didn't do it, and neither did I. That's the truth, no matter what you do to us."

"What about my friend?" Gombei asked Hirata.

"Maybe he likes little girls, nursing mothers, and old nuns," Hirata suggested.

Gombei chortled. "Oh, now that's ridiculous, if you'll pardon my saying so."

"What makes you so sure?"

"I've known Jinshichi forever. We're from the same neighborhood. He's not sick or crazy."

"People keep secrets even from their closest friends," Hirata said. "How do you know what goes on in Jinshichi's mind—or what he does in private?"

"I know he couldn't have kidnapped the girl or the nun. Because he was with me on the days they were taken." Gombei's grin broadened. The gaps where his teeth had rotted out were black holes.

Hirata had expected Gombei to trot out a double alibi. "Which days were those?" He hadn't said. If Gombei knew, that would mark him as the culprit.

"Every day," Gombei said. "We work together."

"There must have been times when you were out of each other's sight. I can ask your boss if he ever sent you to different jobs."

"Ask him, if you want," Gombei said with brazen nonchalance.

"Then again," Hirata said, "why should I bother? I can just ask Jinshi-chi. He's right down the hall."

"Go ahead. He'll tell you the same thing: We were together."

Hirata spied a new twist in the case. "Maybe you were in on the kidnapping together, too. That would have made it easier to grab the women and get them into the oxcart." But Sano's cousin Chiyo seemed to think she'd been raped by one man alone. "Did you take turns? He raped the little girl, you raped the nun?"

Anger erased the good cheer from Gombei's expression. "We didn't do it. I'll vouch for him. He'll vouch for me."

"You're pretty loyal to Jinshichi," Hirata observed.

"Yes, indeed," Gombei said. "Because I owe him my life. We were in the mountains, hauling wood, and my cart ran off the road. I was caught hanging by one hand over a cliff. Jinshichi pulled me up. He saved me."

"That explains why you would want to protect him. Why should he care about protecting you?" Hirata added, "He can say that you kidnapped and raped those women, and walk out of here a free man, while you go to the execution ground."

"He won't. Because he owes me, too. A while back, we went swimming in the river. He got swept away by a current. I saved him." *So there*, Gombei's expression said.

"Old obligations can be easily put aside when new circumstances arise," Hirata said. "You and Jinshichi each have a chance to tell tales on the other and save your own life. Who'll be the smart one?"

Gombei shook his head. "Jinshichi and I always stick together. We always will."

Hirata saw that they had a bond of loyalty as strong as that between a samurai and his master. What threat might change Gombei's story? "I give up, then. I'll let Jirocho decide which one of you is guilty or if both of you are."

Gombei's wary expression showed that he knew of the gangster boss. "What's Jirocho got to do with this?"

"The little girl who was kidnapped is his daughter."

"Well, I'll be," Gombei said, astonished. "Anybody who would touch anything that belonged to him is a fool."

"Indeed. He's looking to get revenge," Hirata said. "Maybe I'll turn you and your friend over to Jirocho. He'll get the truth out of you. Then he'll kill you both, no matter which of you actually raped his daughter and which of you was the accomplice."

Gombei's eyes sparkled with fear of what a gangster out for blood would do. But he shrugged, grinned, and said, "Whatever you want. We all have to die sometime."

Sano, Marume, and Fukida met Hirata outside the dungeon. Jailers escorted new prisoners into the building and led inmates out to go to the court of justice or the execution ground. No one looked happy—not the jailers, prisoners, or Sano's party.

"What did you get out of your suspect?" Sano asked Hirata.

"Gombei claims he's innocent," Hirata replied. "He also says he and Jinshichi are each other's alibi."

"Let me guess," Sano said. "He refused to turn on his friend."

"Right you are."

"So did my suspect." Frustration vexed Sano.

"Those men look like ordinary no-goods, but they're tougher than the rest," Marume commented.

Fukida asked Hirata, "Do you think yours is guilty?"

"Yes," Hirata said, although he seemed uncertain.

"Same here," Sano said. "But there's no evidence. All we have is one witness who saw Jinshichi lurking outside the convent, and one who saw Gombei at Shinobazu Pond."

"Neither man was placed at the scene of the kidnappings at the times they happened," Hirata reminded everyone.

"Or seen in the vicinity when the victims were dumped." Sano had had great hopes for solving the case today, but now the investigation had stalled. "And it doesn't look as if any confessions will be forthcoming."

"If you want confessions, just say the word," Hirata said.

Sano remembered that Hirata knew ways of inflicting pain with or without permanent physical damage. There wasn't a man on earth who could hold out. But Sano said, "No. I'm still opposed to torture. I know those men are guilty, but I won't act on my judgment, or yours, without proof to back it up."

That was part of his code of honor, which seemed particularly difficult to uphold today, when he wanted to punish someone for what had happened to Chiyo and the other women.

Hirata nodded. He shared Sano's principles, if not to the same degree.

"Besides," Sano said, "there's a chance that we're wrong about those men even though we don't think so. If that's the case, it would be a miscarriage of justice for Gombei and Jinshichi to die for the crimes while the real culprit goes free."

"Then we'll find proof." Hirata sounded just as determined to solve the case as Sano was. "Shall I go back to Shinobazu Pond and look for other witnesses?"

Fukida said, "Marume-*san* and I could sniff around Zōjō Temple district."

Sano supposed that he himself could go back to Asakusa, but there must be some other way to quicker results. Into his mind popped a strategy he'd never had reason to use before.

"Not just yet," Sano said. "I have another plan."

20

Along the Sumida River northwest of the castle, upstream from the warehouses and docks, stretched a wide embankment planted with cherry trees. It was popular in springtime, when the trees were in flower and the people of Edo flocked to picnic in the pavilions, drink in the teahouses along the path, float in pleasure boats on the river, and admire the pink blossoms.

But today the blossoms were long gone, the pavilions empty, the sky threatening more rain. The trees, in full summer leaf, shadowed the wet ground. Barges and ferries plied the river, which was brown and murky.

Yanagisawa and Yoritomo were among the few people strolling the embankment. They'd shed their rain capes and hats; they wore dark-colored silk robes without identifying crests. Their entourage waited behind them at a distance.

"What's the matter?" Yanagisawa asked. "You look ill."

Yoritomo's handsome face was pale and sweating; his Adam's apple bobbed as he swallowed convulsively. "I'm just nervous."

"Why?"

"I've never done this."

They were about to embark upon a rite of passage that Yanagisawa had never subjected his son to before. Yanagisawa wondered if he should have scheduled a few practice runs to put Yoritomo at ease. He hoped Yoritomo wouldn't make a bad impression.

"I don't know how to act," Yoritomo said, with shame, "I don't have much experience with women."

That was true. Yoritomo had been sheltered as a child, had lived in an isolated country villa with his mother. She was a distant cousin of the shogun, and Yoritomo the product of a brief liaison between her and Yanagisawa. During his boyhood, Yoritomo had encountered few women except her attendants. Later, his relationship with the shogun had precluded love affairs. Yanagisawa knew that Yoritomo had never experienced sex with a female, but that was, Yanagisawa hoped, about to change.

"Just be as respectful and dignified as you would on any other occasion," Yanagisawa said.

"All right," Yoritomo said, but Yanagisawa could see him trembling. Yanagisawa felt pity for his son, and guilt. Yoritomo's life had been far from normal, and Yanagisawa was largely to blame. "But what should I say?"

"Don't say anything unless somebody speaks to you. If you are spoken to, just try to sound like the polite, charming, intelligent person that you are."

Yoritomo squared his shoulders, bearing up under the weight of responsibility. "Yes, Father," he said bravely. "I promise I won't let you down."

Yanagisawa experienced a love for his son that was so strong his knees buckled. "I won't let you down, either."

Ahead, in the distance, three figures appeared. Yoritomo gulped and said, "Here they come!"

"Relax," Yanagisawa said. "Don't be afraid. We're in this together."

The figures drew closer. "Lady Setsu," emaciated and stern, and "Lady Chocho," her plump, babyish companion, walked on either side of a younger woman. She was unusually tall; she towered over them. They wore dark, modest, but sumptuous silk garments; she wore a robe patterned with green leaves and grasses in brighter tones, appropriate for a samurai lady who was some twenty-four years old. Yanagisawa thought her plain in the extreme. She was all awkward bones. Self-conscious about her height, she had bad posture. Her makeup didn't camouflage her beaked nose or heavy eyelids. Her one claim to beauty was her hair, dressed in a thick knot, shiny and lushly black.

"Greetings," Yanagisawa said as he and Yoritomo stopped face-to-face with the women.

"Why, hello!" Lady Chocho exclaimed. As bows were exchanged, she batted her eyes at Yanagisawa and giggled. "What a surprise to meet you here!"

"A wonderful coincidence," Yanagisawa agreed.

They had to act as if this were a chance encounter. That was the custom for a *miai*, the first meeting between a prospective bride and groom and their relatives. If one side didn't want to go any further, both sides could pretend the *miai* had never happened and save face.

Yanagisawa was determined to see this *miai* through to the marriage.

"What a fine place for walking on a day like this." Lady Setsu lifted the water-stained hem of her robe off the ground. "But I suppose the inconvenience couldn't be helped."

They'd had to pick a location with few people to observe them, where they would be unlikely to meet anyone they knew.

"Will you introduce me to your companion?" Yanagisawa said to Lady Setsu.

She was looking at Yoritomo. The right side of her face wore an involuntary, pained wince. The eye on the normal left side scrutinized Yoritomo closely as she said, "May I present the Honorable Tsuruhime."

The young woman stepped forward, graceless and shy. Eyes downcast, she murmured, "It is a privilege to make your acquaintance."

"And this must be your son." Lady Chocho minced over to Yoritomo, beheld him, and gasped. "You look just like your father! My, you're handsome!"

Yoritomo ducked his head, clearly mortified. Lady Chocho exclaimed, "Isn't that sweet, he's blushing!" She tittered and pinched his cheek. "Oh, your skin is so soft! Just like a baby's bottom! If I were younger, I would eat you up!"

Yoritomo cast a pleading glance at Yanagisawa, who sent him a look that warned him not to rebuff Lady Chocho or do anything else that would offend the women.

"Yes, this is my son Yoritomo," he said.

Lady Setsu's gaze registered shock as it moved from son to father. "'Yoritomo'?" she repeated.

"Meet my daughter," Lady Chocho said, and pushed Tsuruhime at Yoritomo.

They bowed to one another. Tsuruhime wore a sad, resigned expression. Yoritomo regarded her with the look of a man who has come upon a snake that he knows will bite him and wonders if it's poisonous. Not one hint of attraction did Yanagisawa see. But attraction was unnecessary. Yoritomo and Tsuruhime would learn to love each other or not. Other considerations were more important in this marriage that Yanagisawa wanted.

"This boy is the one?" Lady Setsu said in disbelief. "*Him?*"

Yanagisawa realized that this *miai* wasn't going as well as he'd expected. He said, "Why don't we let our two young people go off by themselves and get acquainted." That was allowed by custom, as long as the prospective bride and groom remained within their chaperones' sight. "We can talk things over."

Yoritomo shot Yanagisawa a glance filled with panic. Yanagisawa nodded encouragingly at him. Yoritomo and Tsuruhime set off down a path through the cherry trees. She went meekly. Yanagisawa had seen happier faces than his son's on condemned men going to the execution ground.

Lady Chocho clasped her hand to her bosom and sighed. "Don't they make a lovely couple?"

"Can you really mean to marry him to my stepdaughter?" Lady Setsu stared with shock at Yanagisawa.

"That's why we're here," Yanagisawa said. Her reaction was far from flattering, but he hid the offense he felt. "What objection do you have to Tsuruhime marrying a son of mine?"

"I don't," Lady Chocho said, dimpling at him. "If you were to become my daughter's new father-in-law, I would get to see you all the time."

"No objection against your sons in general," Lady Setsu said, "just that one."

"Why?" Yanagisawa asked.

She laughed, a sour cackle. The muscles on the distorted side of her face tightened. "It should be obvious."

It was, and Yanagisawa knew that if he were in her position, he would feel the same disapproval, but he said, "This marriage is a matter of survival—for Tsuruhime as well as you and Lady Chocho and me and my son."

"Why not one of your other sons?" Lady Setsu said.

Yanagisawa didn't love them as much as he did Yoritomo. They were inferior in looks, and their personalities were less malleable; he couldn't control them the way he could his favorite son. Also, Yoritomo deserved compensation for being the shogun's male concubine. But these reasons wouldn't convince Lady Setsu; they didn't matter in the political scheme of things.

"Because Yoritomo has the right bloodline," Yanagisawa said. "The others don't."

Yoritomo's mother was a Tokugawa clan member, which made Yoritomo eligible for the succession, even though he was far down the list of candidates.

Lady Setsu beheld Yanagisawa with such astonishment that both her eyes opened wide. "So it's not just a rumor," she said. "You do intend for your son to be the next shogun."

Yanagisawa put his finger to his lips. Airing such an intention was dangerous. He glanced around to see if anyone was listening. He saw a few other people strolling the embankment, none close by. "If that happens, it would be the best protection you and your family could have."

Lady Setsu watched Yoritomo and Tsuruhime march grimly side by side along the river, not speaking to each other. "If they marry, it would certainly move your son up in the ranks of the succession," she said, her crisp voice turned acid.

"So we both stand to gain from their marriage," Yanagisawa said. "Perhaps you and yours have even more at stake than me and mine. Do you remember the story of Toyotomi Hideyoshi?"

Some hundred years ago, that famous general had aspired to rule Japan but died before achieving his goal. He'd left behind a wife, and a son who should have inherited his rank, his troops, and his chance to be shogun. But his former ally, Tokugawa Ieyasu, had wanted to eliminate the widow and heir and clear the way for his own rise to power. Ieyasu had besieged their castle in Osaka. Hideyoshi's widow and heir had committed suicide while the castle went up in flames.

"I know that story." Lady Setsu's voice had lost some of its crispness, and Yanagisawa knew he'd scored a point.

"I don't," Lady Chocho said. "How does it go?"

"I'll tell you later." Lady Setsu turned to Yanagisawa. "I suppose you would expect the marriage to be consummated?"

"Of course," Yanagisawa said, although he wasn't sure that Yoritomo was capable. "That's the only way to produce an heir, which is the best guarantee for our future."

"They would make such pretty babies," Lady Chocho said.

Lady Setsu shook her head. "Your audacity takes my breath away."

"Better audacious than dead," Yanagisawa said.

"When should we have the wedding?" Lady Chocho asked eagerly.

"Don't get excited," Lady Setsu snapped at her. "The matter is not settled yet."

"The dowry and other terms are negotiable, but this is the deal I'm offering," Yanagisawa said. "Yoritomo marries Tsuruhime. Take it or leave it."

Lady Setsu frowned, insulted by his peremptoriness. "I require some time to think."

"We have to order Tsuruhime's wedding clothes," Lady Chocho said.

"I'll expect your answer by tomorrow," Yanagisawa said.

From his perch high in a cherry tree, Masahiro watched Yanagisawa and the three ladies walk off in opposite directions. The ladies climbed into palanquins. Yanagisawa and Yoritomo passed directly under the tree where Masahiro was hiding. He could have spit on their heads!

Masahiro almost laughed out loud at the thought. They hadn't seemed to notice him following them from the castle or climbing the tree. If they'd seen him at all, they'd probably thought he was just a boy playing. He'd stowed his messenger's flag and pouch in his saddlebag along the way, and tied a blue cotton kerchief around his head. Now he watched Yanagisawa and Yoritomo mount their horses and prepared to follow them some more. He couldn't wait to tell Father and Mother what he'd seen. He hadn't heard anything, but watching Yanagisawa and the ladies was good detective work, wasn't it?

Masahiro scrambled down the tree and jumped to the ground. But as he hurried toward the pavilion where he'd tied his pony, a hand grabbed his arm. He yelped in surprise.

The hand belonged to a samurai who'd stepped out from behind another tree. His face, his tattered wicker hat, and his worn cotton kimono and leggings were dark with soaked-in grime. His other hand rested on the hilt of his long sword. Masahiro froze and went dumbstruck with terror.

This man was surely a *rōnin* bandit who meant to rob him or kill him, or both.

"Not so fast, Masahiro-*san*," the *rōnin* said.

Astonishment replaced some of Masahiro's fear. "How—how did you know my name?" The man was a stranger.

"I've seen you at your father's house," the *rōnin* said in a flat voice that didn't match his scary appearance.

"You're a friend of Father's?" Masahiro dared to feel relief.

The skin around the *rōnin*'s eyes crinkled with amusement underneath the grime. "You could call me that."

Masahiro was suspicious and wary nonetheless. He tried to tug his arm free, but the *rōnin* held on tight.

"I didn't know Father had friends who look like you," the boy said.

"Your father has all sorts of friends you don't know."

That remark didn't comfort Masahiro. "How did you recognize me?"

"I saw you leave the castle dressed as a messenger boy. A while later, I noticed you in a different outfit." The *rōnin* flicked his finger against Masahiro's head kerchief. "I took a closer look, and I thought, 'That's Chamberlain Sano's son.'"

"Nobody was supposed to know." Masahiro was disappointed that his disguise hadn't been as good as he'd thought. "How did you?"

"You were riding the same black-and-white pony."

"Oh," Masahiro said, chagrined.

Suddenly he noticed that the *rōnin*'s fiercely slanted eyebrows were drawn on his face with charcoal, like those of actors in Kabuki plays. A thought struck Masahiro: He wasn't the only one wearing a disguise. And the *rōnin* was better at noticing things than most people.

"Did you come to visit Father yesterday?" Masahiro asked.

"Yes . . ." Now the *rōnin* looked startled, displeased, and amused all at once. "You were eavesdropping."

The *rōnin* was the spy named Toda.

"But I don't recognize you," Masahiro said. "You look so different today."

"Well, that's the purpose of a disguise." Toda added, "I've learned a few more things besides those I inadvertently taught you. Here's one: When you're watching somebody, don't assume that nobody is watching you."

Toda had seen him following Yanagisawa. Masahiro felt foolish because he'd thought himself invisible and hadn't noticed Toda doing the same thing. Now Masahiro realized that Yanagisawa was getting away from them both.

"Excuse me," Masahiro said. "I have to go."

Toda restrained him. "Oh, no, you don't."

"But we're going to lose Yanagisawa!"

"What do you mean, 'we'?" Toda said with a sarcastic laugh. "*I* am the spy. *You* are just a child. I'm taking you home."

"But Yanagisawa—"

"No buts," Toda said, "and forget Yanagisawa. If I let you keep playing spy, and something should happen to you, your father would kill me. Come along now."

21

Sano returned to Edo Jail that afternoon with his cousin Chiyo and with Reiko. As he rode across the bridge over the canal that fronted the prison, the women followed in a palanquin. Major Kumazawa had insisted on coming along, and he trailed them with his troops and Sano's. The procession halted at the gate.

Inside the palanquin, Chiyo said, "I'm afraid."

"You'll be all right," Reiko said soothingly.

But she was worried about Chiyo, who seemed even frailer than yesterday. Shadows under her eyes bled through her white makeup. When she spoke, tears trembled in her voice. Under her brown silk kimono, her body was gaunt, hunched like an old woman's; she'd aged years overnight. Reiko didn't know how any woman could recover from kidnapping, rape, and the loss of her children. She was afraid that what Sano had asked Chiyo to do would make matters worse, even though Chiyo had willingly agreed to cooperate.

She heard horses' hooves clattering over the bridge. She looked out the window of the palanquin and saw Detectives Marume and Fukida ride up to Sano.

"Where is the nun?" Sano asked.

"She didn't want to come," Fukida said. "When we tried to take her out of the convent, she became upset."

" 'Upset' is putting it mildly," Marume said. "She cried and threw a fit. We thought we'd better just let her be."

"You did the right thing," Sano said, although Reiko could see that he was disappointed. "We'll manage without her."

"Am I the only one?" Chiyo said, alarmed.

Across the bridge came another procession: Hirata on horseback, accompanied by a few troops, escorting another palanquin. "No," Reiko said. "Here's one more."

The troops dismounted, reached into the palanquin, and pulled out Fumiko. Her kimono had new rips and new streaks of mud. Her face was bunched in a murderous scowl.

"She put up quite a fight, but we got her," Hirata said. Fumiko's hands were tied behind her back and her ankles loosely bound together with rope so that she could walk but not run. "I hated to do this, but otherwise she'd have gotten away."

Chiyo gasped. "Is that the girl who was kidnapped?"

"Yes," Reiko said. "Her name is Fumiko." She explained what had happened to the girl.

"The poor thing." As Chiyo beheld the girl, the misery on her own face was leavened by compassion.

"What are we waiting for?" demanded Major Kumazawa. "Let's get this over with."

Sano looked across the bridge and said, "We've got company."

Reiko saw a pudgy, gray-haired man with sagging jowls stalk up to Sano and Hirata. His sharp, gleaming eyes and the cruel curve of his lips brought to mind a hungry wolf. Three big, muscular fellows with tattoos accompanied him.

"It's Jirocho," Reiko said.

"Who is he?" Chiyo asked.

"A big gangster boss. He's also Fumiko's father."

"Papa!" Fumiko cried.

Her wild eyes lit with happiness. She stumbled toward him, hobbled by the rope around her ankles, and threw herself at Jirocho. He pushed her away as if she were a stranger who'd dared bump into him. He didn't even look at his child.

"Papa," Fumiko said, her voice broken by tears.

In the palanquin, Chiyo murmured in sympathy.

"Honorable Chamberlain. *Sōsakan* Hirata. Good afternoon." Jirocho bowed in respectful yet perfunctory greeting. "I heard that you arrested the two kidnappers."

"You get news quicker than anybody else in Edo," Hirata said dryly. "But the men we arrested are only suspects at this point."

"What are you doing here?" Sano asked Jirocho. His manner was cool and calm, but Reiko sensed his anger at this man who'd broken the law many times and punished his daughter for a crime that wasn't her fault.

"I want to see the suspects," Jirocho said.

"Why?" Sano said. "So that you can kill them?"

Jirocho didn't answer, but his jowls tightened and his predatory eyes glittered. His men grouped around him, his wolf pack.

"Stay out of this," Sano said. "If they're guilty, I'll see that they're punished according to the law."

"Maybe I can help you figure out whether they're guilty," Jirocho said. "Maybe I know them. Maybe I've seen them hanging around my daughter."

Sano hesitated, and Reiko could feel him thinking that even though he distrusted the gangster, perhaps he needed Jirocho. He'd told her that the suspects had refused to confess and he had no evidence to prove their guilt. "All right," Sano said. "You can come with us. But keep quiet and don't interfere."

He signaled the prison guards, who opened the gate. He and Hirata led the way inside. As the women climbed out of their palanquin, Chiyo whispered to Reiko, "I don't know if I can bear this."

Reiko took Chiyo's cold, trembling hands in her own warm ones. "I'll be with you. We'll get through it together."

She'd been inside Edo Jail before, and she knew what a terrible place it was, but she didn't see much of it now. When she crossed the threshold, Sano, Major Kumazawa, and their troops closed protectively around her and Chiyo and Fumiko. On the walk through the prison compound, the men blocked Reiko's view of everything except the upper story of the dungeon. But she heard cries from the prisoners, and the stench was overpowering. Reiko and Chiyo held their sleeves over their noses. Fumiko growled under her breath, like a threatened animal. She kept looking over her shoulder for a glimpse of her father.

The group moved into a plain wooden building and down a passage. There were chambers furnished with desks, some occupied by samurai officials. Sano ushered Reiko, Chiyo, and Fumiko, Major Kumazawa, and Jirocho into a vacant room. Detectives Marume and Fukida followed. Sliding doors along one wall stood open to a veranda that overlooked a courtyard with gravel strewn on muddy earth around a fireproof storehouse with mossy plaster walls. Sano positioned a lattice screen across the doorway.

"Stand close to the screen," Sano told Chiyo and Fumiko. "Look outside."

Chiyo and Fumiko obeyed. Reiko stood between them. They peered through gaps in the lattice. Jirocho, Major Kumazawa, and Sano stationed themselves behind the women. Into the courtyard walked Hirata, escorting the two oxcart drivers. Hirata positioned the men side by side, near the veranda, facing the screen. Chiyo uttered a faint moan and recoiled.

"Don't be afraid," Sano said. "They can't see you."

Avid curiosity filled Reiko as she beheld the suspects. The big, muscular man looked at the ground, his heavy shoulders slumped, his low-browed face sullen. His comrade, slight and wiry, smoothed his long, disheveled hair and grinned nervously. Gaps from missing teeth were ugly black holes in his mouth. Reiko had seen many criminals, and her instincts told her that these men were of that breed.

"Do you recognize them?" Sano asked. "Be honest."

Chiyo gazed at the suspects. Her eyes shone with fearful fascination. ". . . I don't know."

"Well? Which one kidnapped you?" Jirocho barked at his daughter. These were the first words he'd spoken to her.

Fumiko turned to him, and Reiko could see on her face her longing to please him, to earn her way back home. She looked through the lattice and slowly pointed at the big man.

Reiko felt her breath catch. Behind her, Sano, Major Kumazawa, and Jirocho stirred. Fumiko's hand moved hesitantly sideways. Her finger pointed at the other suspect. Then she let her hand drop. She shrugged and frowned hard, as if trying not to cry.

"She doesn't know, either," Jirocho said in disgust.

Sano called, "Turn them around."

Hirata gestured his hand in a circular motion at the suspects. They rotated slowly, then faced the women again. Reiko looked from Chiyo to Fumiko. Their faces were devoid of recognition. She sensed their wish to identify their attackers vying with their duty to be honest.

"Maybe if we could get a closer look?" Chiyo murmured.

Sano gave the order. Hirata prodded the two men up the steps, onto the veranda. They stood close enough to touch. Reiko could see the pores in their tanned, weathered skin and smell their odor of urine, sweat, and oxen.

Fumiko shook her head. Chiyo shuddered, her nose and mouth muffled in her sleeve. "I'm sorry. I don't know if it was one of them or not."

The two men exchanged glances. They'd heard Chiyo. The slight one's grin broadened; the big one smirked.

Anger swelled in Reiko. If they were responsible for the kidnapping and rapes, she didn't want them to get away with it. She didn't want Chiyo and Fumiko to have suffered this ordeal for nothing. But what could she do?

A thought occurred to her. "Let us hear their voices," she said to Sano. "Make them say, 'Dearest mother, beloved mother,' and 'naughty girl.'"

Sano gave the order through the screen. "Dearest mother, beloved mother. Naughty girl," the big man said in a deep, thick, scratchy voice. The other man echoed him. Chiyo turned to Reiko in despair.

"I don't think it's either of them," she said. "They both sound too young."

"What do you think?" Reiko asked Fumiko.

The girl shook her head unhappily. Jirocho said, "Well, that's that." His face was grim; so were Sano's and Major Kumazawa's. The two suspects swaggered with glee.

"Have you ever seen them before?" Sano asked Jirocho and Major Kumazawa.

"No," they said.

Reiko tried to hide her own disappointment. She didn't want to make Chiyo and Fumiko feel worse.

Fumiko suddenly said, "Make them take off their clothes."

"*What?*" Jirocho said, incredulous. He grabbed her arm and yanked her around to face him. "What's the matter, didn't you get enough pleasure while you were kidnapped? Do you want some more men? You little whore!"

He raised his hand to strike her, but Sano shoved him toward the door and said, "I warned you. Get out!"

As Marume and Fukida led the gangster away, Fumiko whimpered, "Papa!" then, "I didn't mean it the way he said."

Chiyo moved to the girl's side. "I understand," Chiyo said, putting her arm around Fumiko. "You want to see if we can recognize the men's bodies. Isn't that right?"

To Reiko's surprise, Fumiko leaned into Chiyo's embrace as she nodded. Reiko saw a tenuous bond form between these two women from different worlds. They had experiences in common that no one else they knew could fully understand.

Sano ordered the suspects to undress. They dropped their garments onto the veranda. Major Kumazawa said to Chiyo, "You don't have to look."

Her expression was resigned. "Yes, Father, I must."

The men stood naked. The big man slouched, surly with embarrassment. The other's nervous grin took on a lascivious cast. His organ began to curve erect.

Reiko averted her eyes, sickened by a sudden, unpleasant memory. She'd seen naked men before—beggars on the streets, youths swimming in the river—but only once had she had such a close observation of any except her husband. That had been the man who'd called himself the Dragon King, who'd kidnapped and nearly raped her. Now she felt her heart race and nausea roil her stomach. She kept her gaze on Chiyo and Fumiko.

Chiyo frowned, pondered the men, and said unhappily, "I don't know. I'm sorry. I just can't remember."

Fumiko turned away, her face miserable with disappointment. "He had a big black mole," she said. "They don't."

It was true: Both suspects' penises were devoid of moles.

The big man guffawed and his friend tittered with relief. Fumiko ran out the door. Major Kumazawa said, "We've had enough," and left with Chiyo.

"Take them back to their cell," Sano told Hirata.

The suspects picked up their clothes, and Hirata marched them off. Sano turned to Reiko. "Well."

Sharing his frustration, Reiko voiced the thought on both their minds: "The real kidnapper is still at large. What if it's not one man but three? And how many more women will they hurt before they're caught?"

22

When Sano emerged from Edo Jail with Reiko, he heard screaming and weeping. Jirocho was planted outside the gate with Fumiko on the ground before him, her arms wrapped around his legs. "Papa, please don't be mad at me," she cried as she sobbed.

"Let go, you dirty little animal!" Jirocho shouted, trying to kick her away.

Chiyo stood near them, watching, her hands clasped under her chin. Beside her, Major Kumazawa said, "Let's go."

His face was stiff with disgust at the scene that Jirocho and Fumiko were making. But Chiyo didn't move. At the bridge waited Sano's troops, Jirocho's gangsters, and the palanquins and bearers that had brought the women to the jail. Prison guards peered out of the watch towers.

"Papa, why don't you love me anymore?" Fumiko wailed. "I didn't do anything wrong!"

"You couldn't identify the bastard," Jirocho said, his face purple with ugly rage. "Are you trying to protect him? Or have you had so many men that you can't remember what they look like?" He seized Fumiko by her hair, pulled her head up, and slapped her face. "Whore!"

"Stop that!" Sano commanded.

As he strode toward Jirocho, the gangster pried Fumiko's arms off his legs. "Papa, forgive me, I want to go home with you," she pleaded.

Jirocho beckoned his men. As they all stalked off, Jirocho threw Sano a baleful glance. Fumiko lay curled on the ground and wept. Even though Sano was furious at Jirocho for punishing the girl, he felt responsible for her suffering. If Sano had caught the culprit, maybe Jirocho would have been willing to reconcile with his daughter. A familiar guilt, heavy and sickening as a physical illness, plagued Sano. Another of his investigations hadn't produced quick enough results, and people had suffered.

Chiyo gently lifted Fumiko to her feet, held her, and murmured soothing words. "You can come home with me. Would you like that?"

Fumiko sobbed brokenheartedly, but she nodded. Major Kumazawa exclaimed, "She's not setting foot in my house!"

Chiyo responded with an obstinacy that matched his. "Yes she is, Father." For the first time Sano saw a family resemblance between them. Chiyo helped Fumiko into the palanquin. The bearers carried the women away.

"I'm glad Fumiko has someplace safe to live," Reiko said. "But it must be awful for her to realize that her father isn't going to take her back."

Sano thought of Akiko and couldn't understand how a man could treat his daughter in such fashion, but he'd never walked in Jirocho's shoes. "Maybe Fumiko and Chiyo will be good for each other," he said hopefully. One had lost her parent, the other her children. They might find solace together.

Major Kumazawa glared after the palanquin, then at Sano. "I don't like how your investigation is proceeding."

Sano didn't like how his uncle was speaking to him, and if Major Kumazawa were anyone else, Sano would put him in his place without hesitation. Yet Major Kumazawa was the father of a crime victim, and Sano felt guilty because he hadn't done better by his family.

"I warned you," Sano said. "No promises."

"You never warned me that my daughter would be dragged to Edo Jail to look at naked men. That's unheard of."

"One can't predict what will need to be done during an investigation," Sano said. "Having Chiyo view the suspects was the only way to determine whether I had her kidnapper."

"Well, it didn't work, did it?"

"I explained to you and Chiyo, beforehand, that either of those men could be guilty or not. And she wanted to come."

"And now I have to give room and board to a gangster's brat." Major Kumazawa laughed, a sour, rasping chuckle. "Asking you for help was a mistake. I should have known better than to expect anything good from a son of your mother."

The outright insult stung Sano and drew a gasp from Reiko. He heard Marume and Fukida grumble under their breath. His forbearance toward Major Kumazawa snapped.

"I should have known better than to help a man who's so small-minded that he values pride and convention above his own family." Sano tasted rage, hot as a fire in his throat. "My mother is fortunate that you cast her out. And so am I."

Major Kumazawa started as if Sano had hit him. His features swelled bloodred with fury as he absorbed the implication that Sano had risen higher than anyone brought up in the bosom of the clan. "How dare you—"

"I dare," Sano said, reminding his uncle that he was chamberlain, the shogun's second-in-command. He had another sudden flash of memory. He'd seen his uncle this angry before, on that long-ago occasion at the Kumazawa house. But he couldn't remember why Major Kumazawa had been angry then. "I suggest you improve your attitude toward me. Otherwise, you might find yourself serving the regime in a much lower capacity, far from Edo. Or maybe not serving at all."

Now the blood drained from Major Kumazawa's face: He understood that Sano had threatened to demote him or banish him from the regime to live in disgrace as a *rōnin* unless he showed Sano due respect. Without a word, he turned, mounted his horse, and galloped across the bridge so fast that his troops had to hurry to catch up.

Sano's sense of victory was minimal; he felt as much depleted by the quarrel as angry at his uncle for goading him into showing off his power. Their relationship was going downhill as fast as his investigation was.

Reiko, Marume and Fukida, and Sano's other troops tactfully pretended that nothing had happened. No one spoke until Hirata came out of the jail.

"What do you want to do with the prisoners?" Hirata asked Sano. "Keep them locked up?"

Sano thought a moment, then said, "No. Let them go."

"Let them go?" Reiko regarded him with disbelief. "Even though Chiyo and Fumiko couldn't identify the suspects, don't you think those men are guilty? I do."

"Let them go, but have them watched," Sano clarified. "Do you have any detectives who are good at secret surveillance?"

"Yes," Hirata said. "I'll get them over here."

"If our suspects are guilty, maybe we can catch them in the act of another kidnapping," Sano said.

He looked at the clouded, darkening sky. The guards lit lanterns inside the turrets of the jail. Flames and smoke diffused in the moist air. Sano said to Reiko, "I'll take you home. We've had enough for one day."

Sano and Reiko arrived at their estate as the temple bells tolled the late hour of the boar. Stone lanterns glowed along the path to the mansion. The misty air vibrated with the sound of crickets and frogs in the garden, dogs barking and castle patrol guards calling to one another in the distance, and water trickling. Sano, Marume, Fukida, and the troops dismounted from their horses; Reiko climbed out of her palanquin. Sano's secretary called from the doorway, "Honorable Chamberlain, Toda Ikkyu is waiting to see you."

"Maybe our luck is about to change," Sano said.

He and Reiko went to the reception room. There, Toda knelt in the light from a metal filigree lantern suspended from the ceiling. Toda said, "I know this is a bit late for a call, but I thought it best not to wait."

"Have you brought some information?" Sano asked.

"Yes. I've also brought something that belongs to you."

Toda pointed to the corner, where Masahiro sat in the shadows. His expression combined chagrin and fright. His shoulders were hunched up to his ears, as if in expectation of a blow.

Reiko exclaimed, "Masahiro! Are you all right? Where have you been?"

"You'd better explain," Sano told Toda.

"I was spying on Yanagisawa today. Imagine my surprise when I caught your son doing the same thing."

Sano felt shock drop his mouth. Reiko gasped.

Toda smiled. "I doubted that you would approve. So I brought him home."

Sano strode over to Masahiro and crouched in front of him. "Is this true?"

Masahiro hung his head. "Yes, Father."

"You went outside the castle?" Reiko was aghast. "By yourself?" When Masahiro nodded sheepishly, she said, "You know you're not supposed to do that!"

Sano cut to the more serious issue. "Why on earth were you spying on Yanagisawa?"

Masahiro cringed from Sano's anger. "You wanted to know what he's doing. I wanted to help."

Sano could only shake his head, his mouth open but empty of words. Although he was furious at Masahiro for breaking a rule intended to keep him safe, and for taking such a risk, Sano couldn't bear to scold Masahiro. His son's wish to do him a good deed moved Sano almost to tears.

Reiko grabbed Masahiro by the front of his kimono and shook him so hard that his head bobbled. "How could you be so foolish? You know how dangerous Yanagisawa is!"

"He didn't even see me," Masahiro defended himself.

"Indeed he didn't," Toda said, amused. "Your son's disguise was pretty good."

"But what if he had?" Reiko demanded.

"Yanagisawa is the kind of man who assumes that anyone following him is an assassin," Sano told Masahiro. "If he'd seen you, he'd have killed you first and asked questions later. And that would have made your mother very, very unhappy."

"It certainly would have," Reiko said, "although right now I'm ready to kill you myself."

Masahiro sagged in capitulation and shame. "I'm sorry." Then he brightened and said, "I followed Yanagisawa and Yoritomo all the way to the river. I saw them meet three ladies."

"Oh?" Sano said, his interest caught even though he knew Masahiro was trying to barter information for forgiveness. "What did they do?"

"Don't encourage him," Reiko protested.

"Yanagisawa talked to the two old ladies," Masahiro answered eagerly. "Yoritomo went for a walk with the younger one. But I couldn't hear what they said."

"That's enough," Sano said. "Masahiro, you are never to spy on Yanagisawa or anybody else ever again. Do you understand?"

Masahiro sighed. "Yes, Father."

"Go to your room," Sano said. "You'll stay there until you realize what a reckless thing you did and I decide you can be trusted again."

As Masahiro rose to obey, Fukida and Marume appeared at the door. Sano said, "Organize a watch on my son. Make sure he doesn't leave his room."

"Why?" Marume asked. "Masahiro, have you been a bad boy?"

"I'm sure he'll tell you all about it," Reiko said as the detectives followed the glum, defeated Masahiro out of the reception chamber.

"I hope that will teach him a lesson," Toda said. "If it does, it might add a few years to his life."

Sano didn't want to discuss Masahiro's future with Toda. "Thank you for bringing him home," he said, then changed the subject. "Did you see the three ladies?"

"I did."

"Who were they?" Sano asked.

"I don't know," Toda said. "I've never seen them before."

"What were they doing with Yanagisawa and Yoritomo?"

"Sorry, I can't answer that question, either. They chose a place that had few people and lots of open space. I couldn't get close enough to eavesdrop. But it looked like a *miai*."

"It's reasonable that Yanagisawa would decide his son should marry," Reiko said to Sano. "Yoritomo is more than of age. Maybe the meeting had nothing to do with political schemes." She sounded more hopeful than convinced.

"Maybe not, but then why should Yanagisawa keep Yoritomo's marriage prospects under wraps? I'd have expected him to put out the word that he was looking for a wife for his son and send a go-between to solicit offers from important families. No—there's something fishy about that *miai*."

Sano turned to Toda. "Continue your surveillance on Yanagisawa. Find out who those ladies are and what Yanagisawa is trying to accomplish."

"I'll do my best," Toda said, then bowed and departed.

Alone with his wife, in the quiet of their home, Sano suddenly realized how exhausted he was from the day's endeavors and disappointments. Masahiro's escapade on top of everything else was entirely too much. Sano was also ravenous with hunger.

"Let's eat," he said, "then go to bed."

"That sounds wonderful," Reiko said.

"Tomorrow should be a better day," Sano said. "We'll get another chance to catch the kidnapper. And what else could possibly go wrong?"

23

Morning thunder awakened Edo. Storm clouds obliterated the sunrise. Rain swept the city, drenched people hurrying along streets whose ends vanished into streaming mist. Edo Castle wore a veil of showers that poured down from the sky, rendering the turrets and roof tops invisible from below.

Inside her chamber, Reiko opened the door that led to the garden. She frowned at the rain. Today's journey would be wet and uncomfortable, even more so for her palanquin bearers and guards than for herself. As she closed the door, Akiko toddled into the room and said, "Mama, no go."

Reiko sighed. Akiko often ignored her for days, and Reiko had to work to get her attention. But sometimes—invariably when Reiko had important business to take care of—Akiko couldn't live without her. Akiko had sharp instincts that warned her when Reiko was about to leave the house. Maybe she feared being abandoned again, and her bad timing was perfect.

"I'll be back before you know it," Reiko said as she knelt, hugged Akiko, and tried to soothe her.

Akiko clung and began to cry. Reiko finally had to call the nurse to peel Akiko off her. She left Akiko with a promise to bring her candy. The sound of Akiko's sobs followed her down the corridor. Motherhood and detective work were not always compatible. Reiko swallowed her guilt and went to look in on Masahiro.

He was in his room, practicing calligraphy, supervised by his tutor, guarded by one of Sano's soldiers. When Reiko put her head into the room, he barely glanced up from his work.

"I have an errand, then I'm going to visit your father's cousin," Reiko said. "Be good while I'm gone."

"Yes, Mother." Masahiro looked so unhappy about being confined to his quarters that Reiko felt sorry for him. But she had to uphold the law that Sano had laid down.

"Do you promise to stay home?" she asked.

Masahiro sighed with all the exasperation and impatience that nine-year-old boys could convey so well. "Yes, Mother."

Before Sano could resume his investigation, he had an important meeting with the shogun, Yanagisawa, and the Council of Elders.

In the main reception room in the palace, the shogun knelt on the dais. The mural at his back depicted lily pads and blossoms floating on a blue pond under a gilded sky. Charcoal braziers warmed away the dampness in the air. Sano and Yanagisawa shared the place of honor to the shogun's right. They scrupulously took turns sitting closest to him. Today the privilege was Sano's.

The elders—four old men who comprised Japan's highest governing body—knelt on the floor one level below the dais. A few lesser officials occupied the next, lower level. Secretaries sat at desks off to the side; guards stood along the walls. Everyone was flushed from the heat except the shogun. Although he was bundled up in a thick, bronze satin robe, his complexion had its usual waxen pallor. As Sano, Yanagisawa, and the elders discussed government affairs, he grew bored and restless. Sano could almost see the words going in one of his ears and out the other. When asked to approve decisions, he did so automatically, and the secretaries applied his signature seal to documents.

The assembly reached the final item on the agenda. "His Excellency's pilgrimage to Nikko Toshogu," announced the senior elder.

The Toshogu was a shrine in the city of Nikko, a two-day journey north of Edo, where the first Tokugawa shogun had been laid to rest. Now the shogun perked up.

"Ahh, I've been so looking forward to my trip." He normally preferred not to brave the discomforts of travel, but he was enjoying a rare spell of good health, and it had whetted his taste for adventure. "When would be an auspicious time for me to go?"

The elders didn't answer. Hands folded, expressions grave, they waited for someone else to deliver the bad news.

"Your Excellency, I regret to say that I must advise you against making the trip," Sano said.

"Oh?" Miffed, the shogun turned to Yanagisawa in hope of advice he liked better. "What do you say?"

At one time Yanagisawa would have contradicted Sano to gain points in their lord's favor. But now Yanagisawa said, "I must agree with Chamberlain Sano." The elders looked simultaneously relieved and disappointed. Sano suspected that they missed the excitement of political strife even though they appreciated the peace and quiet. "The trip isn't feasible."

The shogun regarded Sano and Yanagisawa with the hurt expression of a child bullied by his two best friends. "Why not, pray tell?"

Once, Yanagisawa would have let Sano say what the shogun didn't want to hear and suffer the consequences. Instead he explained, "A trip would involve a huge procession, with new ceremonial robes for you and everyone else, plus lodging and formal banquets. That's too expensive."

"How can it be?" the shogun said, puzzled. "I'm rich, I can afford anything I want." Uncertainty crept into his eyes. "Can't I?"

It was Sano's turn to acquaint his lord with reality. "There's not enough money in the treasury to pay for the trip and cover the regime's other expenses."

The shogun wavered between annoyance and dismay. "We've never had this, ahh, problem in the past."

The regime had been chronically short on funds during his rule, and his officials had often tried to tell him, but it never sank in. Ordinarily, Yanagisawa would have jumped at the chance to blame Sano for the shortfall. He'd have accused Sano of squandering and embezzling the money during Yanagisawa's absence. Sano could have accused Yanagisawa of both crimes, which Yanagisawa certainly had committed in the past. But Yanagisawa wasn't doing it now. Sano knew because he kept a close watch on the treasury. Why Yanagisawa now adhered strictly to the rules was a mystery to Sano. So was the reason Yanagisawa didn't seize the opportunity to make Sano look bad.

Sano studied his onetime foe, seeking clues, as Yanagisawa said,

"The Tokugawa treasury has become depleted over the years. The cost of rebuilding Edo after the Great Fire—"

The shogun waved away the Great Fire as if it had been a minor inconvenience instead of a disaster that had killed over a hundred thousand people and laid the city to waste. "That was more than forty years ago!"

"There have been other heavy expenditures," Sano said. "You have many temples and shrines to maintain, as well as roads, bridges, and canals."

"Remember that you're supporting thousands of retainers, including the Tokugawa army," Yanagisawa said.

"Ahh." The shogun hunched his back, momentarily weighed down by the thought of his financial responsibilities. "Well, if I need more money, can't you make me some more?"

"It's not that easy," Sano said. "The yield from the gold and silver mines has been decreasing. We can't just mint more coins."

"Much of Japan's wealth has left the country with foreign traders who sell us goods from abroad," Yanagisawa added.

The shogun pouted. "Then why not just, ahh, debase the coinage again?"

That drastic measure had been undertaken six years ago, when coins had been collected, melted down, and alloyed with base metal to reduce their gold and silver content, thereby increasing the supply of currency.

"We can't do that too often," Sano said.

"It has the unfortunate side effect of raising the price of goods," Yanagisawa explained.

"Why should I care?" the shogun said, confused and vexed.

"Many citizens won't be able to afford food," Yanagisawa said. "There will be famine. You don't want that, do you?"

"No, but I still want to go to Nikko." The shogun's face took on the peevish expression that presaged a tantrum that would end with him threatening to execute Sano and Yanagisawa.

"The people need you to take care of them," Sano said. "That's your duty according to Confucius." The shogun was an enthusiast of the Chinese sage whose philosophy had strongly influenced Japanese government. "Therefore, you must be frugal. As shogun, you're not just a dictator; you're virtually a god, with the power to be generous and merciful."

"I guess I am," the shogun said, preening at this glorified image of himself. In a tone lofty with self-sacrifice he said, "I shall postpone my trip for the sake of doing what's right."

Yanagisawa raised an eyebrow at Sano, suggesting that Sano had laid it on a bit thick, but he didn't complain. No one else in the room would look at them or anyone else. "That's admirable of you, Your Excellency. We must all bow to your superior judgment."

The shogun beamed. Everybody else relaxed. But his mood suddenly darkened. "What is this world coming to?" he lamented. "I'm running out of money. I'm so anxious about the future. When I die, what will become of my regime?"

"Don't worry, you're still young," Sano said. But the shogun's demise was something that everyone in the regime feared. When the reins of a dictatorship changed hands, so could the fate of everyone inside it change for the worse.

"The court astrologer says that the stars predict a long life for you," Yanagisawa said. Had the astrologer predicted anything else, he'd have been executed. And Yanagisawa knew as well as Sano did that they must calm the shogun down or anxiety could bring about another serious, perhaps fatal, illness.

"Everyone dies someday," the shogun said, refusing to be soothed. "And I seem, ahh, destined to go without an heir to carry on my bloodline!" This was a constant source of grief for him. "Ahh, how fate has worked against me."

No one dared point out that his own sexual preference for men had worked against his chances of fathering a son. "There's still time," Sano said, hiding his own doubt.

"Perhaps you could make a special prayer to the gods," Yanagisawa said.

The shogun flapped his hands at the idea. "Nothing I do seems to work. I established laws to protect animals, I build temples." Nobody dared suggest the direct, obvious solution to the problem. "And what good has it all done? My wife is an invalid." She was confined to the women's quarters and rarely seen. "My only son died." Rumor said that the boy, born by one of the palace concubines, wasn't the shogun's. "And my daughter doesn't seem likely to bear a child." The identity of her father was also a matter of speculation, although not in the shogun's hearing. "What have I done to deserve such misfortune?" the shogun wailed.

Before Sano or Yanagisawa could reply, his mood took another turn. "Perhaps it's not my fault. Perhaps I've done wrong because of bad advice from other people."

His glare accused everyone in the room, then focused on Sano and Yanagisawa.

"Chamberlain Yanagisawa has given you the wisest, soundest advice that anyone could," Sano hurried to say.

"So has Chamberlain Sano," said Yanagisawa. "He's devoted his life to your service."

"Oh?" The shogun narrowed his eyes at Sano. "Then what's this I hear about you investigating a crime that I never authorized you to investigate? The abduction of your uncle's daughter, I understand?"

Sano felt the bad wind of the shogun's pique blow harder in his direction. "It's a family matter. I assure you that it has not interfered with my duty to you." But the case had taken time away from his official duties, and the shogun was a jealous man. "May I ask how you heard about the investigation?"

"Yoritomo told me," the shogun said.

Sano glanced at Yanagisawa, who frowned as though genuinely dismayed by his son's actions. "My duty to you is my top priority," Sano assured the shogun. "Should you need anything, I'll drop whatever I'm doing and rush to your aid."

"So will I," Yanagisawa said. "Trust us, Your Excellency, and everything will be fine."

"Well . . ." The shogun vacillated, torn between the pleasure of indulging in hysterics and his liking for peace, passivity, and indolence. "All right. But if I decide that either of you has served me ill . . ."

He didn't need to complete the sentence. Everyone knew that the penalty for displeasing him was death by ritual suicide.

"Enough of all this business, I'm tired," he said. "This meeting is adjourned."

When Reiko climbed out of her palanquin in the Zōjō Temple district, Lieutenant Tanuma held an umbrella over her head to shield her from the rain. He opened the gate of Keiaiji Convent for her, and she lifted the hem of her robe as she walked through the wet garden in her high-soled sandals. The pine trees filled the air with their fresh, resinous scent; their heavy green boughs dripped. The abbess came out on the veranda to greet Reiko.

"May I see Tengu-in again?" Reiko said. "I'm hoping she'll be able to tell me more than she did yesterday."

Now that Chiyo and Fumiko had failed to identify either of the two suspects as their kidnapper, Sano had run out of leads. Questioning the nun one more time was the only way that Reiko could think of to help him.

The abbess's pleasant expression shifted into a frown of concern. "Tengu-in is weaker than when you saw her. Today she hasn't left her bed. I doubt she'll talk to you."

Reiko feared that her previous visit had caused Tengu-in's turn for the worse, but she said, "Please, I must try."

"Very well." The abbess sounded resigned; she knew she couldn't deny a request backed by Sano's authority.

Inside, the convent was quiet; the nuns and novices had left to pray in the temples or do charity work among the poor. The corridor down which Reiko walked was a dim tunnel that echoed with her footsteps and the patter of rain on the roof. Flies buzzed somewhere in the building. Reiko experienced a sudden stab of premonition.

She hastened toward the bedchamber. She ran through the door, breathless with sudden fright, and stopped.

The bed where Tengu-in had lain yesterday was empty, the quilt flung off the mattress. The buzzing was louder here. Reiko glanced around the chamber. She noticed a low wooden table placed in the middle of the floor. A tall, square wicker basket lay on its side near the table as if it had tumbled off. Reiko lifted her eyes above them and saw bare, withered feet dangling.

Her heart clenched; her breath caught as her gaze traveled upward and she discovered what had become of Tengu-in.

The nun's emaciated body, clad in its hemp robe, hung from the ceiling. The stout leather cord of her rosary was looped around her neck and tied to an exposed rafter. Tension had drawn the beads deep into her flesh, which was lividly bruised. Her head had fallen sideways; her face was bloated and purplish, the lips parted to reveal the swollen tongue caught between the teeth. Flies buzzed around the blood that trickled from her mouth.

A shrill scream blared. At first Reiko thought it was her own, involuntary reaction to the horrid spectacle of death. Then she turned and saw a young novice standing in the doorway, stricken by horror. The novice's face turned white, went blank. She swayed, then crumpled to the floor in a dead faint.

24

After their meeting with the shogun, Sano and Yanagisawa walked together, beneath the roof of an open corridor that joined two wings of the palace. Marume and Fukida trailed them. Silvery rain threaded down outside. The palace grounds were a blur of gray and green in which birds chirped, figures under umbrellas moved, and distant voices called.

"Another crisis averted," Yanagisawa said. "Good work, Sano-*san*."

"You, too," Sano said.

"In case you're wondering: I didn't put Yoritomo up to telling the shogun about your investigation. He did it on his own. My apologies."

Sano saw no sign that Yanagisawa was lying. And Yoritomo had reason to do him a bad turn without anyone else's urging. "I gladly accept your apology." What else could Sano do until he knew Yanagisawa's intentions? Sano wasn't afraid to strike first, but he would rather not maneuver in the dark.

"By the way," Yanagisawa said, "I heard about your clever experiment at Edo Jail yesterday. I'm sorry it didn't work."

"So am I." Once again Sano was impressed with how fast Yanagisawa received news. Now he saw a chance to fish for clues about the meeting that Toda and Masahiro witnessed. "Speaking of Yoritomo, I've tried to make amends to him for what happened last year, but he won't even talk to me."

"He's young, and the young take things too hard. Give him time," Yanagisawa said reasonably. "He'll get over it."

"Maybe he would be willing to let bygones be bygones if he had something new to think about." Sano hinted, "Maybe he needs a wife?"

Yanagisawa's calm expression didn't change, although he paused for an instant before he said casually, "I suppose Yoritomo will marry someday."

The space of that instant held everything Sano wanted to know, like a jar whose contents are hidden from view by its thick ceramic walls.

"Someday soon?" Sano prompted.

"Not in the foreseeable future. We're waiting for the right match."

Sano wondered if the young woman that Yanagisawa and Yoritomo had met yesterday had turned out not to be the right one. If so, which side had refused? *Who was she?* Sano could feel Yanagisawa wondering whether Sano had learned about the *miai*, although Yanagisawa didn't ask.

Another question occurred to Sano. "If Yoritomo were to marry, would the shogun mind?"

"Not at all," Yanagisawa said, perfectly matter-of-fact, perfectly at ease. "I've discussed it with His Excellency. He agrees that my son must carry on our family line, in keeping with tradition. His Excellency is fond of tradition. And as long as Yoritomo remains available to him, he has no objection to a marriage."

That was the custom for male lovers: Marriage for either or both didn't disrupt their relationship.

"When I make a match for Yoritomo, you'll be the first to know," Yanagisawa said. As they continued along the corridor, a group of officials approached them. Polite bows and greetings were exchanged. After the group passed, Yanagisawa said, "What's the next step in your investigation?"

Sano noted how skillfully and quickly Yanagisawa had changed the subject. Now he was sure that the *miai* was part of some plan that Yanagisawa wanted to hide. But he couldn't press the issue without revealing that he knew about the *miai* because he had Yanagisawa under surveillance.

"I'll keep looking for the kidnapper," Sano said.

They parted in mutual good cheer that was false on at least one side. As Marume and Fukida joined Sano, a servant from his estate came running toward them.

"Excuse me, Honorable Chamberlain," the servant said. "There's a message from Lady Reiko. She begs you to meet her at Keiaiji Convent right away. She says a nun is dead!"

* * *

When Sano, Hirata, Marume, and Fukida rode up to the convent, they found Reiko pacing the street outside the wall in a fever of anxiety while Lieutenant Tanuma hurried back and forth beside her with an umbrella.

"What happened?" Sano said as he and his men jumped off their horses.

"Tengu-in hanged herself." Reiko tried not to cry. "I found her."

Sano shook his head. The other men looked as appalled as he was. Had the nun been so distressed by the kidnapping and rape that she'd taken her own life? Sano was also dismayed that Reiko had been first on the scene.

"What were you doing here?" he asked.

"I wanted to see if she could tell me any more about the man who kidnapped her." Reiko spoke with sorrow and regret. "Now she never can."

Sano, Hirata, and the detectives strode into the convent; Reiko hurried to keep up with them. Sano said, "Where is Tengu-in's body?"

"Right where I found it," Reiko said. "I told her people to leave everything as it was until you came."

At least the death scene was intact, Sano thought.

The abbess, the novice that Sano had spoken to on his previous visit, and some nuns hovered in the corridor. The novice sobbed in the abbess's arms. "I only left her for a moment," she wailed. "I never thought she would do something like this."

The abbess shushed her. Everyone moved aside to let Sano pass. He and his group crossed the threshold of the bedchamber and gathered around Tengu-in's suspended corpse. Sano expelled his breath in a harsh sigh as they contemplated her limp body and her swollen, lifeless face that swarmed with flies.

"Are we sure this was suicide?" Marume asked.

That had been one of the questions on Sano's mind. He surveyed the room. "It looks as if she pushed the table under the rafter, but she couldn't reach the rafter because the table was too low."

Hirata continued Sano's reconstruction of the events that had led to the death. "So she fetched the basket, put it on top of the table, and climbed on it."

"I would have thought she was too weak to manage that. If only I'd gotten here sooner," Reiko said.

"The will to die can be stronger than the will to live," Hirata pointed out.

"That rosary belongs to her." Sano's gaze took in the leather cord that suspended Tengu-in from the ceiling, the brown jade beads now embedded in flesh, a holy object now profaned. "I saw her praying with it when I was here the first time." He pictured the frail old woman struggling to tie the rosary to the rafter and around her neck.

Hirata continued, "She kicked away the basket, and . . ."

He didn't need to finish the sentence. Everyone could imagine the basket tumbling to the floor, the rafter creaking under the sudden weight, the crack of Tengu-in's neck snapping, her body swinging.

Sano looked around the room, at the bed. "I don't see any signs of violence."

"I asked the abbess, the novice, and the nuns if they'd seen anyone inside the convent who didn't belong here," Reiko said. "They said no. And I don't think they did this."

"Then it was suicide," Sano concluded.

He'd considered the possibility that Tengu-in had been killed by the man who'd kidnapped her. That would have prevented her from ever revealing clues to his identity. Now Sano was as disturbed about her death as he would have been had it not been suicide. The suffering that the rapist had caused Tengu-in had led to her death.

"This isn't just a matter of kidnapping and rape anymore," Sano said grimly. "This is murder."

Hirata, Reiko, and the detectives nodded solemnly. Everyone knew that the investigation had just taken on more urgent importance. Sano thought of Chiyo and Fumiko, still suffering the consequences from the crimes. Would they choose suicide, too?

He gave the nun one last look, then said to Marume and Fukida, "Take her down."

Marume stepped up on the table. He gingerly supported Tengu-in's body while Fukida drew his sword and sliced through the rosary. Beads fell from the cut cord, pattered and rolled on the floor. Marume eased the nun down and laid her on the bed. Reiko pulled the quilt over her, and covered her face.

The abbess entered the room. "May we prepare her for her funeral?"

Her face was so drawn by grief that Sano hated to deny her request. "Not just yet," he said. "I'm sending her to Edo Morgue."

"Edo Morgue?" Surprise lifted the abbess's eyebrows to her shaved hairline. "But surely there's no need." Her voice expressed distaste for the morgue and offense that Sano would send a woman of Tengu-in's rank to a place mainly associated with dead commoners.

"She was a victim of a crime. Therefore, it's the law," Sano said. "Formalities must be observed."

He couldn't tell the abbess the real reason he wanted the nun's body sent to Edo Morgue. And she couldn't refuse. Her mouth tightened with displeasure, but she nodded. "When the formalities are done, will you send her home so that we can lay her properly to rest?"

"Yes," Sano said, although he might have to break his word.

Hired porters carried the nun's corpse on a litter to the morgue, which was located inside Edo Jail. Sano went there by a circuitous, less public route.

After sending Reiko home, he rode to her father's house in the official district near Edo Castle. Inside, he changed his silk garments for the plain cotton clothing he kept there for occasions when he wanted to travel incognito. Then he rode through the city on an oxcart with three convicted criminals. Escorted by troops who belonged to his father-in-law the magistrate, he climbed off the cart inside the gates of Edo Jail.

The troops led Sano past the dungeon to the morgue, a low building with a roof made of sparse, decomposing thatch. The damp weather had given the morgue a new film of green mold since Sano had last seen it, a touch of life in this squalid place.

Sano's arrival coincided with that of the porters bearing Tengu-in's body on the litter. Dr. Ito, custodian of the morgue, stepped out of the building. He was in his eighties, a tall man with thick white hair, his eyes shrewd above the high cheekbones of his narrow, ascetic face. He wore the traditional dark blue coat of his profession. The porters carried the litter into the building, then departed. The troops left to wait outside the jail until Sano was ready to be taken back to the magistrate's estate. As Dr. Ito recognized Sano, his bushy white eyebrows lifted in surprise.

"Greetings, Sano-*san*. I never expected to see you again."

It had been more than a year since they'd last met. Dr. Ito was a criminal, a former physician to the imperial family who'd been convicted of practicing foreign science he'd learned from Dutch traders.

Exile was the usual punishment, but Dr. Ito had instead received a lifetime sentence as Edo Morgue's custodian. Here, he could conduct his studies and experiments on a never-ending supply of bodies. Sometimes he and Sano worked together. But Sano couldn't afford to let his friendship with Dr. Ito become known to more than a few trusted people. Associating with a criminal and collaborating in forbidden foreign science could land him in deep trouble.

"I need help with another investigation," Sano said, indicating the shrouded corpse on the litter.

"I'm glad to be of service," Dr. Ito said, "but how did you get here this time?"

Sano always took pains to conceal his identity and his clandestine visits to the morgue. As he explained, Dr. Ito shook his head in wonder; his face crinkled with amusement.

"Your ingenuity is beyond compare," Dr. Ito said. "Were you hit by any rocks?"

The public enjoyed stoning criminals on their way to jail. "A few," Sano admitted. "Luckily, they were small."

"I suppose that these times call for extreme measures."

Since Yanagisawa had returned to court, Sano had been especially careful not to do anything that could be construed as improper. Perhaps Yanagisawa was biding his time until he caught Sano in a misstep.

"Yanagisawa's spies will be wondering where I've gone and looking for me," Sano said. "We'd better get started."

"Right away."

Dr. Ito ushered Sano into the morgue. Its windows were open to admit fresh air, but the room smelled of decayed meat and blood. Sano greeted Dr. Ito's assistant, who was cleaning the stone trough used for washing corpses. Mura, a gray-haired man in his fifties, had a square face notable for its intelligence. He was an *eta*, a member of the hereditary class that was linked with death-related occupations such as butchering and leather tanning. Considered physically and spiritually contaminated, the *eta* were shunned by other citizens. But Mura and Dr. Ito had become friends across class lines. Mura did all the manual work associated with Dr. Ito's examinations. A man of few words, he stationed himself beside the body that lay under its gray shroud on one of the waist-high tables.

"Uncover the deceased," Dr. Ito said.

Mura drew back the cloth, revealing Tengu-in. To Sano she looked shrunken, an effigy of herself, no longer human.

"A nun?" Dr. Ito asked, clued by the hemp robe she wore.

"From Keiaiji Convent," Sano said, then explained about the three kidnappings.

Dr. Ito moved closer to her, bent over her neck, and studied the reddish-purple ligature mark. "She appears to have been hanged." He peered at the round indentations along the mark. "With a rosary, I deduce. There are no fingerprints on her neck, and no wounds on her hands as there would be if she fought an attacker. I would say this was a suicide."

"That's what I thought," Sano said.

"But if it was, and if you know how she died, then why risk an examination?"

"Because I wasn't able to get any information from her about the man who kidnapped her, and neither was my wife. She was so distraught that she couldn't tell us. I'm hoping her body can."

"It's unlikely after all this time has passed since the kidnapping, but we shall see."

"Don't cut her unless it's absolutely necessary," Sano said. When he returned her body to the convent, he didn't want to face awkward questions about what had happened to it at Edo Morgue.

"We shall hope that a visual examination will suffice," Dr. Ito said. "Mura-*san*, remove her clothes."

Mura fetched a knife, carefully slit the nun's robe down the front, and peeled back the fabric. Naked, Tengu-in was a skeleton clothed in translucent white skin that the sun had never touched. Sano could see her rib cage, her joints, the blue tracery of her veins. Her breasts were small, flat, empty sacks, her stomach concave, her sex a cleft screened by gray pubic hair.

But he saw no trace of any foreign material on her, not even when Mura turned the body. Dr. Ito said, "Whatever the kidnapper might have left on her, it's gone."

Sano endured his inevitable disappointment. He offered a silent apology to Tengu-in, for subjecting her to further indignity, for nothing.

Mura positioned the body on its back. As Dr. Ito reinspected it, his gaze suddenly sharpened. "Wait. There may be something after all."

Hope rose anew in Sano. "What do you see?"

"Mura-*san*, open her legs," Dr. Ito said.

Mura obeyed, with difficulty: The body had begun to stiffen. Dr. Ito pointed between her legs, at ugly red sores on the withered lips of her sex. The white, raised centers of the sores were still moist with pus.

Sano stepped backward, revolted. "What is that?"

"A disease," Dr. Ito replied. "It's spread by sexual relations and common among prostitutes. But it's not often seen in nuns."

Nuns were supposed to be celibate, and by all accounts, Tengu-in had been a virtuous woman. "Then how——" Enlightenment struck. "She caught it from the rapist. He must have it, too."

"That is a logical explanation," Dr. Ito said. "It seems the examination was worthwhile after all. You've learned one fact about the man that you didn't know before."

"Yes. That's good." But Sano quickly realized what else the discovery meant. "He could have given the disease to his other victims."

"If it was the same man in all three cases," Dr. Ito said.

Sano thought of Chiyo, and Fumiko. Would they develop the disease? He found himself hoping that there were three different rapists, even though it would make his job harder.

"Is the disease curable?" he asked.

"Sometimes, with proper medicine." Then Dr. Ito added reluctantly, "Sometimes not."

25

When Sano returned to Edo Castle, one of the guards at the gate said, "Honorable Chamberlain, there's a message from *Sōsakan* Hirata. He has important news, and he asks that you please call on him at his estate."

Hoping that this news was better than what he'd heard so far today, Sano went to the official quarter inside the castle. There, the shogun's chief retainers and highest officials lived in mansions surrounded by barracks with whitewashed walls decorated with geometrically patterned black tiles. Sano dismounted from his horse outside the estate that had once been his own, before he'd been promoted to chamberlain and given Hirata his old position. Hirata's sentries let Sano inside the familiar courtyard, through the inner gate. Sano had visited Hirata often enough that he usually felt little nostalgia upon seeing his former home. Today the mansion seemed smaller, like a shell he'd outgrown.

Sano went to the reception room, and Hirata joined him, bringing two young samurai. They were tall, strong specimens of the warrior class, with intelligence written in the poise of their bodies as well as in the set of their facial features. But they looked utterly miserable.

Hirata introduced them as Kurita and Konoe. "They're part of the team I assigned to watch the oxcart drivers."

A bad feeling rippled through Sano. The men fell on their knees before him and confessed, "We lost them."

They were clearly devastated because they'd failed in their duty. In truth, Sano didn't feel much better about the fact that his suspects had escaped.

"On behalf of my men and myself, I apologize." Hirata looked sober and humiliated because he'd let Sano down. "But I know that doesn't do much good."

Sano didn't berate his friend; that wouldn't do much good, either. "Just tell me what happened."

"The two drivers went to work at a bridge that's being built over a canal," Kurita said. "While we were keeping watch on them, the bridge collapsed."

"There were a lot of men on it," said Konoe. "They fell in the water. The beams and posts fell on top of them. There was so much confusion as people were running to rescue them that we lost sight of the drivers."

"When everything settled down, they were gone," Kurita said.

"Honorable Chamberlain, we've betrayed your trust and our master's," Konoe said. He blinked furiously, but tears ran down his high cheekbones. "We're ready to commit seppuku."

"No," Sano said, adamant. "I forbid it." That would be wasting two lives for one mishap that could have befallen anyone. Sano thought that too many good men adhered too strictly to the samurai code of honor and killed themselves, while too many bad men broke its rules and lived happily ever after. "The important thing is to find the suspects." He still believed they were connected with the kidnappings, and they were his only leads. "I need your help. Now is your chance to make up for your mistake."

"Yes, Honorable Chamberlain," the men said, chastened yet relieved.

Hirata gave Sano a grateful look, which Sano returned in kind. Hirata had once saved Sano's life at serious, almost fatal cost to himself. That alone would excuse Hirata for a million mistakes.

"Where shall we start hunting?" Hirata asked.

Sano cast his mind across the city, which was riddled with places for the oxcart drivers to hide. Conducting a street-by-street search and closing off the highways that led out of town would take too much time. Logic offered a better solution.

"In our suspects' home territory," Sano said.

*   *   *

Instead of going home, Reiko had her escorts take her to Major Kumazawa's estate, where she found Chiyo sitting in her chamber, combing Fumiko's hair. Fumiko wore a fresh white kimono printed with pale blue irises, and her face was clean; Chiyo must have given her a bath. She was actually a pretty girl. She sat quietly while Chiyo worked the tangles out of her hair. Reiko smiled at the scene, which appeared as classic and timeless as one in a painting. She was glad that Chiyo and Fumiko seemed to have found some peace.

Then they looked up at her, and the illusion of peace shattered. Chiyo's eyes were red and wet from crying. Fumiko regained the tense, furtive guise of a cornered animal. Neither of them had forgotten what had happened, not for a moment. Fumiko started to rise, primed to flee.

Chiyo said, "Don't be afraid, it's only Lady Reiko." She smiled, with a painful effort, and bowed. "Welcome. Your company does us an honor. Won't you join us?"

Reiko bowed, murmured her thanks, and sat. Chiyo offered refreshments, and after Reiko politely refused and then accepted, a servant brought tea and cakes. Reiko ate, finding herself surprisingly hungry after the terrible events of the morning. Fumiko wolfed down the food. Chiyo smiled indulgently and said, "She's always ready to eat."

She was making up for months of near-starvation, Reiko thought. "It's good of you to feed her."

Even when Chiyo smiled, the sadness never left her eyes. "Having her to take care of has done me good." Reiko knew she was thinking of her children. "What brings you here today? Is there news?"

"Yes, but I'm afraid it's bad." Reiko told Chiyo about the nun's suicide. She didn't want to disturb Chiyo, but neither did she want Chiyo to hear the story via gossip.

Chiyo looked saddened. "That poor woman. I shall pray for her spirit."

Fumiko didn't seem to care. Chewing the last cake, she started to wipe her mouth on her sleeve. Chiyo gently stopped her and handed her a napkin. Fumiko scowled, but she used the napkin, then carefully folded it. Reiko was pleased to see Chiyo teaching the girl manners. Maybe they would do Fumiko good in her uncertain future.

"Has anything else happened?" Chiyo asked.

Reiko sensed how eager Chiyo was to hear that the kidnapper had been caught and that life would somehow return to normal. She hated to disappoint her. "My husband is pursuing some inquiries." She couldn't tell Chiyo what Sano was doing at Edo Morgue; not even his family could know the secret. "Tengu-in's death may furnish new clues."

There came the sounds of heavy footsteps and male voices from the front of the house. Fumiko sat up straight, her ears perked. "It's my father!"

She jumped up and scurried out of the room.

"What can Jirocho be doing here?" Reiko said as she and Chiyo followed.

They went to the reception room, from which Jirocho's and Major Kumazawa's voices emanated. Fumiko would have rushed inside, but Chiyo held her back, gesturing her to be quiet. Reiko, Chiyo, and Fumiko cautiously peeked in the open door. Major Kumazawa was seated on the dais, Jirocho and his bodyguards on the floor below it. The women stepped back, so as not to be seen, and listened through the lattice-and-paper wall.

"Why have you come to call on me?" Major Kumazawa said in an unfriendly tone.

"Because you and I have common interests," Jirocho said, unruffled by Major Kumazawa's cold reception.

"What might those be?"

"We've both suffered insults to our clans."

"A mere coincidence. It doesn't justify relations between us."

"We have something else in common," Jirocho said. "Neither of us likes how Chamberlain Sano is conducting the investigation."

"That hardly makes us comrades." Sarcasm tinged Major Kumazawa's voice. "Why impose on me to talk about it? State your business."

"I'm here to make a proposition," Jirocho said. "We join forces and hunt down the kidnapper ourselves."

There was a short silence in which Reiko could sense Major Kumazawa's surprise. Major Kumazawa said, "I'm conducting my own search. Why would I want to cooperate with you?"

"Because you haven't managed to catch the bastard yet," Jirocho said.

"You haven't, either," Major Kumazawa retorted.

"True," Jirocho admitted. "I don't have enough men to search the whole city. Neither do you. But if we put our troops together, we can cover twice as much area without going over the same ground twice."

That would surely interfere with Sano's inquiries. Reiko shuddered at the idea of Jirocho's gang and Major Kumazawa's troops rampaging through the city, more avid for vengeance than for the truth.

Major Kumazawa said, "That's not a good enough reason. I know what you are, I know how you do business. Joining forces with you would bring me nothing but trouble."

It might well, Reiko thought. Jirocho said, "Before you refuse, listen to this. Have you ever wondered why you haven't been able to find out who kidnapped your daughter?"

"It's only been a few days since she was taken," Major Kumazawa said. "All I need is more time."

"Have you ever stopped to think that maybe you're not getting anywhere because there are places in the city that you don't know and people who won't talk to you?"

"I know the city like the palm of my own hand," Major Kumazawa said, growing more irritable. "I can go everyplace, make everybody talk."

"You're mistaken," Jirocho said evenly. "You high-ranking samurai live in your own little world. There are many people you never even see because they're careful to stay out of your way. People in my world, for instance."

Major Kumazawa laughed, a sound of pure, arrogant scorn. "Even if that's true, it's my problem. Why should you care?"

"Because I have the same problem. There are places that I can't go, and people who won't talk to me." Jirocho added, "People of *your* class."

Reiko risked another peek through the door. She saw Jirocho lean toward Major Kumazawa as he said, "It seems that there are two different kidnappers. One raped your daughter, the other, mine. What if the man you're hunting is a commoner who's hiding among other commoners, being protected by them? What if the man I'm hunting is a samurai that I can't go near?" His tone grew urgent, intense. "Alone, we're at a disadvantage. Together, we can get the vengeance we both want."

"Oh, I see what this is about. It's not that I can't get vengeance without you; it's that you can't without me." Disdain edged Major Kumazawa's words. "Your offer is an insult. This conversation is finished. Get out."

Jirocho didn't reply, but Reiko could feel his anger and frustration, like heat from a fire burning on the other side of the wall. She and Chiyo pulled Fumiko down the passage, lest they be caught eavesdropping. But as Jirocho and his men stalked out the door, Fumiko called, "Father."

His head turned; he saw her and halted. A strange expression came over his wolfish features. Fumiko didn't run to her father, even though every line in her body strained toward him; she hesitated like a dog whipped too often. Chiyo held her in a protective embrace. Jirocho swallowed; his jaw shifted. His gaze absorbed her new clothes, her clean face. His men looked at him, awaiting his reaction. Beneath his surprise, Reiko detected other emotions she couldn't identify.

Major Kumazawa appeared in the door of the reception room. Jirocho pointed at Fumiko and demanded, "What's she doing here?"

"She lives in this house now." Although Major Kumazawa was, as Reiko knew, far from happy with the arrangement, he seemed pleased to see Jirocho disconcerted.

"Why—how—?" The gangster's face went blank and stupid with incomprehension.

"My daughter insisted on taking her in," Major Kumazawa said. "Have you a problem with that?"

Jirocho didn't speak or move for a moment. Reiko, ignored by everyone, could feel him floundering in unfamiliar waters. It was unheard of for the child of a notorious gangster to be virtually adopted by a high samurai official, and the clash he'd just had with Major Kumazawa obviously didn't make Jirocho any more comfortable with the situation. Reiko watched Jirocho struggle to frame it in a way that made sense according to the laws of his world.

At last he blurted, "You stole my girl."

"You threw her out," Major Kumazawa reminded him. "Which means you haven't any right to object to my giving her a home. But if you want her back, you're welcome to take her."

Reiko felt Fumiko holding her breath, tense with hope. Chiyo hugged the girl close. From the instant Jirocho had first laid eyes on his daughter he hadn't taken his gaze off her, even while he spoke to Major Kumazawa. Now, without a word to her, he stalked away down the hall, his men following. Fumiko hid her face against Chiyo's shoulder and sobbed.

"I'll get my vengeance, and I'll do it without your help," Jirocho said over his shoulder to Major Kumazawa. "And I would wager my entire fortune that you'll never be able to do the same without mine."

26

The road to the oxcart stables led Sano, Hirata, and their entourage past poor tenements that clung to the outskirts of Edo like a dirty, ragged hem. It was twilight by the time Sano and his men arrived at the compound of wooden barns. The yard around them was muddy and trampled, pocked by hoof marks filled with rainwater. The area stank of urine and manure. The fenced and roofed enclosure for parking the carts was empty. Through the open doors of the barns Sano saw empty stalls and idle stable boys.

"I don't suppose our suspects are hanging around waiting to be caught," Sano said. "Their colleagues should be back soon, though. Maybe they can point us in the right direction."

A distant sound of clattering wheels vibrated through the dusk. It grew louder and nearer, punctuated by bellows. The streets around the stables disgorged oxen pulling carts, drivers aboard, returning home for the night. They converged on the stables like a slow, malodorous, and rackety invading legion.

"Divide and conquer," Sano told his men.

They circulated, asking the drivers if they knew the whereabouts of Jinshichi and Gombei. Drivers shook their heads. Finally, Sano's luck changed for the better.

"Jinshichi and Gombei, what a pair of good-for-nothings," said the eighth driver Sano questioned.

Naked except for a dirty loincloth, a rag tied over his head, and straw sandals on his feet, he had skin so tanned and leathery that one could have made a good saddle out of it. As he and his fellows parked their carts under the shelter, he spat on the ground in disgust.

"Why do you have such a poor opinion of Jinshichi and Gombei?" Sano asked.

"They're lazy," the driver said. "They show up late and keep everybody waiting." He unyoked his ox. Other carts racketed into their places in long rows; oxen bellowed and snorted. "Sometimes they leave before the work's done. Which means the rest of us have to haul extra loads. And for what?"

He spat again as he led his ox toward the stables and Sano followed. "No thanks from Jinshichi and Gombei. Lazy slobs!"

Sano was intrigued by this portrait of his suspects. "Where do they go when they're supposed to be at work?"

"Don't know. They keep it to themselves."

Maybe they went hunting and kidnapping women, Sano thought.

"The boss keeps threatening to fire them," the driver said.

"Why doesn't he?"

The driver pantomimed jingling a string of coins.

"Where do they get the money to pay him off?"

"Your guess is as good as mine." The driver prodded his ox into a stall. "But they have more than the rest of us. They even brag about going to Yoshiwara."

The Yoshiwara pleasure quarter was too expensive for ordinary oxcart drivers. Sano began to entertain different ideas about the nature of the crimes he was investigating.

"Can you tell me where I might find them?"

"Sorry."

"Where do they live?"

"Same place as me." The driver pointed toward a street of tenements. "But I haven't seen them around there since yesterday."

Sano thanked the man. As he turned his horse to go, the driver said, "Wait, master. I just remembered something. A while back, I ran into Jinshichi and Gombei at a teahouse called the Drum. I was driving past as they were coming out. Not the kind of place I'd have expected to see them."

"Why not?"

"It's for high-class folks. I was surprised that Jinshichi and Gombei got in. I wondered what they were doing there."

So did Sano wonder.

The Drum Teahouse was located a block off the main street in the Nihonbashi merchant quarter, behind the popular dry goods store named Shirokiya. The shops around it were closed for the night, and no one was around except the watchmen guarding the gates at either end of the road. The teahouse occupied a building decorated with drum-shaped blue lanterns whose cold light reflected in the puddles and cast an eerie radiance into the darkening gloom.

Sano and Hirata left their troops and horses down the street. They entered the teahouse and found a spacious room lit by the blue light shining in through the paper windowpanes. Maids poured sake for the customers, all male, who sat on the floor. Along the walls were private enclosures with curtains drawn across the entrances. The dim light gleamed on the shaved crowns of samurai and the oiled, glossy hair of rich commoners. The blue lanterns colored the men's faces with a morbid glow. Conversation was quiet, minimal. Each man appeared to be alone.

The proprietor stepped out of the shadows. "Welcome, masters," he said with a low, obsequious bow to Sano and Hirata. His hushed voice brought to Sano's mind a lizard slithering under a rock. Dressed in a black robe, he had a narrow figure and a square-jawed head. His eyes had the feral gleam of a nocturnal animal; they didn't blink as they assessed Sano and Hirata. "Please allow me to make you comfortable."

He hustled them into an enclosure, fetched a sake decanter and cups, served Sano and Hirata, then drew the curtains. While they drank, he hovered.

Sano exchanged glances with Hirata: They both sensed something not right about the teahouse. The darkness, the quiet, the mix of samurai and commoners, and the lack of camaraderie were unusual, and there was an odd tension in the air. Sano wanted to know what was going on.

"Won't you join us?" he asked the proprietor.

"It would be an honor." The proprietor knelt beside Sano. As he re-filled the cups, he murmured, "Might there be something else I can do for you?"

"There might," Sano said. "What have you to offer?"

"It depends."

"On what?" Hirata asked.

"On your particular situation."

The proprietor paused, waiting for Sano and Hirata to answer. They waited for a cue from him. His greed for their business triumphed over caution. He whispered, "Is there somebody who's making trouble for you? I can put you in contact with people who can teach him a lesson."

"What if there is somebody?" Sano said. "What would your people do?"

"It depends on what terms you're willing to meet," the proprietor said.

"How much to have him beaten up?" Hirata said.

"Fifty *momme*."

That was quite a bit of silver. Sano began to understand how Jinshichi and Gombei might have come by their extra cash. They were apparently among the proprietor's "people," which would explain their presence at a teahouse whose clientele normally didn't associate with low-class men like them.

"How much to eliminate somebody?" Sano asked.

"That would depend on who it was and how difficult it would be. But the price starts at a hundred *koban*."

It appeared that wealthy folks who didn't want to risk killing their own enemies somehow found their way to the Drum Teahouse, probably by discreet word of mouth. Samurai could kill commoners without punishment, but not one another; for merchants and other citizens, the penalty for any murder was death. The Drum offered a solution to their problems and kept the blood off their hands.

"I'm impressed with your ingenuity," Sano said.

"My humble thanks," the proprietor simpered.

"But you should be more careful whom you do business with," Sano said.

"Allow me to introduce the honorable Chamberlain Sano," said Hirata.

"Allow me to introduce my chief retainer, Hirata-*san*, the shogun's principal investigator," Sano said.

The proprietor blinked.

"Murder for hire is a crime," Sano said. "We're going to arrest you and put you in jail."

The proprietor lunged out of the enclosure as fast as a snake plunging down a hole. But Hirata was faster. He grabbed the man's arm. Yanked back into place, the man struggled until Hirata squeezed a tender spot between his muscles. He let out a bleat of pain and sank to his knees.

"I didn't mean it," he said with an anxious grin. "We don't really kill anybody. It was just a joke. Hah, hah."

"We'll see about that," Hirata said.

His fingers dug into the man's wrist. The proprietor stopped straining to break free. "I can't feel my arm. I can't move." He beheld Hirata with fright and shock. "What have you done to me?"

Hirata had pressed against nerves that controlled sensations and motion in the human body, Sano knew. Hirata said, "It's just a little trick I learned while walking in the woods one day. You run a murder-for-hire business, don't you?"

The proprietor's body sat as still as a corpse propped upright. Only his face was animated, by terror. "No!"

His gleaming eyes darted in search of help. But his soft voice didn't carry outside the enclosure, and nobody opened the curtain to see what was wrong.

"How do you like this?" Hirata changed his grip slightly.

Now the proprietor's eyes and mouth flared wide as Hirata constricted his lungs. "All right," he choked out. "It's true!"

"Kill him," Sano said, "and spare the bother of an execution."

"No! Please, don't!" The proprietor wheezed; his face turned bluer in the blue light. "Let me live, and I'll do anything you want!"

"Let's see if there's something we want that you can give us," Sano said. He usually pitied helpless people and disapproved of physical coercion, but not this time. "We're looking for two men, named Jinshichi and Gombei. Do they work for you?"

The proprietor's face twisted from side to side as he tried to shake his head and failed. Hirata pressed harder on his wrist, and his voice emerged in a strangled croak. "Yes."

"What do they do?" Sano asked.

Hirata eased his grip long enough for the proprietor to gulp a breath and say, "They get women. For men who want special things."

Now Sano understood Jinshichi and Gombei's sideline occupation and role in the kidnappings. Neither of the oxcart drivers had raped Chiyo, Fumiko, or Tengu-in; they'd procured the women for someone else. Someone who had sexual tastes that couldn't be satisfied in Edo's brothels.

172

"Was one of these women a nursing mother and another a nun?"

"I don't know who the women were," the proprietor said, then gasped because Hirata had compressed his nerves again. "No, I really don't, honest! All I did was set Jinshichi and Gombei up with my clients and take my share of the money. What they did after that was between them and the clients."

"Tell me the names of your clients," Sano said.

Fresh terror blazed in the proprietor's eyes. Sano could feel his body shaking inside, vibrating the floor, even though he was paralyzed. "I can't tell you. They'll kill me."

"If you don't tell us, *I'll* kill you," Hirata said.

The proprietor crumpled into a heap as if his bones had dissolved. Sano couldn't begin to imagine what spell Hirata had wrought. The proprietor lay limp, gasping with panic. From outside the enclosure came the voices of the maids, chatting among themselves, unaware that anything untoward was happening.

"All right," the proprietor said. "If you'll just let me go, I'll talk."

27

"You didn't let him go, did you?" Reiko said as she served Sano his dinner at home late that night.

"No, of course not." Sano had begun the story of what had happened at the teahouse. Now he hungrily ate raw mackerel laid on rice balls and dumplings stuffed with vegetables. "Hirata and I closed down the teahouse. We took the proprietor to Edo Jail. Later, I'll figure out exactly what crimes he's guilty of arranging and your father can put him on trial. I've put a watch on the Drum Teahouse, in case Jinshichi and Gombei should show up there."

"Who were the clients?" Reiko asked eagerly.

Before he answered, Sano looked through the open doors that led to other rooms, to see if Masahiro was listening. He'd resolved not to let his son hear any more conversations about detective work. He saw Masahiro exactly where he'd been when Sano arrived home—sitting in bed two rooms away, Akiko curled up beside him. Masahiro was reading his sister a story. Even though he'd spent the whole day indoors, being punished, he seemed contented enough.

"The clients are three individuals who'll be in big trouble if I find out that they touched my cousin," Sano said. "Gombei and Jinshichi did dirty work for some prominent men. I'm not personally acquainted with them, but I've heard of them all. One is a rice broker named Ogita."

"I've heard of him, too," Reiko said. "Doesn't he buy and sell rice from the shogun's family lands?"

"That's him. He's made a lot of money at it." Enough to pay for women to be kidnapped and delivered to him for his pleasure, Sano thought. "The second man is the official in charge of the shogun's dog kennels."

Due to the law that protected dogs, and the public nuisance they caused, the government had established kennels for the strays. Someone had to maintain the kennels, and that duty had fallen to Nanbu Bosai. He was a Tokugawa vassal from an old, respected clan. But good family connections didn't preclude twisted sexual tastes—or crime.

"Who is the third suspect?" Reiko asked.

"A priest named Joju," Sano said.

"The one who's famous for those rituals?"

Joju's unique, extraordinary rituals had captured the attention of the public, which was avid for new diversions. "The very one," Sano said. "But we don't know if any of the three men is responsible for the attacks."

He faced the disturbing possibility that Jinshichi and Gombei had kidnapped the women for other clients that the proprietor of the Drum Teahouse didn't know about. He recalled what he'd seen at Edo Morgue, and another disturbing possibility occurred to him. "Dr. Ito examined Tengu-in's body," he said, and told Reiko about the disease found on the nun.

"Oh, no." Clearly stricken by horror, Reiko voiced Sano's fear: "Does that mean Chiyo and Fumiko might have it, too?"

"Let's hope not," Sano said. "In the meantime, I intend to find out the truth about our suspects tomorrow."

"I must warn you that Jirocho isn't content to leave the investigation to you," Reiko said, and described the scene at Major Kumazawa's house.

Sano was glad his uncle had spurned the gangster's proposition that they join forces, but displeased by the thought of Jirocho running wild in pursuit of blood. "That's bad news," Sano said, "but I won't let Jirocho get in my way."

Hirata raced through the corridors of his mansion. His children stampeded after him, whooping and laughing. Their footsteps shook the floor. Hirata swerved around corners. Taeko and Tatsuo crashed into walls. Midori called from her chamber, "All this noise is giving me a headache!"

But her tone was fond, indulgent. Hirata knew she loved having him at home, romping with the children. He'd been gone for too much of their short lives, and he'd had to win back their love.

He ran ahead of them and darted into a room. Taeko and Tatsuo sped toward him in hot, uproarious pursuit. Hirata jumped out of the room and shouted, "Boo!"

They recoiled and screamed. Now he was chasing them. They all spilled out the door, down the steps into the dark garden. "Try to find us, Papa!" Taeko called.

She and her little brother ran off to hide. Hirata ambled after them. The wet grass soaked his socks. Fireflies glimmered. In their weak, fleeting light Hirata spotted Taeko behind a stone lantern and Tatsuo peeking around a pine tree. He pretended not to see the children, but they screamed when he came near them and bolted. They rustled so loudly through the grass that Hirata didn't need mystic martial arts powers to hear where they went.

Midori appeared on the veranda and called, "That's enough. Come inside. It's time for the children to go to bed."

Taeko and Tatsuo let out woeful cries and begged her to let them play a little longer.

A pulse of energy traveled through the darkness, through Hirata. His breath caught. His flesh rippled as he detected the same presence that he'd encountered at Shinobazu Pond. It was inside Edo Castle, somewhere nearby.

Hirata froze, listening with all his might. The peaceful night vibrated with howls and screeches beyond the range of normal hearing. He moved his gaze from side to side in an attempt to see the invisible threat. His pupils dilated. His vision expanded. The whole interior of Edo Castle, its buildings, streets, and passages, formed an image like a distorted map, composed of echoes and memory, around the periphery of his eyesight. He couldn't locate the presence, but he could feel the danger.

"Taeko! Tatsuo! Get in the house!" he shouted.

He sped toward his children, scooped up Taeko with one arm and Tatsuo with the other. Frightened by his alarm and his rough handling, they started to cry.

"What's wrong?" Midori said. "What are you doing?"

Hirata vaulted onto the veranda and threw the crying, screaming children in the door. He said to Midori, "You, too!"

"Have you gone mad?" she demanded. "What is it?"

"Someone's out to get me." Hirata stood between her and the threat, his arms flung wide to shield her. He gazed into the night, his heart pounding.

"Someone's always out to get you," Midori said. "That's the problem with being the man that everyone wants to beat. Why upset the children?"

"He's here," Hirata said.

"Where? I don't see anyone."

Hirata didn't, either, but the energy still pulsed with ominous power. "Just do as I told you: Go in the house!"

Determined to protect his family, cursing himself because he'd left his swords in the house and there was no time to fetch them, he started down the steps, his body his only weapon.

Midori followed him. "Why are you scared?" she asked. During his time away from home she'd developed a strong will of her own, and she often disregarded his orders. Furthermore, she wasn't quite convinced that her husband lived in dimensions she couldn't see. "You can defeat anybody. Besides, this estate is full of guards. Nobody can get in to hurt us."

Hirata raced in spirals through the garden. He felt like a cat chasing a string it couldn't see, while an unseen hand jerked the string this way and that, just out of reach. The pulse came from all directions and none. As he left the garden and barreled down a passage between buildings in his estate, Midori fell behind. He faintly heard her calling him to come back and calm down. He burst through a gate that led to the street outside the estate.

"Where are you?" he yelled. "Show yourself!"

The sounds of dogs barking and troops patrolling on horseback in the distance were his only answer. The street bordered by the walls of other estates was empty, serene under the moonlit clouds. But Hirata felt no peace.

His enemy had access to Edo Castle. Stone walls and the Tokugawa army hadn't kept him out. He could get close enough to attack Hirata whenever he wanted.

28

Day broke as Sano and Detectives Marume and Fukida and a few troops rode west out of town. The highway extended along a ridge, bypassing the temples of Zōjō district. Bells and gongs tolled. Distant pagodas rose into the humid air and disappeared into clouds edged with gold by the sun.

Sano and his entourage traversed the suburb of Kojimachi, which boasted factories where soybeans were fermented and processed into bean paste. The odor enveloped Sano like a salty, rotten tide. He and his men continued on to the farther suburb of Yotsuya.

He heard the Tokugawa dog kennel before it came into view.

The sound of the dogs barking and howling blared over the roofs of the shops and teahouses that lined the main road, the temples, and the estates that belonged to various *daimyo* and Tokugawa vassals.

"What a din!" Marume exclaimed. "How can anybody stand to live around here?"

The din grew louder as Sano and his men forged onward. The smell hit them as they reached the kennel. One of three maintained by the government, it was a huge compound enclosed by a stone wall, set between the city's outskirts and the farmhouses, fields, and woodland beyond. It radiated an overwhelming stink of feces.

Marume held his nose. Sano tried not to breathe as he rode up to the unguarded gate. His troops entered first. As Sano followed with his detectives, the stench nauseated him and the barking deafened him. Some forty thousand dogs lived here, all strays picked up in the city, protected by the shogun's laws of compassion, kept fed, sheltered, and off the streets. A muddy yard surrounded rows of barracks, their doors open to reveal the dogs in cages inside.

A pack of loose dogs came bounding toward Sano. They were huge, some with shaggy brown or black fur, others sleek and blotched. They barked and growled as they charged. They all wore leather collars bristling with metal spikes. Their teeth were sharp in their snarling mouths. Their eyes blazed with intent to kill.

"Look out!" Fukida yelled.

Sano's and his men's horses shied, whinnied, and reared. A shrill whistle pierced the uproar. The dogs immediately retreated. They stood around Sano and his men, ears flat, growling deep in their throats. Four samurai strode across the yard toward Sano. Their trousers were tucked into high leather boots. They wore grins that said this wasn't the first time they'd loosed their dogs on visitors and they enjoyed the spectacle.

"Greetings," said the leader. About forty-five years old, with graying hair, he was short, but he had a broad build that he inflated by thrusting out his chest and stomach. He walked with his legs spread apart and his arms held away from his body, so that he took up as much space as possible. His eyes sparked with cunning and aggression under their heavy lids. His lips were thick and sensual, his jowls flaccid. He called to the dogs, who crowded around him, wagging their tails. He caressed their heads. "Scared you, didn't they?"

Sano took an immediate dislike to the man. "Nanbu Bosai, I presume?"

"That I am. And you are . . . ?" Dismay appeared on Nanbu's face as he recognized Sano. "Honorable Chamberlain, if I'd known it was you, I wouldn't have set the dogs on you. A thousand apologies."

"Now who's scared?" Marume said with satisfaction.

Nanbu bowed. His three men, all younger than he but cut along the same brutish lines, followed suit. He said, "Welcome to my humble establishment."

Sano heard rancor beneath Nanbu's anxiety to please. The position Nanbu held came with disadvantages as well as a high stipend and respect from the shogun. Nanbu probably couldn't get the smell of the kennels out of his nose, and he was the shogun's chief dogcatcher. He and his assistants had to roam the streets of Edo and capture strays. The law forbade the public to jeer at the dogcatchers, but the law was often disobeyed.

But Sano withheld his sympathy from the man. Nanbu might be responsible for Chiyo's kidnapping and rape.

"May I ask what brings you here?" Nanbu said. "Do you need some guard dogs?"

"Is that what you call them?" Sano looked askance at the animals.

"They're pretty good, if I do say so myself. They cornered you, didn't they?" Nanbu said, not quite in jest. "I train them and sell them. Lord Kii has some at his estate. So do plenty of other *daimyo*. All these dogs eat up a lot of food. Might as well put them to work."

"I don't want a guard dog," Sano said. "I came to talk to you."

"Me?" Nanbu pointed to his puffed-out chest. "To what do I owe the honor?"

To all appearances, he spoke with the surprise and pleasure of any official singled out for the chamberlain's attention.

"We have acquaintances in common," Sano said.

"Oh? May I ask who they are?"

"Jinshichi and Gombei."

Nanbu frowned, in mild confusion. "I'm sorry, but those names don't sound familiar."

Unconvinced that Nanbu didn't know the oxcart drivers, or that the man was innocent, Sano said, "The proprietor of the Drum Teahouse tells a different story."

"The Drum Teahouse?" Nanbu pondered. Sano couldn't tell if he was actually trying to remember the place or planning to teach the proprietor a lesson for informing on him. "He must be mistaken. I've never been there."

"He says Jinshichi and Gombei work for you."

Nanbu shrugged, unfazed. "He must have me mixed up with somebody else."

"I don't think so," Sano said. "I think you hired Jinshichi and Gombei to kidnap women for you to rape."

"Begging your pardon, but you're the one who's mistaken now!" Nanbu regarded Sano with shock that gave way to dawning comprehension and offense. "I heard that your cousin and some other women had been kidnapped and you were trying to find out who did it. And now you want to pin it on me."

His men's expressions turned hostile. His dogs sensed his animosity toward Sano. They barked and growled an ugly chorus of warning.

"With all due respect, I didn't do it," Nanbu declared.

Sano could have spent the day hurling accusations that Nanbu would refute, but he didn't like wasting time, and he was tired of the kennels' horrific smell.

"Fine," Sano said. "Then you won't mind submitting to an inspection by the women. We'll let them decide whether you're guilty."

"Fine," Nanbu echoed with a smug smile. "Whenever you want."

"You seem very sure that the women won't identify you as their attacker," Sano said.

"They won't," Nanbu said. "Because I'm not."

Maybe he was bluffing. Even if he were the rapist, he would know that the victims had been drugged or otherwise rendered unfit to have observed him well enough to recognize him again. But he couldn't know that they hadn't forgotten everything.

Sano decided to try another ploy. "Take your trousers off. Your loincloth, too."

"*What?*" Nanbu's lewd mouth dropped in surprise.

He and his men stared at Sano as if he'd gone mad. Detective Marume guffawed.

"Do it," Sano ordered.

Nanbu recovered, laughed, and said, "Does this mean you're interested in me, Honorable Chamberlain? I didn't know you liked men."

There was no stigma associated with manly love, and the remark didn't bother Sano. "I'm interested in finding out if you raped those women. One look at your private parts should do the trick."

"I'm not giving you a look." Nanbu seemed uneasy for the first time since the subject of the crimes had come up. His chest and stomach had deflated a bit and his arms hewed closer to his sides.

"Why not?"

"Because I don't want to."

"You should be glad to cooperate," Sano said. "This is your chance to exonerate yourself."

Nanbu folded his arms and glared. "I already told you I didn't do it." Sano saw sweat droplets on his forehead. "I give you my word, on my honor. I'm not taking off my clothes."

"Your word's not good enough," Sano said, "and I didn't ask you to undress, I ordered you to do it."

"Want us to help him out of his clothes?" Marume asked.

He and Fukida dismounted and advanced on Nanbu. Nanbu pursed his thick lips and whistled. The twelve dogs grouped around him in a tight, snarling huddle.

"You'll have to get past them," Nanbu said, "and you wouldn't dare."

He was right, as much as Sano hated to admit it. The dogs were a living wall around Nanbu, an army more fierce and loyal than any samurai troops. If Sano and his men tried to penetrate it, they would surely kill dogs in the process; and the shogun wouldn't excuse even Sano, his dear friend and trusted chamberlain, for harming a dog, not when he believed that his chances of getting an heir depended on protecting dogs and earning fortune's grace.

"You win for now," Sano said. He might have risked taking on Nanbu's dogs, if not for his family. If he couldn't talk his way out of the punishment later, Reiko and the children and his other relatives—including the Kumazawa clan—would share it. "But you're in trouble even if you didn't rape those women."

"What are you going to do, cut my head off?" Nanbu laughed recklessly. "You can't touch me. Now get out."

He advanced on Sano. The dogs moved with him, panting for a fight, a taste of blood. Sano and his men had no choice except to mount their horses and let Nanbu and the dogs herd them out the gate.

"What do you think you're going to do?" Sano said, almost angry enough to do something he would regret. "Barricade yourself inside the kennel?"

"That's right," Nanbu said. "If you try to get at me, you'll be the one in trouble."

"You can't hide behind your dogs forever," Sano said.

Nanbu responded by closing the gate in the faces of Sano and his men. Sano, Marume, and Fukida shared looks that brimmed with ire and frustration. Marume said, "That didn't go quite as well as we hoped."

"At least we know one thing we didn't before we came here," Sano said. "Nanbu is hiding something."

"Sores, or a mole?" Fukida wondered.

"That I don't know, but I'm sure he raped at least one of the women. I'm going to find out which."

"Even if he did, how are we going to get the bastard?" Marume said.

Sano told three of his troops, "Stay here and keep watch on Nanbu. If he comes out, arrest him. He won't get away with what he's done."

29

Masahiro meant to be a good boy.

While he ate his breakfast and studied with his tutor, he was serious and obedient. He was careful not to pout while Father's soldiers stood around guarding him as if he were a prisoner in jail. He wanted to convince Father and Mother that he'd learned his lesson, and they would surely ask his tutor and his guards whether he'd behaved himself. But now, as his tutor pointed out mistakes in the arithmetic test he'd just finished, Masahiro itched with frustration.

How he hated being cooped up inside the house! He wished Toda hadn't caught him yesterday. He wished that when he'd spied on Yanagisawa and the ladies he'd learned something so important that Father and Mother would have forgiven him. If only he could help them instead of staying home and doing nothing!

The arithmetic lesson ended. His teacher departed. Masahiro fidgeted while he waited for his reading tutor. The soldier on guard duty this morning was a young samurai named Hayashi, who looked as bored and restless as Masahiro was.

"How about if we play outside for a little while?" Hayashi suggested. "I won't tell your parents."

"All right," Masahiro said.

The words escaped before he could stop them. He couldn't take them back, could he? Because he didn't want to disappoint Hayashi. That was what Masahiro told himself as he followed Hayashi out the door.

The sky was gray and the day warm and humid. Masahiro ran across the garden, enjoying the squishy wetness of the grass that soaked his socks through his sandals. He batted at the low foliage on the trees and laughed as water droplets showered onto him. A teenaged garden boy stood on a ladder propped against the wall. He'd removed his short blue kimono and his floppy straw hat, which lay on a rock near the ladder. Clad only in a loincloth, he pruned the pine trees. Hayashi threw a ball to Masahiro. As they played catch, two young, pretty maids came out of the house, batted their eyes at Hayashi, and giggled. Hayashi dropped the ball and went over to talk to them. Masahiro was left alone. He watched the garden boy climb down the ladder and go off on some errand, leaving the ladder and his discarded clothes. Masahiro's heartbeat quickened; he moved toward the ladder.

Wouldn't it be fun to climb up so high?

First Masahiro picked up the clothes and wadded them under his arm. He didn't stop to think why. He mounted the ladder. The pungent, sharp-needled boughs of the pine tree concealed him from anyone below. When he reached the top rung of the ladder, he couldn't see over the wall because he was too short. He set the garden boy's clothes on the wall. While he grabbed the top of the wall in both hands and scrambled his way up, he heard Hayashi chatting with the maids. His feet bumped the ladder, which fell away from him and hit the ground with a soft thud. Horror filled Masahiro as he crouched atop the narrow wall and wondered how he was going to get back down.

"Masahiro! Where are you?" Hayashi called.

Startled, Masahiro lost his balance. He tried to steady himself, but his scrabbling hands found the garden boy's clothes instead of the wall's solid stone. His fingers slipped. He toppled off the wall and landed on his back in a pile of sand on the other side. The hat and kimono plopped onto his face. Masahiro lay, the breath knocked out of him, stunned.

He cautiously wiggled his body. Although the fall had jarred every bone in him, the sand had cushioned his landing, and nothing seemed broken. He flung the clothes off his face, looked up at the wall and the overhanging pine boughs. He heard Hayashi on the other side, saying, "Where did he go? Chamberlain Sano will kill me!"

Dread flooded Masahiro. *When Father hears about this, he'll kill me, too.* Father would never believe that he hadn't meant to climb over the wall, that he'd fallen off by accident.

Masahiro scrambled to his feet. He was in a passage that divided the mansion's grounds from the rest of the estate. The path between two stone walls had been dug up. The passage was empty except for the sand pile, a stack of new paving stones, and a wheelbarrow. Luckily for Masahiro, the workers had taken a break, or they'd have caught him. But he would be punished no matter what he did next.

Father and Mother would never let him outside again until he was grown up.

Then Masahiro saw a bright spot amid his troubles. Now that he'd escaped, he had another chance to be a detective. What did he have to lose?

He snatched up the garden boy's clothes, which he hadn't meant to steal but would certainly come in handy. Then he ran down the passage before Hayashi could figure out what had happened and come after him. Masahiro would make the most of his freedom. This time he would discover something so good that Father and Mother would be glad he'd broken the rules and he wouldn't feel guilty about his disobedience.

Masahiro didn't let himself think that he must have meant to escape all along.

Accompanied by his two top retainers, Hirata glanced over his shoulder as they rode through Kuramae—the area dubbed "In Front of the Shogun's Storehouses," near the Sumida River. He thought he felt the now-familiar presence, but he wasn't sure.

He'd lain awake for most of the night, his senses straining to detect the slightest hint of his unknown foe. Several times he'd sat up in bed, his heart pounding. But nothing happened except that Midori had grown tired of being awakened. She'd flounced off to sleep in another room, telling Hirata that he was imagining things.

Maybe he had been.

Maybe he still was.

Kuramae was known for its many shops, and particularly for toys. Hirata and his men steered their horses around pedestrians in streets devoted to dolls, kites, fireworks, and *Dagashiya-san*—"cheap-sweet shops"—that sold candy and inexpensive trinkets. Wandering peddlers hawked *kokeshi* dolls, and blowfish whistles. Hirata didn't think of buying presents to surprise his children, as he might have another time. His mind manufactured threats where none existed. Every casual glance from a stranger, every movement or flare of emotion within the crowds, wound his nerves tighter.

He knew that was exactly what his enemy wanted.

The mind was a warrior's most formidable weapon. When it was strong and steady, it could win battles against opponents with better combat skills. An expert martial artist could influence the mind of his opponent by instilling such fear that the opponent became weak, helpless, and easily defeated. Hirata had often used this strategy, but now he was its target. He felt his confidence draining away, his spirit weakening. Although he usually liked to travel alone, today he'd brought Detectives Inoue and Arai. Their company didn't bring him a sense of security, however; indeed, his wish for protection made him feel more vulnerable.

He and the detectives turned onto Edo Street, the main road that led to the northern highway. On the right, between the road and the river, stood the shogun's rice warehouses. On the left side of the road were teahouses operated by *fudasashi*, merchants who delivered the rice to the shogun's retainers for a commission, then bought the excess and sold it at a profit. They also loaned money, another business that made them hugely wealthy.

Hirata dismounted outside the biggest teahouse, which bore the name "Ogita" carved on a discreet wooden placard by the door. Inside, male voices shouted numbers. Hirata and his men entered a room where a rice auction was in progress. Arms raised, waving frantically toward a dais at the back of the room, merchants called out bids. Hirata watched the man at the center of the dais.

Ogita paced, shouted, and gestured like an actor in a Kabuki theater. He wasn't more than average height, but he stood tall. His brown kimono, surcoat, and trousers were made of cotton, in accordance with the sumptuary laws that reserved silk for the samurai class, but his garments had the sheen of highest-quality fabric. His bald head and long, fleshy face shone, too—with grease from a rich diet. His eyes were narrow slits that glinted with intelligence and didn't miss a thing as they darted back and forth, spotting bidders. He wasn't fat, but he had a bulging double chin that seemed to amplify his voice as he repeated bids and demanded a better price. His energy aura was bigger and stronger than anyone else's; he dominated the crowd. But as he studied Edo's top rice broker, Hirata made a troubling discovery.

He was usually good at reading people, but his sleepless night and his state of distraction broke the concentration he needed to assess Ogita. His fear had begun to affect his work. How was he going to handle this interrogation?

The auction ended. Losing bidders left to try their luck at other houses. Ogita and the winners closed their deals by applying signature seals to contracts written up on the spot by his clerks. Servants poured ritual cups of sake. When the customers left, Hirata signaled his detectives to wait by the door while he approached Ogita.

He introduced himself, then said, "I'd like a word with you."

The slits of Ogita's eyes opened wider in surprise. "What about?"

"I'm investigating a series of crimes," Hirata said. "I need your assistance."

If Ogita was alarmed, Hirata couldn't tell. "I'm at your service." Ogita spread his hands in the gesture of a man who had much to give and nothing to withhold.

"Then you'll be happy to answer a few questions." Bereft of the extra sense that usually aided him during interrogations, Hirata fell back on standard detective procedure. He asked Ogita his whereabouts on the days that Chiyo, Fumiko, and the nun had been missing.

He'd expected Ogita to claim he couldn't remember details from so long ago, but Ogita called to a clerk: "Bring me my calendar."

The clerk fetched a clothbound book and handed it to Ogita. Ogita paged to the dates Hirata had mentioned and reeled off a list of activities that included rice auctions at his teahouse, business meetings around the city, banquets, his son's wedding, and drinking parties with customers, friends, and government officials. He smiled and asked, "Is that good enough?"

"That only accounts for your days," Hirata said. "What about your nights?"

"I was at home with my family and my bodyguards." Ogita added, "A man in my position has plenty of enemies, and I'm a target for thieves. My bodyguards stay near me wherever I am."

Hirata didn't doubt that they would confirm his alibi.

"May I ask why you're so interested in my business?" Ogita spoke with mild curiosity, without the caution of a man who was guilty of crimes and threatened by the law. Hirata despaired because he couldn't discern whether Ogita's manner was an act or not. Used to relying on the powers gained from strenuous training and magic rituals, he felt as if he'd regressed to his days as a mere, ordinary human.

"Three women were kidnapped, held prisoner, and raped during those time periods," Hirata said.

"And you think I'm responsible?" Ogita's expression said he thought the idea was so absurd that he couldn't bother to be offended by it. "I am certainly not."

"You haven't asked who the women are," Hirata pointed out. He wasn't so distracted that he hadn't noticed the omission. "Maybe that's because you already know."

Ogita glanced at the ceiling long enough to convey scorn. "No, I don't know, but I suppose I should find out who's been slandering me. Who are they?"

Was Ogita pretending ignorance? Hirata only wished he knew that. "One is the gangster Jirocho's daughter. The second is a nun named Tengu-in. The third is Lady Chiyo, wife of Captain Okubo and cousin of Chamberlain Sano."

The rice broker's greasy face showed no recognition, except a frown at Sano's name. "Well, my condolences to them, but I never laid a hand on them. I don't even know them."

"You should be familiar with Lady Chiyo," Hirata said. "Her father is Major Kumazawa. He's in charge of guarding the warehouses that hold the rice you sell."

"I know him. Not his daughter."

Hirata couldn't have said whether he was lying or telling the truth. "She grew up in the Kumazawa clan's house, which isn't far from here. You must have seen her."

"Seen her, maybe. Anything else, no." Ogita made a negative, adamant, slashing gesture with his hand. Annoyance crept into his expression. "If I want a woman, I don't have to kidnap or rape one. Here, let me show you something."

Ogita stalked to the dais and spread out the rice contracts that lay upon a table. He jabbed his ink-stained finger at the huge sums written on the contracts. "With what I earned today, I could buy ten women for each day of the year, to do whatever I want. You can't really think I would stoop to kidnapping anybody, especially a relative of a man important to my business."

Hirata couldn't deny that Ogita had a point. But a man could become sexually obsessed with a particular woman who was beyond his reach, and none other would satisfy. "There's a witness to the effect that you did."

"Oh? Who?" Anger tightened Ogita's double chin.

Hirata explained about Jinshichi, Gombei, and the proprietor of the Drum Teahouse.

"Never heard of them," Ogita said. "But I'm not surprised that they've said bad things about me. People like to shoot arrows at the highest apples on the tree."

Hirata gazed at the contracts, disturbed because he'd hoped to bring Sano more than the expected denials from this suspect, and to make up for the fact that his men had lost the oxcart drivers.

"That's more money than you'll see in your lifetime," Ogita said crassly, mistaking Hirata's somber expression for envy. He lowered his voice. "I'm going to offer you a deal. You leave me out of your investigation, and I'll make it worth your while."

Hirata stared in disbelief. "Are you trying to bribe me?"

"Let's just call it a little private business arrangement." Ogita smiled.

Nobody had offered Hirata a bribe since his police days. His longtime reputation for incorruptibility, and Sano's, were well known. "Forget it," Hirata said. "You can't stop me from investigating you by paying me off."

"Suit yourself." Ogita's smile persisted, but turned as menacing as a mouth carved in an armor face guard. "If you don't like that deal, then how about this one?

"Three of Chamberlain Sano's biggest allies owe me a lot of money. If you cause me any trouble, I'll call in their debts. They'll be ruined financially, and I'll make sure they know you're to blame. Think about where that will leave Chamberlain Sano."

The allies would surely withdraw their support from Sano. They would also try to influence the shogun to throw him out of the regime, and they would look for another leader.

Who would that be but Yanagisawa?

If three major allies defected from Sano, the balance of power would tip in Yanagisawa's favor, which could give Yanagisawa the impetus to resume his campaign to destroy Sano. Hirata faced a serious dilemma.

"Well?" Ogita said.

In his mind Hirata heard Sano's voice: *I won't give in to blackmail. If I lose my allies and Yanagisawa makes his move, so be it. I'll take the risk for the sake of justice.* Hirata admired Sano for his principles, but his own principles were different in this case. As Sano's chief retainer, Hirata was duty-bound to protect Sano even if it meant going against his wishes. He couldn't allow Ogita to make good on his threat.

As he vacillated, another thought confused the issue: Maybe Ogita wasn't responsible for the kidnappings or rapes. If so, Hirata would have put his master in jeopardy for nothing.

Hirata never knew what he would have said. Just then, the menacing pulse of energy vibrated through the air, striking him dumb. His whole body snapped to sudden, fearful attention. As his nerves began that ominous tingling and his blood raced, he forgot Ogita. His enemy was close at hand. Ears pricked and nostrils flared to catch the man's scent, Hirata silently vowed that this time he would find his enemy; this time they would fight, and he would win.

The pulse emanated from the teahouse's back room. Drawing his sword, Hirata advanced toward the curtained doorway.

"What are you doing?" Ogita said, puzzled.

Detective Arai said, "Hirata-*san?*"

Ignoring them, Hirata yanked the curtain aside. Beyond the doorway was a spacious room for parties. Two maids were rolling fresh *tatami* mats onto the floor. The pulse drew Hirata to another doorway. Ogita and the detectives followed.

"Is something wrong?" Detective Inoue said.

Hirata shushed him with a gesture of his hand. He peeked through the second curtain and saw a large, dim storeroom. Sake barrels were stacked in rows. Three servants unloaded more barrels from a handcart. Hirata slowly put one foot after another into the room. Screeches and howls resounded from other dimensions that impinged on his mind.

A bright flare of energy erupted from behind a row of barrels. Hirata lunged around them toward the energy. The servants yelled in fright, running for cover. Ogita cried, "Have you gone mad?"

Hirata slashed his sword at the place where he thought his enemy was hiding. But there was no one. His sword cut through a sake barrel. Pungent liquor spilled. Sensing the presence behind him, Hirata whirled, charged, and slashed. His blade cleaved more barrels. The space between the rows was vacant.

"Don't just stand there," Ogita said to the detectives. "Stop him before he wrecks my place!"

The detectives grabbed Hirata, but he threw them off. He kept attacking empty air. He didn't know whether he imagined feeling the energy or his foe had projected it toward him, a trick that only the most expert martial artists could manage.

Now the presence seemed to move outside the teahouse. Hirata rushed through the back door, into a yard where fireproof storehouses with iron roofs stood. The daylight on their whitewashed walls struck his eyes. Blinded and reckless, he followed the pulsating energy down a path between the storehouses. At the end of the path, cornered by a bamboo fence, stood a dark figure holding a sword.

Anticipation and a thirst for blood raged within Hirata. He rushed forward and swung his sword with all his strength.

His blade cut flesh and bone. A scream of agony pierced his ears, drowned out the noise in his mind. The pulsation stopped. The blindness and rage cleared from his vision. Triumphant and panting, Hirata sheathed his sword and looked down at the man he'd killed.

Crumpled on the earth lay a peasant boy not more than thirteen years old. His body was cut clean through across the middle. Viscera and blood pooled around him and a broom he'd dropped. His babyish face was frozen in an expression of terror.

Ogita and the detectives ran up behind Hirata. As they all stared at the carnage, Ogita exclaimed, "You killed my servant!"

It hadn't been his enemy he'd cornered, Hirata realized too late. It had been an innocent bystander. The sword Hirata had thought he'd seen was only the broom the boy had been holding.

"No!" Hirata cried. He knelt by the boy, patted his cheeks, and rubbed his hands in a frantic effort to revive him. But it was no use; not even a mystic martial arts expert could bring the dead boy back to life.

Hirata felt the pulse of his foe's energy, fading into the distance, like a taunt.

"You won't get away with this," Ogita said, loud with fury. "Even if you are the shogun's investigator, you'll pay!"

The detectives pulled Hirata to his feet, away from the dead boy. Inoue said, "Come on, Hirata-*san*, we'd better go."

As they led him out of the yard, Hirata realized that his troubles had just gone from bad to much worse. And that was exactly what his enemy had intended.

30

Across the Ryōgoku Bridge from Edo proper, along the Sumida River, spread the city's largest entertainment district. Buildings on either side of a broad, open space housed plays, freak shows, music, wild animal exhibits, and every imaginable sort of diversion. Vendors sold noodles, dumplings, and sweets at food-stalls. Adults stood under eaves and awnings, waiting for the rain to stop, but youngsters roamed, heedless of the weather. Children who worked in the district ran about on errands. Sons and daughters of merchants mingled with beggar children and a few samurai youths in a circle around a man juggling umbrellas.

Masahiro, dressed in the garden boy's kimono and hat, blended right in with the other children.

He was excited because he'd never been here alone. He would have liked to visit the arrow-shooting booth, but instead he watched Yanagisawa and Yoritomo.

They stood near the storytellers' hall, a building plastered with signs that advertised the stories scheduled to be told today. The wall by the entrance was studded with pegs for hanging up the patrons' shoes. Families queued up outside, at a booth where a man sold admissions.

Masahiro was glad that Yanagisawa and Yoritomo had traveled on foot from Edo Castle; otherwise he wouldn't have been able to keep up with them. They were dressed as troops from their own army, but Masahiro had recognized them and stayed on their trail. That wasn't the problem.

The problem was Toda Ikkyu, who must be around somewhere. Masahiro didn't want to be caught again. He'd stayed far, far behind Yanagi-sawa and Yoritomo, trying to spot Toda, the better to avoid him. But Masahiro hadn't found Toda yet. And he had the strange feeling that even if he came face-to-face with Toda, he wouldn't recognize the man. He couldn't remember what Toda looked like.

Here came a palanquin. The bearers were the same ones Masahiro had seen bring the three ladies to the riverbank. Edging closer to Yanagi-sawa and Yoritomo, he waited eagerly to see what would happen.

Yanagisawa and Yoritomo watched the bearers set down the palanquin outside the storytellers' hall. Yanagisawa glanced at his son's rigid, morose face and said, "Cheer up. In a moment you'll be engaged."

"That's what I'm afraid of," Yoritomo said.

Lady Setsu stepped out of the palanquin. She was alone. Yanagisawa knew immediately that something was wrong. She pretended not to see him. She and one of her escorts walked to the booth outside the hall. He paid her admission. She disappeared inside the building.

"Stay here," Yanagisawa told Yoritomo. He hurried after Lady Setsu.

Masahiro tried to figure out what to do. He had to go hear what Yanagisawa and the old lady said to each other, but he might run smack into Toda. Then what?

A peasant family with five children gathered at the booth. Masahiro joined them, hoping he looked like he belonged with them. He fingered a coin in the pouch that hung from a string at his waist. Samurai weren't supposed to carry money—they considered it disgraceful—but after he'd been kidnapped two autumns ago, Masahiro had learned to be prepared for emergencies.

A man cut in front of the family. Masahiro was annoyed, but he didn't say anything; he didn't want to draw attention to himself. Neither did the family speak up. The man wore the kind of fancy hat and clothes that Masahiro had seen on rich merchants, and he acted like somebody important. As he handed over his money, his sleeve rode up his arm. He had a large, brown, irregularly shaped freckle on the top of his wrist.

Masahiro frowned. Where had he seen that freckle before? He sud-denly remembered. When Toda Ikkyu had grabbed him, while he'd struggled to break loose, he'd seen the mark on Toda's wrist. He'd forgotten about it . . . until now.

The man was Toda.

Inside the storytellers' hall, an old man on the stage recited the tale of the Battle of Sekigahara. He pantomimed mounted warriors swinging swords. He performed sound effects—the whinnying horses, the guns and cannons booming. The audience seated on the floor laughed and applauded.

Yanagisawa located Lady Setsu, knelt beside her, and asked, "Where is Lady Chocho? Where is Tsuruhime?"

Lady Setsu's face wore her usual sour, pained expression. The distortion on the right side was worse today, the muscles drawn tight. "They had other business."

Her excuse was unconvincing in the extreme. Yanagisawa said, "What other business could be more important than settling our future?"

A man sat down near Lady Setsu. He looked like a merchant. A peasant couple with six children came in and filled up the space beside Yanagisawa. It didn't matter if these nobodies overheard his conversation with Lady Setsu.

"Settling our future is what I have come to discuss with you," she said. "We need not involve Chocho or Tsuruhime."

Yanagisawa felt a portentous, sinking feeling in his stomach. "You've made your decision, then?"

"I have," Lady Setsu said. "I regret to inform you that we cannot accept your proposal."

Had the outcome been different, she'd have brought Lady Chocho and Tsuruhime, to negotiate the terms of the marriage and plan the wedding. Although she'd expressed doubts the last time they'd met, Yanagisawa was shocked nonetheless.

On the stage, the storyteller howled as he acted out the part of a fallen warrior stabbed through the heart.

Yanagisawa had always believed he could get whatever he wanted. Hadn't he risen from obscurity to become the shogun's second-in-command? Hadn't he survived defeat by Lord Matsudaira and exile to Hachijo Island, then returned as if from the dead? Now he felt as if he'd been climbing a mountain path and Lady Setsu had dropped a boulder from a cliff and blocked his way to the top.

The audience cheered, as if mocking his distress.

"Why not?" Yanagisawa demanded. "Why are you refusing?"

Lady Setsu looked down her dainty nose at his belligerence. "You know the reasons, even though you seem determined to ignore them. Chief among them is the fact that Tsuruhime is not free to enter upon this marriage. She is bound by a previous commitment, as you are certainly aware."

"That's a minor problem." Yanagisawa had to change Lady Setsu's mind. There was no use going to Lady Chocho. Lady Setsu had given him the impression that she and Lady Chocho had made the decision together, but of course they hadn't. She was in control. She was the one Yanagisawa needed to convince. "I can obtain a divorce for Tsuruhime."

Lady Setsu raised her left eyebrow in surprise at his audacity. Her right eyebrow was bunched in a spasm. "People will object."

"The fact that Tsuruhime is childless is a point in favor of a divorce. Would you like to wager that she'll be single by tomorrow?"

"I would wager that you would fly in the face of propriety and break every rule in order to have what you want." Offense wrinkled Lady Setsu's nose, as if she smelled something bad. "But you won't get away with it."

"Yes, I will." Yanagisawa would twist every arm necessary, call in every favor, move heaven and earth.

"Even if you do, a divorce won't remove all my misgivings," Lady Setsu retorted. "It won't change the fact that a marriage between Tsuruhime and Yoritomo would be tantamount to incest."

"Why? They're only distant relatives. People who are first cousins marry all the time."

"You know what I mean even if you pretend you don't," Lady Setsu said. "Considering who she is, and who he is——" Her emaciated body shuddered. "The more I think about it, the very idea of them together grows more repugnant."

Many might agree, but Yanagisawa said, "This is no time for squeamishness." He was losing his patience, his disappointment turning to anger. "All our lives are at stake. If we don't make this match, the troubles you'll have in the future will make incest seem like a blessing from the gods."

"'Squeamishness'? Is that what you call my objection to such a vile, sinful disgrace?" Lady Setsu matched his anger with her own. "I call it honor, respect for tradition, and common decency. All of which you are completely lacking. And that brings me to the last reason why I reject your proposal. I don't trust you to do right by Tsuruhime, Lady Chocho, or myself. You are not a man to uphold his end of the bargain, should it become inconvenient. You would just as soon throw us to the wolves."

She rose. "We have nothing more to say to each other. My decision is final."

On the stage, the storyteller described and pantomimed the rite in which triumphant soldiers paraded the severed heads of their enemies to their lord. The audience cheered. The children beside Yanagisawa laughed. As Lady Setsu walked out of the room, he felt a rage so cataclysmic he could barely restrain himself from drawing his sword, running after her, and cutting her down the middle of her thin, self-righteous back.

When he left the storytellers' hall, Yoritomo was waiting for him. "Father, what happened?"

How could he tell his son that his plans had come to nothing? How could he bear to let Yoritomo down? Hands clenched into fists, jaw tight, Yanagisawa stood helpless and frustrated as he watched Lady Setsu ride off in her palanquin.

"You'll be sorry you disappointed me," he said as she disappeared. "I swear on my life, you'll be sorry."

Masahiro followed Yanagisawa, Yoritomo, and Toda back to Edo Castle. He watched them walk in the gate, then waited until they were safely inside. What a relief they hadn't noticed him! But he dreaded going home. He would be punished for sure.

Hayashi, the soldier who'd been supposed to guard him, rushed out the castle gate, looking desperate. Although he was afraid of what would happen when Hayashi saw him, Masahiro took pity on the man.

"Hayashi-san," he called.

"Young master!" Hayashi staggered with relief. "I've been looking all over for you. Thank the gods you're safe!" He hustled Masahiro past the sentries, who nodded and waved them through the gate. As they hurried along the passages, he said, "Where on earth have you been?"

"The Ryōgoku entertainment district," Masahiro said.

"You went all the way there by yourself?" Hayashi looked stunned, then forlorn. "I've been going crazy looking all over the castle for you. When your father finds out that you escaped during my watch, he'll kill me!"

Hayashi wasn't the only one Father would kill. Masahiro wondered how long he had to live. "Does anyone else know I've been gone?"

"No. I wanted to see if I could find you by myself first." Hayashi had obviously hoped to stay out of trouble. "And your parents aren't home yet."

"Then let's not tell anybody what happened."

"All right," Hayashi said, wiping sweat off his forehead. "It'll be our secret. Pull that hat over your face. I'll sneak you into your father's estate." He added grimly, "I hope your little trip was worthwhile, because the next one will be over my dead body."

But it hadn't been worthwhile, Masahiro thought unhappily. Although he'd heard everything that Yanagisawa and the old lady had said, he hadn't understood what it meant.

Father and Mother were right.

He was too young to be a detective.

31

The temple run by Joju the exorcist was recently built, in a spacious compound within Zōjō Temple district. Sano, Marume, and Fukida walked through a gate whose red columns gleamed with fresh lacquer. Inside the compound, the lavishly carved and painted pagoda rose above grounds lush with flowering shrubs. Crowds of people from all classes streamed in and out of the huge main worship hall.

A servant directed Sano and the detectives to a minor worship hall secluded by a grove of pine trees. Two men who looked like wrestlers disguised as monks guarded the door. They bowed curtly to Sano and his men.

"We want to see Joju," said Fukida.

"His honorable holiness can't be disturbed at the moment. He's conducting an exorcism."

"This is the Honorable Chamberlain Sano, and he disturbs whomever he wants when he wants," Marume said.

The monks stood aside. Sano and his men removed their shoes and entered the hall, a large, cool chamber that smelled powerfully of sweet incense. It was dark except for a single lamp burning at the far end, illuminating a tall man. His saffron robe, his brocade stole, his naked arms, and his shaved head gleamed as if he were made of gold. He seemed to float rather than stand. His face was obscured by the shadows that filled the chamber, whose walls and ceiling were draped in black cloth, but Sano figured he must be Joju. Hands pressed together under his chin, fingers pointing upward, Joju gazed silently at the floor.

As Sano's eyes grew accustomed to the darkness, he saw other persons present.

One lay at Joju's feet. A second knelt nearby. They and the priest occupied a dais, elevated above the floor on which Sano and his men stood. Below the dais, huddled figures sat.

"Want me to stop the ritual?" Marume said quietly to Sano.

"No." Sano knelt behind the audience; his men followed suit. He was interested in what the ritual could tell him about the exorcist.

Joju addressed the figure that knelt by him. "What is your name?" His voice was hushed, but so deep and so resonant that it filled the chamber.

"Mankichi," the figure said in a voice that belonged to a man in his forties or fifties. "I'm a moneylender."

Fukida whispered, "That figures. You have to be rich to afford an exorcism performed by Joju."

Spirit possession was rampant all over Japan. People often attributed illnesses, mental problems, or bizarre behavior to evil spirits that had taken over their bodies. Exorcists enjoyed a flourishing trade, and Joju was in such demand that he could charge exorbitant prices for his rituals.

"Who is this you've brought me?" Joju asked.

"My wife," said the moneylender. "Her name is Onaru." The prone figure was a woman swaddled in a blanket. Her body squirmed like a caterpillar trying to break out of its cocoon. She whimpered and grunted. "She won't eat or sleep. She won't talk. She just makes those noises."

Onaru's head tossed from side to side. When it turned toward the lamp, Sano glimpsed her face. Her eyes were closed, her features sunken. From the audience came the muffled sound of a woman weeping and other people shushing her. They must be relatives of the couple.

"Do you think she's possessed?" the moneylender asked fearfully.

"Do you?" Fukida whispered to Marume.

"I guess we're going to find out," Marume whispered.

There had been a time when Sano had thought that most if not all people taken over by spirits were either faking or deluded. But then he'd gone to Ezogashima and witnessed an actual horrific case of possession that had changed his mind.

"We shall see," Joju said.

He knelt beside Onaru. His face came within the halo of brightness around the lamp's flame. He had features so perfect, so handsome, and so strongly masculine that he looked like an idealized vision of a man.

Sano knew that Joju was well over forty, but in the dim light he seemed ageless. His large, deep-set eyes glowed with wisdom and compassion.

Joju held his hands over the woman, palms down, just above her body. He moved them slowly up and down her length, not touching her. The air between his hands and the woman shimmered. The smell of incense grew stronger, the air thick with smoke. An eerie feeling rippled through Sano. His eyes, throat, and head began to ache. The detectives stirred uneasily. Onaru moaned as if in pain.

"I feel the presence of not one, not two, but three spirits inside her," Joju said.

The audience murmured in consternation. The moneylender said, "Please, can you make them go away?"

"I will try," Joju said.

"This should be good," Marume whispered to Fukida.

Closing his eyes, reaching toward the woman, Joju intoned, "Oh, spirits within Onaru, speak to me."

An orange light flashed to the right of the dais. The audience murmured. The light went out. Its afterimage burned into Sano's vision, trailing streamers of smoke. A blue light, then a red, flared in different parts of the room, then disappeared. A primitive fear crept into Sano. The audience sat in frozen silence.

"I hear them," Joju said. "Honorable spirits, tell me who you are." He listened. "They say they have no names. They are children who died before they were born."

Amazement stirred the audience, even though everyone knew Joju was famous for communicating with the spirits of dead fetuses.

"Children, how did you die?" There was a pause; Joju frowned as if much disturbed. "They were murdered."

Horrified exclamations arose.

"Children, who was your mother?" Joju said.

Onaru gasped and groaned. She sounded as if his outstretched hands were extracting some physical substance from her body. A weird, tuneless music began. Hairs rose on Sano's nape. Fukida nudged Marume, who muttered under his breath.

"I can't hear you. Could you speak more clearly?" As Joju concentrated, the muscles of his face strained. "I'm getting a name. It sounds like *ee, eh*——"

"Emiko!" the moneylender cried in a voice filled with horror.

Joju opened his eyes and asked, "Do you know this woman?"

"She was a maid in my house."

Sano supposed that Joju could have made a lucky guess, and the moneylender had supplied the name. Furthermore, these exorcisms were booked months in advance, long enough for Joju to investigate his clients. But Sano had once communicated with a spirit himself. He knew the dead did speak.

"The children say you are their father," Joju told the moneylender. "They say that after you planted each of them inside Emiko, you sent her to an abortionist. He cut the children out of her womb. They suffered terribly, and during the third abortion, Emiko died."

As the family members gasped, another orange light flared above the dais, accompanied by a soft explosion. In its brightness appeared an image of fetuses. Their eyes were covered by lotus leaves, their bodies severed at the waist and dripping blood. Women in the audience screamed. Fukida and Marume cursed out loud. Revulsion gripped Sano.

The light went out. The gory image disappeared.

"Is it true?" Joju asked the moneylender. "Did you impregnate Emiko, then have her and her children destroyed?"

"Yes," the moneylender said, sobbing with terror and guilt. "I confess. I didn't want a pregnant maid around; my wife would be jealous. I didn't want the children. I didn't know what else to do!"

His story was a variation on a common tale. People succumbed to lust, begetting unwanted babies; married couples had children they couldn't support; prostitutes were impregnated by their customers. As a result, many infants were killed before or soon after birth, and abortionists had proliferated in Edo. The government forbade abortionists to advertise their services on signs outside their shops, but didn't outlaw them. The number of abandoned, homeless orphans was a big problem. And although Sano deplored this widespread practice of killing children, he conceded that sometimes abortion was the best solution.

Some women were raped. Would Chiyo and Fumiko be among those to discover themselves pregnant afterward? Sano hoped they wouldn't have to bear their rapists' children and compound their suffering.

"The souls of your unborn children are caught between the realms of the living and the dead," Joju said. "They have entered your wife's body. She is so weakened by their sorrow and loneliness that she may die."

"No!" the moneylender cried. "I beg you to save her!"

Joju raised his hands and moved them as if palpating an invisible object in the air. Concern darkened his handsome features. "I feel the presence of another spirit."

A rush like wings in flight whooshed over the assembly. Onaru let out a bone-chilling wail. Her family screamed. Sano felt something soft graze his head. As everyone ducked and gazed fearfully around the room, only Joju remained calm.

"It is Emiko," he said. "She is here."

"Look!" cried a woman in the audience. "Her ghost!"

She pointed at the ceiling. There hovered a black, translucent shape that rippled like a veil in the wind.

"Merciful gods," Marume said.

The moneylender threw himself facedown on the dais, his head shielded by his arms, and moaned. Joju lifted his palms to the ghost. "Emiko-*san*, why have you come?"

A low, thunderous sound quaked the room. Women in the audience shrieked; men muttered. Onaru wailed and thrashed.

"She's angry with you," Joju explained to the moneylender. "She wants revenge for her and her children's suffering and death. She has punished you by sending the children to haunt your wife."

Weeping hysterically, the moneylender said, "Make her stop them! Make her go away!"

The thunderous sound rumbled louder. The ghost fluttered with a noise like a monsoon whistling. "I cannot," Joju said regretfully. "Only you can."

"But how?"

"You must repent for your sins. She demands a sacrifice."

"Tell me what it is! I'll do anything she wants!"

Thunder boomed. Joju listened, then said, "You must donate a hundred *koban* to this temple, in order that I may continue helping those in need."

Sano knew that all exorcisms ended like this. The spirits all wanted money, and since they couldn't spend it, the money went to the priest.

The moneylender grabbed a box that had been lying near him in the shadows, opened it, and dumped shiny gold coins in front of Joju. "Here!"

Joju ignored the coins even as they cast glittering reflections onto his face. He addressed the ghost: "You have your wish. Now call your children to come out of this innocent woman." He gestured to Onaru. "You are free to depart to the spirit world, where you belong."

A burst of white light engulfed the ghost. Red, orange, and blue lights flickered. Onaru howled and writhed like a woman giving birth. Screams from the audience drowned in thunder and explosions that rocked the temple. Joju stood, hands spread and face lifted to the heavens, chanting prayers. Acrid smoke billowed while the weird, dissonant music played and Sano, Marume, and Fukida watched in awe.

Then the lights went out; the sounds and music faded. The silence hushed the assembly. Joju announced, "Emiko and the children are gone."

From behind the black curtains stepped monks carrying round white lanterns. Everyone blinked in the sudden brightness. Smoke tinged the air. The moneylender sat up and looked at his wife. "Onaru?"

She lay still and peaceful on the litter on which she'd been brought. "Husband," she murmured.

"Take her home and let her rest," Joju said. "She'll be fine."

The moneylender and the family bowed to Joju. All smiles, they carried the dazed Onaru out of the room.

"Was that real?" Fukida asked.

"I don't know." Marume sounded shaken out of his usual cheer. "But if they're happy, I'm happy."

Sano rose and walked toward Joju, who stood on the dais, hands clasped at his chest. He didn't seem surprised to see Sano; he must have been aware of Sano's presence all along. Perhaps those deep, glowing eyes could see in the dark.

"Welcome, Honorable Chamberlain," Joju said. "Although we've never been formally introduced, I know you by sight."

He didn't look as ageless now. The shadow of black stubble on his head receded far back on his scalp. Lines in his golden skin bracketed his mouth and webbed the skin at the corners of his eyes. His muscles had begun to sag. He also seemed tired from his exertions; he was bathed in sweat. But he descended from the dais with the agility of a young man, and he had an allure that transcended his physical being. He wore holiness as he did his glittering stole. Which caused Sano to distrust him more than he would the usual suspect.

"That was quite a show you put on," Sano said.

Wry humor upturned the corner of Joju's mouth. "I'll take that as a compliment. The salvation of souls can be quite dramatic, as you've just seen."

"Especially with a little help from opium in the incense and a few theatrics?" Sano said. No such theatrics had accompanied the phenomena he'd witnessed in Ezogashima. Sano had more than a hunch that Joju was a charlatan.

Joju laughed, the sound startlingly boisterous. "I see that you like rational explanations. Supposing I did employ the kind of trickery that you accuse me of: Why not, if it drives out the spirits and restores people to sanity?"

"Point taken," Sano said, "but possession by spirits isn't the cause of every illness. It may be rarer than it seems."

"Indeed not. Spirits are all around us, always seeking innocent victims to haunt." Joju opened his arms wide. "We all have the power to communicate with the spirit world, but few of us know how to use it. I am one of the few. I have dedicated my life to freeing humanity from evil spirits and laying them to peaceful rest."

He spoke as if he believed what he said. Perhaps he truly did. "At a handsome profit," Sano commented.

Irritation glinted in the black wells of Joju's eyes. "Not for myself. For my temple. For the benefit of the faithful who come to worship. May I ask why you're here? Perhaps you are in need of my services?"

"As a matter of fact, I am," Sano said.

"Oh?" Joju said, smug because he thought he had the advantage over Sano. "Who is in trouble?"

"My cousin," Sano said. "Her name is Chiyo."

Joju didn't react to the name, but he was clearly a man in control of how he appeared. "What are her symptoms?"

"She has nightmares," Sano said. Reiko had told him that.

"Nightmares are often caused by spirit possession."

"Not in this case," Sano said. "My cousin was recently kidnapped and raped. So was a twelve-year-old girl named Fumiko. I need your help with finding the person who did it."

"I'm sorry, but I don't know what use I could be," Joju said. He hadn't reacted to the mention of the crimes, or seemed to recognize Fumiko's name. "I'm not a policeman."

"You can speak to the spirits. Maybe they can give me some information."

"The spirits speak to me about themselves and their wishes. I can't interrogate them about matters that don't concern them." Joju remained courteous, but impatience tinged his voice.

"Never mind the spirits, then," Sano said. "You can help me in another way."

"How is that?"

"You can tell me about your relations with two oxcart drivers named Jinshichi and Gombei."

Joju looked confused, perturbed. Sano thought he'd finally hit his target, but then Joju said, "They transport supplies for the temple. Are they responsible for the crimes you mentioned?"

"They're suspects." Sano wondered whether Joju's business with the drivers was as innocent as the priest claimed. If not, Joju might have denied knowing them. But he also might have realized that people had seen him with them and it was better not to lie. "Can you tell me where they are?"

"I'm afraid not. I haven't seen them in perhaps a month. If they turn up here, I'll be sure to let you know."

He walked toward the door, drawing Sano and the detectives with him, anxious for them to leave. Maybe Sano had hit him close to home after all.

"They're not the only suspects," Sano said. "Your name also came up in the course of my investigation."

"My name?" Joju's expression altered. Sano saw shock, and an emotion harder to interpret. "You can't believe that I kidnapped those two women."

"Three women," Sano said. "There was another—a nun from a convent near this very temple." Was that fear in Joju's eyes? "No, I don't believe you kidnapped them. I believe Jinshichi and Gombei did. They procure women for clients with special tastes. Are you one of those clients?"

"Of course not." Joju's expression shifted into outrage mingled with disdain. "When I became a priest, I vowed never to harm anyone. I also took a vow of celibacy."

"Vows can be broken."

"Not mine." Joju radiated sanctimoniousness. "The work I do requires me to be pure in mind, body, and soul. If I had committed those crimes, the spirits wouldn't speak to me."

Marume laughed. "That was one of the more original proofs of innocence we've ever been offered."

"It's not good enough. Let's see if you can come up with something based in this world." Sano asked the priest where he'd been during the periods when the women were missing.

"I can't recall exactly," Joju said, "but I was probably praying, conducting exorcisms, and fulfilling my other duties at the temple from sunrise to sundown."

"And after sundown?" Sano said.

"I sleep."

"Can anyone vouch for you?"

"The monks, the servants, and the other priests here. The people for whom I conducted exorcisms. I may have called on some government officials."

"I'll need a list of everyone," Sano said.

"I'll gladly provide it. I'll also provide you a list of good character references." Joju said with a sly smile, "The shogun will be at the top of that list. Are you aware that His Excellency is my patron?"

"I am." Sano knew the shogun was enthusiastic about religion in general and mysticism in particular. But now Sano realized that the shogun's patronage of Joju threatened to complicate his investigation.

The shogun was often more loyal to his favorite priests than to his top retainers. In a conflict between Sano and Joju, whose side would he take?

Joju uttered his boisterous laugh. "Then I needn't warn you to think before you persecute me."

32

Sano returned to Edo Castle after dark, when the night watch patrol guards roamed the passages with torches that smoldered and hissed in the moist evening air. Thunder murmured. As Sano and his entourage dismounted at his gate, Hirata rode up. One look at his friend's face warned Sano that things hadn't gone well for Hirata either.

In his office, Sano poured sake for himself and Hirata. "Any news?" Sano asked.

"My men and I spent the day looking for the oxcart drivers, but we haven't found them yet," Hirata said.

That was bad enough, but Sano could tell it wasn't the worst problem Hirata had to report. "What happened with Ogita?"

"He says he's not guilty. He has alibis." Hirata described his interview with the rice broker.

"We expected as much," Sano said. "Did you check those alibis?"

Hirata hesitated, then said, "No."

"Why not?" Sano asked, surprised.

"Ogita has three of your top allies deeply in debt to him. He said he would call in their debts unless I left him alone."

This was a serious threat with potentially dire political consequences, but Sano insisted, "I won't be stopped by blackmail."

"I knew you would say that," Hirata said, "but as your chief retainer, I must advise you to be careful with Ogita. Besides, maybe he's innocent. I propose that we concentrate on the other suspects first."

"That may be a problem, too," Sano said, and told Hirata about his encounters with the other suspects. "Nanbu is still barricaded inside the kennel with his dogs and refusing to talk. And unless I leave Joju alone, I could find myself in trouble with the shogun."

"That *is* a problem," Hirata agreed. "I must remind you that your ultimate duty is to the shogun, not your cousin or your uncle. Think of what His Excellency will do if you displease him."

Sano didn't have to think. The shogun had threatened him and his family with death often enough. "There must be a way to do right by the shogun and finish this investigation."

"Until we figure it out, we have three suspects we can't touch," Hirata said.

"I did do some discreet inquiries," Sano said. After a long day of meetings at the palace, he'd spent hours tracing Nanbu's and Joju's movements. "I didn't find any evidence to prove that Nanbu and Joju aren't the upstanding citizens they claim to be." Already exhausted, Sano sensed that the day's story of bad luck wasn't over yet. "Have you any more news?"

Hirata bowed his head. "The other day, while I was at Ueno Pond . . ."

He described how a mysterious stranger had begun stalking him, had later invaded his estate, and had shown up while he'd been interviewing Ogita. As he confessed that he'd killed Ogita's servant, Sano listened in dismay, and not only because of the innocent life destroyed.

"Whoever's stalking you, he has the power to manipulate people against their will, to make them do things they ordinarily wouldn't," Sano said. "You're in extreme danger."

"That doesn't make up for what I did." Hirata's stoic expression didn't hide his misery. "And I can't promise that it won't happen again." He said reluctantly, "I must ask you to take me off the investigation."

As much as Sano hated to lose Hirata's help—or to see him suffering because he couldn't fulfill his duty to his master—he knew Hirata was right. "Very well." And he must take additional steps to protect Hirata and the public. "I'm also relieving you of your other investigations and duties until you've found out who's after you and dealt with the situation. Your detectives can handle your work. If the shogun asks about you, I'll tell him you're ill."

Hirata looked stricken, but he bowed in agreement. "May I be excused?"

Sano nodded.

After Hirata had left, Sano went to look for his family. Perhaps Reiko had news of Chiyo. Perhaps the children could cheer Sano up. He found Akiko asleep in bed, but Masahiro was lying on his stomach in the parlor and drawing pictures.

"Is that a cow?" Sano asked.

"No, Father, it's a cat!" Masahiro said. "Can't you tell?"

"Yes, I was just joking," Sano said. "It's a better cat than I could ever draw. What else have you been doing today?"

As Masahiro chattered about his schoolwork, Sano's mind wandered to the investigation. Then Masahiro said, "Father, what's divorce?"

"That's when a husband and wife stop being married," Sano said absently.

"What's incest?"

Sano's attention snapped back to his son. "Where did you hear that word?"

"Oh, I don't know, someplace." Masahiro scribbled on his drawing pad.

"Well, you'd better ask your mother," Sano said, not eager to tackle sensitive subjects.

"She's not home."

"Where is she?"

"She went to visit Cousin Chiyo this morning. She said she would be spending the night."

Sano heard thunder, went to the door, and opened it. He and Masahiro looked at the rain streaming off the eaves. "Well, at least she won't get caught in this weather."

White veins of lightning split the sky above the Kumazawa estate. Rain deluged the mansion. Thunder boomed. The sentries outside the gate stood beneath its roof, while patrol guards inside the grounds sheltered under the mansion's eaves. They didn't notice the man atop the back wall. The lightning illuminated his crouched figure for an instant before the sky went dark and the thunder reverberated. When the lightning flared again, he was gone. The next thunderclap masked the noise he made when he landed on the ground inside the wall.

* * *

In the women's quarters, Reiko played cards with Chiyo and Fumiko. The chamber was stuffy, the doors that led to the garden closed because of the storm. As Reiko dealt the cards, she listened to the rain clatter on the roof tiles. Lightning flickered through the paper window-panes; thunder cracked.

Although pale and anxious, Chiyo made an effort to smile at Reiko. "I'm glad you're here."

"So am I," Reiko said, smiling back.

Fumiko wasn't much for conversation. Intent on the game, she snatched up the cards Reiko dealt her. The women laid out, matched, and picked up cards illustrated with cherry trees, cranes standing beneath red suns, and other suits. Reiko noticed that Fumiko won every round. She began to watch the girl and spied her slipping cards in and out of her sleeves. Fumiko was cheating! She must have learned how from the gangsters. Reiko decided against reprimanding her. Let the poor girl have some fun. And if Chiyo noticed, she didn't seem to mind. There were issues more serious than cheating at cards.

Reiko had a specific one on her mind. All day she'd wondered how to broach the delicate subject to Chiyo and Fumiko, but it couldn't be avoided any longer. "There's something I must tell you," she began. "The nun who was kidnapped . . . she had . . . a disease."

"Oh?" Chiyo said, mildly curious. "What kind of disease?"

"On her . . ." Reiko glanced down, at her lap. "It came from the man who kidnapped her."

Stricken by horrified comprehension, at first Chiyo didn't speak. She looked at Fumiko, who was matching cards and seemed not to be listening. Then she said, "Fumiko is clean. I saw her when we bathed. But I—"

"Do you . . . ?" Reiko couldn't bring herself to ask Chiyo outright if she had symptoms.

"No," Chiyo whispered. "But . . ."

But it was too soon to know whether the rapist had given her the disease or not. Reiko said, "If you find anything wrong, you must see a physician."

"All right," Chiyo said unhappily.

Her duty done, Reiko rubbed her eyes, which were bleary with fatigue. Some two hours ago, the temple bells in Asakusa had rung at midnight. Everybody else in the house had gone to bed.

"If you're tired, you needn't stay up," Chiyo said.

"No, I'm fine," Reiko said. Chiyo had confided that she and Fumiko stayed up late because of their nightmares, and Reiko felt a desire as well as an obligation to keep them company.

As she dealt the cards again, Reiko felt a warm, damp draft on the back of her neck. The flame in the lantern wavered. The sound and smell of the rain filled the room. Fumiko, who sat opposite her, dropped the cards she held. Fumiko gazed past Reiko, her eyes wide with terror.

Reiko turned. A man stood inside the open door, his black garments streaming water from the rain. He wore a hood that covered his entire head, with holes cut out for his eyes and mouth. Raising a sword in both hands, he lunged across the room toward Reiko and her friends.

Chiyo screamed.

Fumiko jumped up to run, but tripped on her hem and fell.

Reiko snatched up her dagger, which lay in its sheath on the floor beside her. She usually wore it strapped to her arm under her sleeve when she left home, but she'd thought she would be safe here. The man rushed at Chiyo. She raised her hands to protect herself, and his sword came swinging downward at her. Reiko whipped out her dagger and slashed at the man. Even as he faltered and turned his weapon on Reiko, her blade cut him across his belly.

He uttered an awful yowl. He dropped his sword, sank to his knees, and bent over the wound. Blood mixed with rainwater spilled onto the floor.

Fumiko huddled nearby, hands over her mouth, staring at him. Chiyo called, "Help, help!"

The intruder glared at Reiko through the holes in his hood, his eyes blazing with hatred and anger. He groped for his weapon, but toppled sideways. The emotion faded from his eyes as he collapsed amid playing cards stained red by his blood.

Reiko heard men shouting and running in the corridors and outside the house. Then Major Kumazawa and his guards were in the room. Major Kumazawa wore a night robe; his feet were bare. He carried a sword, which he pointed at the dead man.

"What happened?" he demanded. "Who is this?"

Reiko couldn't answer. She was suddenly dizzy, gasping for breath. She had a frightening sense that time had folded back on itself and she was reliving an earlier attack, during which her children had almost been murdered.

Fumiko pointed to the mask that the corpse wore. "It's the man who kidnapped us!" she shrilled. "He came back to get us, just like he said he would!"

33

Sano roused groggily from a sound sleep. Into his dark chamber spilled light from a lantern held by Detective Fukida, who stood in the doorway. "I'm sorry to bother you," Fukida said, "but there's an urgent message from Lady Reiko."

Instantly wide awake, Sano said, "What?" He bolted upright in bed. "Is she all right?"

"Yes," Fukida said, "but there's been an attack at the Kumazawa house. She asks you to come at once."

Sano threw on some clothes. Heading for the door, he met Masahiro, rubbing his sleepy eyes, in the hall. "Where are you going, Father?"

"To fetch your mother," Sano said. "Don't worry, she's fine. Go back to bed. We'll be home soon."

He rode through the dark, slumbering city with Marume and Fukida and some troops. The neighborhood gates had long been closed for the night, but Sano and his men wore the Tokugawa crest, and the watchmen let them pass. After a hard ride along the highway, they reached the Kumazawa estate.

It was lit up like a house on fire. Flames burned in metal lanterns along the wall and at the gate; more lights flickered from within the courtyard. Smoke melted into the misty night. The guards let Sano's party through the gate. As they dismounted in the courtyard, Reiko came running out of the mansion. Dressed in a night robe, she was agitated and disheveled, her face bare of makeup, her long hair carelessly braided. But she was indeed alive and well, to Sano's relief.

"What happened?" Sano said.

As Reiko told him about the attack, he listened in horror that didn't ease much when she told him she'd killed the man. Killing was a traumatic experience. Reiko must have been terrified, and she hadn't been the only one in danger.

"Where is Chiyo?" Sano said. "And Fumiko?"

Out of breath from excitement and speaking too fast, Reiko gestured toward the house. Chiyo and Fumiko stepped out onto the veranda. They looked shaken but unharmed. Major Kumazawa appeared behind them, fully dressed in his armor tunic, his swords at his waist, as if ready for battle.

"My daughter and her guest weren't touched," he said. "But they would have been killed if not for your wife."

His tone conveyed some admiration and gratitude toward Reiko but more fury at the attack on his household. "The man climbed over the wall. We found the rope he used. He got past my guards—he killed two of them. He must have been a professional assassin."

"Where is the assassin now?"

"In the backyard," Major Kumazawa said. "Your wife insisted on keeping his body until you arrived."

Sano cast a thankful glance at Reiko. She smiled briefly through her distress. He was proud of her for having the presence of mind to save the evidence.

"Come," Major Kumazawa said, lifting a lantern off a stand and walking down the steps. "I'll show you."

He led Sano around the mansion, across the garden, and through a gate. The detectives accompanied Sano and Major Kumazawa past the kitchen building, to a small, fenced yard. Major Kumazawa's lantern illuminated wooden bins that reeked of rotten fish, and a blanket-covered shape that lay on the ground. Fukida drew back the blanket. Underneath lay a youngish man with the shaved crown of a samurai, a wiry build, and an oval face with long, thick lashes that fringed his closed eyes. His gray kimono and trousers were drenched with blood from the wound Reiko had inflicted on his belly. The clothes had no identifying crests on them. The man was a stranger to Sano.

"Do you know him?" Sano asked Major Kumazawa.

"Never seen him before. Neither have my daughter or your wife, so they say. At first the girl thought he was the kidnapper, but she was fooled by the mask. It must be like the one the kidnapper wore. When she saw his face, she changed her mind and said she didn't recognize him after all."

Marume and Fukida shook their heads; they didn't know the assassin, either. Fukida covered the corpse.

"Do you know of anyone who would want to hurt your family?" Sano said.

"No one with enough nerve to break into my house."

"We need to find out who he is." Concern filled Sano because he was starting to get an idea about the reason behind the attack.

"It'll be day soon," Fukida said. "Do you want us to take his body around the neighborhood and see if anyone recognizes him?"

"Have some of my troops do it," Sano said. It was hardly standard procedure, but there seemed no other way to identify the dead man. Sano hoped it would work better than his experiment at Edo Jail. Envisioning the gory corpse paraded through the streets, he added, "Tell them to keep the body covered and just show the face."

The detectives went off to obey. Sano and Major Kumazawa walked back toward the mansion.

"It's no coincidence that this happened after you started your investigation." Major Kumazawa spoke as if stating a distasteful fact.

"No. I don't believe it is, either." Sano experienced a bad, familiar feeling. Once again, he hadn't solved a case soon enough. "I think the assassin came to kill Chiyo so that she could never identify the man who raped her."

"Do you think he did it?" Incredulity vied with hope in Major Kumazawa's voice.

Sano knew why Major Kumazawa wasn't ready to accept the idea. The dead assassin seemed so ordinary, not an evil monster. And Sano had other reason to doubt that the man had acted alone, on his own behalf. "No. I think he was sent by the guilty party."

"Those oxcart drivers?" Major Kumazawa turned to Sano, his disbelief clear in the light from the brightening sky.

"Not them," Sano said. "While I was looking for them, I found three new suspects."

He told Major Kumazawa about the kennel manager, the rice broker, and the exorcist. Surprise halted Major Kumazawa in the courtyard. "This happened when?"

"Their names came up yesterday," Sano said.

"And you didn't tell me?" Vexed, Major Kumazawa said, "I expected you to keep me informed about your progress."

"I'm informing you now." Although Sano could understand that Major Kumazawa didn't like being kept in the dark, he'd wanted to prevent his uncle from confronting the suspects himself and causing trouble again.

"Nanbu, Ogita, and Joju." As Major Kumazawa turned their names over on his tongue, he looked stunned to think they could have stooped to kidnapping and rape. Then he nodded, aware that even three such important men could have perverted tastes and no scruples. "If one of them wanted my daughter and hired those oxcart drivers to kidnap her—if one of them sent the assassin to kill her—how can I get my revenge?"

Despair pervaded his stern manner. "If I should go after Nanbu, I'll have to kill his dogs. I'm in debt to Ogita. He could make my clan paupers. And Joju is the shogun's protégé." He said bitterly, "I can't touch them any more than you can. I don't care what happens to me, but I can't let my family suffer."

Sano had been in the same position, blocked because his family would share whatever punishment he incurred, too many times to count. But he said, "Let's not give up. Whichever man is guilty—and I'm sure one or more of them is—he shouldn't be allowed to get away with it."

"Shouldn't, but will." Major Kumazawa faced Sano with determination. "Because the investigation stops now."

People had tried to stop his investigations before, but Sano shook his head. "You don't have the authority to call off my investigation."

"Yes, I do," Major Kumazawa said. "I requested your help. Now I'm withdrawing my request."

"You can't just dismiss me as if I were an unsatisfactory servant," Sano said. "I'll continue the investigation until the criminal is brought to justice."

"Even if he sends another assassin who succeeds where this one failed? Even if it means my daughter could die?"

"Another woman has already died. The nun," Sano reminded his uncle. "She deserves justice."

"What in hell do I care about her?"

"And as long as the rapist and the kidnappers are at large, other women are in danger," Sano said.

"I don't care about them, either," Major Kumazawa insisted. "You must stop your investigation."

Under different circumstances, Sano would have respected the wishes of the head of his mother's clan. "I'll continue with or without your blessing," Sano said coldly. "You might recall that my wife was attacked, too. This is personal for me now."

Major Kumazawa stared. Sano saw satisfaction as well as enmity in his eyes. "The longer I know you, the more I realize that you are like your mother. You are just as willful and stubborn as she ever was. Well, that's your choice. But when you choose your actions, you have to take the consequences."

More enraged by the insult to his mother than to himself, Sano retorted, "Willfulness and stubbornness appear to run in the family. It's obvious that my mother and I aren't the only ones who share those traits."

Then he forgot what he was saying, because Major Kumazawa's last sentence had struck a chord in his memory. His anger entwined with the same sense of familiarity that he'd felt during his first visit to this house. In his mind Sano saw Major Kumazawa and his wife standing on their veranda; he heard the woman's voice pleading; he felt the same, dizzy sickness as he had then. Now the vague impressions solidified into a memory of stunning clarity.

"I heard you say that to my mother," he said.

Startled, Major Kumazawa said, "What?"

Recollection flooded Sano, as if a door that sealed off his past had suddenly opened. "I was here. My mother brought me. I must have been four or five years old." Now he knew why she'd defied the ban on contact with her family. "I was sick with a fever. She was afraid I would die." Sano remembered lying in bed, wracked by chills, struggling to breathe. Across the years he heard his mother crying and his father saying they couldn't afford a doctor or medicine. "So she brought me here, to ask for your help."

"You remember?" Major Kumazawa frowned in dismay.

"Yes. I also remember that you said she deserved for me to suffer. You said, 'When you choose your actions, you have to take the consequences.'" Sano's anger burned hotter. "Then you turned us away."

Major Kumazawa wore the expression of a man who'd believed he'd put out a fire and discovered that it had been smoldering underground when it blew up in his face. "I thought you'd forgotten."

"I'm sure you wish I had," Sano said.

He watched Major Kumazawa realize that the incident constituted more than a just punishment of a cast-out relative and her child. Although it had happened in the distant past, it could be interpreted as striking a blow against Sano the chamberlain, the shogun's second-in-command, and the punishment for that was whatever Sano chose.

"I've always regretted what I did," Major Kumazawa said. "I should have helped Etsuko. You were an innocent child; you didn't deserve to suffer. I apologize."

"It's a little late for that," Sano said.

"I only did what was right at the time," Major Kumazawa said, fearful yet insistent. "My parents were still alive. They forbade me to do anything for Etsuko. I had to respect their wishes."

Sano regarded Major Kumazawa with contempt. "Your tendency to justify yourself by blaming other people has made your apology a sham. It's a trait that's even worse than willfulness or stubbornness. So is your belief that you're entitled to things that you won't give to other people. When my mother asked you to save her child, you refused. But when your daughter was kidnapped and you came to me for help, I agreed."

Sano would have been sorry he had, if not for Chiyo, who was as blameless as his own childhood self had been.

"So you're a better man than I am." Major Kumazawa's resentful tone belied the compliment. "Well, if you'd rather not trouble yourself on my behalf or that of my family any longer, then stop your investigation."

"I can't do that," Sano said. "I've already explained why."

The hostility between them solidified, thick as the humid dawn air, as hot and suffocating as smoke. Major Kumazawa said, "Since we'll never see eye to eye, there's no use talking anymore. Be sure to take your wife with you when you go."

The dismissal stung Sano even though he was eager to leave this place and never come back. As he walked toward the house to fetch Reiko, he heard Major Kumazawa call after him, "I should never have broken the ban against contact with Etsuko and her kin. I'll uphold it from now on."

"That suits me just fine," Sano said.

34

The dawn sky glowed iridescent pink and silver, like an abalone shell's lining, as Sano rode alongside Reiko's palanquin down the highway toward Edo. The detectives led the way; Sano's troops guarded the rear of the procession. Sano and his party passed pilgrims walking toward them, bound for the Asakusa Temple district; they followed Tokugawa troops on patrol, nuns and priests headed into the city to beg alms, and porters hauling goods to market. *Eta* trundled nightsoil bins into the fields beside the road, using the city's copious supply of human wastes to fertilize the rice crop. Amid the stench, flies swarmed and buzzed.

Reiko spoke through her window to Sano. "So your relations with the Kumazawa have been severed again." He'd just told her about his conversation with his uncle. "Is there any chance of a reconciliation?"

"Not that I can see. Maybe it's for the best."

Reiko studied her husband's profile as he sat in the saddle and his horse plodded along beside her. His expression was hard. But she knew Sano had hoped to build a relationship with the unknown side of his family, and to reunite his mother with her estranged kin. He must be very disappointed. So was Reiko.

"But you will continue the investigation, won't you?"

"Of course," Sano said, although he sounded less than enthusiastic. "I've made progress." He told Reiko about the three suspects.

Reiko felt alarm creep under her skin. Sano's position in the regime had been secure for a while, but wouldn't be for much longer if he clashed with Nanbu, Ogita, or Joju. Although she feared for her family, she said, "I'll do whatever I can to help."

Sano smiled, appreciative. "There's not much you can do for the investigation now, though."

"Is Hirata-*san* still looking for the oxcart drivers?" Reiko asked.

"His men are," Sano said. "Hirata has run into some trouble."

As he explained, Reiko's alarm increased. Sano said, "We'll catch Jinshichi and Gombei eventually. Maybe they'll incriminate Nanbu, Ogita, and Joju, and I'll have enough evidence to take the three of them down without going down myself." He paused. "In the meantime, you must stay away from the Kumazawa estate. It's not safe there, and you wouldn't be welcome anyway."

Reiko knew the estrangement from the Kumazawa clan included her, too. "But Chiyo and I have become good friends. And Fumiko is there. I need to protect them."

"You're not responsible for that. I'll send some troops to help guard the estate."

Reiko sighed. Although she'd often disobeyed Sano, she had to respect his wishes in this instance. She must put aside her friendship with Chiyo and Fumiko until he and Major Kumazawa made up.

If they ever did.

Her bearers' slow pace made the trip back to the city long and tedious. The journey was lengthened by traffic on the highway, backups at the checkpoints, and crowds in town. By the time the procession reached Edo Castle, it was almost noon. Reiko yawned. She was glad to get home, ready for some peace and quiet.

One of the gate sentries said, "Honorable Chamberlain, the shogun has left a message for you. He wants to see you at the palace right now."

Adrift in a dimension between sleep and wakefulness, she opened her eyes upon a vast panorama of clouds. She floated among them, buoyed by their gray, billowing mass. With every breath she exhaled, they rippled. They shrouded her in clammy moisture. At first she drowsed peacefully, thinking it was a pleasant dream. Then the clouds began to swirl.

They were sucking her into their center. Vertigo dizzied and nauseated her. There was no sense of direction, no landmark to tell her which way heaven and earth were. She felt as if she were falling downward into a whirlpool and upward into a tornado at the same time. Gripped by fear, she blinked hard in an attempt to stop the dream. But the clouds were still there, too dense for her vision to penetrate. She tried to sit up and awaken herself. The clouds swirled faster.

This was no dream.

It was real.

Fright turned to panic. Even as she wafted amid the clouds like a feather in a hurricane, spinning in their vortex, she had a sensation of weight as heavy as stone. She couldn't move. She couldn't see her body, couldn't feel her arms or legs. Her mind and senses seemed cut loose from herself. She cried out for help, but the clouds absorbed her voice. Her heart pounded wildly and her lungs heaved somewhere far away. Her panic evolved into terror.

What was happening to her?

Would she survive, or die?

Even as she feared death, she felt a horrific premonition that something worse was to be her fate.

After leaving Reiko at home, Sano went with Detectives Marume and Fukida to the palace. There, officials stood in clusters about the grounds, their expressions somber.

"I smell trouble," Marume said.

So did Sano. Troops hurried about aimlessly, stopping to talk to one another. Idle servants hovered in the background, as if they wanted to know what was going on but were afraid to ask. The shogun flitted back and forth outside the main entrance, attendants trailing him anxiously. When he saw Sano, he cried, "Ahh! Thank the gods you've come at last!"

"What's happened, Your Excellency?" Sano said.

Out of breath from the unaccustomed exercise, the shogun clutched his chest, doubled over, and panted. His attendants seated him on the steps. He choked out, "My wife has disappeared!"

Sano exchanged surprised glances with his detectives. Lady Nobuko, the shogun's wife, left the castle even more rarely than the shogun did. Her bad health kept her confined to the women's quarters. Sano said, "She can't have gone far. Isn't anybody looking for her?"

The shogun gasped and wheezed. "I'm, ahh, going to faint!"

His attendants pushed his head between his knees. Yanagisawa and Yoritomo strode out of the castle together. When Yoritomo saw Sano, animosity hardened his expression. Yanagisawa looked grave.

"Lady Nobuko didn't disappear from the castle," Yanagisawa explained. "It happened at Chomei Temple in Mukojima district. She went there this morning, to drink from the Spring of Long Life and pray for good health."

Sano experienced a stab of shock tinged with foreboding. "How exactly did it happen?"

"There was a crowd at the shrine," Yanagisawa said. "Lady Nobuko got separated from her attendants. They looked for her, but they couldn't find her. One of her guards just came back to the castle and reported her missing."

Another woman gone missing at a religious site. "Was there any sign of foul play?"

Yanagisawa gave him a look that said he knew Sano feared that Lady Nobuko had been kidnapped. "None that we know of yet. We haven't had time to investigate."

That Lady Nobuko had been kidnapped wasn't Sano's only fear. Maybe she'd been kidnapped by the same man who'd raped Chiyo, Fumiko, and Tengu-in. If so, then his failure to catch the rapist by now had put a fourth woman in peril.

A fourth woman who happened to be the shogun's wife.

"How can this be happening to me?" the shogun lamented. He cared little about his wife—theirs was a marriage of political and economic convenience—but he took every misfortune personally. He raised his head and glared at Sano. "You're my chief detective." In his addled state he'd forgotten that Sano no longer was. "Don't just stand there like an idiot." He flapped his hand. "Rescue my wife!"

And the gods help Sano if the shogun should realize that his investigation had a connection with her disappearance. Once Sano would have expected Yanagisawa to rush to tell the shogun. But Yanagisawa shook his head, silently indicating that he would keep Sano's business a secret.

It was Yoritomo who blurted, "Your Excellency, you shouldn't put Sano-*san* in charge of rescuing the honorable Lady Nobuko. It's his fault she's missing!"

Yanagisawa said, "Yoritomo! Be quiet!" His face mirrored the dismay that Sano felt.

"What? How can that be?" the shogun said, confused. "No, keep talking, Yoritomo-*san*. I want to hear."

Sano was forced to listen while Yoritomo spilled the whole story of the three women kidnapped and raped, Sano's futile attempt to have Chiyo and Fumiko identify the two suspects at Edo Jail, and the missing oxcart drivers. He must have been keeping track of the investigation. Yanagisawa's face was set in an expression of disapproval toward his son. The shogun frowned, trying to understand the story. Officials and troops moved closer to hear, like sharks scenting blood in the water.

"Chamberlain Sano let the kidnappers go." Yoritomo addressed the shogun but looked straight at Sano. "It's his fault that they're at large." Yoritomo's dark, luminous eyes glittered with hatred. He looked disturbingly like his father had in the past, when Yanagisawa had spoken against Sano at every opportunity. "Therefore, Chamberlain Sano is to blame for whatever happens to Lady Nobuko."

"That's enough, son," Yanagisawa said grimly. "Leave us."

Yoritomo walked away, but the damage was done. He cast a triumphant glance over his shoulder at Sano.

"Your Excellency, please allow me to explain," Sano began, wondering how in the world to defend himself when he was guilty of everything Yoritomo had said.

The shogun gazed after Yoritomo in openmouthed shock, then turned on Sano. "How could you do this to me? After all I've done for you!" He struck Sano's chest with his soft, weak hand. "Find Lady Nobuko, and bring her home safe and sound, or I'll put you and your family and all your close associates to death!"

Here was the threat that he'd used against Sano many times in the past, the threat that Sano most feared. Sano felt a familiar, terrible sinking sensation.

"I've, ahh, told you that before," the shogun said, "but this time I mean it." He jabbed his finger at Sano. "Fail, and you all die!"

"I'll find her. I promise." Sano thought of Reiko, Masahiro, Akiko, and all the people whose lives depended on him. In the past, he'd always managed to solve his cases and avert the threat. Could he this time?

"If I may put in a word, Your Excellency," Yanagisawa said, "but this isn't Chamberlain Sano's fault. The real culprit is the person who kidnapped Lady Nobuko—if indeed she was kidnapped, which we don't yet know for sure."

Even in the midst of his distress, Sano noted the irony that Yanagi-sawa was defending him after so many attempts to ruin him. He had to appreciate Yanagisawa's efforts whether he trusted Yanagisawa or not.

"You're right, it's not entirely Chamberlain Sano's fault," the shogun said. "If you had been, ahh, doing your job all these years, there wouldn't be evil criminals around to attack my family." He jabbed his finger at Yanagisawa. "It's your fault, too!"

It was Yanagisawa's turn to look dismayed, and Sano's turn to defend his former enemy. "Your Excellency, with all due respect, Chamberlain Yanagisawa had nothing to do with what happened to your wife."

"I just said he does. That means he did!" The shogun had never been known for rationality, but his word was the law. His tearful glare fixed on Yanagisawa, his old friend and onetime lover. "You let me down. You and Chamberlain Sano must find my wife, or you'll share his punishment!"

He turned and flounced into the castle. His attendants traipsed be-hind him cautiously, afraid of his temper. The troops and officials de-parted as fast as ants scurrying into their hills. Sano, his detectives, and Yanagisawa looked at each other in mutual, dumbfounded apprehension.

"Well," Sano said to Yanagisawa, "hadn't we better get started?"

35

Two armies of samurai on horseback descended on Chomei Temple, from which Lady Nobuko had disappeared. Sano led one army, Yanagisawa the other. They and their troops stopped and questioned people, searched the temple grounds and the surrounding Mukojima district. The afternoon passed; night fell. Carrying torches, the armies fanned out in widening spirals around the temple. They went from door to door, questioning the residents, inspecting the houses. Not until dawn did Sano and Yanagisawa return to Edo Castle.

"Where is she?" the shogun demanded as they walked into his chamber. "Have you found her yet?"

"I'm sorry, Your Excellency, but we haven't," Sano said.

Lady Nobuko seemed to have vanished off the face of the earth.

The shogun pouted as he picked at his breakfast of steamed buns, noodles with prawns, and sweet cakes. Sano's stomach growled. He hadn't eaten since last night.

"Then go out and look some more," the shogun said. "Find her before sunrise tomorrow, or I'll have both your heads."

"Yes, Your Excellency," Yanagisawa said.

He looked as weary and discouraged as Sano felt. As they walked down the palace corridor, he said, "If this case is like your others, then we won't have to keep up the search much longer. With luck, the kidnapper will dump Lady Nobuko near the shrine in time for us to meet our deadline."

"That's not good enough, and you know it," Sano said, testy from fatigue. "The shogun wants her back safe and sound, not drugged and violated."

"Too bad for us." Yanagisawa added, "I didn't put Yoritomo up to telling the shogun about the connection between your investigation and Lady Nobuko's disappearance. It was his idea again. I'm even sorrier than I was last time."

"Do you believe him?" Hirata asked Sano.

They and Marume and Fukida sat in the private chambers at Sano's estate, where Sano had stopped for a quick meal. Hirata had heard about what had happened and was eager for news.

"Yes and no," Sano said. Reiko poured tea for him and the detectives, then served rice gruel with pickles and fish. Marume and Fukida, who'd been working alongside Sano all night, gobbled the food. Too hungry and in too much of a hurry to mind his manners, Sano ate while he talked. "I believe Yanagisawa is sorry for what Yoritomo said. After all, it got him in trouble, too."

"But?" Reiko said as Sano paused to swallow.

"But Yanagisawa has been behind so many plots against me that I'm not convinced he's innocent this time."

"Neither am I," Reiko said. She looked through the open partition that divided the room from the adjacent one and called, "Masahiro, don't you have a lesson now? Go!"

Sano saw their son in the other room, fiddling with his toy soldiers, and pretending not to listen to their conversation. Masahiro said, "Yes, Mother," and obediently left.

"Do you trust Yanagisawa to help you look for Lady Nobuko?" Reiko asked.

"Yes and no," Sano said. "It's in his own interests to find her, but I still think he's up to something. That's why I have to take other action besides our searching the city together."

"What kind of action?" Hirata asked.

Sano could see how much Hirata wanted to participate in it, but they both knew he shouldn't. Reiko poured Hirata a bowl of tea, all she could offer in the way of sympathy that wouldn't hurt his pride.

"Action against three people who thought they were safe from me," Sano said.

* * *

Ogita lived in a modest neighborhood in Kuramae, near his rice brokerage. The two-story houses were respectable rather than elegant, uniformly constructed with brown tile roofs, balconies shaded by bamboo screens, and weathered plank fences. When Sano and his entourage arrived at Ogita's house, Ogita and his samurai bodyguards planted themselves in front of the gate.

"Hello, Honorable Chamberlain," Ogita said. "How may I be of service to you?"

Sano had met Ogita at audiences with the shogun's officials, but they'd never exchanged more than formal greetings. Today he noticed that Ogita wore expressions like layers of clothing. The pleasure on Ogita's fleshy face overlaid apprehension.

"I want to search your house," Sano said. "Stand aside."

The apprehension rose to the surface of Ogita's features like silt in a stream stirred by undercurrents. "May I ask why?"

"I'm looking for the shogun's wife," Sano said. "She's missing, as you may have heard."

"Indeed I have." Now offense hid whatever else Ogita may have felt. "First you think I kidnapped and raped your cousin. Now you think I have the shogun's wife locked up in my house."

"Do you?"

"I'd have to be insane to do such a thing."

"Then you won't mind if I see for myself," Sano said.

Ogita stood his ground. "With all due respect, I do mind. I like my privacy." His features took on a neutral cast, his eyes alert but carefully devoid of emotion. Sano imagined this was the guise he wore when negotiating business deals.

"The sooner I'm finished, the sooner you can have your privacy again," Sano said.

"Didn't your chief retainer tell you what I said when he came to visit me? Before he murdered my servant boy?"

"He said you threatened to call in my friends' debts unless I left you alone."

"I wouldn't call it a threat," Ogita said with a false, congenial smile. He knew, as everyone did, that threatening a top official could mean death. "Just a bit of friendly advice."

"Here's a bit of friendly advice for you," Sano said. "If you call in those debts, I'll seize everything you own."

Ogita kept smiling, but his bulging double chin jerked as he gulped, and Sano could see droplets of sweat on his shiny forehead. Ogita knew the Tokugawa regime had seized property from merchants in the past, for various reasons.

"If I go out of business, the sales of rice will be held up. My customers, including the Tokugawa clan, will be short on cash for quite a while until other brokers can take over for me." Ogita's smile broadened. "Do you want thousands of armed samurai blaming you? How about a famine in the city? You'll be hounded out of the government."

Merchants had gained considerable power because the ruling samurai class had put its financial affairs into their hands, Sano knew. The traditional samurai belief that money was dirty had given the merchants a big advantage. Ogita was right; if Sano shut down a rice brokerage as big as Ogita's, the economy would suffer, and Sano would pay. But Sano's first concern was finding the shogun's wife.

"My men and I are going inside your house whether you like it or not," he said. "We'll kill anyone who tries to stop us."

Ogita's bodyguards looked at each other, shrugged, and moved away from the gate. Ogita dropped his smile just long enough to glare at them. Then he said, "How about if we strike a deal? I convert your rice stipend to cash for half my usual commission, and you leave me out of your investigation."

That discount would save Sano a small fortune, but he said, "Move, or I'll arrest you."

Ogita complied with bad humor. As Sano and his men marched through the gate, Ogita followed with his guards. Sano discovered that Ogita's home consisted of four houses, each at a corner of a square that made up an entire block, built around a central garden and connected by covered corridors. As Sano walked through them, people he took to be Ogita's family and servants scrambled out of his way. Ogita vanished into a maze of rooms crammed with expensively crafted lacquer tables and screens, shelves of valuable porcelain and jade vases and figurines, and cabinets filled with silk clothing that the merchant class wasn't supposed to wear.

"Maybe this is what Ogita didn't want us to see," Fukida said. "He's broken the sumptuary laws."

"Not only the sumptuary laws," Marume said, holding up swords he'd found in a trunk. Martial law said that only samurai were allowed to own swords.

"Never mind about that. All I care about is the shogun's wife." Sano called to his troops, "Turn this whole place upside down."

In a corridor, Sano met Ogita, who said, "Even if I had kidnapped the shogun's wife, surely you can't think I would be keeping her here."

"This is the one place you wouldn't expect anyone to look."

"Look to your heart's content. You're wasting your time."

"We'll see about that. Show me your private quarters."

Ogita led Sano to a bedchamber that adjoined an office and a balcony that gave him a view of his warehouse and the river. The bedchamber was bare and austere compared to the rest of the house, furnished with a few tables pushed into its corners and silk cushions neatly stacked. Sano eyed the cupboards built into one wall.

"There's no room for a person in there," Ogita said. "I don't know what you expect to find."

Sano didn't, either. Gazing around the room, he saw a section of *tatami* that was slightly crooked where the bed would be laid at night. He crouched, lifted a corner of the mat, and touched the floor underneath. One of the boards was shorter than the others, and it was loose. Sano pried it up with his finger and found a square, empty compartment that was about as long as his forearm. He looked up at Ogita.

Ogita smiled. "I sometimes keep money there."

But instinct told Sano the compartment was used for other, secret things that Ogita had just dashed up here to hide. Sano noticed Ogita hovering by the partition that separated the bedchamber from his office. When Sano slid open the partition and stepped into the office, Ogita didn't object or move, but Sano pictured him hurrying to remove contents from the compartment and find somewhere else to secret them moments ago. This was the nearest place, and it offered many possibilities, because the space around the desk was crowded with fireproof iron cabinets and trunks.

"I work at home at night," Ogita said. "I don't need much sleep. That's the secret of my success."

While he spoke, Sano moved around the office. He listened for tension in Ogita's voice and heard it when he drew close to one cabinet.

"That's full of old sales records," Ogita said.

Sano opened the cabinet and saw rows of ledgers. Stuck into one row was a thinner volume with polished teak covers, just the size to fit in the hidden compartment. Sano pulled it out, opened it, showed it to Ogita, and said, "What kind of record is this?"

The book was a "spring book," a collection of erotic art. On the first page was a picture of a woman undressing. A man stood outside her room, peering through the window at her, masturbating his huge erection.

"It's nothing," Ogita said.

Sano turned the page. "If it's nothing, why did you hide it?" The next picture showed the man inside the room. He held the woman and fondled her while she struggled to free herself. His erection pressed against her. Her head was flung back, her mouth open in a scream.

"Every man in Edo has books like that," Ogita said.

"Every man in Edo isn't a suspect in three rapes and possibly four." Sano turned to the next picture. Here, the man straddled the woman. Her legs were spread, his erection thrust into her. She lay limp, her eyes closed, as if unconscious. "Maybe you do more than just look at these pictures."

Obstinacy veiled fear in Ogita's expression. "So what if I do?" He waved his hand at the book. "That doesn't prove I have the shogun's wife."

Marume and Fukida stood in the doorway, craning their necks to get a look at the pictures. "We've finished searching," Fukida said. "She's not here."

"See? I told you," Ogita said triumphantly.

Sano was disappointed, but not ready to consider Ogita exonerated. "What other properties do you own?"

"I have a villa across the river in Honjo and a summer house in the hills outside town," Ogita said. "But you won't find the shogun's wife there, either."

"Excuse me, Lady Reiko, this message just came for you," said Lieutenant Tanuma.

Reiko sat on the veranda, arranging flowers in a vase and worrying about Sano. "Is it from my husband?" Hoping the message said he'd found Lady Nobuko, she accepted the bamboo scroll case from her bodyguard. When she unfurled the scroll, she saw the red signature stamped beneath the characters written in black.

"It's from Chiyo." Reading the message, she raised her eyebrows in surprise. "Chiyo says Fumiko has left the Kumazawa estate. Her father came and took her. I can't believe it! He was so adamant about not wanting her back."

Reiko continued reading, and her surprise turned to concern. "Chiyo says there's trouble. She begs me to come at once. She'll explain when I arrive." Beset by anxiety, Reiko said, "What can be wrong? What should I do?"

"Your husband doesn't want you going back to the Kumazawa house," Tanuma said.

Reiko knew how displeased Sano would be if she went. "But Chiyo needs me. I can't refuse to help."

"Major Kumazawa would probably not let you in the door even though Chiyo invited you," Tanuma said.

"I'll take the chance." Reiko stood. "Are you coming?"

"If you say so." Tanuma had worked for her long enough to understand that arguing with her when she'd made up her mind was a lost cause.

As they hurried off, Reiko hoped she wouldn't be too late to help Chiyo.

Sano and his entourage gathered in the street outside Ogita's house. He assigned a few troops to follow Ogita, in case the rice broker could lead them to the shogun's wife. Fukida said, "Should we go search Ogita's other properties?"

"No," Sano said. "If the shogun's wife were there, he wouldn't have told us about them. I suspect those aren't his only other properties."

"Shall I find out what others he owns?" Fukida asked.

Sano envisioned a long, tedious search through Edo's mountains of property records. "No. We don't have time."

What they did have was two other suspects to investigate.

As they rode down the street, Marume said, "I heard what Ogita said about spring books. He's right—a lot of men have them. You should see the ones in the barracks at home."

Edo had an overabundance of men without women. They were samurai retainers who were single or had left their wives in their lords' provinces, as well as merchants, artisans, and laborers who'd come to seek their fortune in the city and couldn't afford to marry. Under these conditions, prostitution and erotic art flourished. And even rich men, who could have all the women they wanted, enjoyed spring books. But that didn't clear Ogita, not in Sano's opinion.

"I skimmed through the rest of Ogita's book," Sano said. "All the other pictures showed men raping women. Even if Ogita didn't kidnap the shogun's wife, I think he's responsible for one or more of the other crimes."

But so could the other suspects be guilty.

"Where are we going now?" Fukida asked.

"We're going back to the exorcist," Sano said.

36

A group of beggars in ragged clothes loitered in the street outside the exorcist's temple. When they saw Sano's party coming, they held out their hands for alms, but without much hope. Sano and his men proceeded to the hall where he'd seen Joju the day before yesterday. Again, the monks at the door tried to prevent them from entering.

"His Holiness doesn't want to be disturbed."

"Try to keep us out, and he'll be worse than just disturbed," Marume said.

Sano and his detectives went inside the hall while his troops swarmed the grounds and other buildings. He found the hall drastically altered since his last visit. Daylight poured through open skylights. The black drapes, suspended from rods, were drawn back to expose windows cut high in the walls. From one window protruded a wooden bracket that held the painting of bloody fetuses. Through another Sano saw a drum, lute, and samisen in a room where musicians evidently played during rituals. Some windows opened onto platforms. There, monks crouched, setting up flares, rockets, and smoke bombs. More monks leaned out of a hole in the ceiling and lowered a dummy, dressed in white veils, on thin cords. Like puppeteers, they manipulated the dummy; it flew and dived. The scene reminded Sano of a theater undergoing preparations for a new play.

Spying Sano and the detectives, the monks hauled up the dummy, scrambled to close the drapes, and fled through the windows. Marume called, "It's too late." He and Fukida laughed. "We've seen everything."

Joju strode into the room so fast that his saffron robe whipped around his ankles like flames. "What is the meaning of this?" he demanded, his handsome face dark with anger. "Your troops are invading my temple. They say I'm hiding the shogun's wife. That's ridiculous!"

"You've been hiding plenty of other things." Sano gestured around the room.

Joju stopped short, but quickly recovered. "Those are just tools for my rituals."

"'Tools'? Is that what you call it?" Sano said. "I call it 'fraud.'"

The priest put on a dazzling, condescending smile. "The spirits are real. My exorcisms are real. But they work best if people believe in them. The props help people believe."

"I wonder if the shogun will continue to believe in you when he finds out about this," Sano said.

"You wouldn't tell His Excellency." Joju's intonation made the words a blend of question, statement, and threat.

"He deserves to know when someone is taking his money and playing him for a fool."

"Before you do, you should understand that people want to believe in what I do," Joju said. "His Excellency would rather think that I can communicate with evil spirits and solve problems by driving them out, than hear that my exorcisms are fakery and there's no help for people who are ill and troubled."

"You have a good point," Sano said, "but I have influence with the shogun."

"Then let us present our cases to him and see whose side he takes."

"I'll take my chances," Sano said, although he knew the superstitious shogun might well come down on Joju's side. "Are you ready to gamble that His Excellency will continue his patronage of you when he finds out that you kidnapped his wife?"

"I didn't." Joju spoke with obstinate defiance, but Sano sensed his fear that he would be framed.

"Then you should be able to prove you're innocent," Sano said. From outside came the sounds of his troops overrunning the temple grounds, calling to one another, tramping in and out of buildings. "Where were you early yesterday?"

"Here at the temple."

"Have you seen or heard from Jinshichi and Gombei?"

"The oxcart drivers? No."

Sano glanced at Marume and Fukida. He read on their faces the same concern that had arisen in his mind: If Joju did have the shogun's wife, she was hidden somewhere else. All Joju had to do was keep quiet, and Sano wouldn't find her until he let her go. By then, the damage would have been done to an innocent woman, and the shogun would never forgive Sano.

As much as Sano hated to admit it, this was a time for him to compromise. "Listen," he said to Joju. "Give me the shogun's wife, and I won't tell the shogun that you're a fraud. I won't tell him how I found her, either."

Marume and Fukida frowned. They could tell that Sano wasn't trying to trick Joju; this was a genuine offer. Sano knew they didn't want him to let a supposed criminal go free or compromise his principles. Then they nodded in resignation because they knew that what mattered was returning the shogun's wife safe and sound, and Sano had to do what he must.

Joju favored Sano with a smile that bespoke regret as well as offense. "I'm surprised to say that I believe you would actually uphold your end of the bargain. But I can't give you the shogun's wife because I don't have her. That is the truth, I swear by all the spirits in the cosmos."

"I hate to say this, but I think Joju is telling the truth about the shogun's wife," Fukida said.

"So do I," Marume said.

"Maybe you're right," Sano said.

He and the detectives stood in the temple grounds with his other troops, who'd just finished their search without finding Lady Nobuko. By now Sano was so exhausted that he felt his instincts shutting down; he hardly knew what to think anymore.

"Maybe Joju isn't responsible for Lady Nobuko's disappearance or for the other kidnappings." Sano looked around the grounds. He didn't see the men he'd just assigned to keep surveillance on Joju; they'd mixed with the crowds of worshippers. With luck, Joju wouldn't spot them, either. "But I hope he'll lead us to her, if Ogita doesn't."

"If neither one has her, there's still Nanbu," Fukida said.

"He's next," Sano said.

He and his men left the temple. Outside, there was now only one beggar, a woman with raddled skin, lank hair, and feet so calloused and caked with dirt that they looked like hooves. She said something to Sano that he didn't catch. He was so surprised that he paused before mounting his horse. Beggars usually didn't dare talk to samurai.

"What did you say?" he asked.

A closer look at her showed him that her features were delicate; she must have once been pretty. Her voice marked her as younger than Sano had at first thought, in her thirties. Maybe she was bold because she had nothing to lose except her life, which was a burden to her anyway.

"Is he in trouble?" she said.

"Who?" Sano said.

The woman gestured toward the temple. "Him. Joju."

"Yes, in fact he is," Sano said.

She smiled, showing decayed teeth. "Good." Her eyes sparkled with mischief. "I'm glad. I hate him."

"Why?"

"Because he's a bad man."

Here was someone willing to speak ill of the priest that had the shogun's protection, that so many people revered. Now she had Sano's full attention. "Why do you think he's bad?"

The woman's mouth twisted; a tear traced a glistening rivulet down her dirty cheek. Sano spoke to his men: "Give us some privacy." As they rode off and stopped a short distance away, Sano removed a cloth from under his sash and handed it to the woman. She took it, wiped her eyes, and blew her nose.

"What's your name?" Sano asked.

"Okitsu." She offered the cloth to Sano.

He saw grime on it and smelled her rank odor of sweat, fish, dirty hair, and urine. "You can keep it."

With a lopsided smile, she carefully tucked the cloth inside her ragged blue kimono.

"Tell me what Joju did to make you hate him," Sano said.

Her expression suddenly altered into a scowl so fierce that Sano took an involuntary step backward. "He ruined my life."

"How?"

"When I was a girl, I was possessed by evil spirits," Okitsu said. Her scowl faded, but a shadow of it remained, like a warning. "I heard their voices." She raised her head, as if listening for them now. "They told me things."

"What sort of things?"

"They said people were out to get me. They told me to curse at them and hit them. I did it, because if I didn't, the voices would get louder and louder. They wouldn't stop." She clapped her hands over her ears. "My parents took me to see Joju. They begged him to drive out the spirits."

Dropping her hands, Okitsu said, "They didn't have enough money to pay him. He said that when I was cured, I could be his servant. My parents agreed. He did the exorcism. The spirits went away. I went to live at the temple. During the day I washed laundry and floors and cleaned the privies. At night—"

A sob broke her voice. "At night Joju did things to me. Things that should only happen between husbands and wives. Things that priests aren't supposed to do. But I couldn't stop him. I couldn't say no. I owed it to him." She buried her face in her hands. "I was so ashamed."

Realizing he wasn't the most objective judge of Joju's character, Sano cautioned himself against rushing to believe her story, but it resonated with truth.

"After a while he said my debt was paid, and he sent me back to my parents," she said. "But it was too late. I was already with child."

Sano felt pity toward her, and anger at Joju for exploiting a helpless girl.

"My parents threw me out," Okitsu said. "I had the baby in an alley. It died. I almost did, too. That was when the evil spirits came back." She smiled, and her eyes shone with a feral gleam. "They said I must live and be strong. So I did. For a while I sold myself to men. When I lost my looks, I became a beggar. The spirits said that one day I would have a chance to pay Joju back for what he did to me." She grinned at Sano. "They say that day is coming soon."

An eerie shiver rippled through Sano. He could see the evil spirits looking out of her eyes. Then Okitsu turned and shuffled down the street, muttering under her breath. Sano mounted his horse and joined his men. As they rode, he told the detectives what she'd said.

"Well, well," Marume said. "Our friend Joju is guilty of the same sin as the people he exorcises."

"He doesn't seem to be haunted by the dead baby," Fukida said.

"But I'd believe a mad beggar woman over that fake exorcist any day," Marume said.

"So would I." Sano made an effort to hold on to his objectivity. "But even if Joju raped Okitsu, that doesn't mean he raped the other victims. That's not strong enough evidence."

He saw a theme developing. Ogita liked violent erotic art, but so did other men. Joju had exploited a helpless girl, but untold numbers of other men forced themselves on women and society looked the other way.

"It makes him look bad, though, doesn't it?" Fukida said.

"Maybe Nanbu will look worse," Sano said.

"How are we going to get to him while he's protected by his dogs?" Fukida said.

"Thank you for reminding me about the dogs," Sano said. "Before we pay a call on him, we'd better take precautions."

Accompanied by his two chief detectives, Hirata rode along a street that led him past the canals, quays, and warehouses of the Hatcho-bori district.

"Do you feel anything yet?" Detective Arai asked.

"Not yet," Hirata said.

The enemy must be biding his time, letting Hirata's anxiety grow before he made his next appearance.

Since Hirata had discovered that his enemy could reach him anywhere, he'd decided to stay away from home as much as possible. He didn't want Midori or the children to get hurt, and he didn't want a confrontation with his enemy to happen inside the castle, because if he drew his sword there, even to defend himself, the penalty was death. Instead, he must lure the enemy to a place he liked better.

"When he comes, we'll help you take him," Detective Inoue said.

"When he comes, you'll stay out of it," Hirata said. His men were good fighters, but no match for the enemy. Only Hirata stood a chance of winning. At least Hirata hoped he did. "Remember, you're not here to fight."

He'd brought his men to protect innocent people from him in the event that he lost control again. Maybe they couldn't, but it was the best precaution he could devise.

At the ferry dock on the Sumida River, he and his men left their horses at a public stable, then commandeered a ferryboat. They sat under the canopy while the ferryman rowed. The river was as flat and gray as a sheet of lead. It smelled of the brackish water downstream where it met the sea at Edo Bay. Fragments of bamboo, wood, paper, vegetables, and other trash mingled with a frayed sandal, a child's broken doll, and spent rockets from the fireworks display that celebrated the beginning of summer. As the boat glided into the deeper, cleaner water in the middle of the river, the ferryman steered around barges. A light rain began, marrying river and sky. Drops stippled the water, transforming it into liquid gooseflesh. Ahead, at the mouth of the river, loomed two islands.

The southern island was Tsukudajima, a fishing village whose residents doubled as spies for the shogun. Hirata knew that the people in the small boats offshore watched for any suspicious movement of watercraft in the bay and reported it to the *metsuke*.

The ferry stopped at the northern island, Ishikawajima, which was allotted to the controller of the Tokugawa navy. Along the docks, war junks waited for an invasion that might come someday. A shipyard contained vessels undergoing repairs. On a wooded rise in the middle of the island stood the controller's estate. As Hirata and his men stepped out of the ferry, Arai said, "Here, you'll be able to see him coming."

Hirata wondered if the enemy could read his mind and was already here, lying in wait.

A beach separated the shipyard from the village, a cluster of shacks. A crowd of men were gathered at the teahouse and food-stall. Ishikawajima had a reputation as a den of troublesome *rōnin* and vagrants. They came to the island for temporary work and shelter as well as a place to hide from the law. During his police career Hirata had come here once or twice in search of criminals.

Ishikawajima's reputation was one reason Hirata had chosen to come here today. He hoped to accomplish more than a confrontation with the enemy. The other reason was that Ishikawajima had fewer bystanders than anywhere else in Edo, and even fewer who were truly innocent.

Hirata stood on the beach, apart from his men. Gulls picked at dead fish that had washed up at the river's edge. Brackish water lapped at dirty sand. Hirata gazed across the water at the city, which shimmered behind the veil of rain. The ferryboat that had brought him receded toward the opposite shore; no other craft approached Ishikawajima. The sound of hammers pounding and saws rasping came from the shipyard. Hirata breathed deeply, let his thoughts float away, and calmed his mind. He aligned the forces within his body along a spiritual path toward a meditative trance.

His vision expanded until he could see in all directions, the island behind him as well as the river in front of him, red crayfish swimming at the bottom of the river, the sun through the clouds. The gray landscape took on brilliant hues, as if drenched in a rainbow. His nostrils magnified odors; he smelled horse dung, sewage, and garbage in the city, incense burning in the temples, and enough food cooking to make a banquet for the gods. He heard a million hearts beating, and when he reached out his hands, he felt their rhythm through the skin on his fingertips. Closing his eyes, he projected his inner voice across the world.

I'm here, he called silently. *Come and get me.*

He heard no answer from the enemy even though he waited and listened for what seemed like an eternity.

Instead he felt two different yet also familiar energy auras. They pulsed very near him. He opened his eyes, broke his trance. Looking toward the shipyard, he realized that even though one search had failed, the other had borne fruit. There, among the men working on the hull of a boat, were Jinshichi and Gombei, the two oxcart drivers.

37

Sano, his detectives, and the troops walked up to the kennels behind a pack of huge guard dogs that Sano had borrowed from a friend. Three of the friend's dog trainers led the beasts on iron chains attached to leather harnesses. By the gate stood the troops Sano had posted there. The dogs barked and lunged at them while the trainers hauled on the dogs' chains and yelled, "Down!"

"Is Nanbu still inside?" Sano asked.

"Yes," said the troops' leader. "He never left."

"That gives him an alibi for Lady Nobuko's kidnapping," Fukida said.

"It doesn't mean he doesn't know anything about it," Sano said.

Marume pounded on the gate. "Open up!"

First came the sound of dogs barking inside; then a man's voice shouted, "Go away!"

Sano's soldiers jumped off their horses, unloaded a battering ram, and charged. They rammed the gate until it sagged open. Inside it crouched Nanbu's dogs, restrained on their leashes by two of Nanbu's men. Sano's borrowed dogs leaped forward. A frenzy of barks, howls, and shouts ensued as the trainers urged their dogs through the gate and forced Nanbu's men to retreat with theirs. Sano, the detectives, and his troops walked inside.

"Talk about fighting fire with fire," Marume said.

"If dogs are killed by dogs, that's not against the law," Fukida said.

As the two dog packs faced off, Sano raised his voice over their barks and growls. "Where's Nanbu?"

Nanbu's men didn't answer, but one glanced at a building set apart from the kennels. Sano, his men, and his canine army stampeded toward the building. Nanbu's men and their dogs followed. The building was a wooden shack, raised above the muddy ground on low pilings, with lattice enclosing its base; it resembled an oversized privy. The trainers and their dogs held off the other pack as Marume opened the door. Sano and the detectives drew their swords. They looked inside.

A hulking shape moved on the floor. Rhythmic thumps punctuated whimpers and cries. Sano recognized the shape as Nanbu, hunched on his knees and elbows on a mattress. Under him thrashed a girl. She shrieked and beat her fists at him while his body thrust at her and he uttered growls as fierce and bestial as his dogs'.

"Stop!" Sano shouted.

Marume and Fukida burst into the shack, grabbed Nanbu, and dragged him off the woman.

"Hey, what is this?" Nanbu protested. His face was dripping sweat, engorged with lust. His erection showed under his clothes. "Let me go!" As he struggled to break free of the detectives, he saw Sano and exclaimed, "How did you get in here?"

Sano ignored Nanbu and stepped over to the girl. She wept as she tried to cover herself with her torn kimono. He said, "Are you all right?"

Gazing up at him in speechless fear, she pushed long, tangled black hair away from her face. Bruises surrounded both her eyes. Her nose was bleeding.

"Where is the shogun's wife?" Sano asked Nanbu.

"How should I know? Why don't you let me finish?" Nanbu cursed as the detectives hauled him outside and threw him on the mud. The trainers and their dogs surrounded him. "She's just a girl who cleans the dog cages."

"You can go," Sano told the girl. "For your own good, don't come back. Find another job."

She scrambled out the door and ran. Sano left the shack and stood over Nanbu, who said, "I didn't do anything wrong. We were just having a little fun."

"You hit her," Sano said.

"So what?" Nanbu said. The dogs barked and snapped. He cringed. "She got wild. I had to show her who was boss."

His attitude disgusted Sano. "You ought to be ashamed of yourself."

Nanbu looked honestly surprised. "Why? The girl works for me. Besides, she asked for it. She led me on, and then she changed her mind and started fighting."

Sano spotted new variations on the theme. Servants were at their masters' disposal, and Nanbu had only done what countless other men did every day. And many men justified forcing women into sex by saying the women wanted it. However, those excuses didn't make Sano any more favorably disposed toward Nanbu.

"Is that what you told yourself when you violated my cousin?" Sano said.

"I didn't," Nanbu protested. "I told you already." The dogs strained their chains, slavering at him. "Now please, call off your dogs!"

"What's the matter, don't you like a taste of your own medicine?" Marume laughed.

"What about Fumiko and the nun?" Sano said.

"Not them, either!" Nanbu was livid with anger, his hands and knees soiled by the dog feces that littered the ground. "And not the shogun's wife! I've never even laid eyes on her. Why are you looking for her, anyway? Doesn't she always stay inside the palace?"

"She's missing," Fukida said. "We think she's been kidnapped."

"Well, not by me," Nanbu declared. "Search this whole place, search my house, too, if you want—I haven't got her."

Just because he, like Joju and Ogita, indulged in dubious behavior, that didn't mean Nanbu had committed the crimes under investigation. Sano couldn't ignore the possibility that none of the three was behind the disappearance of the shogun's wife.

Then a thought occurred to Sano. What if the oxcart drivers had kidnapped her for another client and hidden her in a secret place? The suspects would know where it was. Sano thought up a deal that might induce Nanbu to cooperate.

"You're in trouble even if you don't have the shogun's wife," Sano told Nanbu. "If she's not found, or if she's hurt, the shogun will blame me. I'll be looking to pass the blame to someone else. You'll make a good scapegoat."

"That's not fair." The horror on Nanbu's face weakened his pose of defiance.

"You want me to be fair? All right, here's a chance to save your life." Sano said, "You tell me where Jinshichi and Gombei take the women they kidnap. I'll let you off the hook."

"I told you I don't know those people," Nanbu whined, but Sano heard the lie in his voice. "You're trying to trick me into confessing."

"Let the dogs have at him," Marume suggested.

"Not yet," Sano said, then addressed Nanbu. "Let's just suppose there have been rumors about two oxcart drivers: They kidnap women and take them to a certain place. Let's suppose you've heard the rumors, even though you've never met Jinshichi or Gombei. Just tell me where the place is. That's not a confession. Nothing will happen to you." Sano hated to play games with a man who might have committed four serious crimes, but he continued: "What do you say?"

Nanbu hesitated. Sano knew that if Nanbu answered, it would mean he was guilty, but Sano would have to spare Nanbu or renege on the deal and violate his code of honor.

"I don't know where it is," Nanbu said slowly.

Sano had had just about all he could take from these men whose true, ugly colors he'd seen even if they weren't guilty of these particular crimes. If Nanbu didn't talk right now, he would kill him. The thought must have shown on his face, because Nanbu recoiled from him in terror.

"I don't know where it is because it doesn't stay in the same place all the time," Nanbu hastily amended. "It moves."

"How can it move?" Sano said, wary of a trick.

"It's a boat," Nanbu said.

When Reiko arrived in Asakusa, she found Chiyo waiting for her in the street a few blocks from the Kumazawa estate. Chiyo clutched the folds of the black drape she wore over her head. She huddled against a wall as pedestrians and mounted samurai moved past her. She looked small, frightened, and vulnerable. Reiko supposed this was the first time she'd left home since Sano had brought her back. When Chiyo spied Reiko's palanquin, she ran up to it and spoke through the window.

"Many thanks for coming. I'm sorry I can't invite you to the house."

"I understand," Reiko said. "What is the trouble you mentioned in your message?"

Gasping, Chiyo bent over and clasped her chest. Not only was she afraid to be out of doors; she was still weak and ill. Reiko told the bearers to set down the palanquin, opened the door, then said to Chiyo, "Come in. Sit down."

Chiyo obeyed. When she'd recovered her breath, she said, "This morning, Jirocho came to the house. My father's soldiers have orders not to let him in, but he stood by the gate and shouted Fumiko's name until she heard him and went running outside. She was so glad to go with him, it broke my heart."

"What changed his mind?" Reiko asked.

"I asked him that. He said he had a new plan for finding out who violated her. And he needed Fumiko to make it work."

Sano wouldn't be pleased that Jirocho had taken the law into his own hands. "What is Jirocho's plan?"

"Jirocho knows about the three suspects that your husband found." The words spilled from Chiyo in breathless haste. "He sent a message, the same message, to Nanbu, Ogita, and Joju. It said that Fumiko has identified him as the one who violated her, and unless he wants her to tell Chamberlain Sano, he should meet Jirocho this evening and pay him a thousand *koban*."

Reiko stared in surprise and confusion. "But Fumiko didn't get a good look at the man. Has she suddenly remembered more?"

"Maybe. I don't know. She wouldn't talk about it," Chiyo said. "Jirocho is gambling that one of those men will think so."

Now Reiko saw Jirocho's intent. "He's setting a trap. He's hoping that whoever violated his daughter will show up to pay the blackmail, and then Jirocho will kill him. But why did he take Fumiko?"

"He wanted her to go with him to the meeting," Chiyo said. "If someone shows up, Jirocho thinks she'll remember, and she's supposed to say whether he's the one. Jirocho wants to be certain."

The gangster boss didn't want to kill the wrong man, who might show up for reasons that Reiko didn't have time to discuss. Jirocho especially wouldn't want to kill someone as important as Nanbu, Joju, or Ogita without being absolutely sure it was worthwhile.

"Where is the meeting?" Reiko asked.

"In the paupers' cemetery in Inaricho. At the hour of the boar."

That was not long from now. Reiko felt a stir of apprehension on Fumiko's behalf.

"I'm afraid," Chiyo said. "If one of those men is the criminal and he shows up, I can't imagine that he'll just let himself be killed."

"Neither can I." Reiko remembered Sano's descriptions of Ogita, Nanbu, and Joju. They hadn't sounded like easy targets, and they surely wouldn't go to meet a blackmailing gangster alone.

"There's bound to be trouble. I begged Fumiko to stay with me, but she'll do anything to please her father. That's all she wants. I asked my father to intervene, but he said it was none of his business." Anxious and frantic, Chiyo said, "Reiko-san, I have no one to turn to except you." She clasped her hands, extended them to Reiko. "Please, will you save Fumiko?"

"Of course I will," Reiko said.

She couldn't bear the thought of the poor girl caught between her rapist and her father any more than Chiyo could. She felt her heartbeat quicken with excitement, urgency, and uncertainty about what to do.

"I'll tell my husband. He'll send out his troops," she said, then reconsidered. "No—that will take too long. They'll never get there in time." Reiko looked at her own entourage of five guards plus Lieutenant Tanuma. She had an army of seven, including herself.

Lieutenant Tanuma said in alarm, "No, Lady Reiko. We're not going. Your husband would kill me."

"I'm going with or without you," Reiko said, "and he'll kill you if you don't come."

"All right," Tanuma said, glum in his certainty that he was dead no matter what he did. "But I have a bad feeling about this."

Reiko turned to Chiyo. "You'd better go home. I'll tell you what happens."

Chiyo stayed seated in the palanquin beside Reiko. "No," she said, quiet but firm. "I'm going, too."

Dismay struck Reiko. "I can't let you."

"Why not? Because we might see something disturbing? Because you don't think I can bear it?"

"Because you're not trained in combat, and I can't promise we'll be able to protect you. You might get hurt."

Chiyo smiled sadly. "What could hurt me worse than what has already happened? What have I to lose?"

"Perhaps much more than you think," Reiko said. "You don't know what the future holds. Your husband and children——"

246

"Are gone for good." Chiyo sounded resigned to the fact decreed by custom. "All I have is Fumiko, and she needs me." Chiyo's soft features hardened with determination. "If you put me out of your palanquin, I'll walk all the way to Inaricho. You can't stop me."

A chamber in the office area of Sano's estate served as a command post for the search for Lady Nobuko. Sano, Yanagisawa, and Yoritomo knelt on the floor while Detectives Marume and Fukida unrolled a map of Edo. The map was crisscrossed by painted blue lines that represented streams and canals. The wider blue ribbon of the Sumida River divided Edo proper from the eastern suburbs. Sano and Yanagisawa pored over the map like generals charting a battle strategy.

"Nanbu said he 'heard' the boat was here," Sano said, pointing to a spot on the Nihonbashi River. "But he also said that was last month."

"At least we know we're looking for a floating brothel and we have one possible location," Yanagisawa said. "Good work, Sano-*san*."

Sano thought how strange it was to hear Yanagisawa pay him a compliment. It was even stranger that Yanagisawa didn't seem to mind that this estate belonged to Sano now.

"Nanbu also gave me a description of the boat," Sano said. "It's approximately forty paces long, with a single mast, a square sail, a cabin with a red tile roof on the deck, and three sets of oars below."

Once the kennel manager had realized that his cooperation could save him from being punished for Lady Nobuko's kidnapping, he'd spewed information so fast that he'd reminded Sano of a horse with diarrhea.

"I've sent troops to seize the boat if it's there, or to trace it if it's not," Sano said. "I expect a report soon."

"In case they don't find it, we'd better start searching all the waterways," Yanagisawa said.

Sano took up a writing brush and dipped it in ink. He happened to glance toward the door and saw Masahiro standing outside the room, watching with avid curiosity. Sano frowned. Masahiro retreated. Sano said, "I'll cross out the waterways that a boat that size can't pass."

"I'll help you," Yoritomo said.

He seemed to have put aside his animosity toward Sano, but then he was smart enough to realize that if they didn't band together and find Lady Nobuko, both families would suffer.

Even after Sano and Yoritomo marked off the waterways that were too narrow or shallow to accommodate the floating brothel, there remained the whole Sumida River, plus wide stretches along other rivers and canals. Yanagisawa took the brush from Yoritomo and drew a line around half the area. "My army will search these," he told Sano. "Yours can do the others."

He and Yoritomo left. Marume said, "I hate to think of how many boats there are that fit the general description."

"And ours has no name or other distinctive features, according to Nanbu," said Fukida.

"Whoever owns it wouldn't want to call attention to it," Sano said. All brothels outside the Yoshiwara licensed pleasure quarter were illegal. Nanbu had claimed he didn't know the name of the boat's owner.

"Finding it could take forever," Marume said glumly.

Hirata entered the room. He said, "Maybe not."

38

Sano and Hirata stood over the two oxcart drivers, who lay in a muddy courtyard inside Edo Jail. Jinshichi's and Gombei's hands were tied behind their backs and their ankles bound with rope.

The big, muscular Jinshichi glowered at his captors from beneath his heavy brow. In the short time he'd spent on the run, his whiskers had grown into a bristly beard. The scar on his cheekbone was flushed red with anger, but he didn't speak.

Gombei, the wiry younger man, squirmed as he said to Sano, "Why are we under arrest again?" He now had three teeth missing. He'd lost another one during the tussle with Hirata, while resisting arrest. His grin oozed blood. His cunning eyes sparkled with fright. "We haven't done anything wrong."

"Then why did you run away from the men I sent to watch you?" Sano said.

"We got tired of being spied on," Jinshichi said sullenly.

"It's not our fault they couldn't keep up with us," Gombei said. Nervousness edged his good humor.

"We're innocent," Jinshichi said. "We already told you so."

"Why were you hiding out on Ishikawajima?" Hirata asked.

Despite some misgivings, Sano had decided to let Hirata participate in the interrogation. Hirata had caught the drivers; he deserved to help question them. And his mysterious pursuer hadn't yet made another appearance.

"We weren't hiding," Gombei said with earnest sincerity. "We couldn't go to work because your soldiers would have found us. We needed to make money."

Sano was fed up with evasions. Instinct and evidence told him the men were guilty of kidnapping if not rape. "What's the matter, didn't you make enough by kidnapping women?"

"We didn't touch those women," Jinshichi said, surly and vexed. "They told you so themselves."

Gombei grinned and licked blood from his lips. "You had to let us go last time."

"Not this time." Although Sano was opposed to torture, for once he must bend his own rules. But he would employ the mildest form of torture, one used primarily for women.

Into the courtyard walked two jailers. They were *eta*, toughs dressed in ragged clothes stained with sweat, grime, and blood from previous torture sessions. Sano said, "Perform *kusuguri-zeme* on these prisoners."

Kusuguri-zeme was the term for torture by tickling. It was considered harmless, and perhaps sexually arousing for male torturers when they performed it on women. The *eta* didn't look thrilled by the prospect of applying it to the oxcart drivers, but Jinshichi and Gombei chortled.

"Do you really think you can tickle us into confessing?" Gombei said.

"We'll see," Sano said.

The *eta* crouched beside the drivers, removed their sandals, and began tickling their feet. Gombei flinched and giggled. A smile tugged Jinshichi's mouth. Soon both men were laughing uproariously. The *eta* worked with grim concentration. Hirata's face was expressionless, his emotions under control. Sano suppressed the urge to laugh. Mirth was contagious.

"Don't let them make you say anything," Jinshichi ordered Gombei as they guffawed and thrashed.

"I won't," Gombei said, gasping for breath. His body jerked involuntarily; distress showed through his humor. "No matter what."

The *eta* proceeded to tickle the men's armpits. Gombei and Jinshichi bucked, contorted, and tried to roll away from their tormenters. Their laughter took on a ragged, hysterical edge.

"Did you kidnap my cousin Chiyo?" Sano said. The men just kept laughing. Sano prompted, "She was the woman with the baby. At Awashima Shrine. You took her, didn't you?"

"No," Gombei blurted between giggles.

Jinshichi shook his head, panted, and roared.

"Suit yourselves," Hirata said.

The *eta* poked their fingers between Jinshichi's and Gombei's ribs, along their waists. Soon the men were covered with mud, sobbing while they laughed. Suddenly it didn't seem funny to Sano anymore. The line between mirth and misery had been crossed. *Kusuguri-zeme* didn't inflict permanent damage, but it caused as much distress as pain did. It was cruel torture indeed. Sano stoically forced himself to watch. He told himself these men were criminals who deserved to suffer until they talked.

"I can't bear it any longer," Gombei whimpered while he laughed and choked. "Make them stop, and I'll tell you whatever you want to know!"

The *eta* looked to Sano, who nodded. They stopped tickling, rose, and backed away from the prisoners. Gombei moaned and wept with gratitude. Jinshichi said to his partner, "You stupid coward." He was gasping as hard as if he'd run all the way across town. Both men's faces were awash in dirt and tears. Sano felt almost as relieved as they did.

"Did you kidnap my cousin?" Sano repeated.

"Yes," Gombei said weakly. "We gave her a potion that we buy from a druggist in Kanda. It makes people go to sleep, and they can't move."

Jinshichi muttered in disgust, but he nodded.

"Who hired you to kidnap her?" Sano asked.

"I don't know his name," Gombei said.

"He's lying," Hirata told Sano.

"Ogita, Nanbu, or Joju," Sano said. "Which one was it?"

Startled, Gombei said, "How——?"

"How did I find out who your customers are?" Sano explained, "I've been checking into your background since we last met. The proprietor at the Drum Teahouse told me about your side business. He was happy to supply the names."

"I'll kill that rat," Jinshichi fumed.

"If you live long enough," Marume said. "Tell Chamberlain Sano which one raped his cousin."

"It was Ogita," Jinshichi said, reluctant to confess, yet eager to avoid more tickling.

At last Sano knew the truth. At last he had a target for the anger he felt on behalf of Chiyo and his newfound clan. He thought of Ogita lying to his face, and an intense hatred filled him like venom infusing his veins, like hot smoke suffocating his lungs. He wanted to lash out at the merchant and strike him down. But Ogita wasn't here, and now wasn't the time for Sano to let loose his temper.

"Ogita wanted a woman who'd just had a baby," Gombei said. "He wanted to drink milk from her breasts while he had sex with her. You can't get that in Yoshiwara. So we went to Awashima Shrine. It always has plenty of new mothers. All we had to do was pick one who looked easy. I pretended I was hurt, I called for help, and she came right to me."

That he could speak so casually about his crime! Sano felt his hatred grow to encompass the oxcart drivers for their part in Chiyo's rape.

"I didn't know she was your cousin," Gombei said. "If I had, I'd have kidnapped somebody else."

Sano wanted to grab the man by his hair, grind his face into the dirt, wipe off its sheepish expression, then cut off his head. But he wasn't finished with Jinshichi. "You did kidnap somebody else, didn't you? The girl Fumiko."

"No," Gombei said. "We never—"

"Was she for Nanbu, or Joju?" Sano said.

Jinshichi said, "Keep quiet! He'll kill us!"

Sano motioned to the *eta*. They moved toward the prisoners. Gombei hastily said, "No! Please! All right! She was for Nanbu. He happened to see her when he and his men were catching dogs at Ueno Temple. He wanted her, but he found out she was the daughter of Jirocho the gangster, and he was afraid to take her himself. So he hired us."

Sano was almost as disgusted by Nanbu's cowardice as by his taking pleasure at the expense of a helpless young girl. "Did he hire you to kidnap the nun, too?"

"No. That was Joju. He likes high-class old ladies."

It was the priest who'd infected the nun with genital disease. He was responsible for her suicide and therefore indirectly guilty of murder. Sano thought about the similarities between the nun and the shogun's wife. He glimpsed a light through the dark tangle of this investigation.

"He's confessed to everything," Jinshichi said with a bitter look at his partner. "Just kill us now."

"Not quite everything," Sano said. "There's another victim besides the three we've discussed. The nun wasn't the only woman you kidnapped for Joju, was she?"

An air of caution fell over the men. They seemed to shrink into themselves under its weight. Their gazes avoided each other as well as Sano and his men. Gombei said, "There were only three."

"Four," Sano said.

"Can't you count that high?" Hirata mocked the drivers.

"Maybe they have short memories and they've forgotten about the shogun's wife," Sano said.

"*What?*" Jinshichi and Gombei spoke in unison; they stared in disbelieving, apparently genuine shock.

"The shogun's wife went missing yesterday," Sano said. "I think she was kidnapped." He pointed at the two men. "By none other than you."

Now they did look at each other, with appalled expressions. Jinshichi blurted, "You didn't tell me she was the shogun's wife."

"I didn't know!" Gombei cried, too upset to deny the charge or keep his mouth shut. "I thought she was just some old lady." He turned to Sano. "I swear!"

"You're in even bigger trouble now," Hirata said. "The shogun will have your head cut off for that."

"Not just yet." Sano addressed the captives: "Tell me what happened."

"We needed money," Gombei said. "We went to see Joju the day before yesterday. He said that if we brought him another old lady, he'd pay us enough money to get out of town. So we went and found her." He moaned. "Of all the women in Edo, it would have to be the shogun's wife. What rotten luck!"

"Your luck is about to improve," Sano said. "Answer a few more questions, and maybe I'll let you live. Here's the first one: Did you take the shogun's wife to the same boat as the other women?"

"He knows about the boat," Jinshichi said dolefully. "He knows everything."

"I take it that means yes," Sano said. "Here's the second question: Where is the boat?"

Jinshichi began to speak, but Gombei prevented him by yelling, "Shut up!" Gombei's eyes shone with desperate cunning. "Even if we tell you where the boat is, you won't be able to find it by yourself. To you, it would look the same as a thousand other boats. How about if we take you there?"

He grinned. Sano knew Gombei was buying time, hoping that on the way to the boat he and Jinshichi would find a way to escape. But Sano had no time to argue or negotiate; without the men as guides, he might not get to Lady Nobuko before the shogun's deadline.

"All right," Sano said, "but I'm warning you: no tricks."

39

The smoke from the crematoriums hung in a cloud over Inaricho district.

Reiko could see the smoke, lit by the full moon, rising like a ghostly fog in the distance as she and Chiyo rode in her palanquin. The light from lanterns hung on poles attached to her bodyguards' horses didn't extend beyond the roadsides. The vast darkness of the rice fields resonated with a cacophony of frogs singing and insects buzzing. At this late hour, Reiko, Chiyo, and their escorts were the only travelers going to Inaricho.

Inaricho was a backwater, situated between two major temple districts. Reiko could see lights flickering far ahead in Ueno to her left and Asakusa to her right, but Inaricho would have been invisible if not for the smoke. It was a perfect location for cemeteries, and for the crematoriums in which dead bodies burned overnight. Inaricho was conveniently near the temples where funeral rites were held and distant from Edo proper, where crematoriums were outlawed because of the fire hazard.

"Jirocho must have chosen the pauper's cemetery because he knew it would be deserted," Reiko said.

"He'll have privacy for his business," Chiyo agreed.

Few people ventured into these parts at night. As her procession entered the smoke cloud, Reiko smelled the awful odor of burning flesh. She and Chiyo held their sleeves over their noses and mouths, but the odor was so strong she could taste it. Her escorts coughed. Their lanterns lit up the smoke and colored it orange. The procession moved as if through fire, toward some hellish netherworld.

The bearers set down the palanquin in the main street, where shops sold altar furnishings such as Buddha statues, candle holders, gold lotus flowers, and incense burners. The shops were closed, abandoned by the living, surrendered to the dead until day came. The bearers were breathing hard, tired from the journey, wheezing because of the smoke. Lieutenant Tanuma dismounted and said to them, "You stay here and guard the horses. We'll walk from here."

Reiko and Chiyo climbed out of the palanquin. As they and the bodyguards raced along Inaricho's back streets, Reiko's heart beat with quickening excitement and apprehension. Beyond small temples and shrines lay the cemeteries, enclosed within stone walls or bamboo fences. The sickening smell of burned flesh grew stronger. Reiko could feel the heat from the crematoriums.

"Which way?" Lieutenant Tanuma's anxious face shone with sweat in the light from the lanterns that he and the other men had brought.

"I don't know," Reiko said. She'd never been to the paupers' cemetery, and there was no one to ask for directions. "We'll just have to look around."

They tramped through the cemeteries. In each stood a crematorium, a massive, outdoor oven built of stone. Each had a shelter where mourners gathered in the morning, when the oven was opened, to pick out bones and put them in an urn for burial. Reiko heard sizzling inside the crematoriums. The smoke that poured from their vents was so thick that she and her comrades groped between the rows of square stone grave pillars carved with the names of the deceased. They tripped on vases of flowers and offerings of food and drink left for the spirits. But they saw no sign of Jirocho or Fumiko. Exhausted, nearly overcome by the smoke, they stopped in an alley to rest.

Bells in the temples tolled the hour of the boar, the time of the rendezvous. As their peals faded, Reiko heard another sound that sent shivers racing along her skin.

"Listen," she whispered.

From somewhere in the distance came the noise of dogs barking. It grew louder, drew closer. Past the alley marched a horde of some thirty men. A few carried lanterns. They appeared to be samurai; they had shaved crowns and wore swords. Ten or twelve held the leashes of big dogs that sniffed the ground and barked. The man with the hugest, blackest dog walked with a swagger, legs spread wide and arms swinging.

"That must be Nanbu," Reiko whispered. "He seems to know where he's going."

She and her companions followed Nanbu and his group to a gate that sagged on its hinges, into a cemetery enclosed by a rough stone wall. Reiko peeked through the gate and saw a large field thick with shrubs and high weeds. Nanbu and his men trudged within the light from their lanterns. Here, in the paupers' cemetery, wooden stakes that bore names scrawled in fading ink marked the graves. Smoke billowed from a crematorium that had no shelter. Firelight glowed through cracks in its walls, like red veins.

"Fumiko must be there already," Chiyo said.

Careless of her own safety, she hurried into the graveyard before Reiko could stop her. Reiko had no choice but to follow, crouching as she ran through the weeds around the perimeter of the field. Lieutenant Tanuma and her other guards thrashed after her, and she prayed Nanbu wouldn't hear them. She caught up with Chiyo and pushed her behind the crematorium. There they hid with Tanuma and the guards. They watched Nanbu's group gather in the middle of the cemetery.

"Where is that cursed gangster?" Nanbu said.

"This was a bad idea," said a bald man with a prominent double chin. He wasn't a samurai; he wore no swords. His cross voice had a deep, carrying resonance. "I shouldn't have let you talk me into coming."

Surprise stabbed Reiko. "That's Ogita. I recognize him from my husband's description. What are he and Nanbu doing together?"

Chiyo whispered urgently, "It's him! I recognize his voice. He's the man from the pavilion of clouds!"

Reiko saw one rapist matched up with his victim, like suits in a card game. Had Ogita, and Nanbu, also violated Fumiko? Was that why they were both here?

"Hey, you came to me when you got that message," Nanbu said to Ogita. "You asked me what to do. This was my solution. If you have a better one, speak up."

However they'd become acquainted, whether they'd both raped Fumiko or not, they'd evidently banded together to cope with Jirocho's blackmail.

"Maybe we should just buy Jirocho off," Ogita said.

Nanbu snorted. "You're supposed to be an expert at business, you should know that won't make him leave us alone. He'll keep asking for more money until he's bled us dry. This is the only way out."

If the presence of his troops and dogs hadn't made it clear to Reiko that he had other plans instead of paying blackmail, his words did. Some of the men must belong to Ogita; he'd brought his army, too. Chiyo had been right: There was trouble coming. Reiko looked at her six body-guards. They were badly outnumbered.

"I don't like this," Ogita said. "We're going to get in trouble."

Nanbu laughed. "We're already in trouble. Or have you forgotten what we had to do to get Chamberlain Sano's spies off our tails?"

"You mean, what you did," Ogita said.

"Hey, you didn't stop me, you stood by and watched," Nanbu said. "We're in this together."

Reiko realized that Nanbu and his men and dogs must have killed her husband's troops. She was horrified because not only were the men dead, but they wouldn't be coming to help.

"Besides, you're the one who sent that incompetent fool to Major Kumazawa's house," Nanbu said. "If he hadn't botched the job, we wouldn't be in this mess now. You need me."

At least Reiko now knew who was responsible for the assassination attempt on Chiyo and Fumiko.

"I never should have gotten mixed up with you," Ogita said bitterly.

"It's a little late for regrets," Nanbu said. "When this is over, you'll thank me."

"When this is over, I never want to see your face again." Ogita ex-claimed, "A curse on the shogun's wife! If she hadn't gotten kidnapped, we wouldn't have to worry about Jirocho."

Reiko began to understand better why they'd formed this unholy alli-ance. If their problems had been only a matter of the crimes against Chiyo, Fumiko, and the nun, the two men could have gambled that Jiro-cho's blackmail attempt was just a bluff and ignored his message. But now the shogun was looking for someone to blame for his wife's disappear-ance. If Fumiko bore witness against Ogita and Nanbu, the shogun would probably take her at her word and decide they were responsible for what-ever had happened to Lady Nobuko even if they weren't. The two men had to destroy Jirocho before he destroyed them.

"We have to warn Jirocho," Reiko whispered.

"But how?" Chiyo said.

They were trapped behind the crematorium, in the radius of its fiery heat. Reiko wiped her perspiring face on her sleeve. If they tried to leave the cemetery, Nanbu and Ogita would see them.

"We won't have to worry about Jirocho much longer," Nanbu said. "Just be patient."

Reiko heard hissing sounds and dull thuds. Men among Nanbu's and Ogita's troops jerked as if they'd been struck. They cried out and clutched at arrows that had suddenly appeared in their chests and backs. Some fell dead or wounded. A dog with an arrow stuck in his side ran off squealing.

"What's going on?" Ogita demanded as his group scattered. He groped after his guards; they drew their swords.

Nanbu struggled to restrain his dog, which lunged and barked wildly. He shouted, "It's a trap!"

More hisses accompanied a storm of arrows that rushed out of the darkness beyond the cemetery. The men raised and swung their lanterns in a frantic effort to see who was shooting at them. More men fell. Stray arrows pelted the grass. As Nanbu's and Ogita's men tried to shield their masters, dark figures climbed onto the cemetery wall. Some took on the shape of archers with bows drawn; others were silhouettes equipped with spears. Some forty in all, they looked like demons risen from hell in the flame-lit smoke that swirled around them. One man wasn't armed. Although short and pudgy, he had a confident, imperious stance.

"Hold your fire!" he shouted.

"It's Jirocho," Reiko whispered.

Laughter and samisen music blared in the moonlit fog over the Kanda River.

Sano, Hirata, Marume, and Fukida walked the two oxcart drivers along the footpath by the water, through the district known as Yanagi-bashi—"Willow Tree Bridge." Here, the Kanda emptied into the Sumida River. Yanagibashi had once been a mere launching point for boats that carried passengers up the Sumida to the Yoshiwara licensed pleasure quarter, but an unlicensed entertainment quarter had sprung up in the area. Some of the boats moored at the docks and some of the teahouses on the riverbanks contained brothels with local prostitutes. But Yanagi-bashi had none of Yoshiwara's glamour.

Cheap, garish red lanterns on the boats and teahouses reflected in the water. Raucous parties overflowed from verandas. Under the bridge, beggars slept. Men stumbled off boats returning from Yoshiwara. Girls called out from windows to them, soliciting their depleted reserves of cash and virility.

Sano had left his other troops behind, at the foot of the bridge, on advice he'd received earlier from Gombei.

"If the owner of the boat sees a big crowd of samurai, he'll get suspicious," Gombei had said.

If Sano were the owner of an illegal brothel boat and saw an army coming, he would cast off and take the boat down the Sumida River and out to Edo Bay. He might even dump the shogun's wife in the ocean.

Gombei led the way with Hirata guarding him; Marume and Fukida followed with Jinshichi, who plodded sullen and silent between them. Sano brought up the rear. They avoided drunks vomiting into the water. Tough young townsmen roved, hunting people to rob.

"Which one is it?" Sano said as they passed boats.

"Farther down," Gombei said.

"It had better be there," Marume said, "or you and your friend are dead."

"It will be. It will be!" Gombei's voice was shrill with his fear that the boat had moved.

Sano felt the same fear as he wondered what was happening to the shogun's wife. But he reminded himself that he had the three suspects under surveillance; they couldn't rape Lady Nobuko. Continuing along the footpath, he observed that most of the boats were small, open craft with a single oar. But quite a few others were larger, some forty paces long, each with a single mast, a square sail, a cabin with a red tile roof on the deck, and three sets of oars below. Figures blurred by the mist boarded and disembarked, customers of the illegal floating brothels which all fit the description Nanbu had provided. The only detail Nanbu hadn't mentioned was the red lanterns that hung from the eaves of the cabins. Gombei had spoken the truth: Without him as a guide, Sano would not have been able to pick out the right one.

Gombei stopped so suddenly that Marume, Jinshichi, and Fukida bumped into him and Hirata. He pointed at a boat moored two slips down the river. "That's it," Gombei said.

"How do you know?" Sano asked.

"Do you see that man on the deck?"

The man stood at the railing, facing inland, his tall, gaunt profile a dark silhouette. He had bad posture, his shoulders slumped, his hips and head thrust forward.

"He's the owner," Gombei said. "He takes a cut of the money our customers pay us for the women."

"You'd better be telling the truth," Sano said.

They strolled casually toward the boat, a party of friends out for the evening. "You stay on the dock and guard our informants," Sano told Marume and Fukida. "Hirata-*san* and I will go aboard."

As they neared the boat, the owner came into clearer view. His long hair was greased back into a knot. His robes hung on him, reminding Sano of a clothes stand. There didn't appear to be anyone else on board, but the windows of the cabin were closed, Sano couldn't see inside it or below the deck. He and his companions had just reached the dock, when four samurai came hurrying down a street that led between the teahouses to the river. The four headed for the dock. When they saw Sano, they stopped in surprise. He recognized them as his own troops.

"What are you doing here?" Sano kept his voice calm. "You were supposed to watch Joju."

"We followed him here from the temple," the leader said. "We just saw him get on that boat."

Shock and dismay filled Sano. The exorcist was already with Lady Nobuko. But that gave Sano the chance to catch him in the act of rape.

Looking toward the boat, Sano saw the owner looking straight back at him. The man had heavy purplish bags under wary eyes; black moles peppered his cheeks. Three more men appeared, climbing up from under the deck, to see what the commotion was all about. They were samurai, heavyset and tough and armed with swords, *rōnin* hired to guard the brothel.

Suddenly Gombei shouted, "Look out! They've come to raid your boat!"

40

In the cemetery, Nanbu called to Jirocho, "What is this?" His face was ugly with anger. The dog on his leash growled. "You told me to come here and pay blackmail, and now you shoot at me and kill my men. Are you crazy?"

"Not crazy, just practical," Jirocho said. Nanbu's men held lanterns up to him, the better to see his face. He posed like the lead actor onstage in a Kabuki drama. The flames and shadows exaggerated his predatory smile, the ferocity in his eyes. "It's obvious you came to fight instead of paying. Forgive me if I changed the odds in my favor."

Reiko counted only twenty men still standing in the cemetery. Jirocho's forces outnumbered Nanbu's and Ogita's by a good margin, and the gangster had his adversaries surrounded.

"I told you we shouldn't have come," Ogita said bitterly.

"Ah, Ogita-*san*. How nice to see you." Jirocho's voice dripped vindictive scorn. "Where's Joju the exorcist?"

"How should I know?" Ogita retorted.

"Two out of three will have to do, then." Jirocho beckoned. "Stop hiding behind your guards. You and Nanbu-*san*, step closer."

When neither man budged, his gang drew their bows, aimed arrows and spears. Ogita and Nanbu reluctantly moved toward the wall upon which Jirocho stood. Peering around the crematorium, Reiko and her comrades had a clear view of them. "Good," Jirocho said, then addressed their men: "Hold your lanterns up to their faces."

"What is this?" Nanbu said again, but he'd lost his bluster. Illuminated by the lanterns, he showed as much anxiety as rage.

Jirocho reached behind him. Reiko saw a small hand reach up from the darkness on the other side of the wall and grasp his. A girl dressed in a white kimono printed with blue irises scrambled onto the wall beside Jirocho.

Chiyo gasped. "Fumiko!"

The dogs began to bark at the girl. She seemed not to notice anyone but Jirocho. She gazed up at him, her eyes filled with adoration.

Jirocho yanked his hand free of hers. He jerked his chin toward Nanbu and Ogita and said, "Which one is it?"

Fumiko reluctantly moved her gaze from her father to the two men. A frown creased her forehead. Ogita said in disgust, "It's just as I thought: She doesn't know. That's why Jirocho blackmailed both of us, and the priest, too, it seems. Nanbu-san, I tried to tell you it was a trick. But you wouldn't listen. Now look at the mess we're in!"

"Shut up!" Nanbu said.

"Open your robes and take off your loincloths." Jirocho was obviously determined to repeat the examination done at Edo Jail, with better results. Nanbu and Ogita looked at each other in consternation. "Do it, or my men will."

Nanbu cursed as he and Ogita stripped. Loincloths shed, they held their robes open, displaying their genitals. Reiko saw the huge, dark mole on Nanbu's penis.

"He's the one," Fumiko said, her shrill voice ringing clear. She pointed at Nanbu.

Reiko saw another pair matched up in the sordid game of criminals and victims. Nanbu had raped Fumiko, Ogita had raped Chiyo, and that probably left the absent Joju guilty of the nun's violation and suicide.

Jirocho fixed Nanbu with a gaze as cold as steel in winter. He said to his gang, "We'll have to kill everybody. We don't want any witnesses."

The gangsters armed with spears jumped down from the wall. As they faced off against Nanbu's and Ogita's troops, Ogita cried, "Wait! I'll give him to you, if you let me go. I promise never to talk!"

His men grabbed Nanbu and shoved him toward Jirocho. Struggling to free himself, Nanbu let go of his dog's leash. He pointed to Jirocho and yelled, "Attack!"

The dog charged. It sprang higher than Reiko had thought possible, up to the top of the wall. Jirocho stepped backward, too late. The dog caught his ankle in its teeth. As it fell, it dragged Jirocho with it. Jirocho yelled and flailed his arms. He and the dog crashed into the cemetery together in a tangle of thrashing, howling, and cursing.

"Father!" Fumiko exclaimed, and jumped off the wall.

A cry of distress burst from Chiyo. She rushed from behind the crematorium toward Fumiko.

"No! Don't!" Reiko drew her dagger and ran after Chiyo.

Lieutenant Tanuma called, "Lady Reiko, stop!" as he and her other bodyguards followed.

The dog savaged at Jirocho's throat. Jirocho shouted, "Help!" and beat at the animal. Fumiko grabbed the dog by its spiked collar. His men hurried to his aid, but Nanbu's troops and dogs headed them off. Chiyo seized Fumiko by the arm. Reiko, close behind Chiyo, saw Fumiko tugging at the dog.

It turned on her and lunged. She screamed and reeled backward, throwing up her arms to protect her face. Chiyo hurled herself between the dog and Fumiko. The dog struck her with all four huge paws, a missile of solid flesh and bone. Chiyo went down. Reiko slashed at the beast, heedless of the laws against hurting dogs. Her blade opened a bloody gash in its side. Now it turned on her. Pure, mindless savagery blazed in its red eyes. It sprang for her throat, its mouth open in a vicious snarl, its throat a gaping red maw. Reiko lashed out her dagger and cut the dog across its belly in midair. It uttered a piercing yowl. Blood and intestines poured from the wound as the dog landed on the ground, panting and squirming.

Reiko hurried to Chiyo. "Are you all right?"

"Yes," Chiyo said while Reiko helped her to stand. "Where's Fumiko?"

Reiko looked around. Jirocho struggled to his feet; his face, neck, and hands were bloody from dog bites. Fumiko stumbled toward him, around gangsters battling Nanbu's troops. Ogita stumbled through the melee, yelling, "Get me out of here!" His guards fought their way toward him.

"You're not going anywhere, you traitor!" Having drawn his sword, Nanbu frantically parried jabs from the gangsters' spears. He ordered his men, "Don't let him get away." A few quit the fight against the gangsters and blocked the gate. "Bring me the girl!" Nanbu shouted.

His men snatched at Fumiko. She dodged. Lieutenant Tanuma called to Reiko, "Take Chiyo outside where you'll both be safe. I'll rescue Fumiko."

He and her other guards ran around the cemetery, lashing their swords at the troops chasing Fumiko, trying to herd her out of danger. Chiyo joined the chase. Reiko ran after Chiyo. They caught up to Fumiko. Nanbu's men surrounded them, swords raised, dogs straining on leashes. Reiko swung her dagger while Chiyo and Fumiko hid behind her. The men laughed and feinted at her; they made her spin, circle, and duck. They were so sure she was a typical, harmless female that they grew careless. She sliced a man on his arm. He yelped in surprise. Another man seized Reiko from behind, picked her up, and threw her.

One moment she was flying through air and smoke; the next, she thudded facedown in the weeds, her breath punched out of her, gasping. Chiyo screamed, "Watch out!"

Reiko raised herself on her elbows and saw the man she'd wounded rushing upon her, sword raised in both hands, face contorted with rage. She rolled out of the way just before his blade came down. It struck the ground where she'd lain. Miraculously, she still had her dagger in her hand. As she regained her feet and fought her attacker, she saw another of Nanbu's men grab Fumiko. He passed the kicking, struggling girl to Nanbu.

"Jirocho!" Nanbu shouted. "I've got your daughter." He held his blade to her throat. "Call off your gang, or she's dead!"

He obviously didn't know that Jirocho had cast off his daughter and had only taken her back as part of his scheme to avenge the insult to himself. Reiko was horrified because she knew Jirocho meant to kill Nanbu and didn't care if Fumiko died, too.

The gangsters faltered and retreated from the battle. Reiko was surprised to see that they evidently weren't so sure of their master's intentions. Nanbu's men maintained their fighting stance. Lieutenant Tanuma and her other guards stood between Reiko and her attacker and shielded her with raised swords. Everyone looked toward Jirocho.

He stood speechless, arms dangling. He beheld his daughter, captured by the man who'd raped her, and his ravaged, bloody face took on an expression of pure anguish.

Shock stunned Reiko. He did care about Fumiko after all. Reiko realized that despite his outlaw status, he was a conventional man who observed the mores of society. He'd rejected his daughter because he felt obligated to, not because he'd stopped loving her. Now he regretted that his plan had put her in danger. Reiko read the other thoughts that he couldn't hide. The child he'd disowned had saved him from Nanbu's dog. Even as he realized he'd made a mistake by casting her off, he feared he would lose her for good.

The crackle of the body burning inside the crematorium was loud in the silence. The people in the cemetery were as still as the corpses that littered the ground. Even the dogs quieted. Fumiko stood in Nanbu's grasp, regarding her father with hopeful anticipation. Everyone waited to see what Jirocho would do.

Gombei ran toward the boat, yelling to the owner, "You have to leave now!"

Jinshichi hurried after him. "We're coming with you!"

"Hey!" Marume yelled. "Stop!"

Sano and Hirata were already racing after the two oxcart drivers. The boat owner shouted commands. Two peasant crewmen bolted up from below deck. One untied the ropes that moored the boat. As Gombei and Jinshichi hit the gangplank, the other crewman tried to raise it. The three *rōnin* on board blocked the gate in the boat's railing. They drew their swords.

"Get off," one of them ordered the oxcart drivers.

"Take us with you, or they'll kill us," Gombei cried.

"You brought them here. You traitors!"

As Hirata caught up with Gombei and Jinshichi, one of the *rōnin* cut the two men across their throats. Blood spurted as they collapsed. The quick, brutal violence horrified Sano even though their deaths were punishment well deserved. Hirata kicked their bodies into the river. Swords drawn, he and Sano clambered up the gangplank, which was slick with blood. Marume and Fukida and their other troops were close behind them. Hirata lunged at the guards on the boat. His blade moved in arcs and slashes too fast for the men to parry. They fell back even as their master shouted at them to stop the intruders. Hirata and Sano leaped aboard.

The crewmen disconnected the gangplank. It fell, carrying Marume, Fukida, and the rest of Sano's men into the river with it. The oars began to move as the crew below deck rowed. The boat pulled away from the bank.

"I'll handle this," Hirata called to Sano as the guards rallied and he began to fight them. "Save the shogun's wife!"

Sano grabbed the boat owner by the front of his kimono and held the sword to his neck. "Where is she?"

"I don't know what you're talking about!"

Sano flung the man into the battle raging between his guards and Hirata. As the boat accelerated down the river, people peered curiously out from the teahouses. Sano saw Marume and Fukida in the water, swimming after the boat. He tried to slide open the cabin door. The wooden panel felt oddly heavy. It was loose in its frame, but locked from the inside. He applied more strength, felt the lock break, and stepped inside.

Dim, silvery light enveloped him. He heard grunts, cries, and rustling that quickly ceased. An odd softness on the floor cushioned his feet. The boat tilted; the door slid shut. Sano found himself in a world of eerie silence. Unnerved, he clutched his sword. As he gazed at his surroundings, he discovered why he couldn't hear any noise from outside.

The walls, floor, ceiling, and windows of the cabin were padded with gray cloth. It glowed silver in the light from a metal lantern suspended from the ceiling. The cloth was ripped in many places, hanging in tatters. There Sano could see white cotton bulging behind the fabric.

He was in the pavilion of clouds.

This was the place where Chiyo had been raped, which she'd described to Reiko. The strange décor plus the drugs explained her memories. The cabin had been furnished to keep sounds from escaping. Sano let out his breath.

He heard someone else breathing fast and hard.

He wasn't alone.

The veils of ripped cloth that dangled from the ceiling partially hid a bizarre tableau in the corner. A naked man with a shaved head lay on his stomach, his muscular legs splayed, arms and hands propping up his body, on a mattress on the floor. His face was turned toward Sano. He didn't move, as if by remaining motionless he could remain unnoticed. His eyes gleamed with lust, silvery reflections, and fright.

It was Joju.

Under him was the nude, emaciated body of an old woman. She lay on her back, her head hidden by the cloth. Alongside her withered limbs and bony torso, a spread of ruddy color glowed, staining her pale, sagging skin crimson. At first Sano thought it was blood and Joju had murdered the shogun's wife. His heart seized. Then she stirred and moaned. Sano saw that the color was Joju's red brocade stole.

"Get up, Joju," Sano said. "Put on your clothes. You're under arrest."

The exorcist slowly pushed himself upright. Sano could see him wondering how much trouble he was in and how to get out of it. His penis withdrew from between the old woman's spread legs. It was limp and shriveled, dripping with semen and blood.

He'd finished the rape.

Sano was dismayed to realize that he'd arrived too late.

But not too late to catch Joju in the act.

Joju yanked his saffron robe out from beneath the woman, who moaned softly. She must have been sedated with the same drug used on Chiyo, Fumiko, and the nun. He pulled the robe over his head and said, "Why are you arresting me?" He'd recovered a semblance of his suave poise. "For having relations with an illegal prostitute?" He uttered a hollow imitation of his boisterous laugh. "That's a minor offense. I'll be let off with a fine. My reputation won't even suffer with the people who matter. You might as well not waste your time."

"I'm arresting you because you violated the shogun's wife and you're a party to her kidnapping. For that, you'll be executed." Sano glanced at the unconscious Lady Nobuko. Her breasts were flat pouches; her rib cage jutted beneath translucent skin laced with blue veins. White pubic hair barely covered her crotch. She looked pitiful and vulnerable. "Now get up." Sano beckoned. "Step away from Lady Nobuko."

Joju didn't move. "You think this is the shogun's wife?" He laughed again, louder. "Well, it isn't."

He pulled aside the dangling cloth that hid the woman's head. Her hair was white, her face as soft and wrinkled as wadded rice paper. She must be in her seventies, much older than Lady Nobuko. The woman Gombei and Jinshichi had kidnapped was someone else. Surprise, disappointment, and confusion stunned Sano.

"Who is she?" he said.

"I don't know. Who cares?"

"Where is Lady Nobuko?" Sano demanded.

"I've no idea," Joju said.

268

If the two oxcart drivers hadn't kidnapped her, then who had? What was happening to her at this moment? Sano had been so sure he would find Lady Nobuko here!

"Why don't we just agree to call this a misunderstanding, and you let me go?" Joju said. "If you don't tell anybody what you saw here, then I won't tell the shogun that you persecuted me and flubbed the search for his wife."

"How dare you try to bargain with me?" Sano's consternation quickly turned to rage.

Joju had raped this woman, no matter that she wasn't Lady Nobuko. And Sano had noticed the similarity between her and one of the previous victims. She was near the same age as the nun, and the unblemished whiteness of her skin indicated that she came from the same high class. Sano remembered his brief glimpse of Joju's penis, now hidden beneath the saffron robe, and further enlightenment struck.

"The blood on you isn't this woman's," Sano said. "It's your own. You're covered with running sores. It was you who raped the nun. You gave her your disease and drove her to suicide."

The look on Joju's face showed his downslide from confident expectancy into apprehension as Sano spoke. His guilt was as obvious as if words describing his crime had been inked on his face, and it was clear that he could tell that Sano had no intention of letting him go. He suddenly snatched at something under the red stole beside the old woman. It was a knife with a shiny steel blade and a black lacquer handle. Even as Sano rushed to grab it and lash his sword at Joju, the exorcist held the blade to the woman's throat.

"Leave me alone, or I'll kill her," he said.

Sano froze, his sword still raised.

"Drop your weapon." Joju's voice and gaze were steady with determination. So was his hand holding the knife.

Sano let his sword fall. It landed noiselessly on the padded floor. Disarmed and immobilized, he cursed himself for underestimating Joju. He knew the exorcist was a fraud and a rapist, but hadn't thought him capable of murder.

"Walk out the door and don't come back," Joju said.

The boat rocked; the door slid open. In came the sounds of feet pounding the deck and blades clashing. Sano heard Marume shout, "Take that!" The detectives must have climbed aboard the boat. Thuds shook the cabin's wall as bodies bumped it. Sano realized that when Chiyo had been imprisoned in the cabin, the door must have opened long enough for her to hear the rain and thunder outside. Then the boat rocked again and the door slid shut, sealing Sano and Joju in eerie quiet once more.

"Be sure to take your men with you," Joju said.

This was a situation that Sano had faced too many times before: A criminal held an innocent person hostage in a ploy to gain his freedom. Counterstrategies that Sano had used in the past raced through his mind, but he couldn't gamble that old ideas would work again.

"Very well," Sano said, thinking fast. He couldn't let the woman die even if she wasn't the shogun's wife. Inspiration arose from his experience with Joju. He backed toward the door, then paused, his chin lifted and his eyes alert, as if at a sudden sound. "Did you hear that?"

41

Jirocho didn't speak the words that would spare Nanbu and save Fumiko. Reiko saw her face briefly sag with disappointment, then transform into a murderous scowl. Fumiko wrenched her body forward. Her sudden movement swayed Nanbu off balance. She thrust her fist backward, between his widespread legs. At the same moment Jirocho raised his hand; he started to speak. Nanbu uttered a bellow of agony. He dropped his sword, let go of Fumiko, and staggered. He sank to his knees, clutching his groin.

"What——?" Jirocho said, his hand still raised, the words he'd meant to speak forgotten. Everyone else stared at Fumiko.

She stood over Nanbu, her face a picture of grim triumph. She held a knife that she'd kept hidden under her sleeve. Reiko gazed at her in awe. Her pose brought to mind a samurai who'd slain his worst enemy in battle. Perhaps Jirocho would have given in to Nanbu, but he hadn't acted soon enough, so Fumiko had taken matters into her own hands.

Blood pumped from the wound she'd inflicted on Nanbu. He roared, a sound as fierce and inhuman as the din of barking and howling that the dogs now commenced. He pressed his hands to the wound, but the blood spilled over them. As his men rushed to help him, he toppled and fell.

Reiko had seen death too many times before. She saw it coming now, in the blankness that obliterated the terror and pain on Nanbu's face, in the inertia that gradually stilled his body. His men saw it, too. Before his last tremors ceased, the cry burst from them: "Avenge our master's death!"

They rushed at Fumiko. This time Jirocho didn't hesitate. "Save my daughter!" he shouted.

His gang fought Nanbu's men and dogs. Fumiko watched her father pick up a club and deliver merciless blows to the enemy troops around her. Her eyes brimmed with adoration. Reiko saw only seven or eight of Nanbu's men left, and only four dogs; the gangsters had killed the rest. Someone bumped into her. It was Ogita, desperately trying to thread his way through the battle, out of the cemetery. He was alone; his guards had died. He collided with grave posts as he neared the gate.

Chiyo stepped in front of it.

"Get out of my way!" he shouted.

She didn't move even though her expression was filled with terror. Reiko couldn't let her friend face Ogita alone. Leaving the gang to defend Fumiko, she ran to Chiyo.

"Who are you?" Ogita was saying.

Chiyo didn't seem to notice Reiko standing by her side. She frowned in dismay and puzzlement as she beheld Ogita. "Don't you know?"

"If we've met before, I don't remember, I'm sorry," Ogita said impatiently. "Now please move."

"You had me kidnapped. You—you had relations with me while I was drugged." Chiyo's voice shook. "And you don't even remember me?"

Ogita narrowed his eyes, took another look at Chiyo. Recognition dawned. "Oh. Yes." A lascivious smile crept across his face. "It's a pleasure to see you again. But I'm in a bit of a hurry, so if you don't mind—"

"I do mind." Chiyo was so pale that Reiko feared she would faint, but she bravely stood her ground. "You will not leave until you explain to me why you did it."

"Enough of this nonsense." Ogita lifted his hand, perhaps to push Chiyo out of his way, perhaps to strike her down.

Chiyo snatched the dagger from Reiko. She brandished it at Ogita and cried, "Don't you touch me!"

Reiko was as amazed as Ogita looked. Never had she thought Chiyo would have the courage to confront her rapist, let alone threaten him. But she came from the same clan as Sano. The same samurai blood ran in her veins.

Ogita recoiled, his gaze darting between Chiyo's tense, white face to the weapon in her hand, caught between her and the battle that still raged on. "All right, if you must know: I did it because I wanted to.

And because I could." He smiled at her shocked expression. "Are you satisfied?"

Such fury blazed in her normally mild eyes that Reiko almost didn't recognize her. Her lips moved, but she could find no words to convey her offense at Ogita's callousness.

"No?" Ogita laughed mockingly. "Well, maybe once wasn't enough for you. Would you like to do it again sometime?"

Reiko gasped in indignation. Chiyo flinched as if Ogita had slapped her and said, "Because of what you did to me, I've lost everything." The dagger trembled in her hands. "My children, my husband, and my honor." Tears glistened in her angry eyes. "And you think it's a joke."

"I don't if you don't," Ogita said patronizingly. "I'm sorry if you're upset, but it's water under the bridge, so let's just forget about it, all right?" He extended his hand to her, waggled his fingers, and said, "Give me that dagger."

Chiyo hesitated. Reiko saw her habit of obeying men weaken her desire to stand up to Ogita. Then she gulped a deep, quick breath, as if she'd jumped off a cliff over the ocean and had to fill her lungs before she hit the water. She swiped at Ogita with all her might. The motion sent him skipping backward and her spinning in a clumsy circle. Ogita chuckled half in shock, half in amusement.

"So you want to play rough?" he said. "Normally, I like a woman with a little fight in her, but I've got to go."

He veered around Chiyo toward the gate. She stumbled in front of him, awkwardly swinging the dagger, totally untrained in combat. Reiko watched in amazement as Chiyo's determination made up for lack of experience. Chiyo chased Ogita straight into the battle. He ran sideways, trying to keep an eye on her and the fighters. Reiko ran after them and grabbed a sword from a dead samurai. How she regretted talking so much about justice! Chiyo had taken Reiko's words to heart. She displayed the recklessness of a warrior on a suicide mission. She seemed oblivious to the swords and spears slicing the air around her. Her desire for revenge on Ogita might get her killed.

Perhaps she wanted death as much as revenge.

Would that Reiko could save her from herself!

Ogita tripped over a bloody corpse. It was Nanbu's. Ogita fell. He sprawled on his stomach over Nanbu. He tried to get up, but the blood was slippery, and he fell again.

Chiyo advanced on him, the dagger raised high. The change that came over her was so startling that Reiko froze in her tracks. Her face was as serene and as hard as a stone Buddha's. Ogita looked up at her over his shoulder as he struggled to rise. All the terror he'd caused her in the pavilion of clouds now glazed his eyes. He opened his mouth to protest, or beg.

Chiyo slashed the dagger down. The blade cleaved deep into Ogita's back. Uttering a pitiful croak, he stiffened. He went limp as he died, lying across Nanbu, his conspirator in sinful crimes.

The unnatural serenity deserted Chiyo. Her face crumpled; she sank to her knees beside Ogita and Nanbu; she began to sob. Reiko moved to console her, but Fumiko came running, cut in front of Reiko, and threw her arms around Chiyo.

"Don't cry," Fumiko said. "They were bad men. They deserved to die."

Now Reiko saw that the battle was over. Nanbu's men and dogs all lay lifeless amid the graves. Only Jirocho and some ten gangsters, and Lieutenant Tanuma and Reiko's other guards remained standing. They were disheveled, bruised, and bloody. In the smoke from the crematoriums and the dropped lanterns whose flames smoldered in the weeds, they looked like survivors of some dreadful catastrophe.

Chiyo wept as though purging all the emotion from her spirit. Reiko felt tears of release sting her own eyes. Jirocho left his gang, walked slowly over to Fumiko, and laid his hand on her hair. He swallowed hard and blinked.

"Don't cry," Fumiko said as she began to sob herself. "It's all right."

"Hear what?" Joju frowned, impatient and threatening, his blade firm against the old woman's throat.

"There's somebody here in this room with us," Sano said.

"There's only you and me and her, and you'll be gone soon," Joju retorted.

Sano gazed around the cabin, lifting his hand, feeling the air. "It's somebody from the spirit world."

Contempt twisted the priest's mouth. "Don't try that on me. I'm the expert at all the tricks. You're just an amateur."

" 'We all have the power to communicate with the spirit world.' " Sano quoted the words Joju had spoken to him during their first meeting.

"But only a few of us know how. You're forgetting the rest of what I said."

"I seem to have become one of the few," Sano said, "and I don't need music or fireworks to hear the spirit. She says she wants to talk to you."

"You're stalling." Joju held the knife firmly against the blue vein visible in the woman's neck. "Get out."

"I'm getting a name," Sano said. "It sounds like . . ." He paused, straining the muscles of his face, concentrating hard. "Okitsu."

"I don't know anyone by that name." But Joju looked as shocked as the moneylender he'd bilked. He obviously remembered Okitsu, the beggar woman Sano had met outside the temple.

"She was once possessed by evil spirits who told her that people were out to get her," Sano said. "Her parents brought her to you. You performed an exorcism on her."

"How——?"

"How did I know? She just told me." Sano cocked his head, pretended to listen. "She says you raped her and got her pregnant."

Joju beheld Sano with the fearful wonder of a pilgrim hearing a Buddha statue at a woodland shrine tell guilty secrets he thought nobody knew.

Sano gambled that Joju hadn't bothered to find out what had happened to Okitsu afterward. "She died giving birth."

"No," Joju whispered. He evidently didn't know that Okitsu was still alive and begging outside his temple.

Sano remembered something else Joju had said: *People want to believe in what I do.* He realized that Joju himself believed, and he was as vulnerable to manipulation by false mediums and spirits as his own clients were.

"What does she want?" Joju said reluctantly, unable to help himself. Sano's knowledge of his past had convinced him that the spirit was real.

"There's another spirit with Okitsu," Sano said. "She wants you to meet him."

"Who . . . ?"

"It's her son." Sano paused a beat. "*Your* son."

"I never had any son." Joju's words were less a denial than a plea for Sano to assure him that they were true.

"Now you know better," Sano said. "He doesn't have a name because he died while Okitsu was having him. She says she's been wandering between the world of the living and the world of the dead, carrying him in her arms. She wants to show him to his father. Here he is."

Sano gestured at the empty air near the bed. Joju's stricken gaze moved to the spot Sano indicated. Sano blew on the cloth that hung from the ceiling over the spot. The cloth fluttered. The flame in the lantern wavered. Joju gasped. Sano could almost see the vision the priest saw—a ghostly woman holding out a baby. The hairs rose on Sano's own neck. The power of suggestion was potent indeed.

"I don't want him," Joju said weakly to the ghost. "Leave me alone."

"She's angry at you for what you did," Sano said. "You caused her and the baby to suffer and die. You doomed them never to find peace. And now that she's found you, she wants revenge."

Joju shuddered as he recoiled from the ghostly mother and child. "Please. Go away," he whispered.

His hand that held the knife trembled. He seemed to have forgotten the old woman was there, but one slip of the knife could kill her. Sano felt an increasing pressure to gain control of Joju, fast.

"Okitsu says she's putting a curse on you," Sano said. "Misfortune will follow you wherever you go. The shogun will turn against you. You'll lose your temple, your money, and your reputation. You'll become a pariah begging in the streets. You'll get every disease known to man. Everybody will shun you. You'll suffer terribly."

Joju glared at Sano as if Sano were responsible for the sins he'd committed, the ills he'd brought upon himself. "Make her stop! Make them go away!"

"I can't," Sano said. "I'm not an exorcist. All I can do is act as a mediator between you and Okitsu."

"Then do it!" Panic agitated Joju.

Sano addressed the ghost he'd conjured up. "How can Joju make amends for what he did? What must he do in order for you to lift your curse and cross into the spirit world?"

He pretended to listen. He forced himself to wait and let the suspense build, while Joju watched him with the helpless faith of a drowning man clinging to a rescuer's hand. At last Sano said, "Okitsu says you must confess your sins."

"All right!" Joju cried. "I took advantage of her. I got her with child. It's my fault they died!"

"She says that's not enough. You have to confess all your sins." Sano asked, "Did you rape the nun?"

Joju hesitated, clearly aware that Sano had led him onto ground where he must dig his own grave. But his fear of the future Sano had painted overcame caution. With a groan, he sank in his shovel. "Yes."

At long last Sano had the admission of guilt that he wanted, but he couldn't stop there. "Okitsu still isn't satisfied. She says that if you hurt that old woman, she'll never forgive you. When you die, she'll lay claim to your soul. You and Okitsu and your child will wander in the netherworld together for all eternity."

The priest gazed at the old woman. She slept, oblivious to the drama taking place. In his eyes warred his desire for salvation and his knowledge that if he gave up his hostage, he was doomed.

Sano pointed at a corner of the padded floor. "Okitsu wants you to throw the knife over there. She says, get up and move away from that woman, or the curse starts now."

Joju's fraught expression didn't change, but Sano felt a dangerous impulse flare in him. Sano ducked at the same instant the priest hurled the knife straight at his heart. The knife struck the wall with a muffled thump; the padding absorbed the blade. Joju uttered a roar of desperate, reckless fury. He lunged at Sano. Sano sidestepped, grabbed Joju by the arm, twisted it behind him, and forced him to the floor.

The resistance leaked out of Joju. Pinned under Sano's knee, he wept, babbling, "*Namo Amida Butsu! Namo Amida Butsu! I trust in the Buddha of Immeasurable Light.*" It was the prayer that the nun had told Reiko he'd forced her to say while he'd raped her here, in the pavilion of clouds.

The door crashed open. The sounds of oars splashing in water accompanied Hirata and Detective Marume into the room. "The boat owner and his guards are dead," Hirata said. "The crew has surrendered, and they're taking the boat back to the dock. Fukida is keeping an eye on them . . ." His voice trailed off. He and Marume stared at Sano holding Joju down, at the naked, unconscious woman on the bed, at the padded walls.

"So this is the scene of the crime," Marume said, dripping wet from his swim in the river. "It looks like you've got things under control here. All's well that ends well."

"Not quite," Sano said. The full measure of his success and failure struck satisfaction and despair into him. "I hate to tell you this, but the shogun's wife is still missing."

42

In the morning, Sano and his detectives arrived back at Edo Castle. His troops had taken Joju to Edo Jail and the old woman to Keiaiji Convent, where the nuns would care for her until she could be identified and returned to her home.

Sano wasn't eager to return to his. He'd missed the shogun's deadline, and now he must face the consequences. He had to save his family, but he was so exhausted he could hardly see straight. He'd hardly slept in days.

Outside the gate, one of his soldiers was waiting for him. "Honorable Chamberlain Sano! The shogun's wife has been found!"

Fukida groaned. Marume cursed and said, "Why couldn't it have happened just a few hours sooner?"

Sano felt as much foreboding as relief. "How? By whom?"

The soldier shook his head. "All I know is that she was found lying in the Ginza theater district."

"That's a long way from Chomei Temple," Sano said.

Her abduction hadn't followed the same pattern as the others, when the victims had been dumped near the places they'd been taken. But the two oxcart drivers weren't the culprits this time. There was another kidnapper, still at large.

"Where is Lady Nobuko?" Sano asked.

"She's being taken to the palace."

Sano and his men rode at a gallop through Edo Castle. They arrived at the palace in time to join a crowd of officials and troops watching four guards carry Lady Nobuko on a litter up the path to the entrance. Her thin body was covered by a blanket, her black hair matted. Her eyes were closed, but Sano could tell she was conscious. Pain, misery, and humiliation played across her pale, quivering face, which was contorted on the right side.

The shogun scurried out of the palace, trailed by attendants. When the guards brought Lady Nobuko to him, he squinted at her as if he didn't quite recognize her. He said, "Take her to her chambers. Call the court physician."

At the entrance, her maids and the other court ladies surrounded Lady Nobuko in an exclaiming, weeping horde.

Then the shogun saw Sano, and his expression turned furious. "My wife is home, no thanks to you! I understand she was found by some policemen who, ahh, just happened to stumble upon her." Sano started to apologize, but the shogun cut him off. "The police said my wife has been violated. I've been dishonored." He seemed more angry at Sano than glad to have Lady Nobuko back alive. "And it's all your fault because you didn't rescue her in time!"

He seemed to have forgotten that he'd previously thought Yanagisawa shared the blame for the kidnapping. Yanagisawa was nowhere to be seen. The shogun jabbed his finger at Sano's face. "You'll pay for letting me down. As soon as it can be arranged, you and your family and all your close associates shall die!"

"Your Excellency," Sano began.

After twelve years during which Sano had loyally, unstintingly served him, the shogun turned his back on Sano and stalked into the castle.

Everyone's gazes avoided Sano. The crowd moved away from Sano, Hirata, and the detectives like the ocean receding from an island at low tide.

Reiko hurried toward him. Her expression said she'd heard the shogun's pronouncement. Masahiro also came running. Sano was aghast that his wife and son had not only witnessed his public humiliation, but would die because he had failed.

"Don't worry," he said more confidently than he felt. He didn't want to frighten Reiko and Masahiro, but he feared that this time they were all lost.

"I have to tell you what else happened." Breathless with excitement, Reiko said, "Nanbu and Ogita are dead."

She poured out a story of blackmail, an ambush and a battle in a cemetery, and the shocking outcome. Sano's men listened with amazement. Sano could barely absorb what he was hearing.

"Where have you been?" Reiko asked.

Sano didn't have a chance to answer, because Masahiro tugged his sleeve and said excitedly, "Father, I've seen that lady before!"

"What lady?" Sano asked.

"The shogun's wife. Remember how I spied on Chamberlain Yanagisawa? She's one of the three ladies he met."

This latest revelation was too much on top of too much for Sano. He and Reiko stared at Masahiro in surprise.

"Yanagisawa had a *miai* with the shogun's wife?" Reiko said.

She sounded as confused as Sano felt. But now Sano began to understand what Yanagisawa was up to. The sheer audacity of it took his breath away.

Masahiro pointed at the crowd of women around the shogun's wife. "And there are the two other ladies!"

Sano spotted an old woman with a babyish face, and a tall, plain younger one. They walked close beside Lady Nobuko as the guards carried her litter into the palace. Sano had never seen them before, but the fact that they clearly outranked the other women told him their identities.

"Who are they?" Reiko asked.

"The elder is Lady Oden, a former concubine of the shogun," Sano said. "The younger is Tsuruhime, his daughter by Oden."

A sudden thought struck him. Masahiro hadn't been the only witness to their meeting with Yanagisawa. The spy Toda Ikkyu had been there, too.

Reiko gasped. "Yanagisawa wants to marry the shogun's daughter to Yoritomo!"

"Yes, because if that happens, it will move Yoritomo way up in the succession," Sano said, enlightened at last. "That's how he plans to seize power." His plan explained why Yanagisawa had stopped embezzling from the Tokugawa treasury: He thought the money would be all his someday. "He had to get Lady Nobuko's permission for the match because she's in charge of all business concerning Tsuruhime, her stepdaughter."

"But the shogun's wife told Yanagisawa no," Masahiro said, pleased by his parents' reaction to his news even though Sano doubted he understood its significance. "He said he could get a divorce. But she said it would be incest."

Sano recalled Masahiro asking him what those words meant. Now he knew why. He also knew why Lady Nobuko had refused Yanagisawa's proposal. "Tsuruhime is already married, to a member of a Tokugawa branch clan. They don't have any children, so Yanagisawa must have thought a second marriage for her would be acceptable to everyone. But a divorce apparently couldn't remove all Lady Nobuko's objections to remarrying her stepdaughter to Yoritomo, who is her father's lover."

"I suppose that could be called incest," Hirata said.

"Yanagisawa was very angry," Masahiro said.

And Yanagisawa never let anyone who crossed him go unpunished. Sano saw a dreadful picture taking shape, a horrifying answer to questions in his mind.

"What are you going to do?" Reiko asked.

"I'm going to have a talk with Yanagisawa," Sano said, "and not just about his marriage scheme."

But Yanagisawa wasn't the only person Sano meant to confront. Sano also intended to get an explanation from Toda Ikkyu.

If he lived long enough.

43

Sano had his chance at Yanagisawa and Toda four days later.

During those days, an upheaval rocked the government's highest echelon and altered the circumstances of Sano and everyone close to him. And although he'd suffered drastic losses, he and his family were alive, and he was thankful.

Now he, Marume, and Fukida stood among a huge crowd gathered in the grounds of Joju's temple to witness the punishment of the famous exorcist.

The chief official from the Ministry of Temples announced, "Joju has been found guilty of *nyobon*." That was the offense termed "woman crime," which meant fornication and breaking a vow of celibacy. "He has been sentenced to *inu-barai*."

"That's a harsh punishment," Marume said as a rumble of awe swept the audience.

"Not as harsh as he deserves," Sano said, "but it was the best I could do under the circumstances."

Joju hadn't actually kidnapped anyone, and although he'd raped the nun and the other old woman, that wasn't a crime under Tokugawa law. Sex in an illegal brothel was a minor offense, as he'd told Sano. And he hadn't actually murdered the nun. Duty-bound to observe the law of the regime, Sano had turned Joju over to the Ministry of Temples, which was responsible for disciplining wayward clergy. Due to testimony from Sano, the ministry had found the priest guilty of the two offenses and imposed the harshest sentence possible.

The exorcist emerged from the hall where he'd once conducted rituals. He was naked, crawling on his hands and knees, with a dead fish crammed in his mouth. Two soldiers led Joju by a rope tied around his neck. They dragged him around the temple grounds three times. Gagging on the rotten fish, hooted at by the mob, he passed Sano without acknowledging his presence. At the temple's gate, the soldiers yanked Joju to his feet; they untied the rope. He spat out the fish and wiped his mouth on his hand. Now his eyes found Sano. They were black with bitter hostility.

The chief ministry official flung a gray hemp robe at Joju and said, "You are hereby expelled from the religious order. You are also banished from Edo."

Joju put on the humble robe. Head bowed, he limped out the gate. The jeering crowd followed him. One woman lingered. It was the beggar named Okitsu. She sidled up to Sano.

"That was worth waiting to see." An impish grin brightened her dirty face.

"It wouldn't have been possible if not for you," Sano said.

Okitsu nodded as though she understood. Then she ambled off. Fate worked in strange ways, Sano thought. Okitsu had gotten her revenge.

A group of male commoners loitered near Sano's party. Four were talking about the scene they'd just witnessed. The fifth hovered at the group's edge. A breeze flapped the wicker hat he wore. When he put up his hand to hold it on his head, Sano saw a large, irregularly shaped brown freckle on his wrist.

"Well, if it isn't Toda Ikkyu," Sano said.

Toda started. "How did you know it was me?"

"Let's just say I've learned a few things from my son." Sano smiled, watching Toda wonder what feature of his Masahiro had noticed and mentioned to Sano. "I've been wanting to talk to you, but you've been pretty scarce lately."

"I've been busy," Toda said.

Sano knew Toda had been avoiding him, with good reason. "You knew who they were."

"What are you talking about?" Toda was all innocence.

"The three women you saw meeting with Yanagisawa," Sano said. "They were Lady Nobuko, the shogun's daughter Tsuruhime, and his former concubine Oden."

The bland expression Toda wore didn't hide his shock. "How did you find out?"

"You said you didn't know who they were. But you did. You know everybody associated with the shogun. You must have recognized them instantly. You lied."

Comprehension glinted in Toda's eyes. "It was Masahiro again. I suppose you also know what became of Yanagisawa's scheme to marry his son to Tsuruhime, ensure that Yoritomo would be the next shogun, and secure his own future?"

"Yes."

"Your son has a talent for espionage," Toda said wryly. "If you'll give him to me, I'll teach him to be the best spy who ever lived."

"My son will never work under a man who double-crossed his father," Sano said.

Toda smiled. "I warned you that I work for both you and Yanagisawa. I try to play fair. I told you about his secret meeting, but I didn't tell you who the women were. I let him know that I was spying on him for you, but I didn't tell him I witnessed his three meetings."

Three meetings? Sano frowned because he'd thought there had been only two. Neither Toda nor Masahiro had mentioned a third. Toda had lied again, by omission. And so had Masahiro.

"So I'm even with you and Yanagisawa," Toda said. "You shouldn't bear me any grudge."

"What you mean is that even if I do bear a grudge, I can't kill you, because someday I may need your services," Sano said. "But next time I'll have a better idea of how far to trust you."

Toda shrugged, his confident superiority restored: He'd successfully navigated another battlefield between two rivals. "That's politics."

He turned and shuffled off, looking for all the world like a peasant to everyone except Sano.

"Don't look now," Marume said, "but here comes another sorry bastard."

The sight of Yanagisawa striding toward him filled Sano with the anger that enflamed his blood every time he thought of what Yanagisawa had done.

"Greetings," Yanagisawa said, smiling as if nothing were amiss.

He'd completely escaped the responsibility the shogun had once placed on him for the disappearance of Lady Nobuko. While Sano had been busy trying to rescue her, Yoritomo had talked the shogun into forgiving Yanagisawa and heaping all the punishment on Sano. The shogun had demoted Sano to his former post of principal investigator. Sano had moved back to his old estate, while Yanagisawa had reclaimed the compound he'd lived in before he'd been exiled. Yanagisawa was now the shogun's only second-in-command, Japan's only chamberlain, once more. That was a crushing blow to Sano, but he knew things could have been worse.

His allies had persuaded the shogun to spare Sano and demote him instead of executing him and his family. They didn't want Yanagisawa in charge of the regime now or in the future. They needed someone to check his power, and Sano was the only man around who had the potential.

"I'm surprised to see you," Sano said evenly. Toda wasn't the only one who'd been avoiding him.

"I had to see this spectacle. Joju wasn't my favorite person in the world."

"I don't suppose he was." Sano knew Yanagisawa didn't like anyone who had strong influence over the shogun. Which was why he'd finally delivered the blow Sano had been expecting.

"Having Joju humiliated and banished was a risky move on your part, since he was still the shogun's favorite exorcist the last I heard," Yanagisawa said. "Does the shogun know?"

"Not yet," Sano said. "In some cases it's better to ask forgiveness after the fact than to ask permission beforehand."

Since he was already in trouble, he'd decided he might as well deliver Joju to justice. That, plus the fact that Ogita, Nanbu, and the oxcart drivers had gotten their comeuppance, was something of a consolation prize.

"That's what I always say." Yanagisawa continued, "I heard about the massacre in the paupers' cemetery. The official word is that Nanbu and Ogita were murdered by bandits. But we both know that the official word isn't always the truth, don't we?"

Sano made no comment. He would never reveal what had actually happened. Neither would Chiyo, Fumiko, Jirocho and his gang, or Reiko and her bodyguards. And all the other witnesses were dead.

"No matter," Yanagisawa said. "Your investigation was a success. Everyone responsible for kidnapping and raping your cousin and those other women has been punished."

"Not everyone." Sano leveled a hard gaze on Yanagisawa.

Yanagisawa raised his eyebrows. "You've accused me of many things in the past, but come now; you can't think I'm to blame this time."

"I don't just think. I know." Sano tried to control his temper. Losing it would only give Yanagisawa more advantage than he already had. "The oxcart drivers didn't kidnap the shogun's wife. Nanbu, Joju, and Ogita didn't rape her. What happened to her was your doing."

"Mine?" Pointing at his own chest, Yanagisawa laughed. "I never touched Lady Nobuko."

"Not personally. You have people to do your dirty work."

Yanagisawa regarded Sano with annoyance, caution, and pity, the kind of look that one gives a madman. "Why would I do such a thing?"

"Because it was the perfect way to sabotage me. You staged Lady Nobuko's kidnapping to look as if it were one in the series I was investigating. You hoped the shogun would blame me. Which he did. Which put me out of his favor." Sano's indignation mounted higher with each consequence of Yanagisawa's scheme he named. "Which is just what you wanted."

"How can you think that? Maybe in the past I would have done it, but since I came back I've done nothing but cooperate with you. Everything that's happened to you was just your bad luck." Shaking his head, Yanagisawa said, "I'm ready to let bygones be bygones."

"You never met a bygone that you could forget," Sano retorted. "Here's another reason you had Lady Nobuko kidnapped and raped: When you tried to marry your son to the shogun's daughter, Lady Nobuko stood in your way."

He watched shock wipe the condescension off Yanagisawa's face. Sano could feel Yanagisawa's impulse to ask how Sano knew about the marriage scheme and who'd thwarted it. In the moment before Yanagisawa regained his usual sardonic expression, Sano knew Yanagisawa was guilty as charged.

"You had an innocent woman kidnapped and raped because she crossed you!" Sano said, letting loose his outrage. This time Yanagisawa had outdone himself in terms of nerve, selfish disregard for human life, and sheer cruelty. "And she's your lord's wife!"

Yanagisawa smiled, his brazen confidence restored. "Let's suppose—just suppose—that I did have Lady Nobuko kidnapped and raped. You have no proof."

"I'm reinvestigating her case. Something will turn up eventually," Sano said, even though he'd been combing the city for four days and no evidence or witnesses had surfaced yet. Yanagisawa had taken pains to cover his tracks.

"Don't count on any help from Lady Nobuko." Yanagisawa's gaze said he knew Sano had asked for an interview with her and she'd refused. Even if Lady Nobuko could recognize the men who'd kidnapped and raped her—which she probably couldn't, because they'd probably given her the same drug that the oxcart drivers had used on their victims— she would never incriminate Yanagisawa. If it was her word against Yanagisawa's, who would the shogun believe?

Probably Yanagisawa.

Furthermore, Lady Nobuko must be aware that no matter how well guarded she was, Yanagisawa could get to her again.

"You won't get away with it," Sano persisted.

"Who's going to stop me? You?" Scorn colored Yanagisawa's voice. "Remember, you have less authority than you once did. I happen to know that His Excellency refuses to speak to you. Meanwhile, my allies are telling him that you're a liability to the Tokugawa regime. When you're gone, I'll still be here."

The genial mask that Yanagisawa had worn for more than a year dropped. At last his face showed his hatred for Sano and his ambition to rule Japan. His dark, liquid eyes shimmered as if with reflections from steel blades.

"Your plan to marry Yoritomo to the shogun's daughter won't work," Sano said. "Try it again, and you'll meet with a lot of resistance."

Sano had told Tsuruhime's husband and his own allies about Yanagisawa's scheme. They'd agreed to block the divorce and remarriage, with military force if need be.

Yanagisawa chuckled. "That's a case of showing up for a battle at the wrong field. Even if I had aimed to wed Yoritomo to the shogun's daughter—which I'm not saying I did—that's not my plan now. I'm exploring other options."

He gestured to a group of samurai who were apparently waiting for him. Sano recognized several Tokugawa clan members among them. Yanagisawa hadn't wasted any time pursuing new, politically advantageous matches for his son.

His son, who'd been his full partner in everything he'd done. Yori-tomo had spoken against Sano to the shogun with Yanagisawa's conniv-ance and blessing, whether Yanagisawa ever admitted it or not.

"I won't be out of the shogun's favor forever," Sano said, "and you won't always be in it. As you've learned in the past."

Yanagisawa contemplated Sano. "Here's some friendly advice." He spoke as if he were so confident he'd beaten Sano, he could afford to be magnanimous. "The game has changed. It's not just about the shogun anymore. This concerns the future, after he's gone. There's no point in squabbling with each other, vying for his good grace." Yanagisawa's tone expressed contempt for such past tactics. "The victor will be the one who insinuates himself into the Tokugawa clan and secures a place in the next regime. And even though I might have failed once, I have a head start on you."

A mischievous smile gleamed on Yanagisawa's face. "I have four sons and a daughter of marriageable age. It's too bad for you that your children are so young." As he strode off to join his allies, he said over his shoulder, "Whatever you think happened, I've won this round."

For four days Hirata had been riding through the city, trying to lure his enemy to him. For four days he'd had no luck. Now, as the twilight descended upon Edo, he found himself in the fish market by the Nihonbashi Bridge.

The stalls were vacant. The orange rays of the setting sun cast long black shadows over the empty aisles. Rats and stray dogs scavenged through heaps of seashells. Hirata climbed off his horse and stood in the center of the market. He projected his senses outward, searching.

Once again he failed to detect his enemy's presence.

Hirata breathed his own desperation, which smelled as rotten as the fish market. He was weak, light-headed, and ill from the fatigue born of sleepless nights and constant anxiety. The old wound in his leg ached. He felt as if the enemy had used his own body and mind as weapons against him, had conquered him without a battle.

That was the strategy of the top martial artists in history. Perhaps it had been his enemy's all along.

Other troubles contributed to Hirata's sorry mental and physical state. Before his death, Ogita had told the shogun that Hirata had killed his servant. The shogun, already upset because Hirata had killed too many other men in duels, had decided that Hirata was too dangerous to be allowed near him. Even if Hirata hadn't had to give up his estate to Sano, he'd have had to move out of Edo Castle. Now he and his family lived in a small estate across the river, banished and disgraced.

But Hirata was determined to make amends and regain his good standing. He meant to fight the enemy face-to-face. If he lost, he would at least see his conqueror and know his name before he died.

"Here I am!" he called. "Come and get me. Or are you afraid?"

His taunt echoed across the deserted market. Hirata listened, then froze alert at the sound of footsteps. They approached from every direction, like a multitude converging on Hirata, but they all had the same stealthy, measured gait; they belonged to one lone man. With them came the unmistakable pulse of the enemy's shield.

Even though the familiar panic surged through Hirata, he didn't turn in circles in a futile attempt to locate the man; he resisted the urge to strike out blindly; he didn't waste his strength. He stood still, looked straight ahead down the aisle of stalls, and simply waited.

A man glided into view at the end of the aisle perhaps a hundred paces from Hirata. By some trick of light or sleight of mind he appeared closer, his size formidably magnified. With the sun's orange glow behind him, Hirata couldn't see his features. He was a tall, black silhouette, his topknot a bulge above his shaved crown, his two swords jutting at his waist.

Hirata felt his heart race and the impulse to flee or give chase leap within him as he and his enemy faced each other. He called, "Who are you?"

The enemy turned away, and the fading sun briefly lit the right side of his face. Hirata glimpsed its high cheekbone and strong jaw, and the curve of a smile that was serene and chilling. Then the man stepped behind the stalls and vanished.

Hirata let him go. He knew they would meet again, just as he knew that the matter of when or where wasn't his to choose. The time and place, the weapons and the circumstances, would be the enemy's decision. And then they would fight to the death.

That was their destiny.

* * *

"Yanagisawa is right about one thing," Sano told Reiko as they sat in their chamber that night. "He has won this time."

"He did it by fighting dirty." Reiko brushed her hair with hard, angry strokes. "He always does." Sano had told her everything, and she was furious at Yanagisawa. For Sano's sake, she made an effort to smile and look on the bright side of the situation. "This isn't so bad. You always liked investigating crimes better than running the government. And we're back where we started, in the place we lived when we were first married."

Sano nodded. But they both knew that things weren't the same as in the past. He'd suffered a tremendous loss of face, a mortal wound to his samurai honor.

"You'll win in the end," Reiko assured Sano.

"I appreciate your faith in me," Sano said wryly. "And I'm not finished yet."

He had to climb back up the ladder of the regime, Reiko knew. Not only did his honor depend on it; people were counting on him to save Japan from Yanagisawa.

"But Yanagisawa is right about something else, too," Sano said.

"What?" Reiko didn't want to hear that Yanagisawa had yet another advantage over her husband.

"We're not just rivals for power in the here and now, but in the future. And maybe the score won't be settled by us." Sano contemplated Akiko playing in the next room with her dolls. "Maybe that's up to our children."

Reiko was dismayed to think the children would inherit the war between their fathers. "How can we protect them? Especially after we're gone?" That time might come sooner rather than later, if Sano didn't regain the shogun's favor. Even if the shogun was on the decline, he still had the power of life and death over everyone.

"It's not too early to think about marriages for Akiko and Masahiro."

Even though Reiko knew Sano was right, she said, "But they're still babies!"

"There won't be any weddings until they're adults. But we could betroth them to members of powerful clans. That's done all the time. It would not only create more alliances for me; it would secure Masahiro's and Akiko's futures."

Reiko sighed; she wished her children could marry for love, not political considerations. But she and Sano had found love in their arranged marriage. Maybe the children would be lucky, too. "A match for Masahiro should come first, because he's the elder."

"Speaking of Masahiro," Sano said. He put a finger to his lips as their son entered the room. They greeted Masahiro, and Sano asked, "What did you do today?"

"I played detective," Masahiro said.

Sano and Reiko exchanged glances. After he'd proved the worth of his talents, they couldn't not let him play his favorite game. Sano said, "I need to ask you a question. How did you know that the shogun's wife refused Yanagisawa's proposal? I thought you said you couldn't hear what Yanagisawa and the ladies were saying."

"I was too far away the first time they met," Masahiro said. "The second time, it was just Yanagisawa and the shogun's wife, and I heard everything because——" He clapped his hand over his mouth.

"The second time!" Shocked, Reiko said, "Do you mean you spied on Yanagisawa again?" Masahiro's sheepish silence was his answer. She turned to Sano. "How did you know?"

"It was something Toda Ikkyu let slip," Sano said. "He wasn't entirely truthful with me, either."

"We forbade you to go spying on Yanagisawa," Reiko reminded Masahiro. "You disobeyed us!"

Masahiro winced. "Am I going to be punished?"

Reiko spread her hands helplessly and looked at Sano.

"You punish him. I don't have the heart," Sano said.

Neither did Reiko, after Masahiro had helped them figure out Yanagisawa's plot. She leveled a stern look on Masahiro. "You were lucky this time, but don't ever do it again."

"I won't," Masahiro said somberly. "I promise."

Reiko heard the echo of her own voice on past occasions, promising Sano that she wouldn't do something or other, all the while knowing that she would. She felt Sano looking at her, obviously remembering that she'd said she wouldn't go to the Kumazawa house again. But Masahiro's actions had made her feel more optimistic about his future. He'd inherited his father's cleverness and her own talent for getting out of as well as into trouble.

"It's time for bed," Reiko told Masahiro.

"Yes, Mother. Good night, Father." Masahiro trotted off before his parents could change their minds and punish him, buying their goodwill for the future.

"If he wants to help with other investigations, how can we say no?" Reiko said ruefully.

Sano chuckled, but his expression turned sober.

"What are you thinking about?" Reiko asked.

"I'm remembering the day Major Kumazawa came to me for help. I thought that all I had to do was find Chiyo. It seemed like the easiest, least dangerous case I'd ever had." Irony provoked a twisted smile from Sano. "Things didn't turn out quite as I expected."

"But you did find Chiyo. You also found the criminals who kidnapped and violated her and Fumiko and the nun." Reiko felt a fierce admiration for Sano. "If not for you, those men would have gone on to hurt other women, and Chiyo and Fumiko wouldn't have gotten their revenge. What happened to you isn't fair."

"Life isn't fair," Sano said, turning philosophical. "I've been lucky until now. I suppose it was my turn for a little misfortune. But I can handle this." He added with regret, "I just wish I could have saved Lady Nobuko and the old woman on the boat."

"The old woman is safe at home with her family. She has you to thank for that." Reiko loved Sano for his confidence, his determination not to complain, and his tendency to think of other people even while he was in trouble. She, too, believed they would weather this crisis as they had others.

"I also wish I could have mended the breach between my family and the Kumazawa clan," Sano said.

Reiko knew that even though Major Kumazawa had treated him so badly, Sano had wanted to reunite the clan for his mother's sake, if not his own. "Maybe you still can."

"That would salvage some good out of everything that's happened," Sano said. "I do have an idea I'd like to try."

Epilogue

The rainy season had ended by the time Sano went to the Kumazawa house again. The mist had evaporated, and the hot summer sun shone above the Asakusa district. When Sano arrived at the mansion, Chiyo greeted him at the door. She was completely transformed since the first time he'd seen her. She'd regained weight and health; her smile was bright. She held her baby while her little boy clung to her skirt and regarded Sano with solemn curiosity.

"Welcome, Honorable Cousin." Chiyo bowed. "A million thanks for returning my children to me."

"It was no trouble," Sano said.

In fact, it had cost him a good deal of trouble. First he'd appealed to Chiyo's husband, but the man still wanted nothing to do with Chiyo and had refused to let her see the children. Hence, Sano had forced a compromise in which the children would live with Chiyo, at her father's estate, every other month. The husband and his powerful associates were now Sano's enemies and Yanagisawa's allies. But Sano thought that was a small price to pay for Chiyo's happiness.

"I'd like to speak with your father," Sano said. "Is he home?"

Chiyo smiled as if she knew a pleasant secret that Sano didn't know. "Yes. Come in."

When Sano walked into the reception chamber, he found a woman sitting in the place of honor in front of the alcove, drinking tea with Major Kumazawa and his wife.

"Mother?" Sano said, astonished. "What are you doing here?"

She smiled fondly at him. "Major Kumazawa sent me a letter, inviting me to visit." Her remarriage and her new life in a country village suited her. She looked almost young, her complexion fresh, the wrinkles filled out. She also seemed happy about her reunion with her brother, in her family home. "I've been here three days. We were just discussing when to tell you." She gestured to the place on the floor beside her. "Please, sit."

Sano remained standing. He said to Major Kumazawa, "I thought we decided it would be best for our families to stay estranged."

Chagrin softened Major Kumazawa's stiff features. "So we did. But after I thought about what you've done for my daughter, and for me, at such a cost to yourself . . . I changed my mind." His speech was devoid of his usual grudging manner. "Besides, I've missed Etsuko. I wanted to see her again."

Brother and sister, separated for forty-four years, seemed to be at peace if not openly affectionate with each other. There was much to forgive on at least one side.

Sano's mother said, "We've been getting reacquainted."

"So I see," Sano said.

"I can see now that you have inherited good qualities from your mother," Major Kumazawa said. "Both of you are willing to risk your own skins to do what you think is right. That's courage. Stubborn and reckless, to be sure, but honorable."

A wry smile tugged Sano's mouth. He knew better than to expect unalloyed approval from his uncle, and he couldn't help feeling pleased. It went some way toward making up for the insults that Major Kumazawa had hurled at him, which Sano would forgive for his mother's sake.

"Join us," Major Kumazawa said.

Sano sat. Major Kumazawa's wife served him tea and rice cakes, the first nourishment he'd taken in his ancestral estate. It slaked not just hunger or thirst, but the yearning for family connection that had spurred him to help the Kumazawa clan despite his misgivings.

"I heard what happened to you because of Lady Nobuko. Your wife wrote to Chiyo and told her everything. I wouldn't blame you for blaming me." Major Kumazawa said gruffly, "I'm sorry."

Here was more sincere remorse than Sano had expected from his uncle. "It's not your fault. The blame belongs solely to Yanagisawa."

"After everything else he's done to you!" Sano's mother blurted angrily. "I could kill that man!"

Sano and Major Kumazawa avoided each other's gazes. They both knew she was fully capable of killing someone she thought deserved it. But that was a story now over and done with. Their family had outlived years of guilt, shame, and discord.

"So you and Yanagisawa are enemies again," Major Kumazawa said.

"We always were," Sano said. Their truces had been short-lived flukes. The war was on.

"That's a hard blow he hit you." To his credit, Major Kumazawa didn't gloat because Sano had been demoted or shun him because of the disgrace.

"I haven't yet met a blow I couldn't recover from." Sano explained that he was gradually working his way back into the shogun's good graces. Oddly enough, that had come about because Sano had humiliated and banished Joju. The shogun had summoned Sano to the palace to give him a tongue-lashing. Some fast talk by Sano had reversed much of the damage done him by Yoritomo and carried the day. "My new task is preparing my family for the future."

"I'll do whatever I can to help," Major Kumazawa said.

Sano's mother smiled and blinked away tears. Major Kumazawa wasn't just repaying a favor, Sano realized. Sano had taken the first step toward mending relations within their clan. Now Major Kumazawa had gone the rest of the distance, by voluntarily welcoming Sano's mother back into the clan. Sano was truly moved.

"Many thanks," he said.

"Just be careful next time," Major Kumazawa said, with a hint of his old, critical tone. "No more foolish heroics."

Sano felt the old offense, tempered with respect and amusement. "I'll try."

This wasn't ever going to be an easy relationship. He and his uncle were too different. Yet Major Kumazawa had taken what he himself probably deemed a foolish risk by allying himself with his unconventional, embattled nephew. They would manage.

Blood was blood.

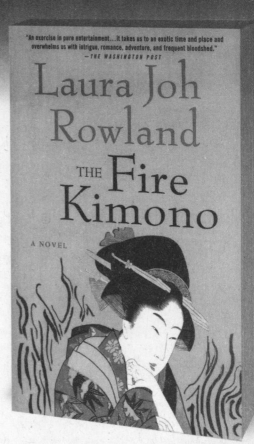